The Ghostly Men

A Magpie Universe Novel

Proof copy

The Ghostly Menagerie

Gary J. Mack

Cover Painting by Rupam Grimoeuvre
Twitter: @grimoeuvre

Cover lettering and framing and additional graphics by David
Collins
Twitter: @DJCollins82

Gary's Twitter @gjm2602
Instagram @garyjmack.

Dedicated to my late great friend Jason. I so wish you could have read this.

Foreword

This book was born from an urge to explore Robert Waterfield's background after I had written his first tale, The Lure of Magpie Farm, which, incidentally, is my favourite tale from Impossible Fruit: A Collection of Speculative Stories.

I knew Robert would cross paths with Masie Price and Harry Morton in The Secret Magpie, and I knew he would have some influence over them in the sequel, The Raven's Message. I'll say no more, as you will have to find out why by reading both. Consequently, this book serves as a bizarre link between the two novels, even though it is set over a hundred years before.

Ghostly Menagerie also sets up a series of novella's about the Menagerie, and they will start to appear in 2025 or so. Hopefully leading up to a planned book called the Supernatural Wars which will close this branch of the Magpie Universe off. There will be hints herein regarding about what *that* is all about.

Having said all that, The Ghostly Menagerie can be appreciated in its own right. You can forget about the links if you want to, and just enjoy what I hope is an emotional and ghostly rollercoaster.

Draw your soul blades, and step into the Hopelessness with me.

Part One: The Menagerie

Chapter One

The Demon of Moseley

Percy, that is my good friend Anna Percival, and I had cornered the Demon of Moseley in the said suburb of Birmingham one cold night in February 1905.

Initially, we were not going to dissipate it, after all it was such a low-level creature in terms of its demonic strength, it was hardly worth the bother. We were just going to shoo it away. How naïve we were.

We had spent a day cornering it, setting a trap, and we were about to throw the lever, as they say, when it appeared from the shadows and showed us its bottom.

Well, I was having none of it.

You don't pull apart your cheeks and let out the Devil's own flatulence in the presence of the fairer sex without there being some form of serious retribution.

It turned and laughed at us. I noticed with some disappointment that Percy was laughing too. Her views on etiquette were broader than mine.

Then the revenants appeared, which wiped away our smiles, and *then* it all went toes up.

Revenants are demon-controlled corpses, by the way, and often tend to be more dangerous than the demon itself, just by way of their sheer numbers.

The Moseley revenants were clearly made up of lots of dead children in different degrees of decay. All with their bloody red pseudo-eyes (their originals had all long decayed) and rapier sharp talons and teeth.

The graveyard of that sorry church must have been mostly populated by the young. It looked like a school trip to Hell.

"Oh, for chuff's sake, not kids again." Percy shouted over the hubbub of the creatures who were marching animatedly towards us.

Percy unfortunately used a lot of colourful language. It made me squirm, if I am honest. If it had been anyone else, I would be warning them about their conduct in polite society, but Percy could curse like a pirate whose grog had just sank through a hole in his hull.

We both pulled our soul blades. Amazing weapons. Percy had requisitioned a set for the Menagerie eighteen months before - upon the creation of our group - and we hadn't looked back. Very good at killing the dead, not good at killing humans.

Soul blades enabled the wielder to access the memories of a master of the sword, who once danced their art with it, whether that swordmaster be currently alive or dead.

My sword was imbued with the catalogue of moves that had once belonged to master Luigi Caruso, a fifteenth century Venetian vampire hunter. Some of Luigi's moves had proven difficult at first until I had worked on my fitness a little more. A word of warning, not even a soul blade can improve stamina.

I pulled my sword, advanced on the small evil creatures, and helped Percy cut a swathe through them like some murderous governess who had become apoplectic at the mess in the classroom. The names Percy called them were fruit-some and not for repeating here. I will not be writing down all her swear words, believe me.

"Die humans." The Demon of Moseley said, although because of his forked tongue it came out as "humanth." We would laugh at itth pronounthiation later.

The child revenants kept re-spawning as fast as we could kill them. I needed to find the source of the demon's death magic and quickly, or we would have been overwhelmed.

Just goes to show, one should never judge a demon by its aura.

"It's using a bone house Robert," the delightful Percy advised. "It can be the only way the little get is so powerful."

I looked about the deconsecrated church to see where the bone-house might be. Normally a bone-house was a cuboid, made out of radius or ulna bones, built around a skull.

The church we were fighting in had been condemned, so it was falling apart and there was little in the way of furniture, but behind the throne the Demon had constructed from decaying human flesh was an old altar; and it was still covered in the holy tablecloth. I bet Percy that the bone house was hidden under there somewhere.

Percy, who had seen where my gaze had wandered, nodded imperceptibly as she skewered a circa three-year-old zombie child through an eye. She struggled to shake its mewling head off her blade, but when it did detach, it sailed in an arc to land with a crunch and a splat and a long vocalised "Weeeee." Vile things.

As I moved off towards the altar, I noticed she pulled her second weapon which was a shorter hand sword, akin to a Roman gladius. She started to spin in a way that impressed me until my stomach tingled in loving appreciation. Unfortunately, I had work of my own to do, so I advanced upon Kenneth.

Yes, that's what the Demon of Moseley was called. He'd clearly liked the name of the man he had possessed, or had forgotten his own ancient guttural moniker.

Kenneth was currently doing a dance, still pants down, this time waving his pathetic John Thomas at me, as if in time to silent music. Wagner, by the look of his exacerbated thrusts.

I raced up the steps and attacked. He dissipated, which was always the cowards way, and reappeared behind me. The blighter pinched my bottom. Laughing, Luigi the swordmaster suggested a feint to the left followed by a sweeping arc downwards to the right.

Success. I managed to carve half of Kenneth's face off. "Bathtub," he screeched like a half-headed harpy and danced back. I was then able to race up to the altar and pull the chalice cloth from upon it's once sacred surface.

I was just about the bend down and look through the shelving, when Kenneth - having jumped super-demonically from his original position, landed with a mighty thud on the altar - and blew another bottom raspberry at me. Thankfully, he wasn't facing me this time.

He'd grown his face back too, well almost. The jelly of his left eye was still congealing like aspic gone wrong. He began to fountain urine at me from his devilish nether regions. I had had enough of his disgusting behaviours, so I thrust the sword hilt at his foul codlings and soon marvelled that I had managed to hit something.

Kenneth's eyes rolled up into the back of his skull and he fell off the altar. This was really proving to be one of the strangest of my adventures - ever.

There was no light behind the altar, so I knelt and scrabbled around for something that might resemble a bone house. I was about to give up when my hand touched on something smooth and cold. I pulled out the cube of stylised bone, as Kenneth rounded on me again. A skull inside the bone house was gnashing its perfectly grinning teeth, and I almost lost a finger or two.

Kenneth shot forward towards me, so I hit him with the only thing I had to hand, as I had sheathed my sword. Whatever magic had created the bone house was not enough to prevent it from shattering on Kenneth's neanderthal-like cranium.

"Thank God for that Bobby. I thought you were about to dance with old Kenneth there. You were taking more time than a French aristocrat in a brothel."

Kenneth was snarling when we approached him. The magic leeching from the bone house had affected him somewhat and he wasn't able to heal his latest injury. A large crack to his forehead was spilling forth a black tar-like fluid which smelt like slurry. The revenants had all long collapsed to decay and dust.

"Let's put him out of his misery." I said retrieving one of our patented demon traps from my pocket. It was just an ink stamp made up of certain angelic sigils that would trap a demon in a rose jar.

I stamped the snarling Kenneth on the nearest bare flesh, which happened to be his left bottom cheek. In moments he was squealing and was reduced to a blue whisp of soul-magic that left poor original Kenneth's corpse behind.

The corpse, which had reverted to human form, flopped off the altar steps with a wet plop. The whisp remained controlled by the magic sigils until Percy flipped the lid of the portable rose jar, and the essence of the creature was sucked inside. Percy screwed the lid tight and put it in her purse which, amazingly she hadn't dropped whilst she despatched the revenants with two swords.

She really was perfect.

I looked at Percy, and she looked at me. We were both covered in gore, dirt, and dust. She started to laugh, and so did I. She put her arms about me and kissed my left cheek, probably, in hindsight, because the left one was the only part of me clean.

I stepped back from her embrace and looked at her. She was so beautiful in that moment. I had pined after her for years at that point. She had helped me get over Eliza. Yet she gave me nothing romantic in return. Nothing to suggest there would ever be anything but friendship.

At that moment I thought there was at least a little spark. A kernel of what could be. We both imperceptibly moved towards each other, led by our lips. I thought this was it. The defining moment. The I heard the words.

"...stop police."

And our brief romantic interlude was over. A possible future shattered.

Within minutes the old church flooded with officers, ably commanded by our erstwhile police liaison officer - Inspector Losenge.

I couldn't blame him from ruining my love life. He was just doing his job. Always too late to help with the monsters, as usual, but always on time to clean up.

Losenge was, ironically, a diamond in a bag of sand. A salt of the earth policeman who cleared up after our fun and games without a word or disparaging remark. He just did not want to know the creepy details, especially by the time we were down the Jug of Ale sipping mild and eating pork rind scratchings.

"Presumably, you will magic up some case notes that suggest our friend Kenneth Bennett was a serial killer who liked to eat the hearts of his victims with a strong cup of tea whilst doing the Sunday Times Crossword?" Losenge gasped sipping the foam off a very full pint. You didn't serve half-measures to the plod, it seemed.

"You really like making up these faux cases don't you Losenge. You could have a career in writing." I suggested.

8

The bespectacled and beardy bald Inspector laughed like an asthmatic cat. "Like the Irishman, Doyle and his Sherlock fellow? What a heap of bloody nonsense. Those tales are so convoluted, you could have rounded up the con by the time you had worked through the clues. As for that Inspector Lestrade, what an idiot. Cases are solved by hard work not listening to some dandy who can tell the make of your underwear from what you find in it."

Percy spat her beer out. I wasn't sure if he had upset her as a Sherlock fan, or she was laughing at Lozenge's faux pas.

"Sorry gentlemen. I need to be going. I have had a little too much."

This was our cue to escape. Our mutual escape phrase. Percy could drink like a fisherman at low tide, so I knew she was getting irritated. So, we said our goodbyes and left the Inspector at the Jug.

"I need to get back to Whitehall, Bobby." Percy said. "Can you take me?"

Percy had got one of her strange messages. It was on the little glowing screen she carried about with her, which I now know to be a mobile phone. It read:

Percy, are you with the Waterfield fellow? We have a new assignment and it's a big one. Come to London as soon as you can.

So, I took Percy into the Hopelessness.

It was this skill that first brought me to the attention of Anna Percival years before. Let me spend a moment to tell you about how I met her.

One strange night in London, Chelsea to be exact. I was journeying from my editorial office to my Kensington pad, when I heard the screams of a young woman.

I raced to the scene to find Percy was being mauled by what I could only describe as a banshee. It was a noisy spirit, all red haired, like Percy, but more ghostly, livid and not as beautiful. It was the banshee that was screaming profanity, but Percy was a good match and was cursing like a navvy who had lost his shovel.

I later found that she was trying to catch the thing in a rose jar with a sigil spell, but it was just not working. They didn't always, particularly if the spirit wasn't inherently evil.

So, I stepped in and took both Percy, the creature and I, into the Hopelessness.

There I subdued the spirit.

I'd always had the knack to do so in the Hopelessness, so Percy was able to capture the creature effectively in the rose jar.

"Where are we?" Percy had asked. She was not worried or phased one jot. Even when the low-level spirits approached her in that place it did not affect her nerve at all.

"This is the Hopelessness. A form of purgatory. I have found I am able to transgress it. I have been able to do so since my Grandfather's funeral, when I was a seven-year-old boy. I didn't want him to die so I went looking for him. I stepped between worlds just like that. I can now, as its master, travel great distances through the realm, so long as there aren't any spiritual barriers. Although I have yet to find a spirit here that I could not subdue."

Percy smiled. It was a smile of understanding, and excitement, if I had read it right. Percy looked at me with an expression one could almost describe as lustful, before she realised her poker face had slipped.

Anna Percival was probably about five feet nine. I never got to measure her, as that would have been ungentlemanly to ask. Being a six foot plus gentleman you tend to notice the ladies who stood at your shoulders rather than your knees. Anna had copper coloured hair and always wore huntsmen's trousers and green jackets when out in the field. She had eyes of the deepest emerald and complexion so fair that she would have looked like a ghost if it weren't for all of the freckles holding her face together.

"I find myself in strange situations all the time, as I work for the Ministry of Mirrors, I have travelled in many strange and wondrous ways, but never as a spirit. Are we dead when we are here?"

I told Percy it was an excellent question, and one I had asked myself many times. The best I could surmise was I was able to convert myself into a form that was able to walk with the dead. I could also take people with me. I was certain our souls did not depart. My body wasn't left behind anywhere. So, I must slip between the veil, from the land of the living to the land of the dead. I couldn't go further. Heaven nor Hell beckoned. Just the middle ground.

Back to the post Kenneth present, I thought of the streets of Whitehall, and immediately we were in a shadow version that existed in the Hopelessness, the buildings had changed around us and, instead of the faded aspect of Moseley- Birmingham, we were in London, near the Ministry.

I then took us back through to the plane of the living and caught the bitter taste of pollutants on my tongue, my nose smelling the effluent that, whilst a long way below us in the sewers, bubbled up on warm nights making the drain grates burp noxious gas.

Percy smiled and squeezed my hand, once we were fully corporeal, then led me to the building that was the Ministry of Mirrors.

Chapter Two

The Ministry of Mirrors

The Ministry's name was purely based on the old adage smoke and mirrors. It was the secret of the secret services, where all things weird and wonderful were monitored.

Britain in the 1900s was rife with supernatural and magical beings. By your time reader, their numbers had waned due to the Supernatural Wars, but in 1905 there was a whole government department, a military regiment, and several police departments which, up and down the country, dealt with the strange. I don't intend to get into the Supernatural Wars in this first journal as it is too convoluted, but it's something we might get into in a later volume.

Only a handful of people knew who the Minister at that time was. I will eventually reveal them, but suffice it to say, he or she allegedly changed, and to tell you a list of names would be neither helpful nor valuable. It would also contravene the Official Secrets Act. During my time liaising with Whitehall, though, it was the same person.

After presenting ourselves at the Ministry, we were taken to a reception room where Percy told some officious old bat, with a face and accoutrements that looked grey and haggard like cracked granite, that she was here to see the minister upon his request. When asked to see the telegram, Percy said she didn't have one. I did wonder why she didn't show Ms Fosdyke, for that was the bats name, the glowing message upon the tiny glass screen that Percy and the Minister used to communicate.

After a visual stand-off that lasted five minutes, Percy was allowed through double doors to the rooms beyond. I waited for Ms Fosdyke to look the other way and I slipped into the Hopelessness. I was sure there would be a spirit about who could tell me a thing or two.

I was startled, as I slipped through the veil, to find there were parts of the Ministry I could not access. It was strange, and this didn't happen often, and was usually because the place was warded against demonic or spiritual access.

Digging into a well of fortitude, I took no heed, but instead tried to peer into the layers around me to see if there was a spirit intricately linked to the building, whom I could coax out and have a conversation with.

At first, I found nothing. It was as if the building were spirit free, but that was nonsense. Buildings were like books, where the stories of spirits and ghosts were written on pages of brick, stone or wattle and daub.

"Even the dead keep their secrets, Mr Robert Waterfield."

The voice was female and rich; she was nicely spoken as if trained to do so. Elocuted, one might say. She appeared seconds after her voice. She was a tall young woman, or had been in life. Spirits could change their shape with ease, although they would snap back into their original form if in my presence.

"What do you seek Robert?"

"Firstly, to make your acquaintance." Ghosts hated ignorance. After all, if you had not been seen for years, you would want the observer to at least acknowledge you and pass the time of day.

She smiled. Her smile made her plain face beautiful. She twirled coquettishly, hands clasped across her abdomen. Her black tresses reflected light that had no business being in this place but, for some reason, helped her glow.

"I am Hannah."

"Please to meet you. May I ask when you were born, Hannah?"

She nodded, still smiling.

Here's the thing reader, ghosts thrive on being remembered. The less remembered, the more transparent a ghost tended to be and its influence upon the spirit world lessened over time. With the merest act of me asking Hannah her name and birthdate, it showed I would remember her, which in turn made her more opaque. She was, after all, too beautiful to be a wisp, as we called the Forgotten.

"I was born to Abel and Hannah Goldman in 1270. We lived as a family on this site; my father was a money lender. We fell afoul of the Edict of Expulsion, and so, when we refused to leave our house, they burnt it."

"Oh Hannah," I said. "I am so sorry." Knowing what was coming.

She smiled again, sadder this time. "They cut my father's throat. The King's guard did it, and yet he was the lucky one. They violated my younger brother and my mother before throwing them back in the burning house alive. Then they raped me. Twenty-three of them, one by one. Then they threw me back. But, during those foul attacks, I had committed their faces to my very good memory." Hannah paused. "You would call it idectic now."

I wondered how she could smile, how she wasn't a screaming spitting vengeful spirit.

"Oh, I didn't die." She said. "I fell through the burning floor into a water-filled cellar. They were all linked in those days, so I escaped through the labyrinth of underground passages. I made my way to friends who knew how to hide me in amongst the riff raff of the underclass. I then met a soldier who I married and who gave me two fine daughters. Eleanor and Matilda. Please think of them."

As their names hit my head, the image of two twin girls appeared smiling, running about Hannah and me.

I grinned, at least there was some sort of a happy ending. Although the story wasn't done.

"My husband's vengeance came under order from a Judge, after our petition, so it was doubly rewarding when I had found Sir Roger had been able to hang every last one of the men my Joseph brought before him, hogtied."

I nodded, I could not criticise her vengeance. I had sent my beloved to Hell for her hand in ten murders. Eliza's death had put me on my current path. It's okay talking about fate and predestination, but times change, someone or something can always put you on a different pathway.

"Thank you for listening to me, Robert. I will now answer your question." Her smile was wonderful, and oh so familiar.

"Are there any evil spirits connected with this building, or creatures of deceit?" I asked.

She nodded to say she understood my question. "No evil, but there is some deceit. There is something alien here, Robert, but it is not evil. Far from it. You are safe in these walls. Stay close to your one sided love though, as she will prove difficult to handle."

Well, that was Percy all right. I loved her and she didn't reflect anything back but friendship and a labourer's arsenal of profanity. I sighed. I understood I could not ask another question, which would need a further boon and I was not willing to lose some of my soul, as was the price for a second query.

"Thank you, Hannah. I may visit you again someday. Or you would be welcome to join us in Birmingham in my reliquary."

"I must remain, Robert. I am near the bones of my Joe and our girls and their girls and so on."

Again, I understood. I wish there had been enough substance to Hannah that I could reach out and hug her. She surprised me by approaching me. Her arms enclosed me. There was no strength, just feeling. Yet how could that be. She would have to be fully opaque to do this. or....

"My Joe was French. From Vatierville in France. Jose de Vatierville or in English, Joseph Waterfield." Again, the beaming smile.

I gasped. I knew it. Grandfather's smile. Tears came to my eyes, yes that could happen in the Hopelessness. All emotions were laid as bare in purgatory as they were in life. I looked at Hannah and she beamed, becoming more and more opaque than she ever had been. Then slowly the outline of a tall man appeared, a burly fellow with a hook nose and a thatch of ash blond hair. Then the two little dark-haired girls grew more substantial. They looked like their father and mother, and one hadn't lived

13

to adulthood by the look of her greater transparency, but that was another story, I would have to save it for another day.

Then one by one they faded. Hannah took longer as she was the most powerful now. Hannah my great times the nth degree grandmother. I smiled at her, then I dematerialised and re-appeared in the real world.

"Mr Waterfield, I presume. Do you have a habit of doing that? Its rather impressive you just disappearing and then reappearing."

The speaker was a tall Viking of a man. He was quite honestly beautiful. His baring was like that of a hairy Greek statue. Gat (who you will meet later) would have boggled eyes by that point.

The Viking wore the smile of a bemused man. The only off thing about him, aside from his mane of hair, was his smell. Or smells. Thousands of delicate smells seemed to emanate from him. It wasn't overpowering or nauseating, more interesting. It was the smells of everyday life brought into stark contrast. They seemed to make his personality.

"I am Lord Magnus. I *am* the Minister of Mirrors." He said holding out a hand that would have shamed a navvy's shovel.

I shook the offered appendage, feeling the power on those forearms. I felt he could have lifted me and broke my back across his shoulders. I could have done with him at university, in the rugger team.

"I want to thank you for the help you gave the Ministry, particularly the Midland's Chapel. Anna talks highly of you. And I have now witnessed the gift you have, that she has told me about, or at least the part where you appear from nowhere."

"I apologise. Its habit, Minister. I tend to check out buildings for evil. Part of my basic survival trait."

"Would you like a drink Mr Waterfield? I could take you to the bar. Anna is somewhat delayed so she said she would join you in Birmingham in the early hours?" He didn't seem to want to tarry so I took the decision off his hands.

"And she sends the Minister as her errand boy to give me said message?"

"Ha." And he did indeed say it rather than laugh it, as if laughing was unnatural to him.

"Percy is somewhat unique in my staff. She is like a daughter to me."

He looked about between twenty-five and a thousand years old. I didn't ask about his age, that would be rude, but he couldn't be a youngster. He was obviously one of the most high-ranking members of the government, not to mention the head of a secret department that could probably bump me off and bury me before you could say boo to a goose.

"I am not a hierarchical man, Mr Waterfield, but I am one who expects loyalty. Percy will come to you tomorrow with the offer of a new case. Your strangest yet."

I said nothing, as I am a man of morals, with no deceit in *my* bones, but I wanted him to tell me more.

"I will leave that to Percy."

Had he read my mind? Hannah had said there was no evil in the building. Only deceit. Was he deceiving me or was he deceiving Percy? I thought I could smell that deception. Suddenly I needed to be away from here. Away from this Viking.

"Off you pop, Mr Waterfield. Maybe we will have that drink someday." The Minister of Mirrors said in a way that would brook no arguments.

So, I did.

I entered the Hopelessness as rudely as I could. And do you know I could have sworn I saw an after image of the Minister, all outlined in blue, smoke rising all about him.

I decided to look up my friend Horace Lightfoot before I made my way back to Birmingham. Horace could always be found in the Duck on Parsonby Street, just off the King's Road.

The Duck was a judge and lawyer's pub and therefore a very safe house.

The manager and staff in the Duck thought I was mad, whenever I visited. I just sat there talking to myself, buying drinks for my invisible companion, whilst sipping dandelion and burdock.

Horace Lightfoot had been my first editor when I began writing my ghost stories, a few years before. I had been about to get my first book commissioned, but unfortunately Horace had a heart attack and died on the way to the Times for the serialisation meeting with the commissioning editor.

As soon as I had heard of his death, I reached out into the Hopelessness to find him. I found him in the Duck in *that* place. I was able then to anchor him to the Duck in the living world. Something for which he said he was eternally grateful. Or at least he would be after an eternity.

"A double whiskey, malt, and a lemonade." I asked the podgy barman who looked sideways at his companion, a haggard woman who could have been his mother or older sister. The barman, who I knew was called Cody, rolled his eyes as if to say the madman was here again.

I was a paying customer, and Horace liked his drink. The bill would be steep, I would be fleeced, and Cody would then be happy.

"Where's your foul-mouthed woman?" Horace asked, becoming solid enough for me to see him in this world, but not for the others without the sight.

Sorry, I haven't explained myself very well. All spirits can appear in our world, but they can only be either seen by those who have the sight like me, a personal attachment to those spirits, or are about to be on the nearly dead end of vengeance. Of course, spirits can be coerced to threaten the living, but that is usually at the expense of some serious blood magic. That is why demons usually used revenants to do their dirty work. It's cheaper. A ghost would have to have a really good reason for tearing your throat out, and be so opaque that they would need an army of worshippers just to keep them visible.

Horace was able to make a ghostly version of his whiskey glass and the whiskey which he tended to gulp. I poured the real thing into the spittoon when the bar staff weren't looking.

"She is over at the Ministry."

Horace nodded. "I thought so. I sensed you nearby. More strange business? I heard that you have just dispatched that little fellow from Moseley. Some of the more opaques were telling me that they felt it in the Hopelessness when you dispatched him. Bone house, wasn't it?"

Horace was always well informed, once a journalist, always a journalist.

I nodded. "He was a dirty little thing. Low power. Good at revenants, though. Showed Percy and I, his bottom."

"Do they eat?"

"Through their bottoms? No, I don't think so." I was imagining the little teeth.

"No. What do they eat?"

"Only souls apparently."

"So why do they need an arse?"

"He had taken a human over." I shrugged.

"So, what's your question then this time?"

"Any mutterings in the ether about magpies, or a Magpie?"

"Capital M?"

"Yes."

"No. You shorted out Isabelle's spiritual strength when you retrieved Eliza's soul from Hell. She is recharging, however. You were stupid to do so. What you would have resurrected would have been worse than the Eliza under that witch's power."

"That's good to know, I said."

"Do not go back to that farm. She will have you. I know that was where you and Eliza set up home, but I can feel it even from here. That place is evil. They say Lichfield is named after a field of the dead, which may or may not be true, but whenever Isabelle wakes, death will follow."

16

Well, I didn't have any intention of going back at that point. For all I knew or cared, Eliza's wedding dress still hung on the back of the parlour door.

Chapter Three

Convergence

Percy had managed to get a message to me before I left the pub. The young man who deposited the note in my hands was very out of breath and waited patiently as I found him a shilling for his troubles.

Robert, the minister really liked you. The commission is worth ten thousand pounds. That should keep you in rose jars for a while. I can't come to you yet. I will see you in Birmingham, but it will be the early hours.

Ten thousand pounds was a small fortune. That would be over two hundred thousand pounds worth of buying power today. And that was what had scared me as I said my goodbyes to Horace. A job fraught with danger, no doubt.

I stepped outside the Duck. It was just a little before one in the morning. Horace had wanted a lock-in and the bar staff were happy the mad man was filling their till with money and their spittoon with whiskey. They probably poured it back in the bottle at the end of the evening.

It was still warm, the air cloying and thick with pollution. It caught at my throat again like badly swallowed food.

London, like most large cities was a smog riddled in the late 1800s and early 1900s. You could have caught the air in an onion bag, sieved it through a sock and it would have made enough coal to power a townhouse for a week. My lungs would have been charcoal branches in their cavity back in those days, if it weren't for my special talent.

So, I slipped through the veil, and used the Hopelessness to stealthily move northwards to my hometown.

Thankfully, as I traversed that ungodly land, a majority of the spirits and ghouls managed to stay in the background. As usual they cursed, spat, and screamed at me, hissing the same vitriol. How could I walk their shadowy pathways, yet still have my soul attached?

A few of the braver spirits detached themselves from the shadows and came to peer at me, but I pushed them back with my subconscious will, a skill I had stumbled upon during one tortuous visit as a lad. I was so used to doing it now, that it was second nature to me - like breathing.

One of the shades tried to subdue me with fear, but his approach was laughable, he was a long-forgotten fade, without anyone left in the corporeal world to remember him; so, he was barely a wisp. I dissipated him easily and he wailed like he was already in Hell, not just purgatory.

I ended my ghost-walk at my residence in Legend Street, Edgbaston, Birmingham, and materialised in one of the underground rooms.

The underground layers of my abode were a warren. I had stipulated the excavation of a whole underground system of caverns and rooms when the row of houses I owned had first been designed and built. I needed to come and go as I pleased, without giving neighbours or day staff apoplexy. I also needed a place for all of the creatures I had captured or those who needed safe haven.

There were things in my cellars that would make gibbering wrecks out of a majority of humans. There were a few in the attic, too.

Postlethwaite the raven was my house guardian. She cawed at me as I materialised. She sat on the threshold of the real world and the Hopelessness, like a guard dog who could sniff out evil either side of the veil.

Like most corvids, Postlethwaite could traverse the living world as well as the Hopelessness, but she was more special than that. Waite had once belonged to Odin. But that is another story. Reader, you might take note here.

"Halt." The bird said as I approached, she was preening her black feathers with her beak. "State your business."

"It's me, Waite. Robert. Mr Waterfield."

The bird gave me a double take as if I weren't really there, although I had materialised.

"The silver man has been screaming in the Cathedral again." Waite said. She had been saying it for a few days and I had meant to question her about who "he" was, but I had been so busy that I hadn't had half a chance.

Anyways, Waite sometimes talked in half-baked Prophecy, and it often took a while to decipher it. She was certainly lost in the codicils at that moment.

"I'll talk to you soon Waite. Promise. I need a cup of tea and then once Percy has been, my bed."

"How can I be nearly dead, Robert."

"You are both alive, and dead, Waite. You are a corvid."

"No. *Foolish man*. That's what *he* is saying."

"Waite, I am in no mood for Prophecy. I promise I will come to you, and we will discuss, but now I am in need of sleep. A new case has arisen. Percy wants to talk to us all, and soon."

"He says one or more of you shall die." Waite cawed, then went silent. She was probably fed up with my ignoring her pleas. Or she was communing with the distant Prophecy. Sometimes she took me subconsciously to places where the codicils spoke from the mouths of other creatures, not that we got anything other than nonsense from them, usually.

Looking back, I probably should have listened to Waite. Instead, I pushed past the bird who guarded my home from evil, then promptly forgot to return. It had been another long night and I had slept truly little for days.

Most of my business, as you can imagine, was, and still is, conducted at night. I worked mainly in the shadows. I wasn't a detective, as such, I was no Sherlock Holmes, looking for a nuanced clue, my business was conducted mostly with the dead, or the absurd.

The house lights always flickered for a while when I materialised into the real world, and they continued as I climbed stairs between the layers. The power supply in Birmingham was poor and intermittent even though I had paid a lot of money to get linked to the brand new Summer Lane power station. It was a very hush hush, and we had a little machine that regulated the current that was ahead of its time, courtesy of Percy, she had got it from the Ministry.

The neighbours would be using gas mantles for years to come.

More opaque ghosts can affect electrical current too, but it wasn't them affecting the power source; my houses were new, and purposefully built far from any cemeteries, so even stray ghosts would not appear in any substance, and the captured ones in the cellars were all warded. Thanks to Gat.

I strode across the arrival lounge, as I liked to call it, a long corridor with a chequered floor with rooms off each side at regular intervals. I pulled open the lead-lined door and quickly ascended three flights of stairs. I heard some of the wailing from the more vocal spirits; there were rows of them in their traps on this level, and I had to mentally switch off, as they can send you mad if you listen long enough.

I fished my keys out of my pocket and inserted a heavy brass beast into the mortice lock before me. With a click the door was open and I entered into the first basement level. I turned and locked the door, and it vanished. I can't tell you how that works. Waite does it all. Doors appear when one of the Menagerie is in need of one.

I reached the ground floor threshold of the house. Waite appeared again, fully corporeal - perch, and all. She wasn't as chatty in her real form. She just followed me with her black beady eyes that reflected the dim light. The next door appeared, and I opened it with my keys.

The hallway grandfather clock struck 2am as I reached the ground floor proper. The house was quiet, but I was not surprised when I saw a light on in the library.

It was more than likely that Gathii Mumbi, my African friend, magical colleague, and fellow scholar - who also resided with me - was studying his spiritual magic from my wealth of supernatural and magic books.

I knocked on the door of the library, with propitious knowledge that I would find Gat leafing through a large tome, his spectacles low on his nose. I wasn't wrong. He looked over them at me, and smiled such a handsome smile.

"Rafiki." He said, in his perfect but accented English. He reached behind himself and rang the bell. "You look in need of tea."

I was always in need of tea in those days. Tea made me human – I rarely drink wine or spirits even now. They fog my brain when it is most needed.

Gat sat there with his pince nez on his nose, his shaven head glinting in the candlelight, the shoulders under his grandad collar shirt looked like his sinew was made from woven steel. A complex character was Gat, his strength a stark contrast to his scholarly ways. Moreover, when he was in Digbeth fighting with some of our Chinese friends, dancing with their complex martial arts, he looked a danger to all who opposed him. Gat was the rock of our Menagerie.

"Did you despatch the creature?" Gat asked, meaning the anchored demon spirit of Moseley.

"Yes, but he was persistent. He used a bone house to secure himself to the poor human."

"I would have burned the whole place down."

"It was a beautiful if un-ordained church."

"A tool of modern social control." He replied with a subtle hint of anger hidden deep within his normal baritone.

I nodded, it was late, but I understood his hatred of all things Church and Government that had long subjugated his people, and so I walked to him and laid a hand of friendship on his arm. He squeezed my hand in return.

"How is Arthur?" I asked Gat, trying to change the mood.

He responded with his wonderful smile. "My love is well."

I laughed, if a little nervously. I was brought up in the Victorian age, after all. Some prudes have been slow to adapt to more modern ways of life, even in the 2020s. I was one of them, in the 1900s. I understood that love between men was love and not perversion, but it took me a time to get that into my thick head – because of the way I was raised - to believe it was a sin, and that many nations punished the sinner with death.

I was also somewhat jealous that Arthur and Gat had each other. I had sent the last woman I loved, Eliza, to Hell. I don't tend to hang around in relationships where the one I loved wanted to put a bullet in my head. Eliza's soul currently sat in a rose jar, on a shelf in my cellar. More of that later.

"Is Percy joining us soon? It is late." Gat put a bookmark in his book, and closed it.

"Yes, she will be coming direct from Whitehall shortly."

"Through one of her holes in the air, it must be important, Robert."

"Yes, we have the offer of a new job." I rubbed my eyes. I didn't dare sit down at that point as I would have been asleep in seconds.

"Any sign of romance?" Gat asked, raising his eyes.

"I truly think she loves me, but like a sister would an elder brother."

"You will find someone soon. I do not have to be Postlethwaite to know that."

I patted Gat's shoulder again and went and sat in one of the high backs by the yawning mouth of the dead fireplace. I *was* soon nodding.

I was roused from embryonic dreams by a kerfuffle in the hallway outside, the front door to the house slammed first, then the twins blew in with the warm night air. Both of them were drunk, as usual. Their propensity to drink so much, and still be alive, amazed me.

I was astounded, as I was every evening, that they remembered to return. Avery and Charlie had no doubt sullenly dragged themselves away from whatever party the fringes of Birmingham society had held that evening. They looked dishevelled; Charlie looked like he (no, she) had been in a scrap, his evening dress was all torn. Avery looked dapper in her (no, his) suit, her short hair immaculate.

Let me explain a little. Charlie and Avery had both decided to switch genders at 12 years of age and had never looked back.

Very few people ever realised they had swapped. They had been twins in the womb after all, but nature had been cruel and they had both been born in the wrong body, or so they said.

I was their Uncle, and they were the children of my dead sister, and I didn't find out until I legally adopted them six years before. As I had said earlier, about my Victorian upbringing they had needed to explain it to me repeatedly. Yet they were family. Family and friends were everything. Prejudice is just idle opinion passed on from one bigot to another, like heavy chains always ripe for breaking. I had to remember the right pronouns, forgive me if I lapse or overstate them.

"Uncle," Avery came over and gave me a big kiss, followed by a hug. He reeked of gin and cigars. His normally sharp hair was dishevelled and lank.

"I could have really done with some help tonight." I said all matter of fact and a little grumpy. I didn't begrudge their fun. I was just exhausted and needed to show that we all should be pulling together.

"Why didn't Gat help?" Charlie piped up. She was lounged in a very un-lady-like manner, her petticoats on show to the world.

"He isn't on the rota. You were." I said a little more bitterly than I needed to. "Luckily, Percy was at a loss this evening."

"Oops. Did you bag Kenneth?" Was all Avery said before crashing into a chair. He was snoring softly in seconds. Charlie was already asleep.

"You know I would have gone with you." Gat sighed shutting his book again. He had given up any hope of reading, for now, by the looks of him. He reached round and rang the bell again. "Where is that bloody tea?"

"The rota is the rota." I said.

"You are always on it. So, it is a mockery. That is why the twins don't engage with it." Gat replied with a tone that suggested I had one rule for myself which wasn't led by example. "Therefore, it is not a rota. More of a constant." Gat was wise for a man in his late thirties, although that was an approximation. I had never asked his age.

Charlie suddenly opened her eyes and let out the most enormous burp. She shut her eyes again and went back to snoring.

"All those lessons in etiquette." I said wearily as I pitched myself into a chair.

"Social control you mean?" Gat intoned.

I wasn't going to win with any response, so I sat there a little forlorn. The front doorbell rescued me from my silence as I realised Wally, who was doing the servants nightshift, couldn't make tea at one end of my house and open the door at the other.

"I'll go." I said. Gat just raised his eyebrows at me and rang the tea bell for the third time.

The front doorbell rang for the second time, and I cursed. Who was making such a racket. Then my tired brain kicked in.

I got to the door and pulled it open. The door was so heavy, and I had pulled with such a force that I nearly slammed into the wall with it.

It was Percy. The woman I adored.

"Bobby, let me in. It's a bastard pea souper out here."

"Are you okay? You could have arrived tomorrow morning, you know."

"I did think that, but after we parted I ended up typing a report for the minister, and then when I went to my room for a shower, but there was no water. I'm sweatier than the doorknobs in a Turkish brothel. I'll need a bath. Will that reprobate Wally sort it for me?" Percy said all this while strolling past me, disappearing toward the library. I watched her hips sway in her manly clothes that garnered many a frown in society. She walked lightly, like a big cat, but she was always ready to pounce. I wouldn't want to be her enemy, let me tell you. I had need of a cold shower before I went to bed.

Apologies for my lewd thoughts, reader. I would edit them out, but they give context.

23

"Oh, all the gang is here - apart from the rude one." Percy said, stepping into the library just in front of me.

"I am right behind you, your chuffing majesty." This voice belonged to Walter, my batman, and the poor staff member on the night shift. Therefore, the maker of tea.

I had met Captain Walter Trevithick in my disastrous stint in the army. Wally was the first to be enrolled in the Menagerie and soon doubled up as my irreverent butler. Wally was five feet seven inches tall, with a massive head and a body like a brick outhouse.

"If I had known it was full misfits night, I would have just put two spoons of expensive tea in the pot. I see the reverse twins are out of it, and the African Prince is drinking the best cognac, so he won't want tea. Just his lordship, and the King's whore."

Gat laughed once sarcastically, which was his way of indicating that he was going to threaten to start to hit Walter if the butler continued on his current path.

"I will tell you now, I have never slept with the king." Percy replied calmly, she never bit at Walter. That was always my job, or Gat's.

Anyway, it was all an act, if you watched them both close enough, Walter and Percy would exchange the odd nod and wink when they were bantering.

"Just serve the tea, Walter. It's late." I grumbled.

"No, it's incredibly early. And I have to be up at the crack of dawn whilst you bunch of miscreants can sleep in. I've got to work with Waite to reseal chamber one. That Bristol Harridan is making a real noise."

"I am afraid I am going to delay your repose a little further. Word from the Ministry; our next adventure. Something is going on in Lincolnshire."

"Oh God, not Lincoln. It's as flat as a witch's tit up there, except for that steep hill. No decent clubs." Mumbled Avery, before returning to a light snore.

Percy sighed, and took a seat. She retrieved a silver cigarette box and offered them around. I refused, but Gat pulled out a cigar instead and lit it before handing the match to a hovering Percy.

"Turn on the extractor if you are going to smoke those foul things in my library."

Gat moved to the wall near the doorway and clicked a switch on the light panel. A light whir emanated from a grill above the door.

Percy had got a technician to install the extractor when I had denied them all smoking opportunities in the library. The library was our centre of coordination though, and we would not meet elsewhere. Some of them needed to smoke to deliberate, so the fan was a happy medium.

"So, Percy, tell us about our next mission."

Percy blew into the air, exhaling intricate smoke rings. "There is something amiss at Lindum Hall. The whole building is possessed. The regiment stationed there, or at least those who were on the outside in the barracks and survived, felt an attack to their minds by some sort of consciousness. An invisible being, it seems."

"I've never heard of Lindum Hall." Gat said. He was attacking the brandy, glasses and decanter chinking.

"It's rather secret. The government have used it for at least two hundred years, as a base to fight and imprison the strange and alien. Human, creature and artefact. It quite possible the only museum with a prison wing."

My ears pricked up. "I've heard of something about this. Didn't they have the Ripper there for a time?" I asked. I'd heard a snifter when I had briefly worked for the Times. The editorial team were warned off of any fact finding on the matter.

"I thought you were sleeping with the Ripper, Percy." Wally alluded to the rumour that the current king had been Jack the Ripper.

I desperately tried not to laugh, even though it was very rude. I almost failed.

"Oh, fuck off Walter dear. Bertie is a friend, not to mention he's also in his sixties. What do you two take me for? I don't need money, or power. Listen, please." It was unusual for Percy to take the rise.

I glanced over at Wally, who just raised his eyebrows at me. He was being deliberately sarcastic as usual, whist being extremely funny. It wasn't his only fault.

"Continue, Percy."

"The Brigadier in charge, Lord Holden, contacted the minister. No one is able to approach the hall, well more like mansion. Its bloody huge looking at the plans. It has an array of underground bunkers and floors.

"Allegedly, there appears to be an invisible barrier all around the complex. And it is impregnable. The army has been trying to blow holes in a vast swathe of nothing for weeks.

"Then, according to Lord Holden, his arsehole-ness, the Archbishop of Lincoln pops over to rouse the troops, as it were, and states instead that the problem is that the place is ungodly and unapproachable under the light of the Holy Spirit.

"His Grace, Canterbury, called Archbishop Lincoln a silly Anglo-Saxon name, apparently and then was ordered to visit by the king himself and came to the same conclusion."

"And that is?"

"The whole building *is* possessed by the Devil."

"I'm not collaborating with any army." Gat announced, all matter of fact.

"Then you will stay here, Gat. If you want to be in the field, you have to adapt your prejudices."

He opened his mouth to argue, but I held up a finger. It was the only time they would all listen to me if I did that. It was my veto, my right as their paying employer-come-shepherd.

"I understand your views about the military, but those boys are just following orders. The corruption is at the top, not the lads whose blood soaks into the earth." I sighed theatrically to add weight to my words.

"Isn't Holden the legendary leader of the Strange Battalion?" Wally said, actually sounding impressed. Wally had, by now, sat down, himself.

I had wanted to meet the Strange Battalion for quite some time. Rumour had it that they dealt with threats from other worlds and planes of existence, Alien creatures and space capsules, like something out of a Herbert George Wells novel.

"He is very well respected." Walter said as he rose again. "More tea?"

"If we accept, and the Minister really wants us to accept, Holden wants us up there by tomorrow morning. Which gives us a few hours' sleep and then a train to Lincoln. We then will catch a Hansom from Lincoln to Lindum Hall for a reconnoitre. We will have lodgings at nearby Pender House, which is on the adjacent estate and also a government owned retreat."

"Thanks, Percy. Gat, you, Percy and I will go with Walter. The twins can sleep off their hangovers and join us later. We will follow normal routes and not travel the Hopelessness. I'd rather not explain how we got there so fast."

"Thank God, that's a relief. I'd rather crawl there on stumps than travel with the ghosts." Walter muttered as he poured more tea.

I looked at Percy and raised my eyebrows, we did share a connection, but she was, as always, oblivious to my affection. One day, Percy, you will see what I think of you - maybe when Hell freezes over, and trees grew on the moon once again.

Percy suddenly stood up; she didn't stay still long at Legend Street. "I had better prepare. I will meet you promptly at the railway station late morning tomorrow." And as quick as she had arrived, she was gone. Her bath beckoned.

"That woman is an Enigma. I'd put the immersion on anyway." Walter said as he tidied up the cups and saucers. When he had left the room, Gat sighed.

"She will notice one day, Robert. Maybe not today, but one day. At least she isn't a hag, like Eliza, looking to claim your essence for her witch." Gat stood and said his good night.

Once Walter had carried the twins up to their rooms and gone to bed himself, I broke into the brandy. I hummed and hawed about going to speak to Waite, but stupidly the tiredness took me, and I floated off. I dreamed of Percy naked in bed next to me on our wedding night, and it would have been perfect but then she pulled a gun from God knows where - and shot me through the forehead.

Chapter Four
A Hellish Journey

Waite was nowhere to be seen when I did go to speak with her. I left her written instructions upon a chalk board near her earthly perch, to let me know immediately if there were any cellar or attic breaches whilst we were away, then I went and met the chaps and climbed into our awaiting cab.

Gat and Walter sat like two opponents before a boxing match, full of respect for each other but waiting to break the other's nose first. Gat, as ever looked over his glasses, book in hand. Walter was doing the Times crossword, or, rather, trying.

I shouted for the driver to take us to New Street Station which, by 1900, had become a busy nexus for travellers. Over forty trains departed every hour from the station, and we were bound for the 10:12 am Nottingham train where we would connect to a Derby bound carriage on route to Lincoln.

St Martin's Church and its surroundings were alive as ever on market day, and as we approached Digbeth the noise intensified. We took a left and made it to New Street. We alighted, thanking the cabbie, and Walter found a trolley for our luggage.

We made our way through the station, which was all bustle and hawking. Most eyes were on Gat, as usual, although he just ploughed ahead ignoring the stares and the infrequent, but bitter name calling. Walter growled at a few of the people we passed, mainly middle-class denizens who could afford to regularly traverse the rails, and were meant to have manners, but were as bigoted as most common British subjects at the time.

I took a quick diversion to pick up a copy of the Times, to read on the way, knowing I would not be able to prise Walter's away from him until he'd filled in every box.

Percy was waiting for us at the entrance to the platform. She was dressed as a young woman, rather than a young man (off to a shoot) as she had been the night before.

She was a vision, in a loose and flouncy blouse above her waist, and tight and bustled grey skirt below. Percy's hair was pinned up intricately atop her head and looked like a delicate pastry. She held a parasol in the same colour as her dress, and she was speaking to a nervous looking porter who stood watching, overloaded with her voluminous cases. She caught my eye and smiled that smile which would have floored stronger men than myself.

Gat looked at me, then Percy, a half-smile threatening to part his lips. He knew my thoughts. He knew they were forlorn.

"Mr Waterfield." Percy said, no public show of affection, just the smile. It wasn't the done thing to kiss in public if one wasn't married, in those days. Even if she had wanted to kiss me. "Gat. Walter. Well, met."

Gat inclined his head, and Walter mumbled. He didn't like being nice to Percy, which quite frankly irritated me. It was a bally good job he was also a man I could not afford to do without in my life. A life I would not have if it were not for him.

"The train departs shortly. I suggest we make our way down to the platform," Percy said, officious as ever, once the pleasantries were over. We were about to be on our way when a young man bounced off Gat.

"Get out the way, you black bugger." The young man said. He was a young office worker, by the look of him. He was all grey suit with a bowler hat, a turned-up nose, and pursed lips that looked like everything he had ever done in life had been given to him on a silver spoon.

Gat stepped back, his hands raised in apology. He knew what would happen if he was seen as an aggressor in such a situation. Walter growled. The young man stood there, fists bunched.

"Leave this gentleman to me." Percy said. The public eye had now turned away from us so, as ever, Percy's timing was perfect. She walked up to the young man.

"I am so sorry my friend got in your way." She purred.

"Friend. You are a bloody whore if you call an African a friend." I was surprised the young man didn't spit. He might have done if Percy wasn't present. Some of his deep ingrained manners were showing through his vibrant true colours.

Percy pointed her parasol at him. Then she threw it up in the air, caught it by the pointy end, and then hit the young man in his testicles ridiculously hard with the parasol handle, with a swing like a boxer's uppercut. She whispered, "you racist little shit," as he collapsed.

"Right gentlemen, we have a train to catch." Percy turned to her young porter whose mouth was open enough to throw stones through. We left the young office worker doubled over, trying to coax his gonads back down as we stowed our bags and boarded the train. Walter did not pitch any comments at Percy for the whole of the day, which was a record, as we now say.

We were comfortable together in a private compartment soon after. First Class, such was the financial might of Percy and her lords and masters. We were served tea and biscuits and I tried to stay awake as we made small talk for the first part of the journey that would take us to Derby.

29

"Brigadier Lord Holden sent me a telegram this morning. Gat, would you do the honour, please?"

Gat nodded then murmured a few words, calling to the spirits of his ancestors, bathing the cabin in a silence that could only be broken by one more powerful than my friend. All the Menagerie had their skills.

"Lindum Hall has been a repository for the strange for as long as we can remember. There has been a house and human-fashioned underground caverns here since the 1500s, when Francis Walsingham, the then Secretary of State decided he needed to keep secrets from the lunatics who wanted to burn everyone and everything that was remotely supernatural.

"Lindum Hall has always been under the authority of the state and the head of the armed forces. Kept secret from the Church and the general public. Although, after Victoria's death, the church were informed. God help us if the Archbishop of Canterbury was able to admit he knew of the site, officially. As it is, he is suppressed by colleagues who know what he got up to when he was a young man."

Percy drew her cup to the mouth and sipped at her tea.

"There have been many supernatural and alien threats to this Kingdom over the years by creatures alive and dead that would make your toes curl just by their description. One such creature seems to have broken its bonds. It has killed, we surmise, the majority of the personnel in the vicinity. It has put up a supernatural barrier whilst it foments its plans. Moreover, it is only a matter of time as to when it makes its next move."

"What magic bonded the creature?" Gat asked.

"Moreover, how did it break those bonds?" I followed.

"The creature has been labelled as Apollyon. Greek for destroyer. Also known as Abaddon. A Hellish demon." Percy continued. "It may have opened the very gates to Hell. A threat of biblical stature."

"There was a Hell long before that storybook was written." Gat said as if he would brook no argument.

"Each to their own belief." I said. "More importantly, Percy, how are we going to deal with such a threat? Gat can channel the spirits, but no one else is a magician."

Percy laughed nervously. "We will have the help of the Strange Regiment."

Gat and even Walter laughed at that for distinct reasons. None-the-less their mirth prevented Percy going on for quite a few minutes.

"This is Menagerie work." Gat said. "No one else has the skills to fight first order demons. If this Apollyon is as powerful as you have said, then the military are out of their depth. Or you will need to bring in the Roman Code, the New Orleans Family, or the Australian Dreamers."

"Lord Holden *has* been advised by Dr Ezekiel Arnold and the Witch Allegra Martineau from New Orleans. It's not a purely magical issue. It is supernatural, apparently."

Gat laughed. "Ms Martineau is respectable and fastidious, but she does not have the power. Arnold is a fraud, you may as well throw mid-west cure-all potions at this Apollyon."

"Lord Holden and The Minister agree that Robert is our best bet to get in there and assess the situation." Percy put her teacup down on the little table that separated us.

"Via the Hopelessness." I had guessed as much when Percy had outlined the situation the previous evening. "It's purgatory, not Hell."

"Yet, there *must* be a gateway." Percy countered.

For moments you could have heard a pin drop. The Menagerie had dealt with some strange things, never one of this import, or a threat from a king of Hell.

"We will need the twins. We will need us all." Walter added.

"They are little more than children, Wally, how can I put them in harm's way without an assessment of the risk? Two children and a handful of us against a potential Satanic being? We will need to have an exceptional plan. We aren't talking level one demons here."

"Of course, it could be all smoke and mirrors."

We all looked at Percy.

"All I am saying is let's not jump to conclusions. We have battled conjurors who have been full of bluster and capable of making a large threat from roman candles, dry ice, and limelight. Not everything we have fought is of death."

I nodded. "Percy is right. We got carried away. Our motto is *sapiens consilium daemonem capit,* chaps. A wise plan catches a demon. Let us get our facts together, and then we will surmise."

Gat and Walter nodded.

We were soon pulling into Derby, to change for Nottingham and onto Lincoln. Derby was quiet compared to New Street, and so we waited patiently for the connecting train. As we sat in the waiting room, I drifted....

...and ended up in the Hopelessness.

I was startled. Not since I was a boy had I arrived in the Hopelessness accidentally. I had always chosen to walk its ghostly paths consciously.

Waite was perched upon the reflection of our cases.

"A spirit calls at Legend Street, Robert Waterfield. You should have listened to the prophecy. It is now in the house. The twins are asleep. He comes to murder."

Immediately, I travelled back to my house in Legend Street, to the first-floor landing where the twins would still be sleeping off their latest hangover. I was about to go corporeal.

"No, it is not alive. It is a spirit. No, it may be alive. I am not sure." Waite cawed, flustered. That was so unlike her.

"Bring forth Raven, your human avatar must protect my twins, Postlethwaite. I will not fail them again."

Waite transformed, splitting into two beings, into her human avatar - a spirit I knew as Hrafn Gunnarsdottir, who we called Raven. Waite fluttered onto her perch after the separation.

Raven smiled at me, as she loved to travel to the land of the living, and she drew both her soul blades whilst she stepped into corporeality, leaving me alone.

I followed into the real world and ran to the twin's bedroom, throwing open the doors. I could feel a spirit, yet it was both alive and dead. No wonder Waite had been confused.

Maisie, it was a strange one.

It had the body of a man, and the head of what could only be described as a street lantern.

A four-sided, lantern-headed man-creature.

Looking closer, I could see it was dressed as a policeman, down to the epaulettes that designated its rank as constable.

It turned to me, and I felt the strength of its will. Unlike anything I had felt before, and I had dealt with evil on many levels.

The lantern-head hissed and rattled with the sound of a burning mantle. The light at the centre of its visage flickered.

The creature then became faint for a second, and I thought like most spirits it had worn out its welcome. I tried to banish it, but then remembered that only worked in the Hopelessness.

The creature flickered like a flame in a breeze, or a poorly connected electric light, then suddenly there were two of them. They hadn't split, one hadn't grown from the other. It just came to be. A twin, born of peculiarity.

Both the lantern-heads stepped forward. I pulled my soul blade from its imagined space upon my back. The twins were at risk, it was time to fight.

Raven engaged with one of the lantern-headed creatures, her soul blade only just scraping it's lantern glass. Then there were three of them.

How could they reproduce so? I had not come across anything that could do so in such an immediate fashion. Not even revenants.

The room was then a flurry of movement. I immediately engaged one of the creatures. Its rasping hiss was like water on a heated rock.

"Twins, wake up. It is Uncle Robert. Danger level one. *Surgit.*"

We used latin code words for immediate flight or fight reactions in dangerous situations, and imprinted them on our subconsciousness, this was one of Gat's tricks. A word to wake us, a word to sober us, a word to sleep, and one never used; a word to die.

"You bugger." Avery swore, jumping up. "*Sobrii.*" She shouted, and pulled her sword from its subconscious sheath. Charlie did likewise, which was a good thing because two of the Lantern Heads had been budding doppelgangers. Charlie held a long sabre, and a long fighting knife with a wide guard to block other weapons.

I looked to one side. Young Raven had decapitated one opponent and faced another. Waite was not a young bird, but her human avatar looked so.

Raven looked to be about sixteen. In life she had been a Shield Maiden and she had died in Lincoln in the tenth century, where Postlethwaite took her spirit to preserve it as a favour to Odin.

Raven was a wonderful, yet terrifying fighter, a whirling dervish, a tornado even. She took out another opponent, and then killed the one I faced. We both turned as one to help the twins, but needn't have bothered. Both Avery and Charlie had done their duty.

"Morning uncle." Avery said like he had just got out of bed. His silk gentleman's pyjamas damp with sweat. Charlie hadn't got undressed and so she wore her undergarments and petticoats from the evening before.

"Thought you were in Lincoln, Uncle?" Charlie said, sheathing her soul blades.

Raven morphed back into Waite, who had appeared on the dressing table between the twins' beds.

There was a low boom from somewhere deep in the bowels of the house.

"Diversion." Waite cawed, and flew off.

I began to follow. To the twins I said. "Change and pack. Civilian dress for now but put your combats in. We will have to travel the Hopelessness when this is over. If I am not back in half an hour raise the alarm. Call for Gat. Then follow me down. Do not follow me alone."

They both nodded and I stepped into the Hopelessness, down to the lower levels of the house.

The cellars were lit but only with low electrical light, it was not helpful for navigation and threw terrifying shadows.

I heard a caw, and I followed the sound. It was a warren I knew well, each alcove, nook and cranny. I knew what those rooms did to sound.

I found Raven engaging another of the lantern-heads in the vast rose jar room. The place where we stored the high danger but captured spirits.

It was holding a jar, one of many that lined the walls. I could now see there was a gap on the middle shelf of five. It had surely been targeting an individual rose jar device. The creature was after someone in particular.

The Lantern Head budded and so there were two for me to battle. Raven engaged without being asked.

"Persistent, aren't they?" She said, winking as she lifted her ethereal sword.

Raven had a great personality. Waite must have had a sense of humour, deep down, to trap a moribund avatar with the same name as its race, and then give Hrafn Gunnarsdottir the ability to show her wonderful persona.

I never ever said this to Waite, up to that point, but I had sometimes wished Raven were the primary personality of the raven Postlethwaite. Raven was far more balanced and less in the prophecies.

Raven danced with her swords. It is the only way to describe how she moved. I wasn't sure if it was the soul blades that did it, or her own training; perhaps both. Her moves were beautiful, but deadly. The creatures in front of us that night were fast, but Hrafn Gunnarsdottir was quicker.

I lost ground on the creature facing me. It blocked my attacking blow and its reflective, rasping maw came face to lantern with me. I could hear its mantle chugging on an unconnected gas supply. Yet there was another sound present in the background, I had heard it with one of the earlier ones. A familiar sound. Yet at that time, I couldn't place it.

The knowledge of The Great Caruso, Italian swordmaster of the 1480s filled my head.

Step back, move to your left side as it approaches from the right, turn, and then skewer.

My body followed those instructions, I stepped and turned, and it moved past me, its momentum carrying it forward. Then I stuck my sword in what would have been its right kidney. It staggered.

Take its sword arm. Then head.

I did so, and it came off at the shoulder, falling to the ground with a clang. Metal.

Steam. That was the noise.

Strange.

It moved clearly with some sort of combustion. I then arced my sword back-hand and took its head, which fell and shattered. As I watched it's then recumbent hissing form, it dissipated.

I turned as Raven finished the other one before it could bud. Then she leapt forwards and caught the rose jar before it hit the floor. Like a cat, rather than a bird, she rose and gave the jar to me.

"Mr Wakefield. He is not the only jar taken off the shelf."

I walked over to the wall at the side of the room which was lined with those glass receptacles. There was a principal place where I kept the most evil of them. The room had been warded, yet the Lantern Heads had broken it easily. That was not what was troubling me. In a setback alcove under another layer of Gat's magic was an incredibly special jar I should not have been able to handle, or even know it was there.

Yet, now with the magic dissipated, I knew what jar was missing. Eliza's, containing the miserable soul of the woman I once was to wed, who killed many men, as well as her parents. I had brought her soul back from Hell in order to spare her, yet I couldn't separate her from the evil bestowed by the witch Isabelle of Stafford.

Why had they taken Eliza?

My Friend. The train comes.

That was Gat. I would have to travel to Lincoln, and, on our return, we would have to look for Eliza's rose jar and hope to God that whoever had taken it could not get past the rest of the wards set by Gat.

"Protect my house, Hrafn Gunnarsdottir."

"I am Raven now. Call me so, Robert, and I will protect your house for eternity."

I smiled. "Thank you, Raven."

Chapter Five
She's a Vampire

We didn't linger in the Hopelessness, the twins and me.

Firstly, they were always nervous in that place, particularly Charlie. Secondly, I always feared the revenants their parents had become would try one day to take their children back via that place. Ridiculous as it would seem, I feared it would be so. They were young adults, but that fear was always present when I took them to that place.

Avery and Charlie did not know their parents had been revenants. It hadn't been my secret to keep either, but their grandmother, the infirm Lady Amelia Curzon – not of the famous Curzons, from Kedleston Hall I might add, who are wonderful people - had made me swear I would not reveal their parents' fate, just in case it affected their development.

I was brought up to believe truth was the best policy, but we won't dwell on that now as you will find as you read on.

We stepped into the waiting room at Derby station and were immediately whisked away by a lingering Percy.

"Its cost me ten pounds and a letter from the Home Secretary to delay this train. We cannot wait any further." Percy seemed irritated until I briefed all my colleagues on the train what had befallen us at Legend Street.

"Eliza could ruin everything," Percy said through gritted teeth. "You are vulnerable around her."

Looking back, it hurt me a little, the woman I now loved suggesting the woman I *had* loved was still a factor in any future possible failure on my part. I wasn't a man who shed tears, I never had been, but at that point my throat caught. Gat looked across at me with an imperceptible shake of his head.

Be strong my friend. I could imagine him saying. He was my rock at times.

"We do not have the time to go find her rose jar now. We will see what's what at Lindum Hall , survey the situation, and then I will assess the risk of one over the other."

"Robert…"

"No Miss Percival, I am clear. Eliza can wait. The things that took her clearly had purpose. I can only hope it's not the witch Isabelle of Stafford pulling the lantern-head's strings. Although, from what I can gather, Isabelle is bound to the earth presently, and cannot walk among us."

"Isabelle is part of an anchor binding spell, my friend, however badly her younger self had executed it. Eliza cannot go back to that farm lest she be obliterated. Someone else, or something, had stolen the rose jar with Eliza's spirit within in it. Mark my words." Gat offered.

I nodded at Gat. We had put Percy in her place, I didn't like doing it, but Percy was impulsive. She would be expecting to fight on two fronts, but from what I had heard about what was going on at Lindum Hall, we needed all hands-on deck.

"What about these lantern-heads?" Percy said. She was always like a dog with a bone, she wouldn't let anything go.

"I will search the Hopelessness at some point." I said almost angrily. The Hopelessness wouldn't reveal any secrets unless I had more distinct information. Those creatures are clearly fuelled by steam and some sort of ethereal power, was it magic?

Percy looked at me. She knew I was giving her short shrift, and I would pay for that. Eventually.

"How about we ask my Arthur to contact our friends at the ministry. They could look into the lantern-heads, and also keep an ear to the ground concerning Eliza." Gat offered most helpfully.

Thank-you, I mouthed as Percy looked away. "I will also ask the agency to put someone on it. I am not happy with Eliza's soul on the loose. Nor these so-called steam-powered creatures."

"I agree, but we need this commission, Percy. The coffers are running dry. I need to finish this job before we look nearer home."

"And you will be paid handsomely by the Ministry of Mirrors. Yet, we will be expected to find that rose jar. It's not all about you and your failed engagement, Robert, but she could let Isabelle's magic loose on this world."

That hurt. I might have then sulked for a while as we disembarked the handsome cab.

The rest of the journey passed with no further incident. We alighted at Lincoln and were soon greeted by a certain Captain Sidney Knowles. He was a very handsome ash blonde haired fellow with high cheekbones and a chest you could have fashioned barrels around. I noticed Gat's eyebrows rise, as well as Percy's.

Percy and I rode with Captain Knowles, whose life story was vomited up to us covered in sugar. He had been part of the Staffordshire regiment before he had been taken on by Brigadier Lord Holden, because of his ability to work well in a crisis. He had worked out that the barrier was affecting the world around them, as well as blocking their entrance.

"Gravity was off." But he said it as "orf."

"He was about as Staffordshire bred as the King's balls." Percy had whispered.

"I noticed that I could jump higher than normal," he continued, "lift things that had been far too heavy for even me to do so before, even though I spend an inordinate amount of time in the gym. Then I found the anomaly in the chapel crypt."

He paused for effect, like a cheap vaudeville comic. Knowles was not a natural storyteller, he had paused for effect for far too long and even the former simpering Percy was getting annoyed.

"Well man. What was it?" She pleaded.

"We don't know. Suddenly the place began to shudder. We evacuated the grounds and left. Even now we can only get as far as the outer wall of the estate. There is some sort of impenetrable barrier surrounding the place. Like an invisible wall." Knowles had clearly trod the boards at Oxford or Cambridge, probably an early member of the Footlights. He tried to summon up an air of marvel and wonder as he hit his mark. It didn't work.

Percy looked at me and, in that glance, she managed to convey her feelings that this man was in fact a plum-sucking inbred aristocratic moron. His aunt was probably his mother.

"So, we do not know anymore? Has Lord Holden ordered any intelligence missions?"

"We cannot get through the barrier."

"That doesn't mean there are no clues." She said as if Captain Knowles was fresh medical student meat at a post-mortem.

"Above my rank, Miss Percival. Above my rank." Knowles repeated as if that explained it all.

Then the conversation stalled. Percy was not impressed with either me or Knowles by that point.

We arrived at our lodgings, which were immaculate. Pender House was on the Lindum estate, and had been a large abode built for the future Dukes of Lindum to stay in with their new wives, away from the hustle and bustle of the main estate. It was red brick, not that it made it look any less imposing. It was a four-storey affair, made up of four gabled facets in a rectangular quadrant. It was stunning.

Knowles left us at the steps, and we were taken into house by the Head Butler, Sergeant Davies, a no-nonsense ginger Welshman who looked at Captain Knowles like he would have him for tea. Davies led us through to a large sitting room.

Davies turned to Gat and said. "You can take your master's bags upstairs. I will show you the way."

You could have heard the intake of breath from Walter, Percy, and the twins over a grenade going off.

"His Highness Prince Gathii is a member of the Investigation Team, Sergeant Davies. My name is Captain Walter Trevithick. You will take the Prince's bags *upstairs*."

Davies went green. He looked at Gat and bowed rather comically. I saw my friend's lips twitch despite the slight. "I apologise, your Highness. I will arrange for the bags to be delivered to your rooms."

"See that you do, son. The Brigadier and I go back a long way."

I looked at Walter, in fact we all looked at him. He winked. He was such a liar. He hated rank. He hated hat he had been a captain because of his birth status. He had spent thirty years rubbing the shine off his accent and etiquette ever since.

Our rooms were splendid and extremely comfortable when we eventually reached them. Lord Holden asked Percy and I to attend his office as soon as we were settled.

Percy was still a little off as we walked down the main stairwell to the lower floors. I was likewise hurt by her earlier words and was not going to broach a conversation with nonsensical small talk.

Brigadier Lord Holden's offices were normally situated at Lindum Hall, but since it had become sealed off by the strange possession, he and his men had set up a control centre on the ground floor of Pender House. I knocked lightly on the door.

Someone shouted "enter", probably the Brigadier's adjunct.

It was imposing as we moved through, the fine panelled double doors opened up into the most wonderful library I had ever seen. I noticed with some jealousy that it was far more grandiose than the one at Legend Street.

It had wall to wall books. Gat would have broken out in hives if he knew we were in there when he hadn't been invited.

The room – and there was little of it without bookshelves – was decorated with carved oak borders, and on each of the four walls was a single bas-relief panel surrounded by shelving.

It was quite a remarkable set of images. I could see a death figure with a scythe, I could see a figure killing others from atop a horse, I could see a pile of bodies behind a pock faced creature, and a crowd of starving figures holding empty bowls out to a gaunt laughing woman. The four horsemen of the apocalypse.

"Charming, aren't they?" The Brigadier said, heavy with sarcasm, from behind a leather embossed desk that sat in the middle of the library, like a hamstrung titan.

A pretty red-haired woman dressed in military attire stood to his left, a notebook in hand. "Lord Pender was a bit of a black magic aficionado. He surrounded himself with people who were said to be witches or wizards. If I weren't the commanding officer here at Lindum, I would have said he was a nutcase. Unfortunately, he was more on the ball than his

39

eighteenth-century Enlightenment contemporaries gave him credit for. Apparently, Newton had a soft spot for Pender. He also had him exorcised and locked up for study.

"Welcome to Pender House. I am hoping you are going to help us seize back control of our HQ. Captain Wright, will brief you shortly on recent developments."

I had heard that the Strange Regiment had, for many years, allowed women to enlist. I saw Percy's reaction when Holden announced her as Captain Wright.

Holden continued. "May I introduce Colonel Robert Waterfield, Colonel, Captain Claire Wright."

I shook Captain Wrights hand. She was delightful to look at, even though she was dressed as a squaddie. No feminine accoutrements to be seen, just a naturally handsome woman. Percy was beautiful, but Captain Wright had something about her that I couldn't put my finger on at the time. An effervescence

"Colonel?" Percy laughed.

"Yes, but only briefly." I said to Captain Wright, as if that would assuage her. I barely thought about my time in the military. I certainly couldn't talk about it in present company. We will re-visit those days at some point, but not yet.

"Hush hush stuff, Miss Percival." The Brigadier tapped his nose. "Colonel Waterfield is a man of secrets, however I will honour his veritable discharge papers and call him Mister. And so will Captain Wright."

"I am not allowed to use my rank outside of the regiment either, Colonel. My lips are sealed." Captain Wright smiled again. I was immediately taken.

"Anyway, enough of the pleasantries. Take a seat, both of you. Captain Wright will tell you what we know."

We were seated without refreshments, which I thought a bit rude, then Captain Wright began.

"Our problem is named Apollyon. After the sculpture that adorns the reception hall of Lindum. Upon the Greek statue, as we were fleeing, were carved the three words. "I am Here.""

"We lost thirty-two personnel. Seventeen remain in the property, left behind as we evacuated. Some volunteered purposefully, some accidentally. Fifteen souls have been lost after various attempts to break through the barrier. It is as if it reacts like a threatened living thing if we get too close. It pulps its victims, and they explode into a fine mist. It is very, very unwholesome.

"The last time it happened, a group of us had managed to breach the barrier, led by the witch Arabella Pear. She was able to make a conduit through, momentarily, though we thought the breach would hold. But then, one by one, they vapourised. Ms Pear too, eventually. Her screams were pitiful. It could have so easily been me.

"We haven't seen any apparitions, nor heard any voices in days. It has all been as silent as the grave. Lindum Hall has never been silent. When you work at Lindum you get used to the noise of the strange - ghosts and spirits. There are over sixteen fully opaque spirits in the upper house, relocated from elsewhere. Hundreds of transparent beings, and a forgettable number of whisps. All contained and friendly. The damaged spirits, demons, aliens and undead creatures are on the lower floors, below ground in the bunkers. Whatever this Apollyon is, it came from those depths, perhaps even from below decks. Possibly one of the earliest creatures the regiment captured, or something that has used one of those creatures to break through. We have no way of knowing which one. The records were not well kept, in the early days. Trying to find a scribe with no firm links to the church was problematic in the 1700s.

"I have two eyewitness accounts of lower floor spirits and demons screaming for re-location, so as not to be left in there with Apollyon. Screaming. What would scare Hellish creatures so?"

Captain Wright sighed the sigh of the exhausted, and I immediately felt for her.

I took a moment to look at Lord Holden. He was a thick-set bulky man, who had been well muscled before the spread of middle age came to him. His hair was battleship grey, and carefully combed over his pate. His left eye twitched every now and then, particularly if he didn't like what he heard. He wouldn't be a good poker player, I surmised.

"We are out of answers Waterfield." Holden banged his desk in frustration. "We are hoping that you and Prince Gathii can help. You are renown for your prowess at such matters. An outcome of a chance meeting between Percy and the Secretary of State recommended we try your outfit, Waterfield. I am not sure what we will do if you are not successful. Do you have any thoughts?"

"From what you have said, we need to reconnoitre. I need to attempt to breach the barrier through the Hopelessness."

"What?" Captain Wright asked.

I sighed, I wasn't used to talking about my talent to strangers. "I can access the spirit world. I am not what one might call a magical being, but, since my youth I have been able to step between the veil. I can walk the fields of the shadow of death, as it were. I can commune with the Hopelessness and those who dwell within its purgatory. I should be able to breach the barrier."

"I was surprised to hear about your abilities, Waterfield?"

"Yes, Brigadier, they are under the line for many reasons. My ability has been struck from all official records, sir. Redacted, as it were. For my

41

sins, I consult with the Secret Service, and Percy, here, is my handler. I have only been working in such a way for a few years. I got into the business of the strange after my fiancée became possessed by a witch, and killed ten people, and then tried to shoot me. I thought my ability to walk the Hopelessness brought me closer to the spirits than any other man. Imagine my surprise when I realised such creatures were living amongst us and that ghosts and spirits walked the world in numbers."

"And am I right you are able to trap them in rose jars, too?" Captain Wright asked.

"As I believe you do here. We just have a tame witch who spells the glass." Percy said quite snappily.

"Yes, but are you constantly warding the jars, the magic breaks down so easily, it seems."

"Yes, Gat takes care of that for us, too. Not every creature needs warding, but some do."

"When things are right, we could do with your help cataloguing the creatures at Lindum. If we could subdue some of them, rather than having them walking though you all day." The Brigadier said light heartedly. "Makes you want to throw up your breakfast. Pardon the imagery, ladies."

"I am sure we can help. I'll lend you Gat."

"Marvellous." The Brigadier mumbled, he looked at his watch. "Actions, then?"

I sighed, there was only one thing to do. "Gat and I will enter the Hopelessness, we will then attempt to breach the barrier. Tonight."

Percy nodded, it seemed she had reached the same conclusion.

"I would like to accompany you." Captain Wright asked.

"Travelling the Hopelessness can be difficult for the living." I said. Although, on one level, I admired this woman's bravery.

Then Captain Wright dissipated.

That was the only word for it. She turned to mist. Then she re-materialised behind the Brigadier.

"I am not human, Colonel Waterfield."

"Dear gods." Percy screamed. "She's a chuffing vampire."

Chapter Six
The Barrier

How Percy kept a full ten inch stake in a handbag so small was beyond me.

Whilst I was more experienced in dealing with the ghostly, spiritual side of things, Percy was very experienced in ridding the world of the undead. Vampires were rare, but they appeared every now and then. Shapeshifters were more than common, half human, half demon creatures were less so.

Percy was skilled in the capture and destruction of such blood sucking creatures, which was how she had worked her way up through the ranks of the Ministry of Mirrors, apparently. Although, come to think of it, her stories didn't always match. More of that later.

It was probably why Percy suddenly leapt toward Captain Wright; a stake upraised in her left hand.

Captain Wright dissipated again, and coalesced behind us.

"Stop." Commanded Holden.

Percy came to a halt just feet away from the pretty captain.

"I am not a Vampire." Wright muttered. "And I would ask you not to utter such a flagrant profanity." Captain Wright's voice was forceful, unafraid. "I am descended from an elemental creature. I have certain anthropomorphic talents passed down via my female line. I am not an undead Miss Percival, just Elemental."

"Stand down Ms Percival." Barked the Brigadier.

The stake flew from Percy's hand, pulled by some unseen force, and ended up held in the closed fist of the captain. As we watched she brandished it before herself, holding it aloft as it began to glow. I watched as twigs erupted from the stake, and leaves began to grow from it.

"Would a vampire give life like this, Ms Percival?" The Captain asked.

Percy stood there mouth open, a little redder than a few moments ago.

"If you are here to help, Miss Percival, you have to realise not everything strange is dangerous. We do not trap everything in a jar." The Brigadier was angry, pointing his stick at us. I noticed it didn't have leaves on it. Captain Wright had obviously not handled it for him.

I held my hands up in front of my chest in supplication, and although she looked like she didn't want to, Percy apologised. Although it was the merest of mumbles.

Captain Wright dispersed again as if to prove a point, and re-materialised in front of me. So, near me in fact, I could feel her breath. It smelt of spearmint and Parma Violets. She handed me the stake, which not only had little branches and leaves on it, but it also had a root system. It was like one of those little bonsai trees one could see in a Japanese exhibition.

"Plant her, she will bring you luck."

Involuntarily, I smiled at her. Captain Wrights reciprocal smile took my breath away. Her eyes became the deepest emerald, her hair seemed to glow like embers. I was at that point captivated.

"Sir, I will join Mr Waterfield and Prince Gathii later, if that is acceptable." The captain said to her commanding officer, then turned to me again. "I have colleagues who are like me, who may well be able to provide us with some support if we are able to break through the barrier into the Hall."

I nodded. "Percy will no doubt join us, too."

"Just ask Miss Percival not to stake anyone."

I wanted to laugh, but when I looked at Percy she was seething.

We spent another hour with the Brigadier, who read us the riot act and then told us that he would not appreciate us jumping to conclusions about any of his staff, and that we were not to kill any of them either. We were instructed to inform our companions likewise. We left his presence with our tails between our legs, and went to find Gat, Walter, and the twins.

We found the twins first, sitting watching a drill on one of the large front lawns. Percy excused herself and stormed off, still hot under the collar. "I am going for a lie down."

Percy was usually queen bee, but she had been put in her place by Brigadier Lord Holden, who had gone to Eaton with the Home Secretary, who no doubt would have her job if he were to write about her discrepancies.

"What's with Miss Prissy Bloomers." Avery asked. He was wearing a military-like outfit. Avery was good at that, managing to blend in with the locals. He had probably talked the quartermaster into it, he had a fearsome ability to persuade. So full-on, and charming.

Charlie, on the other hand, was dressed in casual ladies hunting tweeds and a flat cap.

I couldn't help but smile. "She picked a fight with a vampire who wasn't a vampire."

"What?" Avery jumped up from the red and white deck chair she had been lounging in.

Then I started to laugh even more. "She got a bally stake out of her handbag. Captain Wright, by the way, is an elemental spirit. She is of the wood folk. She took the stake from Percy, and turned it into this baby tree."

I brandished the little thing in front of them. Charlie cooed over it in a very Charlie fashion. Avery had eyes of warning. It wasn't until I looked up that I saw Percy had been there all along.

"We convene at three PM to try and breech the wall. Try to have your wits about you then, *Colonel*."

My cheeks went red as Percy turned her back. Charlie and Avery began to laugh.

"Feel up to joining us in the Hopelessness?" I asked the twins before leaving to freshen up. "We are going to attempt to breach the barrier."

They both nodded, but I saw Charlie looked less than eager.

Back in my room I slept for about an hour, at least, dreaming forgettable dreams. I thought about Eliza's spirit being at large and so I dropped into the Hopelessness and fast-walked to Birmingham.

Waite was on her perch in the cellars of our home.

"He isn't dead, Robert."

"Who?" I asked. I had forgotten about the words Waite had said to me the night before.

"The splintered soul. He is calling you."

"What does that mean?"

"That is all I have. No other context. It comes to me from the codicils. I have nothing else. It is like a dripping tap of consciousness."

"Well, keep me updated."

I moved into the real world, and Waite followed. As if sensing that I wished to speak to Raven, the girl appeared.

"I should be with you in Lincoln. There are dangerous creatures there, even on the side of good."

I looked at Waite's pretty teenage avatar. "I fear Eliza may return."

"You should never have tried to bring her back." Raven finished.

"Foolish man." Waite offered.

"A moment of weakness."

"More a moment of stupidity, dear Robert." Raven placed her hand on my heart. She liked to feel it beating. Raven no longer had one of her own.

I sighed. I had been stupid. The dead should not return to the land of the living, particularly the serial killing kind. I thought I could cleanse Eliza of the evil that Isabelle had planted within her. I had expected that Eliza would suddenly have no evil. I was foolish to think that the venom in her was solely because of the witch. No, Eliza had been born like that.

"Go back to Lincoln, Robert. I will watch and report back."

I nodded my thanks and dipped back into the Hopelessness. Raven flowed into Waite, and the bird flew onto her perch.

I heard the knocking before I left the Hopelessness Lincoln end.

45

I materialised as Gat entered the room.

"There are some strange folk here, Robert." He said mischievously. "I have just been conversing with Captain Wright. She seems rather taken with you. Have you fallen out with Percy?"

"Did she tell you about the vampire thing?"

He nodded with a chuckle. "We will use it against Percy for the rest of her life, no doubt. If she is speaking to us." He laughed his deep laugh. "We are needed. It is three o'clock."

Gat led me down the main stairs and out of the front entrance of Pender House to a set of carriages that would take us to the grounds of Lindum Hall.

I sat in the carriage with Gat, Captain Wright, and Walter. Percy, the twins, and the Brigadier were in the second carriage, and there were four members of the Strange Regiment in another. The journey was a short one.

The final part was on foot, as we needed to cut through the woods that sat at the back of the estate. As we neared to the invisible barrier, I could feel the evil ahead of me. I wasn't fearful or apprehensive, but there seemed to be a hanging pall of malfeasance.

"Goodness me." Percy whispered. She wouldn't look at me direct since the incident with Captain Wright earlier, but she did glance back.

"It gets worse as we approach." The Brigadier explained.

I saw the twins glance at each other. Gat was muttering in his native tongue. Walter gave a shake of his head.

"Can you get us all into the Hopelessness, Mr Waterfield?" Captain Wright asked as if annoyed by her commanding officer's warning.

"Not all in one go. If I take Gat through with you and your soldiers, Captain, I will then return for Miss Percival, and the Twins."

"Make it so." The Brigadier said. "I will remain here with Captain Trevithick and Sergeant Ross."

The nervous looking green gilled sergeant nodded, but said nothing. I hadn't even noticed his presence until his name was mentioned. Walter did not look happy at being left behind, nor being called Captain Trevithick.

Captain Wright introduced me to Corporal Coppice and Private Beech, the two other elemental beings she had mentioned earlier. I explained that we didn't need to hold hands, but the others needed to separate from us by less than a few yards.

I concentrated, it was easy for me to slip through the veil on my own, or with those I knew well. For new acquaintances, I needed to get to know them, however briefly. Gat surmised that I broke myself, and any that travelled with me, down into sub-atomic parts to slip through the gap between the real world and the Hopelessness. It wasn't until much later, watching Star Trek, that I utterly understood what he meant.

I took us through, but it was like wading through treacle, or fighting against sinking sand. When we appeared the other side, the spirits reacted to unseasoned visitors to their realm.

Who has come.
Why can they be alive here and not us.
Their souls are still attached.
Catch one, cage it….
…use its soul.

I could see that, for the three elemental spirits, their trip to the Hopelessness was a shock. I could see Corporal Coppice staring into the distance. His knees were literally shaking.

"Robert." Gat said. "Look. The barrier."

And there it was in all its glory. Or its ugliness. A wall of naked human flesh. A composite of bodies forced together in a Hellish manner. Mouths moaning, calling, screeching. It was like the worst of charnel houses. Blood poured from the joins in that barrier of flesh where the dead bodies had been mashed together in merged horror. Even I was shocked.

How would we get past this? Beech was retching, and Captain Wright gasped.

"Gat, call your magic, we will need to protect these people whilst I am gone. Remain in the Hopelessness, but behind one of your barriers."

He was muttering his undecipherable words before I had ended my sentence. He drew pictures in the air that sparkled and left after images on the retina. He always said his magic was controlled by the earth, and now it seemed more elemental. Gat and the soldiers winked out of existence. I could feel no trace of them, and hopefully neither could the spirits.

I stepped toward the barrier and told Percy and the twins to be ready with their swords.

What surprised me was that the Hopelessness was silent. Not that it talked, it was more of an absence of something when it communicated. Like the anti-whisper of lost secrets. It always goaded me. This time it was as quiet as the grave.

We re-appeared in front of Gat and the soldiers, and I nodded at my friend.

"Fucking Hell." Percy said in her non-lady-like manner. I usually found it exciting, but in the company of Captain Wright and her soldiers it seemed dirty now.

"Look." The Captain said.

I looked at the barrier as part of it, a human shaped part, broke away. The thing had once been a man. Yet, although his skin had been flayed, you could tell he was male. He was tall, and his grey eyes were bright compared

47

to the redness of his lipless grinning head. He was horrific. Then he resolved into something more human, although not quite.

He moved like a ballet dancer, one foot placed carefully in front of the other in a majestic balletic walk. I pushed at him with my mind, and he stopped. Then he laughed.

"I am not any old transparent spirit, Mr Waterfield. You will not dismiss me, nor my Master with ease. You may have free reign in this realm, yet my Master has the realms beneath, and he will push through into the real world. We will eat you all. We will chew on your bones, suck out your marrow, we will take your souls, and the bodies of your children, and we will take them as our own. Their childish minds will flee, and we will return."

Despite the words of the nearest man, he was not able to move to me. So, I approached him.

"Colonel." Captain Wright said. "Mr Waterfield. Please."

"He knows what he is doing." Gat replied.

Percy just laughed. "He is making it up as he goes along." And that hurt.

"What are you? Who is your master? Apollyon?"

It threw back its head and laughed, and in that time, I watched him, I could see blood continuously pumping though near transparent vessels that had none of the protection of skin.

"Your names for him, human, though ancient, are immaterial and do not do him justice. He is the Burning Flame, the Spear of Hell, Lucifer's Sire. He will claim your world and he will devour you."

I suddenly had a thought. In the Hopelessness I could usually tell if something was opaque enough to interact with. Normally I could feel it, like a hum, a kinaesthetic talent I had never explained nor written down.

I swept my hand out in front of me. It passed through the creature.

"Illusion." I said. "The Barrier is just an illusion."

The flayed man dissipated with a cackle, and I strode forward. "Come on." I shouted to my companions.

I marched towards the barrier of bloody sewn-together corpses, and, despite the stomach clenching smell and the radiating horror, I passed through it, and out the other side.

I was in the deep vaults of Lindum Hall's mirror image, in the Hopelessness. My companions came through soon after me.

Immediately, the creatures attacked.

Chapter Seven

The Vaults

There were five of them. All dressed as soldiers, because that was what they were. The remainder of the Lindum Hall forces, the remains of those who were not able to get out when Apollyon broke through his containment, no doubt.

They were undoubtedly revenants, they were horrific in their own right, but they had been chewed upon by something, or some things far worse, by the look of them. They came at us slowly poised with claws held forward uttering rabid snarls.

Captain Wright and her soldiers started to fire, but the bullets just went through those creatures, not having any effect, merely taking morsels of meat with them. My Menagerie companions held up their soul blades.

The twins, as usual, were the first to engage, eager as ever, spinning and dancing with their blades shining, like light from heaven.

I went for the one nearest creature to me. He was tall, a sergeant by the look of his epaulettes. He would have been blonde and handsome once, I could tell this from the side of his face that remained, the other side of his skull, including brain tissue, was gone. The separation had left the neatest of bloody lines.

The blond soldier flickered, and suddenly he was someone else, something else. He was now a Roman foot soldier. He pulled a gladius of light from the scabbard at his waist, then charged.

"I am Marcus Veritas Albus, my blood runs in the veins of my descendant, Sergeant William Hibbard. I am a blood spectre. I can be any of my descendants, or antecedents. I pick the most efficient of warriors to engage with you."

Well, Marcus (formerly William) talked too much. I had my soul blade instructions in an instant and so I took the other half of his face off with a step backwards and right handed forty five degree pivoting swipe. Marcus's half-bonce bounced on the ground a few times, making grinding sparks. His headless corpse fell over sideways, then it, too, dissipated.

The twins had dispatched their revenant blood spectres, Percy hers, and Gat his. It was too easy. Captain Wright had backed away with Beech and Coppice as their guns would not work on such creatures. These were supernatural beings, after all.

I turned to see Captain Wright smiling at me, relief etched on her fear worn face. She and her fellow soldiers visibly relaxed. Unfortunately, they should not have stepped back into the shadows away from the light of our soul blades.

I saw more revenants materialise behind them. I watched as claws grew from their fingers in the space of a heartbeat. Beech and Coppice were immediately impaled and ripped apart; four bloody halves of two men thudding to the vault floor, like sides of beef in an abattoir.

Captain Wright screamed in grief, rather than in fear, but then one got her. She turned to emerald mist and reappeared next to me. I caught her and saw she was bleeding heavily from a cut in her side.

Charlie and Avery had already engaged and dispatched those new creatures.

Then more appeared.

"Retreat." I cried over the hubbub. "Gat, you and the twins engage them." That was my first mistake.

Without further ado I took Captain Wright and Percy back through the veil, stepping out in front of a surprised Walter, and the Brigadier.

"Look after Captain Wright." I shouted to Wally. He was also a fine medic and so I knew Claire would be in safe hands. Yes, I started to call her Claire at that point.

I stepped back through to the Hopelessness immediately. There were too many of the blood spectres for us to cope with. I called to the twins and Gat, and they turned and ran towards me. But Avery tripped.

In seconds, the Revenants were upon him.

"Go. There are too many." Avery shouted.

"Uncle, help him." Charlie screamed.

I was in two minds. I took Gat and Charlie out into the real world.

Mistake number two.

I stepped back though the veil, heedless of the dangers. I pulled my soul blade and fought my way to Avery, who had managed to get up, valiantly fighting the creatures around him.

"Avery, to me, my man." He looked over at me, his bright blue eyes alive with the thrill of battle. He beamed. I had addressed him appropriately it seemed. I had made his last day, by the look of his smile that soon became a grimace as the talons ripped into his leg.

Avery swiped with his sword and cut down one that had attacked him, then it dissipated. I fought towards him, but they were trying to pull us further into the vault.

"Try to fight towards me, Avery." I shouted as a blood spectre came at me, flickering between a seventeenth century cavalier, and a uniformed private from the Strange Battalion. I dispatched the sorry creature, and I was nearly by Avery's side.

50

Then a spectre caught him with one elongated talon. It thrust it through Avery's lower chest.

The noise it made was meant only for a slaughterman in a charnel house to hear.

Avery's eyes widened. Then they were upon him. His screams were awful. They would haunt my nightmares.

Instinctively, I asked the Hopelessness to dispel those revenants. The evil flesh barrier was humming louder at my back. Eventually the blood spectres dissipated.

Avery was rolled up in a ball. I knew before I reached him that he was dead. A life taken supernaturally.

Avery's spirit stood.

"Well, that's embarrassing, Uncle Robert. I've never lost a soul blade battle."

Something I may not have told you before now is that I rarely cry. Yet I felt the tears wet upon my cheeks instantaneously.

Avery had already started to fade. Yet he had also started to change. His features that had always been softer than Charlie's and more feminine began to become more angular. Avery was changing. His face became that of a male. Avery was at last a "he" in form as well as thought.

"I'm me. For the first time in my life. Isn't it ironic that to be whole I needed to dead." Avery screamed with joy in the face of death.

I took in that monumental statement and my heart wrenched. I knew the twins had each other's bodies, in effect, somehow in the womb they had been mixed up. The latent Victorian in me had refused to acknowledge that Avery was a man to all intents and purposes, and Charlie was a woman. Now I could.

"It's a bit shitty I had to die for the changes to fully take hold." Avery sighed, without lungs.

I couldn't help but sadly laugh, although snottily, as the tears were flowing, still. Avery faded further. I lent him some of my power, and he solidified a little more.

"It's okay, Uncle Robert. I am at peace. Tell Charlie what happened, and she will find it easier to cope with. Or be so jealous she'll haunt me. Actually, wait a minute, I can haunt her. Remember me. I don't want to be a bloody whisp."

More laughter, And then Avery was gone. One of the twins was dead. Dear God.

I stepped out of the veil, worse for wear carrying Avery's remains. Charlie came towards me screaming because she had twigged that her brother, her other half, was with me only in body. I stood there as she pounded my chest with her fists. I pulled her close and looked at my companions. Gat had a single tear tracking down the left-hand side of his face. Percy would not look at me. Walter took Charlie from me and turned her into his arms, and she continued to sob.

For the first time since we had come together, I had lost one of my Menagerie.

Worse, I had lost one of my wards. My nephew. I put my head in my hands. Then I stepped through the veil and travelled to my home in Legend Street, howling all the way.

A while later, Raven came to me as I downed my third large brandy. It burned my hoarse throat, but I didn't care. It did little to soothe me. She approached me carefully as a cat would approach a fellow feline, wary but ready.

I looked up at her and she smiled sadly. The ghost of a young Viking shield maiden. How bizarre my companions were.

Raven then held me as I cried. It was ironic. The being who looked about sixteen and had died over a thousand years before, held me, a grown man, as I cried and cried.

I then spoke to her of Avery's death.

"He was brave, a warrior. He died in glory. He will fight with my ancestors in Valhalla." Raven said as she stroked my hair.

Reader, it's probably fair at this point that I tell you more about Raven. Or Hrafn Gunnarsdottir.

Waite had trapped Raven's spirit a thousand or more years ago, at a point in the middle of the tenth century in the place that would become the grounds of Lincoln Cathedral.

It was not unusual for a Viking to have black hair, but Hrafn had been named so because of her thick raven-like tresses.

Because of the connections between ravens and Odin, Hrafn had been trained as a warrior and she always fought in the vanguard as she was seen as lucky and able to deliver the message of war.

Waite, ancient in her own right, had found the young Shield Maiden bleeding heavily on the battlefield and had bound Hrafn's spirit to herself. Waite had asked the dying girl's permission. And, allegedly, Odin had given his blessing as well.

They had lived in a symbiotic state for centuries.

I first met Waite and Raven in the Hopelessness, just after my eighteenth birthday, prisoners bound by a rather evil bogle I had traced back to a lost soul linked to the real world.

I found out during the rescue that Waite could live on both sides of the veil, like me. We were of the same ilk, bird and man. Waite decided that she owed me a debt of protection for her rescue, and agreed to guard my new home on both sides of the veil - and had done so for the subsequent years. Raven was always happy to help.

Waite herself, was normally remote and, in the codicils, and usually Raven's visits were brief ones. Over time, she seemed to be staying longer and longer. I didn't think I would ever get to understand Waite, nor Raven, but in the hours after Avery died, I knew there was plenty of empathy and care in the spirit-avatar.

Waite and Raven were not just repaying a debt, I think they liked me, and liked being with me.

"He is still screaming." Raven said as she rocked me.

"Who?" I asked a little disjointed.

"We have been trying to tell you for some time, unfortunately the information keeps sliding from your mind. The man who is the Order Soul."

Well, I was certain I had never heard Raven or Waite mention the Order Soul.

"What or whom is the Order Soul?" I asked, wiping my eyes.

"He calls to us, from the boundary of time, where all paths converge, and the truth is known about everything. He is the balancer."

I looked Raven in the eyes, eyes that had glazed over like cataracts the colour of shark bellies. This wasn't Raven talking. It was Prophecy, I had seen it before. Usually, Prophecy spoke nonsense. That day she conversed.

Then I was pulled to a place along with Raven. It was a place beyond comprehension.

It was nothing like the Hopelessness, it was a place that was so very welcoming; like a space where you knew all your questions would be answered truthfully, where sense was made, and chaos hid in the shadows in fear of being sorted out.

It was a bright church - of sorts. High vaulted ceilings of white marble stretched into the ether. Although that place was not measured in earthly dimensions, it was perfect and complete, but it was so massive I could not see the apex, just a vanishing point.

It was strange that in the last few hours I had been in a vault both below ground and high above. Both supernatural places too, it seemed. Was this some sort of parallel world, or place?

"This is the Cathedral of Truth." Raven said, the Prophecy talking through her, she swept her hands out before her dramatically, like a bad Shakespearean actor trying to give depth to their stage. "A place of purity. Nothing like the shadow world you walk, nor is it like Apollyon's grotesque lair."

"How do you know all this?"

"This is where I am from. I know all that has happened, all that will happen, and what might happen. I weave the threads for the Librarian - my Order Soul - to weave together into the books of Truth."

I looked for somewhere to sit down. I was so tired, and overwhelmed. I could have easily slept, but there were no pews to rest upon, no screens in this Cathedral to lean on, no altar nor lectern where I could have perched. I thought I might be dreaming but Prophecy shook her head.

"You are fully awake, Robert. Here in the realm of truths, few sleep. There have only been a handful of mortals who have walked these corridors. I would welcome you to stay for longer, Robert, for you are now an agent of Truth, but we must not tarry. The books have stopped writing themselves, they must resume, and soon."

It *was* a place of books. I could see them all now. The high, many-levelled walkways lined every part of this Cathedral. Wall to wall books, wall to wall truth, like God's own library. My guess was not that far from its real purpose.

"This is a place where all the Gods, old and new, past, present, and future come for advice. They read the books of truth and decide which of the truths to implement."

The Prophecy was really building up its part through Raven as she danced about, like a trainee ballet dancer. I was trying not to laugh. Although then, with fear, I realised Apollyon's spawn had moved like this.

"You think me a fool, Robert? A mummer? I only have the skills of Raven at my disposal. She is a warrior, not a dancer."

I did not want to insult the Prophecy further, especially if it was used to advising Gods, for I was not sure of its power, nor its intent. It might have vaporised me in a blink of an eye, or more probably wiped me from the pages of Truth, if I didn't tone down my scepticism at that point.

"No. Forgive me, I apologise. I have recently suffered loss. It has overwhelmed me."

"We feel your pain. Your nephew is at rest; we know he fulfils his destiny. But it is nothing compared to this."

A figure appeared, high above our heads, a man of sorts, but he was made perfectly of metal. It took me a while to assess his aspect because his sudden screams shook my very soul. There was something through his side, a lance maybe, and it was all that attached this metal man to one of the cathedral columns between two vast walls of tomes. Viscous silver blood issued from the wound and dripped like quicksilver tears. He was like some bleeding metal Jesus, screaming for the sins of man.

"He is the Order Soul, the Librarian of the Cathedral of Truth. Sometimes known as Endure." Raven said as the Prophecy.

"How long has he been like this, and who did this to him?" I asked, ever the questioner.

"Allegedly, a minion of Apollyon did this. Yet I cannot be sure. Your bravery at moving through the barrier helped you gain access to the Truth, Robert. We see you as one of us now. Find this murderous agent, they hold the secret of Apollyon's demands, they know where Eliza is held captive. Two birds with one stone. They are with you at Lindum Hall."

"What?" I asked with venom.

"One of your companions is evil, Robert. You must break the barrier, send back Apollyon by meeting his great need, then find the traitor, and free my Order Soul. Fail in any one of those tasks and the world will cease to exist."

I was a little overwhelmed, but thought I may as well ask about the other mysteries that were rife in my head.

"Is this Isabelle?" And I knew from the silence to move on. "And who sent the Lantern Heads?"

"Isabelle of Stafford is too interested in her own corporeality for now. As for the Lantern Heads, they are new, alien. Without my Librarian I cannot tell you the truth of them."

I sighed. "How do I kill Apollyon?"

The thing that spoke through Raven laughed. "*You* cannot kill what is celestial, only contain it. Find the traitor, they have taken books of truth, bring them back. Save my Order Soul. Make him complete. Without him I am not able to see. For whilst I am Prophecy, I am chaos without my Librarian. I need my Order Soul to put my prophecy in order. I will then tell you where Sammel is, for that is whom Apollyon seeks. "

Prophecy was almost pleading. It sounded sad, if you could measure sadness in the tones of eternity.

"You need help, Robert, and I will support you. I grant your Raven a boon for being a servant so readily. You will know soon what it is. Furthermore, she will help you and the people of the future, for whom you write this journal."

Well, when it said that, I thought - I am not writing a journal. I had never written one. It was Prophecy talking, after all. We are all bound by the codicils it seems.

I was about to ask another question when suddenly I was back in my house, in the parlour, where Raven had held me as I cried. She looked up at me, her eyes now clear.

"That was beautiful, but sad. It felt like Valhalla." She said. "How he screams. I want to talk with the Order Soul when he is healed. I want to ask him questions. I want to save him, Robert. I wish to return with you. I will help you find your traitor."

I was about to say to Raven that I would be happy for her to stay and protect the house, the souls we had caged, for fear that they, too, would be released.

"The Prophecy of the Cathedral of Truth always grants a boon to those it speaks through. It asked, and Waite agreed."

I frowned, and looked at Raven carefully. There were tears rolling down her face. "Sorry, what do you mean?"

A nimbus suddenly surrounded Raven. I wondered what was afoot. I had seen so many strange things in that long twenty-four hours, what else could be happening?

Raven and Waite came together again, Waite had flown off her perch and they merged. Then they separated, but not in the normal fashion. They were, for an instant, both occupying the same space and time, then they were forced apart - very separate.

"We were one, and now we are two. Sisters. Raven and Waite. The Prophecy has granted us both a life on this plane."

I was staggered. First Avery taken and then Raven given life? As if things were balancing.

"I will guard your house, Robert Waterfield." Postlethwaite said, "and my sister will now guard *you*. Trust no one but us. As the Prophecy said, you have been deceived. One of your companions has deceived you. One of them has also killed. They might be the same person."

I gasped, there was no other word for it. I walked over to Raven and hugged her. She was softly sobbing.

I then went to the drinks cabinet that sat next to my personal bureau and I opened the door, pulled out a new bottle of brandy, and poured two slugs, offering one to Raven. I necked mine in one go. I gasped, as I have said I don't often drink. Raven took hers well.

"No drink for me?"

I ignored Waite's sarcasm. "Gat, Charlie, Percy, and Walter. One of them is my betrayer. How can this be?" I thought aloud.

I searched my mind for hints or clues, and I could find none. No doubt it would sow the seeds of mistrust, this knowledge. I would rue finding out that someone was working against me, someone I would have trusted with my life.

"You have a difficult road ahead." Raven said. "I will help you all I can."

I smiled at the young woman. The former Viking shield maiden. My new protector.

Chapter Eight
Best-Laid Plans

I took Raven through the Hopelessness and back to our rather wonderful billet at Pender House. Not that glorious surroundings could take the edge off my angst. I spent the next couple of days in my rooms, grieving.

Only Raven and Captain Wright were allowed to cross the threshold. My mood had already found the traitor in each and every one of the Menagerie, rightly or wrongly.

Was it the presence of Apollyon that was affecting me, or was it something else?

I tried to speak to Charlie, but Charlie blamed me for her brother's murder and spent the hours I tried to console her reminding me that I had failed Avery in every way.

I took to the Hopelessness on the second evening and taking Raven with me and also - in agreement with the Brigadier - Captain Claire Wright - who I agreed to call Claire so long as she dropped the Colonel nonsense.

I had served for three years in my twenties, and I had barely got to the rank of Major. The rank Colonel was more of a hierarchical thing put upon me by the crown as my early work with the secret service meant I came across rank-proud types who were mostly ex-military. Those were secret times that predated the Menagerie. I will say very little about those times.

We were soon back in the vaults. There was no sign of the revenants this time. Whilst Raven scouted ahead, her sword drawn, Claire decided to try and bring me out of my funk.

"It wasn't your fault." She said.

I was still amazed at her bravery in coming here, considering two of her men had been torn apart on the very spot we were conversing. She had been injured, but seemed to have recovered well.

Claire's preternatural green eyes looked at me with compassion. It might have been something more, but I was too far into my depression at that point to notice.

It was only much, much later in my life that I realised Claire Wright was my saviour at that point. She was my anchor to the real world. Despite her preternatural origins.

"No, I am guilty of a great sin. I have lost one of my wards. Charlie believes I left her brother here to die."

"Wasn't Avery in fact a woman? In male clothing?"

I could have got angry at that response until I realised, I had offered no explanation to Claire. And I reflected that I, too, was still so Victorian myself.

"Twins born in the wrong bodies. They knew from a very young age that they were so. My sister couldn't accept it. Their father was broader minded, but he never lived long enough to help his wife accept their children. I can't imagine our society accepting them. So, I needed to protect them. On one count I have failed."

I realise I was revealing my woes to a complete stranger, who I had known for less than a whole day. Yet I felt Claire was a kindred spirit and she would understand being different as she was mixed species. Few in society will accept the unaccepted, reader.

"Nature is strange. I can believe it. My mother was part tree. How could I deny the twins their gender?" Claire had said.

I was pleased for the change of subject, and a glimpse into Claire's psyche.

"Until recently I thought elemental creatures were a myth. The Fae. Are they really all around?"

Claire laughed a deep throaty laugh. I liked her tone, deeper than most women. It had an honest quality to it.

"You deal with ghosts and demons, and yet you hadn't speculated about the Fae? Have you never met a white witch? They like to tell everyone our secrets."

"No. I have met but one witch and she wanted to peel the skin from my back. I have never met any of the Fae before now. You were the first. Coppice and Beech, of course. Why aren't you named after something tree related?"

Claire laughed again. "Their names are pure coincidence. No more than the places their ancestors lived. Near to trees, how else would their forefathers have coupled with dryads?"

It was a convincing point and not for the first time that day I felt foolish.

"Robert."

Raven's voice cut through our small talk. We hurried to where the shield maiden was observing a door at the back of the vault where we had fought the revenants.

It was not solid, but nothing was in the Hopelessness, so I quickly slipped through to the real world to see if it existed there. It did and there was no sign of any creatures, so I brought Claire through. Raven, we found, could flit through the veil, herself, and followed my lead lessening my burden.

The real vault was musty, like all ancient burial places it smelled of dust and death.

In the real world the tombs were all capped with the medieval stone likenesses. Ancient members of the original family to have lived near the Abbey that had become the vast Lindum Hall.

"Sir Robert De La Ville." Claire read. "They became the Deville's. The fifth Duke of Wimborne granted the house to the military in 1790."

"So, the Strange Battalion have been here a hundred and fifteen years, or so?"

"Yes. I have been with them from the start."

"You are that old?"

Raven looked at me, her eyes wide in warning.

That was a slip. I felt terrible until Claire laid her hand on my arm.

"I am older than even that. It is my nature. I will live hundreds of years."

I smiled at her forgiveness and turned back to the door.

"The door is a portal to elsewhere. Look at these marks."

"Biblical Aramaic." Claire said.

"That's impressive." I said, a little impressed, although on reflection from these times a little patronising.

"I am a tree. We have learned man's languages by our scars, thousands of years of carving on our trunks and branches." Claire barked the word *man* but followed it up with a smile. "It says that this is a Passage for Angels."

I had seen only one of these before, during a case the Menagerie had worked on behalf of the French government. The portal had been sighted in the larger grounds of the Notre Dame Cathedral. It was now locked away below the Louvre, in the vaults where the republic's magical artefacts were kept. Following the Supernatural Wars there were no angels nor demons left to use them.

"Wait, there is another phrase. Welcome to the Son of Dawn. Morning Star. Lucifer's father. The Fallen."

"Like Hel." Raven said. "Daughter of Loki."

"You might both be right." I said, "now it seems it is called Apollyon."

At the mention of the name the portal flared, just once. A mist of sparkling motes appeared floating in front of us. Raven had already pulled her sword.

As we watched, the motes formed into a naked figure. He was like an alabaster Greek statue, but no less explicit in his nakedness. Like some raunchy Raphaelite carving.

"You have broken through the barrier." It said in a matter-of-fact way. Voice emotionless. "Apollyon is impressed. And although he cannot stop you from moving through this place, and what you call the Hopelessness, he does warn that he will kill you, if you wander too far. Thank you for feeding his revenants, although they are creatures of instinct and therefore without control. He apologises for your personal loss."

"Who are you, and what does Apollyon want?" I growled.

"I am Candour, and He seeks the truth about his son Sammel."

That name again. I saw Raven look over at me. That look confirmed my worst fears. This was all so very convoluted.

"And what truth might that be?" Claire asked. "The truth that kills my brethren?"

The alabaster being looked across at Captain Wright. "We have no argument with the elementals, half-dryad. However, if you come to dance with the humans against our revenants, they will treat you with the contempt you deserve."

"Apollyon wants to know the fate of his son Sammel. He invaded this place to call you here. You must find Sammel, then Apollyon will leave."

"He killed all these people to bait me?" I was revolted.

Candour ignored me. "Unfortunately, to work on his behalf you would have to prove yourself to him. He has a thing about loyalty."

Just like me. I wondered of his friends had betrayed him.

"Why can he not just break free and find Sammel himself?" Again Claire.

"Apollyon is bound to his own level of reality. If he leaves, he can never return there. But if he does leave, he will destroy everything in his path in payment for the deceit of mankind. If you can give him the whereabouts of Sammel, if you can locate his son, you can send them both back. He knows you have been to the Cathedral of Truth. He knows you have seen the Order Soul. He knows you seek a traitor. He knows your boon for returning the books of truth will be the whereabouts of his son."

Claire gasped. I looked at her, and nodded. How did Apollyon know this, unless the traitor was working for him? Or was it someone known to Apollyon.

The naked statue being chuckled. "The traitor is not his, the traitor belongs to someone else. Apollyon is a god. He can access the Cathedral, but he cannot enact any part of this in that dimension, or this one."

"How do we know that's true?" Raven was fierce in her challenge. Living up to her role as my champion.

"I cannot lie. I am an avatar belonging to the Lord Apollyon. I simply do not lie. That is why I am named so. "

I could not cope with so many twists and turns when I was younger, Reader, so I almost screamed, letting out a gasp that was angst personified.

"I think it speaks the truth, Robert." Raven said. "It is the servant of evil, yet it cannot lie. Evil needs duplicity to trap its victims, but its most trusted servant cannot operate in duplicity itself. For Apollyon would be in danger of betrayal all the time."

"So, if we prove ourselves, find the books, receive Sammel's location then find your master's son and bring him here, then Apollyon will leave this world."

"Yes." The statue being replied. "And he will free the souls of those taken in battle."

"Battle?" Raven asked.

"Humans took his son. A human agent tried to kill the Order Soul, it seems, although we are at a loss to understand how. Apollyon is at war until Sammel is retuned. Who has the power to visit the Cathedral of Truth other than Gods, or Prophecy and her guests? I will help you find out. Apollyon can help you test them, if you bring them before him."

"And will you be on hand to answer my questions?" I asked a little calmer by that point, although I was nowhere near relaxed.

"Yes."

"Answer me one final question and I will give you an answer as to whether I will bring my companions back here."

"Ask."

"Is there more than one traitor? Has more than one of my friends attacked the Order Soul."

It was Candour's turn to show something like frustration or anger. "The Order Soul has been injured by something created in this reality. It is against the laws of the universe. If the Order Soul perishes, then no one will know truth from lie. So, you need to decide quickly whether you will find the books, then find Sammel for my master, especially if the capture of this traitor heals the Order Soul."

"Please answer my question."

"Only one of your human friends walks a traitor's path. Although most will deceive, and more than one may die. Your love for them will die with your answers, then grow with newly found trust."

"I wanted truth, not riddles."

"To prove yourself to Apollyon you must find out the truth for yourself. Find your traitor, then the books, free the Order Soul, ask for Sammel's whereabouts as your boon. Apollyon will then depart back to his realm and take his minions with him."

I looked across at Claire, then Raven, to get some sort of unspoken agreement. Was it a trap? I raised my eyes as if to ask their opinion. They both nodded.

"I think it must speak the truth." Claire said.

"Come back with the candidates in two days, at dawn. I will come to you and bring the Truth of Apollyon. It will reveal your friend's deepest secrets. Do not discuss what you are doing with any of them. They will be tested, but so will you. Your mind may not survive the test. You may find things out from the past that will affect you forever. Are you willing to do this to find your traitor?"

Claire touched my arm, Raven nodded.

Candour stood awaiting my decision. Oh, how I wish I could have consulted with Gat or Walter. But then either of them could be the guilty party. The one who had the power to injure the Order Soul. Otherworldly? My betrayer. They may also have had Eliza, and I needed her back in the vaults, safe, and secure. I needed to know how to find Sammel, and then Apollyon would leave. The world would then be safe.

Easy.

That was sarcasm by the way, reader. It comes more with age.

I nodded to Candour. "I agree, but if you are to appear in my presence again, servant of a god, or not, I implore you to wear some trousers."

Candour nodded at me, and I definitely saw some sort of smile hooking up the corners of his alabaster lips.

Then we were suddenly back in my rooms.

"What do you think?"

Raven sheathed her sword. "The creature told the truth, Robert. I had enough ability left over from my possession by the Prophecy to know that." She poured herself a large measure of brandy. "It is medicinal," she said, in response to my raised eyebrows.

Claire gave me a smile. "Candour was telling the truth, as far as I can decide, too. I have certain elemental powers, but they are only residual, beyond my shape shifting ability. I could not detect any lies. Although I cannot read minds, I can quickly get the measure of any being, mortal or otherwise."

I then told her and Raven about Eliza, and how I had once built a life on lies, and that how I had found it difficult to trust anyone outside my circle of friends. Then I expressed my angst at knowing one or more of them would betray me.

I told Claire about the rose jar that contained Eliza's spiritual remains, being stolen, and that Eliza may well have had help to escape her spiritual bonds.

I needed to ensure Eliza's return to magical custody. My once fiancé was most likely as dangerous dead as she was alive. A serial killer who preyed on young men and also killed her parents. Isabelle had called Eliza, her Magpie. I would only realise a hundred years later what that meant. Reader, you will likely know by now, too, having fought a Magpie, yourself.

"Aside from you both, and Postlethwaite, I have four friends, no family – five counting Avery – who I would have trusted with my life, who I had jokingly called my Menagerie. We are all bonded. We are a team, a family. Now that could all be in ruins. One of us is dead, and If Candour is right, then others may perish. Another is a traitor, and all are duplicitous, at the least."

I felt my head hanging again. Then what seemed like hours later, but was probably seconds, someone sat next to me on the couch. The warmth of arms wrapped around me. A kiss on my cheek. I looked up to smile at Raven, to find it was Claire. Those green peaceful eyes were safe, like the canopy of a forest in the rain.

I looked up at Raven, who had her sword half drawn, but I am not sure Claire noticed. Her empathy at that point was much needed.

"I will brief the Brigadier, Robert. Get some sleep. I am sure Raven with her half-drawn sword will watch over you."

I looked at Raven, and shook my head. Raven sheathed her weapon, and nodded back at me, imperceptibly. She would protect me, or die trying.

Finally, I nodded. I had two days to prepare. I would talk with my Menagerie and try and see if I could find any clues as to the identity of the traitor. First though, I needed to rest. Grief came upon me again like a fog and I do not know how I ended up undressed and in my bed.

I slept for twelve hours.

Chapter Nine

The Evening Before the Test

"What is happening, Robert?"

Gat came to see me the night before the testing would commence. I was in one of the common rooms contemplating my next moves. It took all of my willpower not to cave in and tell him what was happening.

"Why is she here in this form?" He nodded at Raven, who just smiled at Gat like a cat who was hatching a plan for world domination.

"She is here to make up the numbers."

"Robert, can you hear yourself. Avery died. Charlie is beside herself. We should throw the towel in, let Charlie grieve. Damn it, Robert, we should just let…."

"We need to rid this world of Apollyon. He is too much of a threat. If we can save the Order Soul, it will give us the means to find Sammel, and Apollyon will leave."

"And you believe that?"

"Gat, it was the Cathedral of Truth who set me upon this path. Candour, Apollyon's servant, cannot lie."

"And you will believe that he tells the truth on behalf of Apollyon because a tree spirit and a raven's avatar have told you so? Robert, I am seriously worried about your judgement."

It was at this point there was a knock at the door, and Percy entered.

"Are we still going in tomorrow morning?" Percy had a very matter of fact face and stance. I really wasn't up to challenging her.

Percy hadn't questioned me at all that morning when I had told her we were going back through the barrier. She just looked at me sadly. Whether that was pity, or whether I looked like I was grieving for Avery, I wasn't sure.

I didn't have the time to ponder on intentions. One of the Menagerie was a liar, and an attempted murderer at least. How long had the traitor been working with us all. Had they killed before? I couldn't believe it might be Walter, Gat, or Charlie, therefore it had to be Percy. Although I didn't really believe it was her, either.

"It is foolish. We should return to the Cathedral of Truth and get more answers." Gat was quite annoying by that point.

"No." I said a little too quickly. "Someone has grievously injured the Order Soul. The Prophecy will not let us through until we know who. I need to find that agent."

"And this person is going to just surrender these Truth Books?" Gat said almost incredulously. I had loved him as a brother, but he was like a terrier down a rabbit hole when he had his chance. "Robert, if there is something you are not telling us…"

I *had* said *no* too quickly, he knew something was up.

"What did the Prophecy say? Word for word."

I was about to speak but Raven jumped in. "Find the perpetrator. Return the Truth Books, the Order Soul will recover, and the whereabouts of Sammel will be revealed."

"So how the heck did the father of Hell and his son get out?" Percy asked as she sparked up a cigarette. Smoke gathered round her head like a halo. Was that a premonition?

"He isn't out. His son has been taken." Raven said.

"Stop the riddles, young lady." Gat spat in frustration.

"I was eleven hundred years old when your mother opened her legs. Prince Gathii. Apollyon isn't out, but he could be, and if he decides to do so, he will render this world with death and destruction."

"Why is this spirit talking for you, Robert?"

"Enough." I barked. "Gat, just go with us on this."

"Why is it that things are never simple around the Menagerie?" Gat said angrily, and at that moment I could see on his face that he was grieving for Avery too.

We all were.

Yet one of our merry group might attempt to kill, one of us would die, and another would be duplicitous. The menagerie would in effect be down to three. Like when we started out, before the twins came of age.

"Have you spoken with Charlie?" I asked no one in particular.

"I have." Gat said. "She is torn apart, Robert. Her brother taken from her so soon. It could affect her mentally. Are you sure she must enter Lindum Hall, go past the barrier."

"She must." I said.

Gat shook his head and growled.

"That's stupid. She could stay with Walter at the house. We could go in, take Raven instead." Percy had joined us shaking her head.

"We will need Raven as well. Claire Wright, too."

"Why the tree lady, Robert? She is not used to our work methods, she could be a liability."

"She is half elemental spirit. I lead the Menagerie, Percy, not you, nor the Ministry of Mirrors. Claire will be useful."

"We are dealing with demons, Robert, not people. Why are you locking yourself in your rooms, and treating us so? Raven is allowed entry, this Captain Wright, too. It's as if it is us on trial, not that creature beyond the barrier." Percy was really angry.

I thought she had guessed my plan, that there was more to it all, and my heart went in my mouth. I looked at Raven, who gave a slight shake of her head as if telling me to let it go.

Percy sighed. "It is unfair. *You* have lost your nephew, one or more of us may not come out of this alive. I could go to the Minister, he can call in another team." This was the closest I'd seen Percy to tears. She was wringing her hands, sweat had appeared on her brow, despite the room being cool. This wasn't like her. Especially when she then strode over to me, and hugged me.

Quite frankly, I wanted to be intimately close to Percy, but once she was in my arms, I didn't know what to do.

There was another knock at the common room door, Claire entered. Her timing couldn't have been worse, seeing me embracing Percy like that. Not that there was anything at all beyond her kind words of consolation between us. We had only known each other for a few days.

"The Brigadier wants to see you, Mr Waterfield." She said curtly, her face stern. Not Robert, nor Colonel, but Mr Waterfield. I saw her look Percy up and down.

"Percy, the Menagerie is needed. We collectively are the only people who can do what we do. I am the only person who can get us all into the Hopelessness. If we go in ones or twos, we will be vulnerable. All or nothing, my dear."

She looked up at me, and smiled. There it was again. That look in her eyes, just like in Moseley, when we nearly kissed. A spark? It was fleeting, then gone. Percy was all business-like again. She pulled down her jacket in a perfunctory manner, and swept out of the room.

"Let's not keep the Brigadier waiting." Claire said.

I made my way with Claire, to a different room this time, it was late, and Lord Holden was still on duty. Did the man never sleep?

I knocked, and entered another wood panelled room. It was lined with maps of the region. There was a topographical war board on a large table, a filing cabinet, desk, and chair – nothing else. The air was oppressive, and I could smell the sweet smell of expensive tobacco.

Holden was in his shirt sleeves, they were rolled up but, despite the heat, he still wore his tie.

"Robert. Thanks for coming to see me. Please, sit down. Wright, please wait outside."

Claire nodded, and left.

"Brigadier, Lord…"

"Edward, please. Robert, I am so sorry for your loss. I would fully understand if you wanted to stand down. I am sure the minister would understand. Whiskey?"

"Just soda, please."

The Brigadier squirted me a glass of soda from the siphon, and poured himself a large shot of whiskey.

"Robert, are you sure?"

"I don't drink that much."

"No," he said, walking over to hand me the glass of carbonated water. "Are you sure you want to do this?"

"As I have said, just a few minutes ago to my companions, Edward. Only I can take us all in."

"Claire, Captain Wright, has said that if we can find this Sammel, his son? Dear god, I didn't know the things had sons, or daughters for that matter. If we can find him, then Apollyon has said he would leave here."

I nodded.

"Why then does he want you to go back in if his son is out there?"

He was another Gat.

"There is one of us who is not being truthful." I explained. Trying to make my mistruth as simple as possible so it was not discernible from the lie. "Apollyon will not let one who is a deceiver look for his son." Although I was stretching the truth so much, I thought it would soon snap like a rubber band.

"Amongst your friends? You think one of them is a liar, possibly a traitor? And what will *he* do, kill them? Will you kill them? Are you willing to lose your niece? Your African friend? Lady Percival? Captain Trevithick? Dear God, man."

"I have to find out who it is, Edward. A traitor has no place on my team, and I want them to reveal themselves. Then we can return the missing Truth Books. Then the Order Soul will grant me that boon."

"And those books prevent the Cathedral of Truth operating? And there could be nothing to tell truth from lie? It's a bally far-fetched mess this, Robert..." Holden sat down heavily, and put his feet up on his desk. "And I have seen a lot of weird and wonderful things as the leader of the Strange Regiment."

I sat, myself, and sipped at my soda. It was bitter, just like my soul that evening.

"There is something you are not telling me, Robert." Holden opened a box on his desk and took out a cigar. He offered me one, but I declined. It took him an age to light the damn thing, and then I was choking.

"If your secret is germane to your own business, and it does not get my soldiers killed, then you can keep it. However, if Claire or any of my men are to be in danger because of what you are holding back now, I demand to know." Holden looked me in the eye like a Rhino about to charge.

I shook my head. "I am holding a secret, Edward, but to reveal it I would put all that I have invested in this mission in jeopardy. Trust me, Brigadier. I will die before I let anyone else perish."

I said that knowing I would lose other friends if Candour's prophecy played out.

"Do you have any children, Robert?"

I shook my head.

"Never married?"

"No, the only woman I truly loved ended up a mass murderer."

Holden spat whiskey back into his glass. "You really have had it difficult. I never married. These soldiers are my children. I have lost so many already during my career. Those trapped in the house that became those revenants, Claire described. Too many lost. I will trust you to get rid of this bloody demon, Robert. Do you promise me? Before any more of my children die."

I looked at him and lied again. I didn't know if I would keep all his soldiers alive. I just didn't know if we would be successful, or whether Apollyon was leading me a merry dance. "I'll do my best," I said.

"You defeat grief one day at a time, Robert."

"Yes, Edward." I was just agreeing with him. My grief was threatening to overwhelm me.

"Go and get some sleep, man. You look like you have saved a fortune by marrying a whore."

That was a new one on me. I actually laughed as I left Holden's office.

I checked in on Charlie before I went to bed. She was in one of the sitting rooms, at the front of the house. Walter was with her. She gave me a black look as I approached.

"Charlie."

She was somehow even more feminine than before, as if losing her other half had confirmed her sex, her place in space and time.

"Uncle. I am coming with you."

I nodded as I sat next to her. I took one of her hands. It was perfectly manicured and lacquered.

"I am so sorry about Avery. If I could have done anything, I would. When I returned, he was long gone." Another lie. They were sprouting like leaves on a tree of mistruth.

"I am sorry for hitting you. For saying you did it. I know now it wasn't your fault."

To be truthful, I relaxed somewhat. There was only one thing worse than losing Avery and that would have been losing Charlie because she blamed me for her brother's death.

"You are a brave woman, Charlie. I would welcome you on our mission."

"Good. Because I am going to kill Apollyon for what he did to Avery."

This last sentence was said with such bitterness I almost recoiled. I saw Wally sit upright, alert. He only did that when he was shocked.

"We will help Apollyon find his son, and let them leave, Charlie. Apollyon is too powerful for any one of us to face."

"We will find his son. You will ask him to leave, but you must help me avenge my brother. We were born together, we should have died together. He should not have left me. I. Am. Incomplete. Apollyon must die."

Wally stood now. He was as uncomfortable as I was. Charlie was no longer sad or tearful. She was vengeful.

"Miss, you need to get to bed. You are tired."

"I am having a drink. Then another. Walter, you either join me, or go to bed. Uncle, goodnight."

And with that she stood and went in search of the mess. It would be open still, no doubt.

"Robert. This mission is a mess."

I nodded, I couldn't disagree.

"We should abort."

"And leave this creature here, threatening our very existence? It will leave as soon as we have found his son."

"His? His?" Walter shook his head. "We have already lost one of our own. Your nephew, Robert. How can you carry on?" Tears were clouding his eyes. Walter had always been emotional. Well, as soon as he had left the army behind, that was. "Little Avery. Gone."

I took my friend in my arms. Unsure if he was a liar, or not, and held him as he quietly sobbed. Friendship is hard to break.

Grief hits us all in many different ways. It is as separate as each of our identities.

Part Two: Deceit

Chapter Ten
Gat's Lies

The flesh barrier was all that I could smell as we slipped back into the Hopelessness. The crushed-together naked bodies writhed and glistened like an animated butcher's window.

"Are we all okay?" I asked them. The Menagerie all nodded.

Claire would not look at me, not since she had seen me embracing Percy the night before. Which was strange, because, at that point, there was nothing between us.

She had seen the kind smile Percy threw me after I had asked if they were all okay, and her face became blank.

Typical, I had now offended my new friend, someone who clearly thought a lot of me. But, As beautiful as Claire was, I couldn't escape the feelings I had towards Percy.

I realised then, in front of that horrific fleshy wall, how similar Claire and Percy were. I stopped myself, horrified, I was comparing the beauty of two women, as that horrible crush of lost souls writhed in front of me. I shuddered as if someone had walked over my grave.

"I need to know you are all okay to proceed." I repeated more business-like. Feelings towards beautiful women, and their possible perceptions were quickly put to one side.

They all answered in the affirmative. So, we then made our way past that horrible fleshy wall again. Apollyon had promised that there would be no more revenants, and I prayed that he was holding up his end of the bargain.

We came once more to the vaults, and the doorway Candour had appeared from. It was open and beyond we could see a large room.

It had a grand chequered floor, and a mezzanine gallery for viewing. This was clearly a ballroom.

We all filed through the doorway. I went first and looked back as my companions were due to walk through. Only Gat arrived.

"It's a trap." Gat shouted trying to turn back; but where there had been a doorway, there was now only a barrier. He turned to me.

"What is going on, Robert?" His face painted with suspicion.

I shrugged, all I knew was this was probably the beginning of Gat's test.

Yes, it is time. Apollyon affirmed, but only to me, via a mental projection.

Then suddenly, our surroundings changed. The scenery flickered like an expensively staged illusion.

I was standing next to Gat on a beach. The sand was light purple, as were the cliffs that loomed over us like patient sentinels. The sky was a lime green. Two suns hung in balance, one dim and red, the other bright orange. The heat was stifling.

"No." Gat said. "Not here. I cannot be back here. Not after all I went through to get away. Dear Goddess. I am going mad. Robert, please."

His voice had changed, his normally buoyant demeanour deflating as I watched. A rough London clatter replaced his African tones.

The first of his deceptions.

"No, it's just Apollyon testing us. Or rather, testing you, my friend."

Gat looked at me, horrified, then instantaneously where there had been a separate Robert and Gat - there was only Garrett N'Dour.

It was hot, even for a Praxian summer's evening. The trade war between the Praxians, Earth, and Leilanth was spiralling out of control. The whole planet was in danger, and I needed to get off that forsaken rock. However beautiful it was, and however much it felt like home, my life with Ayel was more important. And we needed to get off-world quickly.

I toyed with the idea of just activating the portable Simba Gate module I had as a standby, and to go instantaneously back to Earth. One push of a button. Just one step through, and I would be home. But how could I leave Ayel?

Ayel was my beautiful Praxian. He was my rock. I was falling in love with him, he was so strong mentally and physically, that it took my breath away just to think about it.

The strongest partner I'd had in all my five hundred years, was Ayel.

I suddenly looked up. The sky was full of battle craft; their powerful weapons spitting fire and causing death. I had to be quick before the horror started to rain down from that heaven.

Ayel worked in the Earth ex-pat district as a masseur, but I was well aware that he was quite a way away from me on that day, he was on a job up in the hills.

How dare there be war in the sector. I had almost made enough money, over the last century and a half, to fund my escape. All those diving lessons for ex-pats – struggling to finance my own galaxy class Simba module, so I could jump sectors away from Ancient Earth. I was sick of the colonialism, slavery, and trade with planets who still exploited other beings.

I needed to keep calm. Whilst on the surface I was a mild-mannered diving instructor, I would never have made the money for a Simba module just by holding the waists of rich folk up in the water.

I was also feeding intel back to the Earth Government through an information hyper-router about those very ex-pats themselves, especially those who were indulging in slavery and profiteering from the illegal smuggling of aliens from other planets.

So there lay my second reason for not immediately jumping off planet. My list of perpetrators was locked in a bank vault.

You don't want to leave that sort of shit lying around. It would get someone killed – probably me.

There was a huge spurt of water in the bay, I was standing next to an array of rich people's boats. A large chunk of fuselage from one of the frack-off spaceships had just hit the water next to a grand yacht. The next piece hit a clipper further up the bay. It exploded once, then twice as the fuel cells ignited.

The resulting boom sent up a massive spray. People all around were screaming as they were hit by shrapnel and burning debris. It was sure feeling like the end of the world.

I needed to find my man, get my info crystal, and get the frack off the planet. I guessed I couldn't upgrade my Simba sooner than planned as my funds wouldn't have cleared. So, it would be a short jump back to Ancient Earth, then to my place on Lunar, and then a bigger jump out into the unknown of another galaxy. I wanted to be the only human in the place I was going with Ayel.

I started to make my way around the beach headland and towards my skimmer. It was moored by a bar from where I operated the diving school. I needed to try and get onto the main autobahn and towards the human quarter, I just hoped Ayel had returned home and had not done something stupid, like joining the Praxian navy, in a fit of valour. The Praxians were like that, all honourable, heroic, and a little thick-skulled. Ayel would get himself blown up, I was sure of it, just to prove a point.

There was a huge detonation above. It seemed one of the Leilanth craft had fired upon a large Praxian navy ship. It was a huge sub-space goer, probably had a personality. Looking up, I flipped my lenses dark to shield my eyes when the ship's core exploded.

It was like a mini nova.

There were screams all around as people went flash-blind for a short period, yes, it was that bright.

I just kept going. There would be more bits of debris falling soon and, depending upon all sorts of factors, such as atmosphere, weather, and combustion, we could be sitting ducks awaiting our first and last fireball.

Those ships were a mile or two across, with enough downward momentum, to create the power of thousands of mega-tonnes.

The bar was almost deserted when I reached it. Giulio, the bar manager, was packing up his things, but he didn't see me as he operated his portable Simba gate and stepped through. I stepped onto my skimmer board, a little antigrav plank, basically, and tapped in the coordinates for Ayel's place of work. First, I needed to get my imprint-drive from the banks, so I set the sub-destination via the People's Bank.

I had to back-track in order to head into the centre of the local provincial town of Akhet. The People's Bank was a human-led organisation, so I wouldn't have any problems getting in. Although, like a lot of the ex-pats, the staff might have already headed off through their Simba gates.

I dropped the skimmer in the narrow bay. Then I ran up the esplanade and through the double doors of a large green building. The place was empty with no living souls as far as I could see. I could have robbed the place, but to be honest, I just wanted to get the data crystal.

I made my way up to the first floor, and towards the personal banking store where all the retinal-coded safety deposit boxes were located in a large vault. I accessed my box and took out my finance implant and crystal. I slapped the implant onto my left hand, opposite my everyday implant, and turned to leave as it sank into my skin.

Unfortunately, two noticeably big and rough looking humans were barring my escape route.

Sodding typical.

I recognised one of them as Malen Tom, a particularly nasty member of Earth mafia.

And his name was on my secret list. He no doubt knew he was on it.

Before Tom jumped back to Ancient Earth or one of the colonies, he obviously needed to make sure he wasn't blacklisted. That meant he needed any incriminating evidence to go away. Killing me would do just fine.

"You have led a lot of us a merry dance, Garrett, you nonce." He drew a disruptor from his left hip.

You might be thinking that he was being a little un-PC with his comments, and he was, but a nonce, to many ex-pats, was anyone who slept with a Praxian.

"You don't seem to be walking like you've been buggered by a big blue man." Tom sneered. "Do you only give out the punishment?"

"Hey," I said, "mind the children's ears," I nodded at his fellow. The other man was as bald as an egg, and as broad as he was tall. I was probably going to get hurt for that comment, but, as usual, my mouth gets in the way before my brain engages.

"Ha!" Tom laughed, yet it didn't hit his eyes. "Barry, here, loves the boys. Particularly the African type like you, Garrett. It didn't take much persuading for him to go into deep cover. Pretend to be a blue alien."

No.

It couldn't be. I suddenly felt extremely sick. Had I repeatedly shared a bed with that brute.

The air about Barry suddenly shimmered and he morphed into Ayel. My lover. I gagged. Then I vomited up my lunch.

The two men laughed, and it was enough of a pause for me to act. I tapped my neck, and a force suit covered me in moments. Like a second skin it would enhance my speed and strength. It was military grade, and well, I had spent quite some time in the Ancient Earth navy. You don't think I would spy for the Ancient Earth Government without getting a few perks.

So, the best form of defence was attack, they say. I caught up with Barry in a moment and I hit him so hard his feet lifted off the floor and he flew backwards, at least unconscious, possibly dead. His disguise dissipated. I was in combat mode, I didn't care.

I turned to throw a punch at Malen Tom, but he had suited-up, and I just hit a force-wall that jarred my whole being. Then I felt a massive impact that drove me backwards as he palmed me in the solar plexus.

Gasping for air, I converted the kinetic force to throw myself into a backward somersault, I executed it perfectly to land in a crouch, steadied by one hand. With the other I fired a subdermal missile round at Tom. Well, not *at* him, exactly, but the ground just in front of him. There was always a chance that the ordinance would pass through the individual, wounding, but not fatally injuring. If it hit the surrounding area, the shrapnel or debris could just take him out. The ground mushroomed just in front of Tom, but he walked through, unscathed.

"More than just a chancer then, Garrett?" The big criminal said. "What are you, ex-army? Navy? Secret Service?"

"All of the above, shit-face." I bigged up my part. Winning in a duel is half skill, half bravado.

I then ran past Barry, who was breathing, according to my HUD, but still unconscious. I couldn't believe I had fallen so easily. I was never the mark. I did the marking. It was the first time in centuries anyone had got one over on me.

I activated my codes, I reached into the bank AI with my imprint. I uploaded the information, used my Simba module to open up a micro wormhole, and sent the information to my Ancient Earth account. At least my paymaster would be able to retrieve it if I couldn't get back.

I had hoped Ayel would be there with me. Clearly, he was just a ruse. "Stop. Garrett."

Would I shit. There was no way I was going to let Tom catch up with me, he was wearing some serious kit if he was able to knock me flying in my exo-suit.

"I've got the real Ayel."

He was lying. I was sure of it. There was just enough in his voice that meant I believed him.

"Give me the information, and I will let lover-boy go."

I pulled my momentum up, converting my energy from the kinetic, and into storage. I turned to face Tom, who had just caught up with me.

"How do I know this isn't another ruse?"

A wormhole opened up beside Tom, and someone pushed Ayel through. My heart nearly burst with relief until I saw through to the state of him. He looked roughed up, the bastards had obviously beaten him to get my daily whereabouts. My stomach and heart felt better that I hadn't been sleeping with the delightful Barry all this time, but it ached to see the sight of Ayel so mistreated.

"Don't give him the information, Gat." Ayel shouted. "I'll go to the Goddess Elchamber with my pathway laden in gold and jewels, and my immortality guaranteed."

I smiled at my love. If I gave away that information, then hundreds, if not thousands, would die: all the undercover agents working to pull down the intergalactic slavery ring, funded by the Leilanth and supported by many corporations from Ancient Earth, would be compromised.

I loved Ayel, but I couldn't let him live at the expense of thousands of others. He knew that too. He was a brave man. Which was why he snatched the other gun Tom had at his side, and shot the big man.

It wouldn't kill Tom, but it would disrupt the suit. I stormed forwards with that converted energy as thrust. At the same time, I fired micro grenades at the criminal.

"Get clear, Ayel." I shouted and watched as the grenades exploded in front of Tom, knocking the wretch into the air. He spiralled backwards, like a casually thrown child's doll. I reached him and punched his head, once, twice, then the third time. The suits were good, but they would deactivate if there was a chance of suffocation. They were skin-tight, not much room between for the recycling of air. Add a liquid like blood and you could soon drown.

Tom screamed, as the head of the suit opened up. I punched Tom again twice. The third time I heard his skull crack.

Then I heard a scream.

I turned in horror. My lovely Ayel was standing with a length of metal thrust through his chest. Behind Ayel was Barry. I fired off a compressed round of multi-shot. The rounds reached Barry's head as soon as I reached Ayel, turning the former's skull and brains to vapour. Barry's body poleaxed.

I caught Ayel before he fell. Even with the help of my suit he was a big, heavy lad. *My* big heavy lad.

"Let's get you somewhere. Fix that up." I said. I had pulled my suit-visor down for fear of drowning in my tears. I struggled to lay him down with the metal sticking out of his chest. So, I snapped as much as I could off either end. Blue blood welled around the entry and exit wounds.

He turned to look at me, and the effort was writ large upon his pained face. "I think it's a bit too late for that. My main heart has gone. I can feel my secondary pump faltering."

The Praxians could self-monitor their own internal organs. It was a marvel. They could self-diagnose, and get their systems repaired if needs be. We were too far from a hospital though. My Simba portal was likely no use for short hops. I checked it as I moved Ayel towards me. Multi-mode was not available, the battle up above must have disrupted things.

There was another large explosion, Ayel jumped, half unconscious, I saw a massive piece of debris hit a building behind the bank. The bank just began to crumble. Dust blew past us, thick and choking. I picked up Ayel and sped back towards the sea. Back to the bar.

I lay Ayel down on arrival, and plugged my device into the bar charge unit. I looked up. I could see the flash and coruscation of Simba modules creating their mini wormholes as people left, or as emergency services arrived to carry the fallen away. The sky was now full of ships. Earth Mind-Goliaths, Leilanth Whales, and the smaller Praxian Yachts.

Ayel's breathing was shallow as I knelt by him. I scanned his body. He was in shut down. His secondary heart was about to fail.

No.

All I could do was comfort him.

I sat and put his head in my lap.

"Remember when we first met. You arrested me for vagrancy because I was drunk and sleeping on the beach, I'd lost my job a few weeks before, and had been turned out my apartment." I said to him. Ayel's mouth twitched as if he were about to smile.

"You never went through with the arrest, as it was your last day on the job. Instead, you took me back to yours, tidied me up, and took me out for a slap-up meal. You got me into recovery, got me off the drugs, and turned me into a better man. I will always love you for that."

A tear left the corner of his right eye and tracked a darker blue line down his light blue skin. He shuddered a little as he grabbed me, as if to hold onto life. He smiled for he had died in combat. He would live forever, as he believed, in the halls of the Ancient Warriors.

"You were the one Ayel. In five hundred years I have never known anyone like you. You knocked me off my feet. I will love you forever."

There was a large detonation above us, and we both jumped, even Ayel who had so very little life in him.

"Go." He whispered, blue blood upon his purpling lips. "Go now."

He was looking upwards. I glanced above too and saw the biggest piece of debris coming down, plummeting towards us.

"I can't leave you.

"Go. My. Love."

He shuddered, and my HUD said he was dead. I didn't even have time to mourn. My tears were dried by the air above me being superheated. I pulled the suit back over my head.

The sky darkened. Whatever was falling had by then blocked both suns.

I dashed to my Simba Module, and slapped it onto my suit, funds had cleared, multi and long distance modes were now available to me. A bit of luck at least. So, I thought of the coordinates of the family farm where I had grown up.

I could go see my family. Hopefully spend some time with them before I left Ancient Earth for good.

The wormhole opened with a brief flash of blue-orange coruscation.

Unfortunately, something powerful hit the wormhole as I stepped through.

It hit me too. Hard. I spun into the void like a trapeze acrobat who had missed the safety of his fellow's hold.

Blackness came for me like a long-lost friend. I would be joining Ayel after all, it seemed.

Yet destiny dealt me another card.

I came to in a field in the English countryside near my father's farm, but where it would be in centuries time. My suit was ruined, it had enough power to tell me the date, the time, and the temperature. It was the fourteenth of February 1789, half past three in the afternoon and seven degrees Celsius.

I was trapped, my Simba module useless. I tried to find the World Net, the secret source of Gaia's life power. I tapped into it and healed myself.

There were some benefits to being a child of Ancient Earth. But not many.

Then I sat down and cried.

Interlude One

I opened my eyes. I was surrounded by my friends, all of them were standing. All looked asleep, or possibly unconscious.

"How was your first experience, Robert?" It was Candour, the alabaster being, naked apart from some sort of loincloth. He shimmered like a pool reflecting the bright light of the sun.

"That was the first test. Did you find your deceiver?"

I did not know what to say. I was thoroughly discombobulated at that point. My head was swimming with questions.

"Apollyon will speak with you soon, Robert, but he wants you to see through the eyes of all of your friends. This is your test, as well as theirs."

I nodded reluctantly. Could I live even a few short hours in the minds of my other friends?

I felt dirty at the intrusion.

Gat wasn't Prince Gathii. Gat was Garret N'Dour. Was that my secret to reveal though? Garret was from the future, and had come to the past as part of a traumatic event? What led him to become Prince Gathii? Where did his magic come from? I now knew it wasn't supernatural, he had linked to Gaia's Net? Was our planet actually called Gaia? No matter. Gat had lied. For years. Gat had gone to University with Abel. Robert had met Gathii through his beau. Twelve years ago.

Gathii was a lie. Garrett was real.

Had Garret N'Dour attempted to take the life of the Order Soul? Was he trying to get back to the future? Was he behind the abduction of Eliza's rose jar? Was he linked to those Lantern Heads that I knew were tied up in this betrayal?

Yet Garrett had seemed such a worthy soul in that short space of time I had been in his head. He had been fighting against the bonds of slavery, still so painfully rife in Earth's future. He had risked everything for his blue-skinned lover. My throat caught with emotion at the thought of that large blue man skewered by the length of metal, dying in Gat's arms.

"I haven't seen enough to know if Gat is the traitor. I presume I will live an episode in the life of another of the Menagerie quite soon?"

Candour nodded. "Do you have a preference as to whom it might be?"

I just wanted Percy to be faithful. She may not return my love, but I had worshiped her from afar for years.

Neither did I want my friend Walter to be a traitor. Or Charlie. Dear gods.

"Are you ready?" Candour asked. "Apollyon is impatient."

I nodded.
Then swiftly, I was in someone else's head.

Chapter Eleven

Percy's Lies

It's my birthday today. And I have just realised that I am bloody ancient.

It's also been an age since I wrote in this voice-journal. LP will kill me if I don't document stuff.

When I look in the mirror, these days, I see a young woman in her late twenties, possibly thirty. I am not sure how old I actually am, but a rough estimate would suggest over fifty thousand years.

I was born in 1867, the third daughter of Lord and Lady Percival. The former, who I never met because he was always in Africa, at the head of some imperialistic army. Daddy is still there, in his grave, killed in my first year by those he and Britain tormented. As for mummy, well, she was dead by the time I was four, and I have no memories of her either. Mummy's wealth had always depended upon the opium trade, and she had succumbed to its usage.

I was eventually brought up by the dowager Lady Percival. My grandmama. She's the one I get my filthy mouth from, and my fighting stance.

To cut a long story short, I ended up working for the British Secret Service because of Grandmama, who had been an agent herself. Then I was poached from the British Secret Service by Perfume Factory Large Pockets, the alien Zenobart who spent his days protecting the Earth from threats of creatures from parallel worlds and bubble universes.

I then became one of the Chosen, a group of humans from my version of Earth selected by the Universe, for all I can gather, to travel to a magical planet. Then I became a goddess, some followers called the Gypsy, others called me the Traveller.

I then, in a fit of pique, and with a bit of help from a chap called Flynn (quite a hottie by the way – sorry Arthur) opened up a wormhole back here to Earth, as I had learned my Arthur was still alive.

I was recruited once more by the Minister of Mirrors as he had felt the time disturbance caused by my return to the real Earth. I'll let you into a secret, The Minister and Large Pockets are the very same. Within weeks LP assigned me to watch over a debonair ghost and demon hunter, Robert Waterfield.

I had been assigned to watch Robert, as he was the owner of a very unusual power that intrigued LP. Robert could slip between the worlds of the living and the dead.

LP was worried that this might link back to certain events that awoke dark powers on our Earth making it a favoured destination of evil beings throughout the multi-verse. We were on the cusp of the Supernatural Wars, but no one would have known at that point.

Robert is a lovely man, by the way. Handsome, like my Arthur, but Robert is much more mature. Built like a brick shithouse, too. I have often imagined him naked, looking at the contours of that well-honed body. Well, what's a girl to do when her husband has been missing for most of her ancient life?

I haven't had a shag for eons.

One of Robert's worst kept secrets is that gym in one of his many basements. I wonder what he thinks we think he's been doing when he reappears above ground sweating like a murderer in a court dock.

Unless he is partaking in the pretty opaque ghostlings. No, that is sick, he is a good man. Maybe the best Earth has to offer in this period.

I think he wants me, and he would be a catch, and although I haven't seen you, Arthur, for tens of thousands of years, in relative terms, I am still married to you in the eyes of the Universe. Love never dies; it just changes.

I've watched Robert from the time he left Magpie Farm. If he knew I was outside that building when his harridan of a fiancé had begun shooting at him, he would be distraught.

I very nearly broke cover at that point. Thankfully, LP had assured me that his life would not be in danger. So, after I saw him leave the house with that boy's body wrapped in those bloody bed sheets, I watched to find more out about the man himself.

The boy had been Eliza's tenth victim, according to the case files I read later. She had killed her parents, too. It could quite have easily been Robert wrapped in those sheets, rather than that boy.

I paid Robert's bail when they arrested him for the murders. Idiots. Of course, the police didn't think it could be the lovely Lady Eliza Bell who had killed so many young men and her parents. That was compounded by the disappearance of Eliza herself. Robert was guilty in the eyes of the law.

The ministry eventually intervened and proved that Robert could not possibly have been the murderer as, in the end, we fabricated Eliza's demise with an unknown body, which police fished out of Stowe Pool in Lichfield with the murder weapon in her petticoats, and a letter of confession to all of the killings.

The majority of police of the 1900s were not ready for the truth about supernatural beings, and their like. Forensic evidence didn't even exist.

Over time, it became clear Robert's talent to travel to the Hopelessness was inert, unthreatening, and very personal. It could only aid us in our missions.

We haven't as yet enrolled Robert in the Chapter of the Worlds of Our Faltering Hearts, (known so because Arrythmia was the reward for those of us who travelled to lots of alternative timelines and dimensions via those artefacts) instead we encouraged him to engage with more common horrors.

I now act as an intermediatory between LP as the Minister, the police, and the Menagerie, of which I am an honorary member.

It is an appropriate name. Each one of us is a strange creature in our own right. I am clearly a strange ancient woman who keeps returning to the world of my birth to save it.

Whilst he was dating Eliza, Robert had also been investing in property. His ghostly, and once very rich grandfather, had secreted plenty of money away in places only Robert could find. It was quite an investment plan.

Robert invested in a new development in Edgbaston, Birmingham, on Legend Street, just at the turn of the century, and by then he had his Bat-Cave ready. Apologies, Arthur, for the references to future fiction, but having lived across various timelines, there are things that have become groundings for me. My love of twentieth century comics being one of them. More about them in future entries my love.

I first met the rest of the Menagerie one January. LP asked me to engage Mr Waterfield's services as a test, to see if he was worthy of a link to LP's Ministry of Mirrors. As in smoke and mirrors.

I took a late night single carriage train from Euston to Birmingham, and made my way to Edgbaston. It was cold and LP had needed to pull a lot of strings to get the train to run on New Year's Day, in the first place. I could have used future technology to step through a portal, but LP didn't want us being too ahead of our times, too often. It made the dimensions wobble.

I knocked loudly on the door of 42 Legend Street, not knowing at the time it was an interconnected complex of ten buildings, as from the outside, it looked like a normal Victorian terrace.

It was a while before Robert trusted me enough to tell me what he had below the house, or rather houses. Eventually, I found that it was cavernous down there, and I was sure its dimensions were affected by the bird Postlethwaite, who lived on the cusp of life and death guarding Robert and his manse.

Robert had quickly filled the guts of his complex with captured evil spirits; some that he was worried about despatching, some of whom he should have, but was too kind to do so, and many revenants that were impossible to destroy.

I am sure there are other things down there he has never told me about. Vampires, werewolves, or other supernatural creatures, judging by the silver doors I saw.

Back to that cold January, and my first visit.

Walter opened the doors of number 42 - good old dependable Captain Trevithick. Hero of many secret missions. He could have gone onto great things if he hadn't left the army the same day young Robert had.

Robert had been forced into the military by his father at the age of eighteen, with a bought commission. Mr Waterfield senior had influenced his son's career with money from afar. He sent the war office money from the Americas, and Robert had been over-promoted - much to his embarrassment.

When Robert's was twenty-three, his father died. Robert left the army as one of the youngest majors ever to have graced the South Staffordshire Regiment. He hadn't fought in a single battle, he hadn't gained a single medal, he had been a desk officer. The later title of colonel bestowed so he could interact with the highbrow idiots at Whitehall was more of an embarrassment to him, and a stone around his neck.

Robert doesn't know I know all this, by-the-way.

"Can I help you?" Walter asked that cold early morning.

"I am here to see Robert Waterfield." I said with my best and brightest ancient girly smile. "It is the most utmost emergency."

"They often are, Miss." Walter said, unphased by what I did with my eyelashes. It wasn't the answer I was looking for. I was aristocracy on Earth, and I had been a goddess on Nova Gaia, so part of me still needed servants to bow and scrape and move when I said they could. Walter had obviously not grasped this.

"May I wait for him?" I asked, fully expecting to have to find some guest house that would allow me to stay over without thinking I was one half of a jilted sexual tryst.

"He may be some time, miss. Although, I do have ways of contacting him."

That was better. "Don't mind if I do?"

"Come through to the library, *miss*. Let me take your hat and coat." His sarcasm was thinly veiled.

I was then availed of my outer shell, and Walter took me through to the library. It was huge and, by now, I had realised the dimensions of that house were definitely off.

"Are the houses knocked through?" I asked.

"Yes, madam. They are all knocked through my soul. Mr Waterfield needs quite some space to operate his business. I spend my days talking to contractors and architects about his devious schemes. That is why I look sixty when I am only actually twenty-five."

84

I snorted. Walter raised his eyes in a way only the lower class could show the upper class how privileged, but stupid they were. To be honest, my way of snorting with laughter hadn't impressed my worshippers on Nova Gaia, either. The Travelling Gestalt on my previous world were fundamental in their religious beliefs. It was somewhat ruined, on one occasion, when the Goddess Gypsy (not my choice, by the way, as I've said) had snorted holy ale through her nose by mistake when the archpriest had tripped over his vestments, and had skewered himself rather that the sacrifice.

"Tea, miss?" Walter asked. It seemed he had lost all respect for me because of that one snort. He can be a bit of a wanker, at times. Not much of a sense of humour outside of the lowest form of wit, the sarcastic get.

"Yes please."

I sat in that vast library for hours. I memorised the books on the shelves in that time. There were four comfy chairs at one end, and a nice leather embossed couch. It sat just in front of an open roaring fire. I nodded off a few times under its warm glare.

I was told later that there was a protection spell over those books. I had presumed any rare or expensive tomes were archived, the heat and air, I supposed, would do them a mischief. LP would have had a fit. The University libraries were fitted with condensers and air conditioning. I could see LP pouring water over the fire, and then bricking it up.

"Miss." Walter said, making the word seem very dirty. "I am Captain Trevithick. I am not a butler. I am happy to serve you tea, but I do not subscribe to the divine right philosophy of the aristocracy. Cutting to the chase. If you want sugar, feel free. I shall be in my room doing the crossword. Mr Waterfield will be here presently." The fact he had answered my comment from hours before showed how much of a tosser he was, back then. He became a loveable tosser, eventually, but back then he was a real grade-A sarcastic nob.

He left me again, for hours. I had drunk two cups of tea, and I was about to pee in one of the plant pots when the most beautiful boy and girl swept in.

Thing is, when you have been around as long as I have, you pick up on certain clues.

Charlie, as she introduced herself was dressed in a fitting powder blue dress. It was lower than formal wear, but none the less very Edwardian. Avery was dapper, taller than me and extremely handsome. Quite foxy actually. I immediately knew there was something different about them.

After having had a toilet visit, I politely conversed with them as we waited for Mr Waterfield. They told me their hobbies and what their aspirations were. Charlie wanted to help the poor and Avery wanted to go off and join the military. A fine upstanding pair of twins I thought.

Then I realised what was up. They were identical, in every way. For a set of male/female twins they were like mirrors of each other. It was quite astounding.

I realised they were transgender. Even during the future (and I have visited it a few times) when such body swaps, and genetic manipulation was available, never had I set eyes upon such perfect representations of the opposite sex. Charlotte had been born a boy and Avery a girl. They had wanted to swap bodies, I think, ever since.

Then two gentlemen entered, covered in the snow that was promised by the orange skies a few hours before.

The first was a tall African gentleman. Quite dishy and to be honest, I'd already switched over to swoon mode, when he introduced himself. Prince Gathii. He was clearly not from that time or that version of Earth.

He was putting on an act - as was I.

We were two peas in a pod in that respect, and whilst my magical powers did not work on my home planet, I could read him like a book. I just winked at him. *I am on to you sunshine.* I tried to relay.

Then there was Robert. You forget how big he is. His kindness shrinks him.

Since the first time our eyes met in Chelsea something had changed in him. That day he looked tense as he entered the room as if there was a massive burden hanging over him like some great weight or a great hurt - maybe a bereavement. Yet, when he looked at me, he visibly melted.

"Lady Percival, it is so nice to see you again, apologies that I wasn't here when you arrived."

"You were not to know I was coming. A bit of a whim. I am on the business of the Minister of Mirrors."

"We are not working cases based on whim." Walter said as he arrived back at the library with more tea for the others.

"Seconded," Gat said being mother.

Robert shushed them and then pulled a seat over to join me by the fire, flicking dark looks their way.

"Ignore the Menagerie. They are, particularly testing. Please let us know why you are here."

So, I told him. Boy, Robert is the easiest person to open up to. I had seen him many times from afar, he had always looked so imposing, but here, his friendly rosy-cheeked face lit by the fire was hypnotising. It was like he could see my very soul. Of course, he probably could, or would be able to when I corked it.

"Of course, we will help." Robert said and we continued chatting into the late morning. He offered to put me up, to save me travelling through the snow, and then and we had a delightful New Year's Day Roast magicked up by the then yet to be seen cook.

86

The next day we went on a walk through the snow, and we got to know each other much better. I outlined some of the plans the Ministry had, if Robert was amenable to helping out with more cases. He said he would be happy to accompany me back down to London once he had dispensed with the ghost of St Chads in Lichfield. It was apparently a weaselly little wraith. Well, I knew, because we had planted it. LP had used it to test Robert and his gang.

Of course, the Menagerie was a well-oiled machine, and the creature was captured and stowed below Legend Street ready for further study by Gat.

On the way back to Legend Street from our promenade, we heard a horse whinny and the coach Robert, and me were travelling in must have hit the curb. We were thrown about and, with an almighty screech the coaches axel must have split. We were surely going to crash, according to the shouts of the driver, who was then thrown. I waited for the collision.

Then we were somewhere else.

Robert had used his trick with me for the second time and we had landed in the Hopelessness. It was more horrible than the first. Robert's shock at the crash had dropped some of his personal shields.

I must have been there for all of two seconds, yet it seemed that all of the evil I had ever encountered was there waiting for me. I could feel it hiding in plain sight.

I was still screaming as he brought us back into the snow on the Hagley Road, next to the mangled carriage.

I have been back to the Hopelessness many times since, and I can also get there on my own with some thought, now, but I will never forget that second time.

Robert then explained to me, back in the library, about the Hopelessness, and how his wards stop the wraiths and spirits attacking him, and that he must have been so discombobulated that his protective shields had fallen. He apologised profusely as I held a brandy in a shaking hand, and promised that I wouldn't be afraid on my next visit.

Diary, I think Robert has been in love with me since. And I like him; he is a dear friend, but he is not what I would call right, for me. I'd be happy to jump his bones, but that is probably language I picked up from my Skyflier chums and it doesn't belong in this sexually simpler time. He is not you though, dear Arthur.

Onwards and upwards. Diary, journal or whatever you are called, I have work to do. If we get rid of this Apollyon, I intend to go and try to find Arthur. Last seen in Alberta, a crazy parallel version of Victorian England, where she got assassinated and the German consort became king.

Although not working with Robert in the future will be wrenching. He is like the brother I never had.

Percy out.

Interlude Two

I physically staggered, looking for a place to hold myself up.

Like Gat, Percy was a living lie. She had never loved me. She had a long-lost husband, she had lived for centuries; had been a goddess. To be honest I would have agreed with her deity when I was at the height of my love for her, yet now I would never truly be able to love her like I thought I had. It was clear that as I felt her re-live her story as she spoke it in her diary; that she had a lot of affection for me, but she did not love me.

Was that worse than realising she could have also betrayed me?

No. Percy hadn't. Surely.

I felt tears on my cheeks.

I barely had chance to focus on reality when Candour appeared.

"Have they all deceived me, Candour?"

"Deception is just another version of a personal view, frame of mind, or reality."

I couldn't fault his logic, but I felt stripped bare. I had seen Gat's desperation on the Praxian world, I had seen the eons Percy had lived through, got flashes of quite different worlds, future and past.

"The traitor is neither Gat, nor Percy?"

"I am giving you the truth, you must interpret it as you will."

"Is Apollyon going to put in an appearance soon?" I said, sighing.

"How do you know he hasn't?"

"Why has someone taken his son."

"Power. The Nephilim are the most powerful beings on the planet. With that power you could challenge Mother Gaia."

"How was he stolen."

"Through a hole in the air."

I thought about that for a moment. Then all thoughts were shelved as I was pulled into someone else's memories. It had to be Charlie, or Walter's.

Chapter Twelve
Little Wally's Lies

I ran through the streets of East London as quickly as the weather conditions would allow; if I didn't get back to Old Giles with his daily quota of purses, then I would be flayed alive.

"You've dallied again, Little Wally." Giles would put the emphasis on the *little* all of the time.

The snow had started to fall. It was cold, and my toes were poking out from my worn boots that had been open to the elements for quite some time. I'd nearly caught frostbite on a few occasions and had cuts on one or more of the three remaining stumpy toes that poked out, often.

Giles always said that if you weren't speedy enough, then the Shadowman would get you. The Shadowman was faster than everyone, and knew everyone's intentions. The only way you kept the Shadowman at bay was to do as you were asked by you elders, and betters.

Giles was older, but not better. He was creepy. The things Giles did to young girls was only imaginable by interpreting their screams. Wally had heard two of Giles's henchmen calling the old man a pervert, I didn't understand what that meant as a boy.

I wasn't certain the Shadowman was real, with bravado I, like my peers, poo-poohed the idea, but late at night, as I shivered under newspaper, or huddled next to a friend, I would imagine a shadowy hand reaching down like a claw to take me in my sleep.

Thankfully, Giles did not know Lizzie from the Market End. Pretty Lizzie who managed to look her best despite the challenges of being a street urchin. Like him, Lizzie had no folks, they had died of the pox, or the gin. Most of her brothers or sisters had starved to death like mine, or had been hung for stealing a morsel of food.

I dreamed of getting away, becoming a soldier in the Queens Army, having a shiny uniform, a wage, and the ability to buy Lizzie flowers when I was on leave. I would always give pennies to the starving children if I were earning.

I had to be careful though, mixing with the Market End as a River End child could be dangerous. The bigger children and young adults were not averse to cutting a throat and leaving a young body bobbing in the Thames, one of her tributaries, or the sewers.

Most days I would sit on the edge of the market and watch, hoping for a view of Lizzie. Often, I would see her with Barrow, the boss of the Market End. Barrow was a strong man in his thirties who was one of Giles's fiercest rivals. Their opposition was coming to a head, I could feel it. I hoped, no, prayed Lizzie didn't get caught up in it.

I eventually reached the lean-tos, a rabbit warren of shacks and runs you could get lost in if you weren't careful. I actually think that this might've been the whole idea.

Giles held court in an old church ruin, a church the families of the dead had obviously forgotten about. The broken walls with their remaining stained-glass windows jutted up like the many broken teeth Giles had in his head.

Giles sat on his throne, a beggar king, surrounded by young girls and women. Two of his Rabid Guards stood watch over proceedings. To be a Rabid Guard was a privilege, you could participate in Giles's drinking sessions and also spend time with his hand-me-down whores.

I almost skidded into the court. The ground was icy, and un-salted. We only had salt when one of the boys had knocked off a barrel from the docks, or the slaughterhouse. I came to a halt before I fell into Old Jennie's lap. Old Jennie was only nineteen, which might tell you a thing or two about his lordship, King Giles.

"Fuck me, it's the little 'un." Giles had been a mummer before his times went hard. He still had the skill of captivating an audience and throwing his voice to the crowd.

"Any of your girls found his willy, yet? You won't in this weather."

There was a large guffaw from Giles's, what did he call them? Hareem. That was it. The two Rabid Guards were laughing, too. Not sure why Cody was, he had nothing between his legs on a warm day, but I wasn't going to join in that sort of gutter humour. You might be born with the turds, but you didn't have to always talk their shit.

"What have you got for me, little 'un? Come closer. I don't bite. Do I, girls?"

"No," the girls chorused. "Not unless we bite you first."

That was Giles's court down to a tee. He set up the jokes, and his retinue delivered the punchlines in the manner of the Vaudeville Theatre that would be so popular twenty years later.

So, I sidled up to the old man. You could smell his breath from ten yards away. *Midden breath* we called him. Not to his face, or to one of the Rabids or one of his guards. We were not stupid.

I had done really well that day. Four purses. My quota was two purses. I gave the old man three. I had secreted the fourth away somewhere for a rainy day, for six years' time when I could enlist in the Queens Own. I was still thin enough to squeeze between the bars of the main sewer overflow

91

shafts, and so, I would climb down the rusting ladder into darkness and the foetid stinking air amongst the rats; to put my takings behind a secret brick.

"Call the older ones in, Rabids." Giles called. I could smell his breath from where I was standing.

The rank and file who were not out working, but waiting at Giles' beck and call, gathered in the courtyard.

"Are we all here?" Giles asked, his voice carrying across what would have been the nave in this ruined church. "Good." He nodded.

"The little 'un has collected three full purses. Bring them forward, my lad."

I piled the purses on Giles's lap, exactly where he beckoned for me to do so.

"You see, if this little runt can collect three purses, then all you lot can too, thanks to the little 'un, the quota has been raised to five."

The Rabids and Giles's girls cheered. The others looked at me with hate.

With those few sentences Giles made me everyone's enemy in that court. If anyone, including myself, didn't get five purses the following day, then we would be whipped. Or worse, depending on the shortfall. One lad, Bobby, had been kicked to death by the Rabids for failing to get his quota. Bobby was six.

"Get out." Giles said sometime later, once he had had enough of his own act. The rank and file left immediately, many sparing a glance my way. "Not you. Wally. Come here."

I walked up to the old man. It was all I could do not to gag, and I'd only had a mouldy potato to eat in the last few days.

" 'Ere boy. I want you to go a little further afield tomorrow. I want you to collect your quota in the Market End." Giles smiled, his teeth had long ago rotted away to stumps. "If you can get me three purses from the Market End, and not cause a fuss, then you can have a week off. You can also sleep with one of the girls. I don't care if you bang her, or use her to keep you warm; that is your reward. If you get caught though, don't come back."

I got out of there as soon as I could, and went to the market perimeter. I sat on the steps of a derelict townhouse that had burned down the summer before last, it was next to a whorehouse where I used to run errands for Giles, when I was younger. The girls were always polite when they came past, smiling at me.

A skinny redhead with a few too many mouth sores ran her fingers through my hair at one point. Her name was Annie. "It won't be long before you'll be popping in for a bit of how's your father, Wally."

I smiled, it paid to be polite, you never knew when you might need to hide under a whores bed, away from some cutthroat or bully. People tended not to enter a house of sin without an appointment, because they often ended up in old father Thames.

Annie was probably only twenty or so, but she looked ancient to me. Nothing like Lizzie. My Lizzie.

I sat around for probably an hour or so and thought I had better find somewhere to sleep for the night. The gas lighters were out, although they didn't light many in the slums. Who needed light in Hell?

I found a couple of the younger boys had stolen a bottle of gin and were sipping it whilst trying to keep warm under newspaper blankets near abandoned cellar flat stairs. I snuggled up with them for the night, taking a swig or two of gin in exchange for a few crusts of stale bread I had managed to pick up earlier in the day. Then I slept the sleep of the cold and hungry, yet again.

I awoke shivering, nothing new there, it wasn't even a cold spell, the wind just had that northerly chill the rich folks talked about when I was amongst them, unnoticed. I wrapped my tatty scarf around my head to keep my face warm, but to also disguise myself a little better. I then stepped out into the streets near the market where the less salubrious hostelries and inns were located.

My first mark was drunk. I used to hang around outside a brothel where they catered for men who liked boys. Firstly, I would look for one that was drunk, I would never approach a sober nonce. I would then track the mark out of the market area and back towards the East End proper, or wherever they were headed.

Mr Rich Pants was a small pot-bellied fellow, not much taller than me. He was dressed in clothes that were expensive, but had seen better days. His shoes were scuffed and, because he was three parts to the wind, he wasn't watching where he was treading. Those shoes were absolutely caked in seven shades of shit by the time he had exited the second street.

I knew what would happen. It always did. It was just the timing. There was a slope on Keen Street where the cobbles were worn from the dray men who delivered barrels. If you didn't know that you would slip on the shiny surface when it was icy, or when your shoes were caked.

Down went Mr Rich Pants, like his ticker had given up. I once saw one of Giles's mates go like that. His heart stopped, and he fell straight forwards, his head popped when it hit the cobbles, like a pomegranate.

"Are you alright, sir?" I asked with my poshest voice, I might add.

"Young man. Help me up. Help me up, and I will be eternally grateful. I will reward you for your service, young man. In ways you couldn't imagine."

Well, first of all, I felt sick. I knew what men like that did to boys, and no, I'll never talk about it, ever. So, I cut his purse with my old fruit knife before I'd even helped him up. It was stowed down the front of my breeches with my other 'valuables.'

"Don't worry about the reward, sir. I am praised enough with the gaze of Jesus."

"You one of those Methodist boys then?" Mr Rich Pants asked, his voice with inflection. I didn't like what it suggested. "Are you an altar boy?"

I looked around. There was no one about. So, I kicked him on the side of the knee. The place that easily dislocates if you hit it exactly right. There was a crack. The pervert looked at me cross eyed, and then fell back into the shit.

I was away from there before the sick bastard screamed.

The purse was loaded, so I made my way to my sewer entrance at Curtis Street, and climbed down. I had a couple of spare empty smaller purses for just this occasion. Giles would get his purses, but only on my terms. That meant I had three makeshift purses. I now needed two more.

I had a spare groat and so I decided to visit the bun vendor on the Market. I would be all right buying things, but if the Market End thugs thought I was working their patch, then they would kick me out, or worse, to death.

I chomped on an Eccles cake, and went and sat back out by the whorehouse. I could see Lizzie selling flowers. I had just finished my cake when I saw a young man approach her. He bought a dozen roses, but I noticed him being too busy with his hands about Lizzie's person. I was having none of it.

I hightailed over to where Lizzie was trying to protect herself. I picked up the biggest handful of horse manure I could, and I threw it at the young man. As he turned at my screaming approach, I realised my mistake. It was Giles's business partner, Mr Norrin. The shit hit him square in the face, and his mouth was open.

I immediately feared for my life, despite my laughter, so, I ran.

Straight into Giles. "However fucking funny that was to see, boy, you will probably hang for that."

The Rabids soon locked me in the vault underneath the church. It was cold and scary. I was shivering, and I was crying. My life wasn't great, but that didn't mean I wanted to be hung or, at best, whipped. I sat there for such an exceptionally long time. Until I was pulled out of the crypt. I was pulled before the whole of Giles's entourage.

"What do we have 'ere, then?" Giles said to the congregation. "Where's my five purses. You only brought me three. And you chucked shit at a gentleman. Mr Norrin has gone home for a bath. He wants to return tomorrow to look at your body before we drop you in the Thames, to be with the fishes."

The Court of Giles laughed raucously at that. They were all jostling for a better place to see me as I was led by the Rabids into the last light of the evening.

"What shall we do to him, kidduns?" Giles asked his people.

"Strip him. Naked." Someone cried.

"What about his girlfriend?"

I went cold. What did the old bastard 'mean girlfriend?'

"Mr Norrin has had his fill of little Lizzie. After all she was the reason little 'un here went to her aide and chucked shit at a gentleman. Bring her out here."

Poor Lizzie was in a tattered shift. It was barely sparing her blushes, although I realised at that point all of her blushes had been taken along with her innocence. I would kill Norrin, and then I would kill Giles. I would kill the Rabids and the whores who laughed at poor Lizzie.

"Bring her here." Giles said. "Let me have a look at you. You look like you have been a busy Lizzie."

The crowd roared with laughter. Lizzie was sobbing, although she had cried all her tears, it seemed. Snot was bubbling from her nose. She knew, like I did, that we were not going to see another dawn. It was all over.

That was when all hell broke loose, and Barrow and the Market End boys attacked.

I ran once I saw Lizzie being led to safety by a boy who I thought looked like her. He was a handsome lad of about fourteen, or fifteen. One day he would be my brother-in-law, I stupidly thought, but at that point I didn't know the future. I just knew he looked kind and so like Lizzie.

I went and slept in the sewer that evening. I would need to get away from this part of London. I was a marked man, or rather boy. I didn't want to die, I wanted to become a soldier, and go into the army. I gave up my dream of ever being with Lizzie at that point.

I emerged the next morning, and it was snowing heavily, I made my way towards the Market End and noticed, whilst blowing into my hands, that there was a commotion. It was early, and they were still setting up some of the barrows, and some of the regular hawkers were not yet in place. There was a crowd gathered in the square.

As I moved closer, I noticed Lizzie's brother. He was beside himself, crying and rocking. There was someone in his arms. My heart went colder than the previous evening when Giles brought Lizzie out to parade her in front of his court.

Lizzie was looking at me. Those beautiful eyes staring deep into mine. I could have believed, perhaps, that if it weren't for the bone-deep gash between them. My Lizzie was dead. And I knew who had done it.

I moved in closer. There was another dead body, but this one was strung up from a lamppost. Barrow, the gang leader of Market End was swinging in the breeze. It seemed Giles had increased his territory.

I blinked away my tears and locked my sorrow in a box in my soul and ran. I ran until exhausted. I ran across London. I ran until I collapsed, and some missionary took me to the local church Workhouse. They looked after me for a few weeks until a young woman came to visit me. The Governor was most surprised when she turned up.

That was the first time I saw Lady Percival. Anna took me from the workhouse to a family in North London called the Trevithick's who had just moved down from Norwich. They were childless and wanted to adopt. Something that was almost unheard of, then.

Percy has forgotten, however.

You might think that was the end of this little chapter of my life. And yes, Mr Waterfield, I know you are in my brain. And that is good. Because, you see, I am going to die.

Before I die, I will finish my tale.

I went back to my old haunt, on my first leave. I did some research just before I went over to Africa, to fight in the first Boer War. I found where a certain Mr Norrin lived. I staked out his house, and I watched him for a day. I broke in at an opportune moment, and I cut his throat.

Then I found Giles, who was still alive. I killed the two Rabids on duty with a knife in their ears as they snored.

I then found Giles and first chased away the whores. Giles recognised me and he was still defiant, the bastard. He was an old spindly man by then. He still called me *little Wally* even though I towered over him. He was still laughing as I squeezed the life out of him.

So, as you rifle through my thoughts, Robert, my friend. You see I also lied. All those times I told you not to kill. That it was not the right way.

I killed for vengeance. That is the worst kind of premeditated murder.

Interlude Three

I gasped and looked at Candour, who I knew would be there.

"Walter. Will he die?"

Candour nodded. "He is the victim."

"I need to save him."

"One of you must die to reveal the traitor. Was that not the Prophecy?" Candour asked. "Even though I can only tell the truth, I will not reveal a prophecy as lies."

"At least Walter did not betray me." I said, thankfully. A chair appeared in that room, and I sat down. They might not be my memories, but I had felt them all. I had run where little Wally had run, felt the emotions he had felt, suffered the losses he had suffered. "Can Apollyon not help me?"

"You would make a deal with the Devil."

"Thought that he was a God?"

"There is more than one God. There are multiple deities, Robert."

"So, Apollyon *is* a god of sorts?"

"There is no *of sorts* about it."

"Are you saying that because he is your master?"

Candour laughed. Not sarcastically, but like one who knows so very much more than you. "Apollyon is not my only master. I serve all the gods and goddesses. I serve the Pantheon. I am their truth."

"You didn't say that at first."

"You didn't ask."

"Would Apollyon save Walter if I save his son?"

"That was not the agreement. Only Gaia can bring the dead back without them being un-dead. Find Sammel, and Apollyon will leave this place. He does not make bargains he has not instigated, himself."

I really did not want Walter to die. Although as I was about to plea further, I felt the pull of another's memories. Was this Charlie's mind I was being drawn to?

Chapter Thirteen
Solo Missions

How could I tell Uncle Robert that Charlie was a murderer. I looked at her, as I sat in our dressing-come-sitting room, puffing on a cigar whilst darning. Butter wouldn't melt in her mouth.

Last night, I saw her kill a man in cold blood outside the Bacchus club, near the viaduct.

"Avery dear, pass me the paper. I want to see what the girls will be wearing this season."

I did as was asked, I was busy hemming my floaty trousers ready for our evening at the Council House in Honour of the Coronation of the King and Queen. I wasn't going to look a state. Not if I was going to make an impression on Violet Priestly. Oh Violet, I know we can never be together, especially if you get a gander below the belt, or under the shirt, before the wedding. But, just to dance in your arms just for one evening. Before Charlie is locked up for her crimes. They will find out she is, under the law as he, then they will look at me as her twin and my secret will be out.

"Damn."

"Are you alright, sweet pea?"

"I've just lanced my bloody finger with a bobbin needle."

"Ouch, here, let me take a look. I'll ring for Walter, he will have a field dressing."

"I've got blood on my slacks. I am going to have to soak them, and hope it comes out."

"Who is going to see a speck of blood on your turn-ups, some amorous woman who inspects the bottom of people's trousers. Mind you, I have seen everything in Birmingham. Particularly in the Bacchus. So, it wouldn't surprise me."

How could Charlie carry on as if nothing had happened.

So, I am now writing this down in case anything happens to me - not that I would think Charlie would kill me, or have me killed - but as I've already been poking my nose in, I had better be prepared.

Anyway, I am getting ahead of myself.

It all began when we were in the carriage, on the way to the bar. It was the only place in town where we could feel at home, amongst the so-called homosexuals and deviants who otherwise would be roaming the streets of our fair and smoggy city. The officials turned a blind eye so long as we stayed there and did not infest the rest of society.

Neither Charlie nor I identify as homosexuals, we are just victims of being born in the wrong body. Our souls obviously got mixed up in mother's womb, and out we popped. I was born without a few bits, and Charlie was born with too many. It's not like anything could sort us out, short of God or serious magic. Unfortunately, I believe in neither.

"You seem quiet, Charlie."

"I am marvellous. Hogey is going to be there this evening."

"He is a complete fruit."

"My, my, Avery, it takes one to know one. Hogey knows a Spirit Witch who can help us. I am not really after his body. Well, I might be using him a little bit."

"A Spirit Witch? Not this again. There is no magic on Earth that can give us what we want.

"You have heard the things Uncle Robert has experienced. Surely somewhere, somehow, there is something that can help us. Switch our minds, or our souls. We could have each other's bodies. We could be free."

"Of course, dear, but it is mumbo-jumbo. You asked Gat, and he is a sorcerer. He said it was impossible to switch the essence of two people from one body to another, even with the most powerful spiritual magic."

"And do you think Gat knows all there is to know about magic because he is an African mystic? I wouldn't be surprised if he were born in Leeds." Charlie swiped.

I laughed. There was something about Gat that was as false as the bottom of a magician's top hat. Uncle Robert could never see it. Why did he spend all his time in the library looking at science books if he was supposed to be an African mystic? There was also the tattoo on his wrist that looked like a pocket watch with strange numbers. He hid with that ridiculously thick leather band. I wondered if Robert had even noticed.

Uncle Robert looked at hearts and minds rather than people.

I remember having a conversation with the snooty cow, Anna Percival. At least she didn't bat an eyelid when I spoke with her about us wanting to change bodies. Her response was as pragmatic as usual. "One day they *will* invent a way to set people like you and Charlie free, Avery. It's probably not going to be for an awfully long time. So, you need to find your way in life and find people you can share it with who will not exploit you for what you are."

What really annoys me about the pretty heifer is that I agree with her, even though I want to punch her in the face when she is being all know-it-all government agent, and I know the King and the Home Secretary horseshit.

We arrived at the Bacchus club that night. I had already arranged to meet my chum, Paul Thompkins. Paul was neither homosexual nor in the wrong body, he was just one of those people who identified better as *different*. He was a writer, and Uncle Robert had edited one of his adventure books. Paul was one of those voyeurs. He gravitated to the unusual, it stretched the boundaries of his craft, he said.

Paul was standing at the long bar. It was a grim affair, with a poorly lit dance floor, and a small stage for a band. There was a cloakroom at the narrow entrance, as well as ambiguous bathrooms, where all sorts of action could be had.

"Curzon. My old chap." He said.

"Tommo." I replied. "No sketch book, tonight?"

"No. The last time I was here I drew someone who was a bit near the royal family to be reproduced in such a way. He was riding the son of the Mayor of Birmingham, at the time. Wouldn't be good to have a recording of that, according to Inspector Losenge. He also waved the Obscene Publications Act at me, so I had to destroy it, and promise I wouldn't bring my pencil in here."

"I am sure if you waved your pencil, there would be a few who would be interested in you sketching them."

"I am an artist of the moment, and you are crude. I like to work spontaneously, not arrange a tableaux. How effete. Gin and tonic?"

"Don't mind if I do."

Paul and I sat by the dance floor, and waited for the band to strike up the music. It was all vaudeville tunes. *A Bird in a Gilded Cage,* and other sweet ballads.

It was Paul who noticed who Charlie was with.

"Isn't that your sister with Hogey Marsh?"

Marsh was one of the sons of the famous Birmingham gang-land family. They supposedly wore blades in the peaks of their caps, although Hogey, a nickname for Adolphus Marsh, was far more stylish than his thuggish brothers. Why was Charlie getting mixed up with him? Okay, he was quite different to his brothers, who wouldn't be seen dead at the Bacchus. But he was still a Marsh.

"She needs to choose her companions a little better." Paul said.

"Yes, I will be having a word."

At that moment she shook her head at Hogey Marsh, and stood up. Hogey put a hand on her arm, but Charlie pulled away and slapped him before storming out.

"Stay here, Paul. I don't want you involved." I said, standing up. The Marshes were crazy. I didn't want Paul suffering because of Charlie's poor decisions.

I dashed across the dance floor, towards Hogey who was following Charlie outside. I elbowed through the incoming crowds. I fought against the tide, all the way down the stairs until exited the club and saw Charlie racing ahead. What was she doing? I kept my distance and watched. Charlie, once in the alleys, had her soul blade out.

It was so unlike her.

As I approached, Charlie peeled away, and moved further into darkness. Hogey hesitated, this was strange behaviour, it was as if he did not know what was going on. There was a scream. It was male.

Hogey turned and dashed past me, oblivious to my presence. He didn't go back to the club, he kept on running, his face ashen. I stayed in the shadows and waited. Eventually, Charlie walked past sheathing her soul blade. She dusted herself off and walked stridently back into the club.

I could make out the shape of a young man lying in a puddle. I could see he was injured, his abdomen had been cut horizontally, he was failing to hold his intestines back with one of his weakening hands. They were like glistening sausages in the moonlight. The puddle was his blood.

I knelt by the young man who was breathing in shallow gasps. He looked at me and there were tears in both his eyes. He really was too young to be dying. He looked no older than sixteen.

"Why did you meet Charlie?"

"You the police?" He whispered.

I nodded. He grabbed me with his clean hand.

"She wanted a jar. I stole it for her."

"What sort of jar?"

"I don't know, but I stole it from her house."

Well, that threw me. I thought of how he'd got past Waite, Walter, Uncle Robert, and Gat.

"How did you get in?"

"She gave me some keys. I went into the back of the 'ouses, where the bird ain't. It's so big. And filled with 'orrible noises, Voices. Creatures." He gasped.

"Was it a rose jar?" I asked.

"I don't know. Can you help me, sir? Are you a doctor, or the police?" His voice was fading.

"What did the jar look like, was it like a large teardrop?"

"Yes. A tear…"

Then he died. His remains vanished. The soul blades tidied up after themselves where creatures were concerned. He couldn't have been human, or fully alive, yet Charlie had still ended him.

I looked around me. I could do nothing for him, and if Hogey Marsh had told anyone what Charlie had done, then the Police would be on their way here, not that they would find anything. I kept to the shadows, and made my way back into the club. I sat down next to Paul, who nodded at me.

"Everything alright, old chap?"

"Yes," I said, trying to keep the panic out of my voice. "Lovers tiff."

Charlie was back at her table with Hogey, who I thought had done a runner, quite honestly, he looked out of it. What the bloody hell was going on?

The rest of the evening was uneventful, and then it was time to return home. I was quite drunk by that point, and so was Charlie. Hogey had been carried out off his face, as Percy says. She was grinning all the way back, which was Strange. Charlie never grinned and, after what I had witnessed, she really didn't have the right to grin.

"Why did you leave the club tonight?" I asked her.

She laughed. "Hogey wanted to show me something."

"I have no doubt he did." I said. Charlie was giggling now. She was a pretty convincing liar. It hurt, despite the alcohol levels in my bloodstream. We never kept anything from each other. Yet, Charlie didn't confess, even though she was almost incapacitated from the liquor. When we got back, we made our way to the library.

Charlie collapsed in one of the long chairs. I hugged Uncle Robert, and said something nice to Gat before I heard Walter come in with the tea. I barely drank any before I went up to bed. God knows how Charlie got up to her room.

"Is it still bleeding?" Charlie asked, bringing me back to the present. I'd been sucking my finger, and it had stopped.

"No. Its fine."

"What happened last night, Charlie? Who was that dead boy?"

"What dead boy?" She replied quietly almost convincingly.

I looked up at her. I had fixed her with one of my legendary stares.

There was a really long pause.

"If you must know. He threatened to attack Hogey and so I had to deal with him."

"Deal, Charlie?" I shook my head as I stood. I didn't want to be near her. "He was eviscerated."

"He pulled a gun on me, and I panicked. He was a half-spirit, moribund, anyway."

"I don't remember seeing a gun."

"I disarmed him. It's probably still there on the floor. He wanted to sell me a rose jar. He said it contained the spirit of a witch called Isabelle. The witch who took control of Eliza Bell, Uncle Robert's fiancé. When I said no, he pulled the weapon."

"He said you got him to steal it. Do you have the jar?"

102

Charlie walked over to her vanity table and opened one of the neatly piled hat boxes. She retrieved a tear-shaped bottle and handed it to me. Was she telling the truth. Was this Isabelle's jar, or someone else's? I didn't recall Uncle Robert saying he had trapped her. If fact I distinctly remembered him saying she was still tied to the magic on that God awful farm, he described. I tested the jar later it was empty.

"You need to tell Uncle Robert about this. How did that boy get into the house?"

"He said he had taken some keys from the table just inside the front door."

Was that another lie? I didn't know who to believe. I should believe in my sister rather than a young criminal. I was doubting Charlie. Walter nor Waite would leave the security of the house so open.

"Speak to Uncle." I told Charlie. She nodded. I would mention it to him later, but not before I had checked to see if there was any evidence of a struggle remaining in the daylight.

So, I feigned tiredness, and escaped the house via the back entrance. I tried to work out as I went how easy it would be for someone to navigate the corridors if they did not know the layout of the house. I always got lost in the lower levels.

I sought out Postlethwaite. I had go down a good few levels to find her, but at least she wasn't morphing into the tiresome teenager, Raven.

"Wait." Waite said for a change. "Avery Curzon. How may I help you?"

"Has anyone entered the house in recent days who you have not recognised? Maybe they used a key to get in?" It was to the point. The bird was creepy, less time spent with it the better.

The raven cocked her head to one side. "Impossible. The keys are all linked to the masters and mistresses of this house, they are isomorphic. It is impossible for anyone else to use them. Should someone do so I would be alerted. Unless, of course, there was magic involved. It would have to be strong magic. Waite is not a pushover. Raven can feel the magic of those who have passed, too."

So, Charlie was lying.

I left the building, and hailed a cab over to Digbeth, to the viaduct, and the Bacchus Club. I asked the cabbie to wait. I wouldn't be long. I just had a wander over to where I found the boy who had been eviscerated with Charlie's soul blade. Of his remains there was nothing left, as I mentioned earlier, so I started to look in the scrub for the gun.

I walked in steady lines backwards and forwards. The land enclosed by railings, next to railway sidings, so there was only a finite area I had to cover. Of course, the boy could have thrown a gun over the railings, but would he have had time?

103

My search of the waste-ground proved fruitless, and cabbie dear was harrumphing loudly. I was about to call off the search, when I saw something gleaming in the long grass, on the other side of the railings, on the left-hand side. I reached through the struts, but I couldn't quite reach. I fished in my coat for my fountain pen, I managed to hook the trigger guard with it. Even I could tell, as I pulled the firearm under the gap in the boundary, that it was a Smith and Wesson. It had that distinct shape, with the wooden grip. I had used one in my police firearms training Uncle Robert allowed us to attend, put on by the redoubtable Inspector Losenge.

On the journey back to Legend Street I found myself conflicted. There was a gun. The boy could have threatened Hogey with it and, therefore, Charlie may well have opened him up like a banana in self-defence. Conversely, we had been taught that life was sanctified, and not to be ended willy-nilly. Even if it had been a spiritual life.

I arrived back at Legend Street and alighted, I let myself in the front entrance and went to find Uncle Robert. Instead, I came across Walter, who was carrying a silver platter's worth of teacups.

"Is Uncle Robert in, Wally?" I asked him.

Walter shook his head. "No, young master, he has just taken up his case in Moseley with the foul-mouthed woman."

"Bugger." I said. Then suddenly I had the fiercest of pains in my head. And momentarily I was elsewhere. I was in Charlie's head. She was with Hogey. She was kissing him, they were naked in a bed, but then she took out a knife and slit his throat.

Walter broke through the miasma. "Avery, what ails you?"

Of course, he was a great help, and always an ally. Walter was a good source of advice and guidance, and had been so for the last few years.

And I tried to tell him what I had just seen. I really did. For the life of me I couldn't remember what was what. Well, I could, but I couldn't say it. It's only now, as I remember, that I can reach for the words, or the images. Everything around seems transparent. It's like I am dead.

Interlude Four

I felt Avery's mind fading.

I glanced at Candour.

"How could I see the memories of a dead person?"

"Because they are memories that have happened, and you have been in physical contact with Avery in the last few days."

I felt the pain of sorrow again. That biting, heart-aching loss. Avery, who I left with the revenants. Avery' who had been lost. It had been my fault he had died.

"I need to speak to Apollyon. I want him to bring Avery back."

"That is not the bargain. As I have said, only the power of Gaia can do such a thing. Find the Books of Truth of the one that tried to kill the Order Soul. Find Sammel. Apollyon will leave this place. I will reiterate, my master only wants his son back. He is not interested in conquering the world of man. He is in emotional schism. Moreover, there are threats to this world that make Apollyon pale into insignificance. My master would rather be in Hell than have to fight the evils that lie in wait for you, Robert Waterfield."

"You are such a positive light, Candour."

"I speak nothing but the truth, Robert."

"So, when can I speak to your master?"

"There is one episodic recollection left. After that you will spend time with my master."

"Presumably, Charlotte's story. I wonder what subterfuge she holds for me. Avery's episode just gave me more puzzles. Will I get any more answers? I think I know who the traitor is, and then the next episode reveals another. Have I always surrounded myself with such duplicitous people?"

"I am afraid I am not at liberty to answer your questions. Apollyon may well do so. Or he will take you to find out. Solve it, and you will have the Books of Truth. Take the Books of Truth back, and the Order Soul will heal. Once he heals…."

"I will be granted a boon. Believe it or not, Candour, I am able to follow a simple cause and effect pattern. I cannot, though, without time to think, make notes, fully ascertain the mystery at hand. I should have read more Conan-Doyle." I looked at the near-naked being who was irritating me somewhat. "Why do you not wear any clothes?"

Candour tilted his head onto one side. "I am the anthropomorphic representation of truth. Clothing covers the truth. My naked form does not lie, therefore I have no need of garments. Am I that disgusting, Robert?"

I felt terrible then. Despite Candour being probably nothing more than a figment of my imagination, or the very least Apollyon's, I was still not one to criticise, or feel disgust at the appearance of another person's nakedness.

Suddenly, I was elsewhere. In Charlie's mind, this time. Although I desperately wanted to get back to the real world.

Chapter Fourteen

Charlotte

The day was going horribly wrong.

I'd received the letter from William Marsh, Hogey's brother threatening to out me as a man who wore women's clothing. A sissy, a queer, or a nonce were the words. I read the letter on the way home from the meeting of the Women's Guild. Martha Marsh, Hogey's sister, had handed it to me with a sneer you could have cut bread with. Hogey knew my personal secret, and still loved me. Avery had been suspicious of Hogey's intentions, but they had always been sound. Hogey was strong, yet gentle, he would be distraught to think I was being blackmailed, especially by one of his own family.

When the moribund boy put the gun to my head on the doorstep of 42 Legend Street, I thought that my number was up. Then momentarily, I thought he might be a ghost. As I watched him for those seconds he held me at gunpoint, he was blending into the background. You would have had to have looked very carefully to see that he was there at all. I think there was some magic involved. The Marshes obviously had some powerful allies. Or they were pawns in someone else's game.

"I want a rose jar." The boy said.

Firstly, I wondered how he knew we had those on the premises. Secondly how did he know what a rose jar was? It wasn't common knowledge.

"You can get them from Birmingham Market for a penny a piece." I replied, humour always being my go-to when I was scared.

"It has to be Isabelle of Stafford's spirit." He said, as if it was being read off a list. This boy had learnt his lines by rote, it seemed. "Take me to the rose jars. No one will see me."

Well, I still didn't have a clue. The only Isabelle I knew was the one who allegedly possessed Uncle Robert's fiancé, Eliza. Why were they after her spirit? I wasn't sure that Robert would keep such a thing anyway. I was almost certain he said she was tied to Magpie Farm, where he used to live, because of deep-rooted curse magic.

I crept through the house. Only Walter was at home, or so I would have imagined, at that time of the day. I took the young creature down into the depths of Legend Street, and into what I called the vaults, or the catacombs. The main room that held the rose jars was a massive, converted wine cellar.

108

There were rows and rows of the things. Robert had always said they could do with being relocated.

I searched the catalogue. No Isabelle. I searched all of the shelves. Almost three hours with a gun pointed at my head. No Isabelle.

The boy suddenly looked very strange. Like he had been frozen in amber. When he un-froze he said. "Isabelle is not here."

Well, I could have told him that again. And had done so many times in those three hours.

"I will take the jar belonging to the Bordesley Child Killer. Sir Jonah Wakefield. Isabelle…influenced him."

I checked the register again, and almost immediately found Sir Jonah's Rose Jar. It was next to Eliza Bell's.

I switched the bottles and gave the boy Eliza's rose jar whilst pocketing Sir Jonah's. I would find out what the Marsh's needed with the spirit of a dead serial killer. Presumably, nothing good.

I was led back to the front door by him, and the boy left, leaving me with my conundrum and a tension headache.

Should I alert Uncle Robert? Tell Avery? I had let someone into our house, I had possibly endangered everyone. I had given out Uncle Robert's fiancé's rose jar. What would he think of that? Although he always said he needed to be rid of Eliza, and he and Gat should never have rescued her spirit from Hell. He had kept her for a reason, surely, but I had given her away whilst pocketing Sir Jonah's.

Robert would be both angry and distraught. For whilst he was always sure to show us his hatred of Eliza, I knew he still wished he could have cleansed her soul. To have her with him once again. Well, I supposed it might stop him mooning over Percy.

I immediately went for a lie down. We were meant to be at the Bacchus later that evening, and I couldn't find myself going, feeling as low as I did. I would have to confront Hogey, and tell him what had happened. First, I needed to sleep, so I drew a bath, put on my sleep attire, and went to bed.

I woke a few hours later. Avery was pootling about in our shared living quarters, whilst we didn't share a bedroom, we did share adjacent sitting and dressing rooms. I found him puffing on a cigar, in a cloud of smoke, like a dirty halo about his head.

"Charles." He said, in that irritating manner, as if my dress and adopted gender was just an affectation. I was always so careful to call him Avery, and 'he,' and not mock our birth-rendered predicament. He always shunned this in favour of a cheap gag, wherever possible. Soon he would make a mistake in public, and we both would be outcasts.

"Do you have to smoke in here? it will play merry Hell with my dresses and hats."

"We're still going to Bacchus tonight. I don't want to be tired for the Coronation Celebration tomorrow evening."

"Yes." I said firmly, even though I had almost talked myself out of it, earlier. "I need to go and see Hogey."

"Oh, not the Marsh boy. He is only one short step away from villainy. You need to end that, Charles, or I will have to tell Uncle Robert that you are mixed up with the Marshes."

"You will not. I'll not be policed by the likes of you, nor Uncle Robert. You know Hogey is not like his brothers, he is a kind and thoughtful decent boy. I like him a lot."

"Well, I am going to call on Paul, I will need a companion to help me cope."

"Think about our predicament, Ave, we should not be disrespectful or prejudiced."

"I am a man in a woman's body, you are vice versa. We are not homosexual."

"We would be treated as so. Lambasted as queer, bizarre, or weird. One wrong decision, and our secret would be out before we have been able to swap bodies and live as we should have been born."

I should have told him that the reason I wanted to get near to Hogey was because his brothers knew people. That's why I knew the invisible boy from earlier was linked to them. The Marshes knew people with magic. If I could get our bodies swapped, we could be far away from here. Away from this tiresome life, far away from the management of our affairs by Uncle Robert. I love him dearly, but I didn't want to be hunting monsters the rest of my life.

"I am going to recharge my batteries before we have dinner." Avery yawned, stubbed out the barely smoke cigar, and left.

Dinner was uneventful. Robert and Percy were out and about fighting ghosts and ghouls and, before I knew it, the carriage had arrived. We entered Bacchus, and Avery went to find his charming friend Paul; I went to Hogey's usual table. He was sitting there, swigging back a soda, his handsome face always beaming, nothing like his two brothers, who were vicious individuals. If they knew Hogey was here with me again, I would have thought we would be both for it.

"Sweetie," he said, as I approached. He stood and pulled back a chair next to him for me to sit upon. He clicked his fingers at the bar, one of the staff nodded and said they would be with us next.

I just put Martha's note in front of him. "Read." I said.

He did so and then looked up at me. His eyes were glistening. "Darling Charlotte. I am so deeply sorry. I will tell her to desist, immediately. It's my brothers. They would never waste their time to confront a mere

110

woman, so they have roped Martha in. Did she send her invisible boy – Sonny?"

"He put a gun to my head. If he, or either of your brothers come anywhere near us again, I will not be responsible for my actions."

"That is going to be a little difficult, when you have hired them to contact the Spirit Witch."

He was talking really loudly and thank God he hadn't uttered her name. Helen was the woman who could allegedly switch our souls between bodies. For a price.

You said my name, boy-girl.

I looked at Hogey. Had he just spoken?

I am Helen, the Spirit Witch.

Shit. I thought.

Shit indeed.

Why had everything stopped around me? My surroundings all fell away, and I was suddenly in a stone cottage somewhere.

A woman appeared. She was a dainty thing, dressed in scarlet satin, and black velvet. A stereotypical witch, if ever I saw one. She was covered in gold, earrings, bangles, bracelets and rings.

"This is your subconscious. I also see your Uncle Robert, watching in the distance."

"He is always watching." I said. It was the first thing that came to mind. I did feel terrible for thinking so, but I so wanted to be away.

The witch made a tea pot appear on her large wooden table that looked like it held the contents of an apothecary upon its thick oak top. She poured tea into the two cups.

"If you want me to help you, you must first help me."

"What must I do?" I asked, my eagerness driving the need for me to be female.

"You must kill. I need the blood of that moribund boy, Sonny. He is a liability now."

"I cannot kill. I am not a killer."

"Yet you can kill the undead, the revenants?"

"They are already dead. That is not murder."

"Tell that to a vampire sire when you kill his children. A werewolf mother when you have shot her cubs full of silver bullets."

"They are all dead."

"You are a boy."

"No, I am a woman." I screamed.

"Your hands are large, your feet are large, you have codlings. You are about as much a woman as the King of England is."

I paused, getting my anger under control. Helen was playing back my own frailties. I could make myself look feminine, grow my hair long, paint

111

my nails, rouge my cheeks. Yet, as I grow old, my hair will fall out like papa's. I will most likely become broader, and stronger.

"I can make you a woman." Helen said. "I need three souls for the magic. One now, and two in the future."

"Who?" I asked, not believing I was asking that question at all.

"I want the soul of the boy as I have said. I can use the spirits of children for strong magic. Later today, he will come through a tunnel to confront you about the rose jar you switched. You will need to cut him down. He will appear away from the Bacchus in order not to be spotted. As soon as I send you back to reality, you are to go and kill him. He will try to shoot you, so please be quick."

"What about the other two murders?" The word was like iron, no blood in my mouth.

"I want you to kill one of your father's friends. I do not mind which. Then I want you to kill Hogey once you have escaped your Uncle's clutches."

"No."

"The only future for you is in the employ of Lord Ainsworth. He has a machine that can switch your bodies. All you have to do is provide me with three souls, and make sure your brother/sister doesn't die until then."

"What does the Home Secretary have to do with this? I can't kill. I will not commit murder in order to…"

"Become *you* for the first time?"

Time seemed to stretch forever. I began to cry. Tears were streaming down my face. "Why Hogey?"

"One who is loved by others, one who is loved by the self, and one who carries power. That is the destiny I have read for you. Three deaths equals the blood power to switch the soul of you, and your brother."

"I cant. I won't…."

I was back in Bacchus. I looked about me, then, over at Avery who was in conversation with Paul. He glanced over at me. I turned to Hogey.

"Darling, why are you crying are you wishing you were a girl again?"

I stood, slapped him and ran, racing out of the club, back down the stairs, past those who milled towards the entrance. I followed the road around to the sidings. I seemed to know the invisible boy would appear exactly there.

He stepped out of what looked like a tunnel. He was a handsome thing, probably not yet sixteen. He was shirtless and if he turned a certain way he would almost disappear.

"Bitch-boy," he screamed, reaching into his pocket for the weapon I knew he would draw. "You gave me the wrong rose jar. I need the right one."

He raised his gun, although I had already pulled my sword. I knocked the gun out of his hand with an ancient move passed down to me by my swordmaster. Then, on the returning stroke, I nearly cut the boy in two. His belly parted like a surprised smile, and his innards spilled out. He tried to catch them, but they were like so many steaming sausages that looked ready for the pot.

He fell, I ran. I stowed my sword away as I did so. Avery ran past, in the shadows, but he thought I hadn't seen him. That murder was for both of us, Avery. You will never know, though. I willed the boy to die and dissipate before Avery got to him. I think he may have spoken to the dying child.

"Darling, what is wrong?" It was Hogey coming towards me. My next but one victim.

Soon Charlotte, but not yet. I suggest you enjoy him until then.

"No, just needed some air. Felt a little queasy."

But Hogey had seen the boy, he ran off. It took me an age to calm him down. Show him no one had died.

Good girl. Said the Spirit Witch, Helen. I could hear her gold jangling.

I returned home with Ave a few hours later. The next day, Avery started to ask me about the boy, but I managed to fob him off.

The boy I had killed.

I am a murderer. I will have to do it again.

To be free of this body.

I will lose my soul.

Somewhere underground, in the distance, the witch Helen laughed. Her name was Madam Or. Robert knew that Charlotte had been duped, but not by whom. And yet she had killed, and might kill again.

Chapter Fifteen

Apollyon

"Robert, my boy. Come here, sit upon my knee."

Grandfather Edmund was still dead. Yet he visited me from time to time, or I visited him, I was never really sure which way around it was.

At first my beloved grandfather didn't tell me much about the Hopelessness, then, after I had been walking its tunnels for some years, he visited more often. It was early in my ghost hunting career. I hadn't teamed up with the Menagerie by that point, but I was realising my plans were too big for one person.

I had been tracking a soul who was, for some unknown reason, anchored to a particular prayer book. The bloody book was indestructible. I had tried to salt it, and burn it, I had tried holy water, I had tried acid, and I had tried to boil it. All to no avail.

So, I stepped into the Hopelessness to see if I could find a saner portion of the soul. They tended to be tormented on Earth, but in the Purgatory that was the Hopelessness, they seemed to be more rational. Ironic, considering the Bible's version of purgatory. I presumed, and it was a long jump, that after this place came Hell, and these souls ultimately would be tortured in perpetuity, by Satan and all his minions.

"It is more complicated than that, young Robert."

Suddenly, I was back in my grandparent's parlour. I was sitting on his grey couch that was rough like hessian, crisp ironed white linen antimacassars in place to stop the grease from visitors' hair making marks upon its expensive surface.

Grandfather was smoking his pipe, sitting in his corner chair by his bookcase. I could smell his favourite brand of tobacco, so familiar, like a mixture of cinnamon, toffee apples, and cow pat. On this occasion, his wife, my Grandmother, wasn't present.

"The Hopelessness is a conduit. A link to the many levels of existence between Heaven and Hell. It's not just Purgatory. You could meet any level demon, or any type of angel."

"I've never met an angel." The seven-year-old me said. I wasn't sure why I was rationalising myself as such a young age. I was thirty-odd by that point in my adventures.

"Rare as hen's teeth, bab." Grandfather said, in his native black country accent. "You aren't likely to see one very often. Now that Order Soul who works in that Cathedral of Truth, he was part angel. He was a Nephilim. His father was an angel, and his mother a human woman. Strange creatures, those Nephilim, can be as powerful as gods themselves. He is an automaton, now. Anyway, that is a story for another day."

"How do I find an individual soul, Grandfather?" I asked him as if it were the most natural question a thirty-year-old man being represented in the body of his seven-year-old self could ask.

Grandfather laughed. He had been miserable in life. Grandmother had died young, and he had pined for her. My father, his son, was a disappointment, more interested in prospecting in the new world markets than marketing the family canal haulage business.

"You always asked the pertinent questions, even when you were young as you look now. Turn yourself into a man Robert. You know how."

I thought about my outer shell in the Hopelessness, and warped it to how I should have looked as an adult. I was malleable. It was just when I was in Grandfather's presence I seemed to snap back to that little boy.

"Is it to do with the cables I can see. The black for evil, the green for strength, red for greed, and the white for life?"

He tapped his pipe into an ashtray, and smiled again. His missing teeth made his smile look comical. He only ever smiled for me in life, after Grandmother died that was.

"Look carefully for the person you want to identify. Look for your late father's thread. You know what he looked like, you also know what he was really like."

My dad was mixed up in all sorts of things none of us knew about until he died. He had been shot in New York by a gangland boss who had tried to extort him. Father had acted the big 'I am' he thought he was, then bang, it was all over. He had been a strong-willed man, slightly on the side of evil from some of the drug and people-trafficking accusations that came to light from the NYPD. He had no doubt walked over a lot of people, maybe even killed a few, himself.

So, I looked for my father's mix of colours. I pulled on those threads. Suddenly, there he was. Maurice Waterfield. My father. Well, it wasn't my father, just the ghostly representation of him, his soul was off elsewhere.

"Top marks, my boy. Let that fool go." Grandfather said. "Now find the one you want to locate. Do you have the prayer book with you? This should be easier than finding your daddy."

I let father dissipate, I had no urge to look upon him for much longer. He really didn't have time for me at all, in life.

I pulled out the book from my pocket, and suddenly there were millions of glowing threads of all colours and shades about it, flowing up and down, left and right, into tangential infinity.

"Look for the darker threads. The spirit who is anchored to it will have primacy over the other souls that have touched it, alive or dead." Grandfather guided.

So, I looked closer at the book. Beyond the macro, to the micro, what in the present day we might call the quantum. I pulled at those strings until a face appeared, then a name, and then a personality.

Carlton Holmes, once a curate at the Church of The Latter-Day Saints, snarled at me. Until I pulled at the evil black strands and severed him from the book and the influence had held over certain family of parishioners for almost a hundred years. Carlton screamed into the void as he faced an eternity of horror for those actions carried out whilst alive and latterly dead.

"My clever boy." Grandfather said. Although his voice had changed. The tone, the accent, and the intonation.

I looked up at him whilst remembering that what I had experienced was a memory all along. The man I saw in his place was quite beautiful. Angelic.

The man's eyes were piercingly grey, his short black hair and beard were well kempt, with touches of grey. He didn't look old despite the fact he was clearly ancient. This was, without a doubt, Apollyon. He was very sharply dressed in a light grey tweed suit, it had fine mustard lines brought out by a mustard tie. It was a more modern look than the Edwardian.

"Welcome, Robert." Apollyon said, or he might have just put the words into my brain. Still to this day, I am not quite sure. "I love how you are telling this tale about something of the past to someone in the future."

Apollyon knew then that I was going to leave this tale for others to read.

"I see all things, Robert. I once guarded time for God until he cast me down. You do not lose the knack."

I knew in an instant that Apollyon could end me with a thought, a whisper, or a scream. I would have just dissipated, like motes of dust on whatever breeze was present here.

"It is exceedingly rare that someone alive has so much sway over the world of the celestial and the dead. I honestly think you might be able to pull my threads apart."

Our surroundings suddenly changed, the room I was in warped. Apollyon sat on a stone throne before me. Candour, to his left. Another naked figure on his right. She was quite beautiful, but green in hue, she looked like she had scales, as opposed to the alabaster sheen of Candour.

"This is Whisper, my other guardian."

The beautiful woman inclined her head, and I tried so very hard not to look at her nakedness. It was the Edwardian era, we would get an urge over a bared ankle, in those days.

116

"He looks good enough to kill and eat, with a little bottle of red."

"Oh please, Whisper, please do not bring everything back to murder, and horror." Candour jabbed.

"Our Lord is a Devil. He would normally allow it. It's been so long since I ate a human."

"Our Lord is also an angel. He wouldn't dream of such evil."

"I *am* here, my guardians. You *can* talk to me, rather than around me." Apollyon held both his hands out, pointing either side at the alabaster and green beings. "As you can see, Robert, Candour serves as my conscience, Whisper is my guilt."

He smiled. It was captivating. I was expecting someone dragon-like, at least spiny, horn-ed.

"I scrub up well, don't I? I can look like however I wish."

He didn't seem like a Devil pining after his son. If Apollyon were an angel, that would definitely make Sammel…

"Nephilim. Correct. His mother was human."

I jumped, I took a step back, Apollyon had just spoken to me in his true voice. In it was all the power, and all the sorrow of eons. I managed to keep control over my bladder. It was a close thing. I was, from that moment, both horrified and in awe. In that moment I saw the true Whisper, a face of fangs and forked tongue, no doubt she could have shred my soul. Then I looked at the very human face of Candour, who brought the balance of humanity to a fallen god. I could see that if anything happened to Candour; Heaven, Hell, and Earth would be in danger.

"Return my son, Robert. If you do not, I will torment you for eternity. I will let Whisper have you for her plaything. Could you imagine fornicating for every second of an eternal existence as pleasure becomes pain then horror? I have shown you your friends, and their deceit. Sammel was lured to the surface by some power that defies me. That attempted to murder the Order Soul – the best of us."

In that moment, the barriers in my mind fell away. I saw the truth Gat had failed to tell me. I saw the deception in Percy's heart, and her lack of love for me. I saw Walter's early life shaping his soul into a premeditated killer, and before all those times he told me not to kill. Then the twins, those poor, tortured souls. How I failed them. The memories of Avery recently gone, and the hatred of me that seemed to be growing in Charlie. I was looking for someone who had killed, and who had tried to kill the Order Soul.

"Enlightened, you move to the final part of my puzzle; before you have to go and solve one of your own. Get my Sammel back, Robert. I cannot have him lost. Those who have taken him are shrouded from me with magic that is indescribable. Yet, there are links between you, and them. Threads."

I was moving backwards as Apollyon talked at me. He had risen from his throne. His image had changed. I saw the demon then, the torturer of souls. Half beast, half man. Father of Satan.

Then he was back to the sharply dressed cat. "Satan is just a name for the King of Hell. Sammel is his successor. Some have called me and Sammel, Lucifer, although that is wrong too. The Bible isn't the whole story, you know."

I nodded, gasping. I thought I was a goner for all the time he spoke with *that* voice.

"I will *find* you your son, Lord Apollyon." I said, meaning it. Well, I didn't want my eternal soul tortured by Whisper. However much a man of my age might be turned on by the thought of eternal sex.

He laughed. "Good man. I will stay connected with you. With your permission. Until you deliver my Sammy."

I could *do* nothing but nod.

"Thank you. Now, to the next part of the test. Who attempted to kill the Order *Soul*, and why? Who took their books from the Library of the Cathedral of Souls before their time was up? Two of them apparently. Connected. Lots of questions, Robert."

I wondered just what Apollyon had up his sleeve, and whether I could trust him.

"You don't have to trust me. I will play no part in your decision making. It will be made for you, in any case. I am going to lend you Candour and Whisper for a short while. They will help you work out the traitor. Is it Percy, Charlie, Gat, or Wally?"

I swallowed. This was the part I was dreading. All my so-called friends had deceived me in some way, or another.

And before I knew it. I was back amongst them.

Chapter Sixteen
Rise of the Lantern Heads

I was back in the Vault behind the wall of flesh. I could smell sweat and fear. Did my friends know I had experienced a part of each of their lives?

They were looking at me, amazed. Then I realised I had Candour on my left, and Whisper on my right. I looked at them both. but thankfully they were both clothed, and in human form. They were clearly far too beautiful to be human, much like their Lord and Master, Apollyon had appeared to me.

Only Walter could look me in the eye. I was watching him as I remember him saying he had been stabbed when I was in his mind.

"Are you okay, Wally?"

He nodded as I move towards him and grabbed his hand to shake it.

"I am going to be killed, aren't I? In the future, that is?" He whispered.

I nodded, sadly. "I fear it will come about my friend. I am so sorry."

"Robert, what do you mean?" This was Percy. She approached me, but I held my hands up to stop her.

"One of you is about to kill again. My dear friend Walter is the victim. You cannot run, Walter. This has to come to pass. It is a fixed event."

Apollyon had put those words in my head.

Walter didn't look scared. He probably thought his past indiscretions were coming back to haunt him. He nodded at me to say it was alright.

"From what I have seen, you all have blood on your hands. As do I. One of you has planned to murder one of us here, today. The way reality is warping tells me it may well have happened already." I explained.

"Clever boy." Whisper said. She undulated forward, looking each of my friends in the eye.

"I never meant to cause you stress, brother." Gat said. "I was stranded here, in my past. I needed a way to live. I seemed to graduate to the strange. I love Abel, none of that is unreal. I love you too, Robert, as a brother. I would never harm you. That is why I never told you."

"How could we have seen Avery's thoughts, his episode of this madness. He is dead. I do not remember killing that moribund boy. I am not a killer. It is clearly made up." Charlotte screamed. "Deception."

So, everyone had seen everything.

Candour came forward. "Apollyon retrieved your brother's thoughts before his moment of passing."

"But all that nonsense about magic. That did not happen. I had something with Hogey Marsh, but the killing of that boy just did not happen!"

"Yet the rose jars belonging to Eliza and the Bordesley Killer were missing from the archive after the Lantern Heads invaded. You and Avery were the only people there that afternoon as we pursued the Moseley Demon. No wonder you were avoiding the rota. It clashed with your visit to Bacchus, no doubt." Whisper hissed.

"Raven would have been there." Charlotte parried.

"Raven was an avatar at the time, incapable of independent thought or reason." Candour said this again, so I could judge that it was true. If I could believe him. This was a servant of a Devil, a Fallen Angel. "I cannot lie." Candour said, looking at me.

"Uncle Robert. How is it that we are not fighting this Apollyon? His revenants killed my brother. Avery is barely cold. How could I contemplate killing others? I'm devastated. And Hogey is still alive. I did not kill Hogey." Charlie was crying now. Big massive sobs wracked her body. Percy came over to hold her. "I only wanted us to be healed. I only wanted us to be in the right bodies. I only wanted us to have normal lives. I wanted to marry, give birth to children. I did look into spiritual magic, but I hit a brick wall. Some of what we saw was made up. I never met or spoke to that witch."

"Apollyon is merely protecting his realm, and his ability to find some way to retrieve his son." Candour said, as if it were plain fact. "And why aren't you already mourning Walter, Charlotte. Your guardian is about to die. Did you not hear your uncle?"

Screaming, Charlie went for the being in a way I have never seen her react before. Hands outstretched like claws. "Your master has ruined my life. I will destroy him, if it is the last thing I do."

Candour caught both her hands, and she was immobilised. I could see the being had immense strength. Charlie was exerting the maximum effort against the minimum intervention.

"Stupid child. Did you think you had the ability to affect Apollyon's servants, let alone his godliness?" Whisper said this to Charlie, but it seemed she was addressing a wider audience.

"What of the woman who wanders time?" Whisper then asked of Percy, as Charlie slumped against Candour, who put her on the floor in a careful way.

Percy just stuck out her chin. It was no surprise she was like she was. She had lived in the future, it was obviously a place for stronger women at some point. That was no bad thing for me to contemplate, even with my old Victorian soul.

"Keep quiet, celestial. This talk of Walter already being killed is stupid. Even you, a child of a demon, knows that even whispers of the future can wipe out whole timelines. If any of us knew of events before they took place, then the future would unravel. Then, which of our actions, or movements, breaths, or sighs altered the pattern of behaviour that led to one civilisation crumbling, and another growing. Robert, you have to believe me, there are things even the gods aren't party to, that I know. I had to keep secrets. LP and I protect this world from invasions from different dimensions, alternative timelines, creatures that are born in a moment and, if allowed to grow, they would overwhelm us all. There are different versions of me active in different timestreams, all at once. I am betraying many more Roberts and Gats, pissing off many more Walters with my bad fucking language. It's who I am. I am married to another, Robert. You have heard of him – Arthur Poke. I am currently searching for him, he thinks I have been lost. I haven't seen him for fifty thousand years. I wielded power on a magical world for eons, defeating evil, time and time again. I am a Chosen, I am eternal. That is my curse. I love you, Bobby, but just not like that. I am not your traitor."

Walter approached me, and this time I let him get close. He put his hands on my shoulders. I let him. "Robert, you saw those things I did as a boy. They *were* premeditated, but they were also necessary. Yes, I told you not to kill unless it was really necessary. I told you that because I didn't want you to live with all of the guilt. In our minds, we are sometimes a little more relaxed in our way of processing things. That was me as a twelve-year-old. It is true, I have never regretted killing Giles, or his henchmen. He was evil. I would do it again, in a heartbeat. I am happy to die if it moves things along. I deserve it."

"Can we leave this realm?" I looked to Candour and Whisper, who both nodded.

"I want to question my friends in the real world. Away from any other spiritual influence."

I took us all back to the barrier.

Raven was there, as was Claire.

"Thank goodness you are all okay." Claire said, her smile cutting away some of the hurt that attached itself to me. I could have sworn that she made to approach me, and throw her arms about me, but stopped as she was, of course, on active duty. I could have imagined that, of course, in my heightened state.

I turned to my friends. "We are all tired, after our experiences, please get some rest. I will meet with you all at some point later."

"Who is this other creature?" Raven asked. She hadn't been keen on letting me go into the Hopelessness without her. Her swords were both drawn.

121

"Warrior." Whisper said.

"Prophecy unraveller." Candour added.

"Minions of an evil god, Hel herself perhaps?"

"Your Viking god Hel has other names: Apollyon, Abaddon, Morningstar, Daemos, Shaitan, Kali – my master is named as such, and is none of those, Shield Maiden."

"Yet *he* is influencing things more than he is letting on." Raven added. "I have danced in Asgard, I know their games."

"For once, I cannot argue. You are known to us. Protector of the Veil Lord."

"Veil Lord?" I asked Whisper.

"You are the Veil Lord in Prophecy, Robert. The Walker of Purgatory." Candour explained.

"Well, I am no Lord. Just a human who wants to keep this world safe from evil. Including Apollyon. I am still wary of his role here. Candour, Whisper, I know he is listening. He said he would be with me. Our deal is that I bring Sammel back, and you leave. Any deviation from that pattern and I will go to war with Apollyon and all his minions. Is that clear?"

"The Lord Apollyon agrees." Candour relayed his masters affirmation.

"Although he says it with a smile. You double cross him, Veil Lord, and he will turn you to dust." Whisper looked like she would eat me.

"Agreed. Enough now, I need rest." I said. I'd had my fill of celestial beings. I looked at Claire, who was smiling at me.

To Raven I said, "Take Candour and Whisper, and ensure they are comfortable. See to any needs they have until we reconvene tonight. I need to think about who our traitor might be."

Raven nodded.

"Then, watch the Menagerie. Confiscate their soul blades, Raven, make sure you hold them in check. Do not kill anyone."

Raven nodded again. It was good knowing I had such fine protection.

I, of course, had no clue who the actual traitor was. I could surmise, but it could have been any of them. I had never felt so alone. Even my niece and nephew were strangers to me, at that point. My friends were shadows of the people I had thought they actually were. Candour probably saw through my bravado, as if I were made of clear glass. I didn't care. I needed sleep. It would give me more time to think about who the traitor in our midst might be.

Claire walked back with me, to the house. It was nice to be with someone who was neither part of the Menagerie, nor linked to Apollyon.

"Are you okay?" She asked.

I could have broken down quite easily at that point. My stiff upper lip was about to go flaccid, my mental reserves were about to dry up.

"I think maybe not. Those who I have held closest have lied to me. Percy, Gat, Charlie and, to a lesser extent, Walter. I have seen that Walter is dead, in some kind of uncertain future. Avery already gone."

Claire said nothing at first, she just wrapped her arm about me.

"Come this way, Robert, let's take the long way round, through the woods. Then, if you need to blow off some steam, you can."

I smiled at her, then. She was astute as well as lovely. What she said next, and how she said, it surprised me.

"Are you in love with Anna?"

I stopped. Half irritated, half filled with that feeling of the promise of something nice in life coming my way.

"I was, once, although I have recently found out that she has been married for an awfully long time."

"Child bride?" Claire asked, smiling at me. The intonation of her comment rising in mock surprise.

"She is ancient. She has lived a thousand lives. I think I am incidental. Who can I trust?"

"We elemental folk do not beat about the bush, Robert. I have barely known you, but I want to love you. Not forever, unless you wish it so, I am not talking of marriage, if you are opposed to the idea. I know you are the one for me, for now."

She put her hands either side of my head and pulled me towards her. Our lips touched, and we shared a slow lingering kiss. There had been so much power on display recently, from so many celestial beings, one forgot what the true magic was. Claire almost cleared my head with one kiss.

"Do you want to share your experiences with me? One kiss, and I feel what you have felt. It's not reading your mind, exactly but it's a pattern of emotion I can interpret."

I kissed her. I needed to share my loaded brain.

She stood back, gasping. "Dear Goddess, Robert!" Those three words conveyed her shock, and all of the duplicity I had endured.

That was when the tears came to my eyes, and I started to sob. Claire held me tightly for a few minutes as I cried and cried, getting a brief respite from the stress by allowing my emotions to overspill in a very non-gentlemanly way.

Then I heard a sound, one that I had heard recently, but couldn't put my finger on it. It sounded like the mantle in a gaslight. The hairs on the back of my neck stood on end.

"Robert?" Claire whispered.

I turned to look upon what she could see. Two of the Lantern Heads stood looking at us. Their fluttering, mantle-like, wheezy laughter sending shivers down my back. They sounded like they were mocking us.

"Are those them?"

"Lantern Heads. Yes." *Raven. Come. Candour and Whisper, watch my friends.*"

I pulled my soul blade. I was really up for a fight, after the day I'd had. I charged at them without a thought.

They both held out their hands. They grew long metallic claws from their nails, highly polished, and sharp looking. They were ready to engage. I hit the one on the left with as much force as I could muster, it just blocked me, and I had to spin away.

"I am here." Raven said. She was beside me, and that was good because the two Lantern Heads had become four. She engaged two of them, and I attacked the others.

Then there was a hiss from behind us. Another person had joined us. I looked to my left, briefly. It was Whisper. She was holding two fiery green battle axes. She was spinning them with ease, like it was all a circus act. There was fire in her eyes, too, and a broad smile.

"Are these creatures yours, or your masters?" I asked her, surprised at her joining the melee.

"Neither. Apollyon has nothing to do with this kind of hybrid, industrial magic. Their maker took Sammel. Apollyon is sure of it now." Whisper crashed into one of the creatures, and smashed it apart with her weapons. It dispersed on the breeze.

I hit another one with my sword. It staggered backwards, but rallied. Its rattle became louder, almost mocking. *Weak human.* Then it split apart into two, but the one that had just materialised was in-turn split in half by Raven. I speared the other one shortly after.

I heard Claire scream "no" and then gunshots as she pumped bullets into one of the monsters. Another was reaching for her neck with its sharp talons.

I immediately responded to the attack, and took the head off the Lantern Head that was reeling about, having been shot by Claire. I watched it just as I decapitated it. It was a thing of flesh and bone, but also threads of evil magic, steam and clockwork parts. A strange hybrid. Why did the corporeal elements dissipate so? They were certainly bound by magic. One would have expected the brass mechanics to be left behind. It was all very curious, particularly if I were to believe Whisper that they were not creatures of Apollyon.

I turned to engage with the others, but it seemed Raven and Whisper had things in hand. The last of the creatures was despatched.

Those creatures are not mine. They are not celestial in origin, Robert. They were invented with earthly magic and science. Evil. Lingering evil.

It was the voice of Apollyon.

I think we will find Sammel where those creatures originate. They are forged with blood magic and metal. Supernatural, industrial, not celestial like Whisper, or Candour.

Apollyon's presence left me as we trudged back through the woods towards Pender Hall. I was thoroughly weary, now, but we would need to brief the Brigadier to be on alert from more attacks from the Lantern Heads. Not only would we have to find the traitor, return whoever's life books had been taken and then find Sammel, I would need to solve the mystery of the origins of the Lantern Heads. I couldn't have them popping up all over the place, threatening the citizens of Great Britain.

Claire caught up with me, and put a hand on the small of my back. "Get some rest." She whispered. "I will see you later. You need strength for what lies ahead."

Raven didn't leave my side, she/they marched me up the stairs, to my room. As we approached, Percy was coming the other way. She smiled at me, but I didn't have anything left to give, ashamed, I lowered my head like a coward.

Once Raven was gone, I stripped, bathed, and then I put on a set of pyjamas. I lay down marvelling at the events of the day, I plumped up my pillows, and lay back down. I was asleep as soon as my head hit the pillow.

Chapter Seventeen

Dinner, Deception, and Just Desserts

Claire had been kind enough to organise a dinner for us all. The atmosphere was not conducive to friendly chat, and the seating arrangement had put me as far away from Percy as possible. It didn't help that Candour and Whisper stood in the corner of the room, watching us all like sentinels.

It was Charlie who piped up first. "So, these creatures of Apollyon remain, despite his other servants ripping my brother apart? Please can you let me know where the sense is in that."

I looked up and managed to make eye contact. "You all deceived me and one of you is a murderer. You, Charlie, in those memories were tasked by Helen to kill two others. Sonny, Hogey Marsh, and another."

"Those memories were fabricated, Uncle, I do not remember them as such."

"They were truthful." Candour added.

"Or so you say." Walter came in, dabbing at his mouth with a napkin. The soup really was good but watery "Your master is a fallen angel, yes?"

Candour nodded.

"And he just so happens to be one of the Lords of Hell. Yet he commands a creature who tells no lies. Satan is the lord of lies, is he not? Has he lied about my death?"

"Satan is just a name, human. Candour and I are his truth and judgement. Our master is not lying. He is beyond lies, although he can torment your soul in perpetuity if you are evil. He is allowed. Maybe, little Wally, you fear you have carried out too much evil in your time on Earth?"

"Silence." I commanded, it was as much as I could do not to vomit. I barely touched my food that day. "You are here because you are my friends. All of you kept things from me. The Prophecy says one of you will die at the hands of another, and that another will deceive me in such a way it will hurt me the most. Percy, I think you own the latter deception, never have I had someone I have trusted with my life keep so much away from me."

I had never seen Percy become emotional, but she was near to tears. "Robert, I am so sorry. I serve a higher power. I was not allowed."

"Yet you wove a fabricated story of lies about yourself. You knew I loved you, yet you didn't tell me you had a husband. You didn't tell me you had lived for eons as a goddess on another world. Gods, I can't even believe I am saying that bit. The Minister is also another worldly being interfering with our planet."

"Protecting it. As do I, Robert."

"All smoke and mirrors?" I said, fundamentally understanding the name for the ministry, now.

"Walter, my friend." I turned to him. "Out of everyone, your deception is the noblest. And it seems you will pay for that, and I am not allowed to intervene with what might happen for fear of not finding my traitor. How could I fault what you did as revenge on Giles and those wicked people? What a life you lived. You are completely forgiven. I wish for you to work alongside me until we are both old and grey. Although it seems unlikely, now. I just need to know one thing. Have you ever killed anyone who wasn't deserving of it, who wasn't an abuser, or evil to the core?"

Walter smiled his smile that usually preceded a barbed comment. Slightly misaligned on his face. "Never. Although I have been tempted."

I looked to Candour. The alabaster being currently appearing as a well-dressed gentleman gave me an almost imperceptible nod of his head.

"Gat, or Garrett?"

"I prefer Gat, these days."

"Please drop the false African accent."

"Sorry Robert, force of habit."

"When and where were you born?"

"2564 Hayes, England. I lived a lot of my early life in London City."

"Why could you not tell me?"

"I didn't think I would believe."

"Does Abel know?"

Gat sighed, and he nodded.

"So, I have another old friend that has kept things from me. Please tell me you love him, and he is not part of your disguise."

"Yes, I love Abel. The African element was cover, but drawn from my father. I always thought I would find a way back to the future. I was waiting for a moment to broach the subject with Anna, but I never had the chance."

"I could get you back, Gat, if you truly desired it."

Gat sighed. "I have too much here now."

I looked again at Candour, who nodded.

Claire squeezed my leg. It was so difficult opening up and watching them open up, in turn. Never had so many tears been shed at a dinner party.

"Let us come to Avery's memories." I looked directly at Charlie. "He observed the Moribund boy, Sonny. Did you?"

Charlie stood up. She was laughing.

"Yes?" Her voice was different, however. Deeper. More evil.

128

"I wanted to hear it from you." I turned, and looked at the others. "Friends, move away from her. I am not sure that is Charlie. *She* will kill."

"Uncle Robert. Do you know how likely that it will be you? I had secured a way to transfer my body into Charlotte's then Avery's, and vice versa, yet you went and let him get killed, you stupid bastard. I can hear Charlotte screaming inside me. Percy never loved you, but you could not see it. You now know Gat was a student of science, not mysticism, you missed his obsession with the science books, his magic comes from that tattoo on his wrist. Walter always liked Avery better than me, I was never comfortable in the company of the so-called Menagerie. There was never anything for me. My parents were killed by revenants, you are probably to blame for that, too."

Those last words were a scream. Charlie, or whatever was possessing her pulled out her soul blade, even though we had agreed not to bring them into this room. She launched herself onto the table. Plates, cutlery, condiments, and dishes went everywhere.

There was a dull thud, and two gateways opened either end of the room. Lantern Heads flooded through. We were sitting ducks. Raven had appeared, too. I had told her to stay away, but keep a watch for anything out of the ordinary.

Charlie came at me, and swung her sword. Raven blocked her, but was knocked away. Charlie, it seemed, had gained in strength. Charlie came back at me, and I knew her shimmering pink blade would get me, I would not be able to get out of the way in time.

Suddenly, I was shoved to one side. Claire had physically pushed me. I marvelled at her strength. As I looked back, my heart went in my mouth as the arcing thought blade approached Claire's head. Claire just dispersed and the blade passed through nothing but green mist.

It was chaos.

Whisper, Candour. Aid them.

Apollyon had granted us the help of his minions, and we needed it. I had quickly dawned on me that Charlie, or clearly now, the thing possessing her, was in some way in league with these creatures, and that when we first fought them together, she had probably known they would come after us, then. How long had she been possessed?

Charlie locked her eyes on me again. Walter had pulled one of the ornamental swords off the wall and was in a defensive stance. He was unlikely to be a match for someone with a soul blade. Raven had joined them on the table. It was sturdy enough, I'd hoped.

I should have known there was more to Percy. She availed on us these magical weapons with some ruse that they were from the ministry, and I had accepted that without question. Indeed, we all had.

I was so gullible.

129

There was a clang as soul blade met metal. Then the doors to the room opened, and a small troop of soldiers led by Claire entered. I heard her tell them to aim for the Lantern Heads, but to not endanger civilians.

Percy had ignored the no-weapons clause as she pulled hers, but she also dug into her pocket and threw me a soul blade handle. It was my own.

Clang. Walter had blocked another blow, and Charlie was cursing horribly at him. She backhanded Raven, and my young protector was flung from the table. She collided heavily with one of the dining chairs, almost unconscious.

Walter had fought in real battles, he probably wasn't as disadvantaged without a soul blade as I had given credit for.

Clang. The sounds of percussive weaponry filled the air. Between the minions of Apollyon and the soldiers, the Lantern Heads were pushed back. There was a scream as a young soldier fell to the claws of one of the creatures. Suddenly, there was also one upon me. I hadn't pulled my sword in time as its claws raked the air towards my face.

I fell into the Hopelessness.

As usual, I was in the same place physically, but everything was calm. I saw a brief whisp of the young soldier as he followed the light. Presumably off towards heaven.

"Uncle Robert." Said a voice. It was the ghost of my nephew, Avery.

"It's not Charlie, the thing possessing her *is* evil, Uncle Robert. She/it called the revenants to kill our parents. She is possessed by a powerful creature, Uncle, you must put a stop to this evil. They do have Sammel. He is in such pain. I can hear him…"

Avery screamed, and was dragged away. I stepped back out of the Hopelessness, into the melee. It was a big risk, but I immediately pulled my sword. I swung it at the back of the Lantern Head before me, and it dissipated.

Charlie and Walter were locked in their fight, still. There were four or five of the Lantern Heads left. Candour pulled the head off one. Whisper punched through another.

Gat used his wrist tattoo to fire what I had once believed to be his spiritual magic. That power hit one of the creatures, and it seemed to crush it into a ball, getting smaller and smaller until it winked out like a turned-off star.

Then the thing using Charlie took Walter's head clean from his neck.

It landed with a heavy wet thud. His body fell the opposite way to the killing stroke.

"No." I screamed. Yet I was furthest away. Although I never wanted to look at my friend again for fear of what the vision of his headless body would do. I raced towards him.

Percy, who was nearest the dining table, engaged Charlie after she dispatched her last opponent. Charlie looked assured, strong. There was an incandescence to her. Then she flickered. Percy got in one block before Charlie pulled another weapon and chopped into Percy's side. Percy fell badly from where they had engaged.

Charlie jumped from the table, and ran towards one of the gateways. She looked back at me, laughing.

"It will be you next, Uncle. Enjoy burying your friends."

Then Whisper was upon her. She punched Charlie soundly whilst avoiding those magical blades. Charlie barely missed a step. She crossed her swords over so fast it was a blur, then she closed them in a scissor movement, taking Whisper's head off. Charlie was getting used to decapitating her victims, it seemed.

NO!

That was Apollyon's scream, and in his wail, I heard the disbelief that one of his celestial minions could die.

The Charlie-thing had the audacity to sheath her swords and give a little wave as she stepped though the gateway. It snapped shut.

An eerie calm hit the room, aside from the moans of injured soldiers, and the dissipation of the final Lantern Heads. None of the strange creatures made it through the gateway with the Charlei-thing.

I went to the corpse of my friend, Walter, and I shifted to the Hopelessness. I hoped I was in time.

He was there waiting for me. He was smoking a ghostly cigar. The light was forming above him. He would be opaque. I would remember.

"Well, it was fun whilst it lasted, squire." Walter said.

I choked, not knowing what to say.

"Sorry I lied, Robert. I warned you about killing people because I had already done so. I regret not being more open."

"You didn't lie. It's how you coped, I can see it. There was no shame in what you did to Giles and his team. He abused you for years. I would have done the same to him. I think that judging by the light gathering above you that you are on to better things."

"I'm going to see Lizzie for a while." He said, dropping his ghostly cigar, and putting it out with a ghostly boot heel. "See you later, Squire. I'll rattle a rose jar soon. Make one up for me."

Then he was gone.

Robert.

I didn't have time even to grieve for the loss of my friend. Apollyon was in my head. It cleared of all immediate sorrow, this was probably the demons doing.

You must find Sammel, then kill the Charlotte thing. That bitch-creature has ended Whisper. How was she able to do that? A mortal finished my Whisper. I must have her corpse when you have defeated her, Robert. I must know how she did it. Use Candour, he is at your disposal.

At the time I did not have any qualms with that. I agreed. Apollyon vanished, and my grief flooded back.

Percy had been fatally injured, too. So, I stepped back into the real world to see something truly strange.

There were two Percys. One lying bleeding profusely. Another standing nearby. The one on the floor started to shimmer, and then she faded.

Percy came over to me, and hugged me. I let her.

"How can there be two of you?"

"Future me. It took me months to heal from that wound. The Minister thought you might have needed me sooner. He rigged a portal to bring me back. And before you ask…"

"You can't bring Avery nor Walter back."

Percy shook her head.

"The minister and I have agreed on something."

"What about?" I asked. This was cryptic for her, she normally cut to the chase.

"After this is over, we will part ways. He has granted me leave, to go and search for my Arthur."

I smiled at her.

"Will you forgive me enough to let me have one more adventure with the Menagerie?"

I kissed the top of her head.

"Of course. I need all the help I can get solving this one, rescuing Sammel, and finding out who is really behind Charlie's behaviour. This is not my Charlotte. She has been turned, possessed."

Gat came over and begged my forgiveness, which of course, I gave, but with a clear order that he would divulge everything. Percy and Gat went off to get some medical help as my big friend had a nasty gash over one eye.

Claire had arranged for Walter's body to be removed. Then a handful of duty officers led us out of the dining hall so they could tidy things up.

I went to see Raven, who looked like she had broken an arm. If there were any doubt, she wasn't still a ghostly sentinel herself, this was it.

I found Candour weeping, sitting in a chair. He looked up at me, he seemed very human at that point.

"Hundreds of thousands of years ago, my master created Whisper and I to aid him, following his fall. Doomed to judge over the evils of this world he has been very much mistaken and maligned. Whisper and I balanced him. But now she is gone. What will happen to my master? What will happen to me without her?" Candour made full eye contact. "Will you help me, Robert?"

I nodded. I had enough grief for a thousand people, but I took on the sorrow of one more. If we were to get to the bottom of this, and survive, I would need Candour.

"Robert?" It was Claire. "We have had Charlie's room searched. We found these."

At first, they looked like everyday books, but as Claire gave them to me, I saw that they weren't really in my hands at all.

"Hold on to me." I said.

We both dropped into the Hopelessness. The books were clearer there.

"Their Truth Books." Claire said, reading my mind.

"Whatever is possessing Charlie must have taken them from the Order Soul to aid their body swap. Injuring him in the process. If we return them, we will be granted our boon. We can then go and rescue Sammel." They were well rehearsed words, but needed saying again.

It was strange to think we had come to Lincoln to deal with a threat and that that threat wasn't the main danger after all.

"There are so many questions, Claire. Who had Charlie sided with? Who is the maker of these Lantern Heads, and what is their aim? How were they able to capture a Nephilim? Why have they got Sammel? Who would want to garner the wrath of a former angel, a demi-god?"

"Well, Robert, let's find out. First, you need some rest."

We stepped back into the real world.

"And there is another thing, Robert. I'd quite like to join the Menagerie for this one adventure. Brigadier Lord Holden has already given me a leave of absence."

I smiled. I had brought us back to the hallway outside our rooms. "We will probably need the Brigadier's help too."

"Finally, Robert, there is another thing."

"Yes?" I asked and she whispered in my ear.

"Can you indulge a Dryad's needs."

I nodded. This move to physical love was speedy. Yet I needed it.

I was not alone that night with my grief. Claire Wright stayed with me kissing the tears away.

Chapter Eighteen
More Than One Boon

I'd had enough of Lincoln, and I wanted to be home. Too much had happened, and I wanted to be in a place of familiarity and of safety even if it were just for an evening before we went to London.

Percy said she was needed in Whitehall, for a time, so I took Claire, Raven, and Gat back to Legend Street. Candour said he would join us as soon as he had mourned Whisper with his master.

I brought us back to one of the lower levels and we climbed. We left our baggage in the hallway, and separated.

Gat had spoken truly little to me over the last few days. Whereas before we would discuss politics, history, and philosophy for hours. Looking back, it would be fuelled by lots of questions from Gat. He had been trying to hide the fact he was from the far future, and my times were ancient history to him.

Mrs Lark, the day cook, had prepared a breakfast for Claire and I. Gat didn't join us, and Raven said she wanted to commune with Postlethwaite.

I knew we were going to have to go to the Cathedral as soon as possible, but I wanted a little bit of normality.

I looked at Captain Claire Wright, the red-haired, green-eyed lady across from me. I had known her for a few days, but already found myself quite smitten by her. She had lain by my side the previous evening, and had listened to me pouring out my heart; first about Eliza and then Percy. And bless Claire, she listened to it all whilst holding my hand, whispering calming and encouraging words to me as she did so.

"We bond quickly as a people, but if I am going too quickly for you, Robert, I will understand." She had said.

I nearly told Claire how much I was ready for there to be someone else in my life, but I think she'd realised that already.

"I am old, Robert, will that be a problem?"

Percy was over fifty thousand years old. Claire was a girl compared to her, how could I reject her based on age? If I had known, then that I would be compiling these journals at the age of one-hundred and sixty then I certainly would not have had an issue with Claire's age.

Once breakfast was over, we returned to my room. Claire had brought her bags up; she wasn't going to let me out of her sight. I lay on the bed almost drifting back to sleep.

I heard the sound of the shower and felt the change in temperature in the room as the steam curled under, and around the door. I smelled perfumes, and a scent familiar to a forest after a rainstorm.

Claire entered the room minutes later with a towel wrapped about her. This Victorian gentleman would not make eye contact, in fact I was almost horrified, she had suggested showering in my bedroom ensuite. I looked everywhere but at Claire.

Claire laughed and dropped the towel.

Well, you can imagine what a fully naked beautiful half dryad did to me at that point.

Time slowed. And I really needed that slowing of the frenetic pace of the last week or so.

We lay together for most of the day, getting to know each other in the most intimate of ways. It was getting on for early evening when we decided to shower together, and get ready for dinner.

We dressed semi-formally, as we were not receiving guests. I saw Mrs Lark raise an eyebrow at Markham, the day butler. Claire caught it too, and raised her own eyebrow at me.

Dinner was braised beef, with shallots in a red wine sauce. It was delicious, and Claire complimented Mrs Lark on her food, which was a good thing. Mrs Lark would be your best find forever if you said her cooking was good. Mr Lark had the most terrible gout apparently and it was no surprise she hadn't been arrested and imprisoned for killing more people with food.

We retired to the library; each with a brandy. It was a cool evening, so Markham had put the fire on. It crackled and popped. We sat near each other, hand in hand. It was momentarily bliss. I forgot for a short while about the loss of the twins and Walter. I would have to make the arrangements for Avery and Wally's funerals, but they could wait until tomorrow. Walter wouldn't mind. He was a pragmatic fellow, and I had already made my peace with Avery, even if my guilt remained.

I was about to fall into a funk when Raven appeared. She didn't use the doors, she just materialised, I didn't know she could do that still. Then I realised it might not be Raven.

The Prophecy had her.

"I have come to take you to the Cathedral of Truth."

Claire looked at me, her hand tightened on mine. "Robert?"

"Its fine, my love, we need to go there. Did Raven bring the books?"

Raven nodded her head, but it was the prophecy talking through her. "The books have been returned. One to the section of the living, the second to the section for the dead. Although neither sits well on their shelves. Are you willing to come?"

I looked at Claire. "You can stay if you would rather?"

135

She shook her head, so I nodded at the Prophecy in Raven's body, and then we were elsewhere.

There was the Order Soul, looking much healthier hovering in mid-air, in the same space he had occupied before, legs together and arms out like a living metal cross.

Candour was standing below him, but not moving or indeed participating in anyway as if he were an automaton, and switched off. I couldn't help thinking how similar Order and Candour were.

"I thank you, Robert Waterfield, and your Menagerie for restoring my missing books. As you can see, I am healed." The Order Soul, Endure, said.

"And I am pleased to see that you are." I said.

"I would like to give you your reward. What boon would you ask of me?"

I paused, not for dramatic effect, but because I felt like I was on a hamster wheel, repeating myself time and again.

"I would like to know the whereabouts of the being Sammel, son of Apollyon." I managed to say.

"Beware the Lanterns." Prophecy offered from Raven's mouth.

"It's a bit late for that." I replied sarcastically, but the silver fellow just had that half smile on his face. Raven's possessed face remained stoic, like my sense of humour was wanting.

"Forgive my Prophetic friend, Robert, Claire. She has a habit of dropping bad news when all you want is good. The son of Apollyon can be located in Alexander's Castle. London."

"You will struggle to find him though, Robert. Another will appear. Sammel's choice will threaten the make-up of the whole world, possibly the universe." Raven muttered.

I wanted to be away from Prophecy.

"Thanks, Endure. I hope to meet you under better circumstances, in the future. Will you allow us to depart?"

The Order Soul smiled. "Because your boon has been met with some negativity, Robert, I would like to grant you two further things."

Well, if there was anything to help on this damned quest, I would be happy to bite the Order Soul's hands off.

"Firstly. As a champion of order, you are granted access to the Cathedral of Truth whenever you need it in the future. Just close your eyes and call me."

Whoopee, I thought, unkindly, then put as much sincerity into the thanks I gave, just in case my appreciation looked fallible.

"Secondly, I grant you temporary conditional access to The Net. The world's power grid. Like your friend Garrett, you will also be allowed to call to Gaia, and she will help, if reluctantly, during times of need."

Then I felt a surge, like I was too near an electricity source all statically charged with the hairs rising on my body.

"What has just happened?"

"Gaia says her power is only to be used in protection of this world. It is quite miraculous, even if it has some side effects."

"Side effects?"

"Prolonged life increased physical strength, and stamina. Angel power, in effect. Very few humans living can tap into the source. You are a champion of this world, Robert. Use it wisely."

"What if I do not want it?"

"It's too late, I have given it to you."

"I might be allergic." I said, stupidly thinking I was a child refusing a horrible foodstuff.

"Dear Robert, this is the power of stars, the energy of the universe. Not a bag of peanuts."

"Robert, it is a great honour." Claire said.

"Sallandra Oakroot." The Order Soul said as if seeing Claire for the first time. She had shared that name with me the previous evening but had sword me to secrecy. She told me not even to think that name amongst others.

"Endure." Claire said. "We all know a few secrets biological angel android."

"Touché." Endure, the Order Soul said with a vaudeville campness. He had gone from a mortally injured statue to an effete showman. "How is your mother?"

"Entrenched within Sherwood. Again."

"Old Sherwood's a handful, darling."

"He is indeed."

They chatted for a while. I looked at Raven, half expecting some doom and gloom.

"It's me again." Raven said through gritted teeth. "Can we go? I hate being possessed. It's happened three times in the last week. My frigging toes are curling."

"You may depart, friends. Hrafn Raven Gunnarsdottir, I apologise for Prophecy using you so. I promise it will not happen again. Well, perhaps not for a while."

Candour snapped to attention. He looked around at us like a child who had fallen asleep and lost his bearings in the space between dreams and live thought. "Apologies. I was communing with my master. He is not happy that you have given Robert access to the Gaia Net."

"It is a good job I serve a higher power than Apollyon, or his peers." Endure said. "Otherwise, I would be quaking in my boots. I'll see you soon brother. Robert, Claire, and Raven. I hope you find what you are looking for."

We shook hands, and then we were transported back to Legend Street.

Raven went to check in with Waite, and Claire went and rang the bell for tea. I needed to make my peace with Gat. I really had ignored him since I had found out he might be the traitor. My head was still full of images of his life in the future; that wonderfully coloured planet Praxia, that was all pistachio sky and emerald sea.

Gat was sitting in the library. He had books open. His sleeves were rolled up, and I suddenly realised I had never seen him without a shirt on, nor his arms exposed. The tattoo on his arm was like the belly of a rainbow trout in its iridescence, it was like some elongated jigsaw piece, there were lines of metallic surface that grew into his skin.

As I approached, the thing went ping, like the cloakroom bell at the Grand Hotel. He looked up at me, and grinned.

"Roll your sleeve up, my friend." He said. It was strange, he was speaking in a London accent now, not with his African dialect.

I did so. I had felt some momentary discomfort earlier and a godsforsaken itch. I unbuttoned my cuff and rolled up my sleeve. There on my left wrist was the same sort of metallic jigsaw piece.

He stood up from behind the desk and strode over to embrace me. He gave me a very unmanly kiss to the neck which would have seen him arrested anywhere else but his home or a rugby pitch.

As he pulled away, he had tears in his eyes. "I am so sorry, *man*." His accent was even more London, rougher. The original. I was astounded.

Gat had misled me for his own safety, and I had seen him as a traitor, yet he had not betrayed me like the creature possessing Charlotte, or even to the degree Percy had pulled the wool over my eyes.

"It is I who should say sorry. We are brothers now." I said holding my wrist up. It wasn't some bonding over beer statement. I felt we were joined in some way.

"Here." Gat said, "touch your imprint with mine."

I did so touching the strange metallic jigsaw piece to his.

Then I was in his mind, growing up on the streets of a future, unrecognisable London. I was then a commander on board a fighter class Mind Ship called *The Success of the Introvert,* whose pilot was an avatar utilising the mind of someone whose body had died but whose brain had stayed functional.

Then I was back.

"Oh, dear goddess. All those things you said about Elizabeth. And that witch, Isabelle." Tears were still in Gat's eyes. He had seen the sorrow of my life, and I had seen his.

Bonded.

138

It was my turn to hug him, and we stayed like it for a time. Then I heard a feminine throat clear.

"Do I have competition?" Claire asked of Gat.

He was wiping tears away as we parted, but he came to embrace Claire.

"I hope you will both be so happy together." He said kissing her head. He towered above her.

"Its early days, he hasn't got me killed, nor introduced me to a dead witch, so we should be okay."

Claire's jolliness helped to break the mood, and we began to laugh and joke with each other. We had a nice evening; we needed to relax and enjoy some time away from the strange, for tomorrow we would be going to London, and threats anew.

Part Three: The Gold Lord Cometh

Chapter Nineteen
The Ministry

I asked Raven to stay at Legend Street, mostly because of her injury, but also because I needed someone to protect the rose jars, artefacts and alert us, should there be further incursions.

Claire, Gat, and I went to London via the Hopelessness, as soon as we had all packed. Strangely, my wrist imprint tingled as I crossed the veil, and surely there was a connection between the power of the living Earth and the beyond. I was sure I would find out at some point.

Gat eventually pointed out he felt the same, and probably could have crossed over to the Hopelessness on his own, but he found it 'creeped him out' a little too much. He was full of future sayings, by that point. They don't speak proper in the future, I had to say, in a mock cockney accent. He just laughed.

We met Percy at Hampton's Tea Rooms, off King Street, after taking the tube to South Kensington and dropping our bags off at the hotel Percy had arranged; at the ministry's expense. Percy looked beautiful and refreshed and nothing like a gal fifty thousand years older than me. She was dressed in another glamorous emerald dress. Thankfully, Claire had changed into her blue one, that would have been a faux pas to blow a man's mind.

We ordered tea, and lemon drizzle cake, and then we told Percy about our latest trip to the Order Soul. She listened intently and made a note of the address we would find Sammel.

"Let me check this Alexander's Castle out with the ministry. Just in case. Agreed?" Percy offered.

I nodded my affirmation. Gat and Claire did likewise.

"I'd like you to come to the Ministry. I think the Minister would like to meet you all. In the flesh, as it were. Or the fur, in his case. I think he would like to apologise for our approach, Robert." Percy said as she sipped from a bone China cup.

"You mean for watching me?" I replied smiling.

Percy's face went blank at that point. It seemed I had hit a nerve.

"Please, Percy, there is no need. I am over my fit of pique. I am pulling your leg." I had overstepped the mark with my humour, it seemed.

"I am the one the prophecy said would disappoint you most." Percy put her cup down loudly. I winced, and it must have been evident to Gat and Claire who had remained silent.

"Let us all let bygones be bygones." Claire said, which made Percy look at her like she was dog mess on her shoe.

"I think I know Robert better than someone he has known less than five minutes, Claire, I have reparations to make. Let me make them."

"Well, I hope that doesn't involve Robert, himself."

That made both Percy and Gat's eyebrows rise. Touché Claire.

"Oh, come on, you do not think I meant it like that, do you? I may be part elemental, but we aren't all sex mad."

This time Gat did spit out a little bit of tea. Claire made firm eye contact with Percy, as if to say, 'you had your chance love, now move over.' Whilst I still loved Percy, in my own way, she was never going to be the one. Claire might well be. She had won the exchange in the tea shop.

We ate and drank what was left, exchanging pleasantries before a ministerial carriage turn up to collect us. It was one of those new-fangled motor carriages, a Rolls Royce Silver Ghost. It was a prototype the minister had acquired, a full year before they hit production. I eventually found out he had gone forward in time and purchased it as they didn't really start to enter the mainstream until 1906/7. It made a hell of a noise, but it was fast, and it carried the four of us in style.

We approached the War Office, which is on the junction of Horse Guards Avenue and Whitehall, and in the early 1900s it was not as busy as it would become just ten years, or so, later.

Percy explained that the Ministry of Mirrors, proper, could be accessed via a secret hall at the back of the War Office. My previous visit had only been to a faux reception.

Well, it was far stranger than I had guessed. We were led to a corridor that looked more like a dowdy suburban set of offices than a government mainstay. Our chaperone left us by a large mirror that covered the whole width of the wall. As we approached, Percy did not slow, instead she stepped into the mirror and vanished. A second later she stepped back.

"Come on, slow coaches."

And like my original journeys into the Hopelessness, the Cathedral of Truth, and any of the other strange places I had visited, I stepped into another new world entirely.

If the War Office corridors had been dowdy, the Ministry of Mirrors was wondrous. We stepped into the most opulent of rooms. It was a grand reception room. It was lined with bookcases.

"It's a Library palace." Gat exclaimed. He *was* in awe.

"Welcome to the Ministry of Mirrors, or for those of us that know it better, the Nexus of the Worlds of Our Faltering Hearts."

142

I must have looked puzzled. I had seen some of this in her mind. Percy explained as we walked back the way we had come, but in a parallel opulence.

"When we travel through time, and parallel planes, it gives us a sort of arrhythmia." Percy explained. "We have to ground ourselves in the world of our birth in order to survive. Usually, we all return to our true homes or birthplaces on our given birthdays. We then briefly celebrate our long-lived and multi-dimensional lives there."

"How did you survive for fifty thousand years on that other world? The magical one?" I asked her, believing her immediately rather than questioning something Jules Verne or Herbert George Wells might dream up.

"I had to be exiled from Gaia. I was chosen by that world, New Gaia, or Nova Gaia, as it became. All of us who went there from an alternate timeline did so. It had its own power NET."

Percy spoke as if thinking about that place pained her. Had she left so much behind? She had lost her husband before that, so she had been without her loved one for all that time.

Percy linked arms with me. "I have come to terms with my return, Robert. I need to find my Arthur. He's not much more than a boy, and he is lost, somewhere. I did leave many good friends behind on Nova Gaia, though - alive and dead."

Rather than roll her eyes, Claire looked heartbroken for her.

Gat sighed.

We came to an elaborate shallow staircase which branched upwards in three directions. Forward, left, and right. Percy angled for the left corridor, and we all followed.

We came to another mirror, and we stepped through. The next place was like some futuristic ship; all gleaming white.

"The Minister has a passion for the fictional bridges of ships-" Percy didn't finish her sentence.

"This is the USS Enterprise." Gat said. "This is the bridge, and that is the ready room of Jean-Luc Picard. In my time they reconstructed this as part of the naval fleet training sims. It was a curio, and became a faster than light hotel."

I didn't understand one word, but have subsequently caught up with Star Trek. At the time, I found it noisy and distracting, with a lot of whistles and whirring noises. The adjacent 'ready room' doors whooshed open, and what can only be described as a big blue furry monster walked out.

Although I had already seen Perfume Factory Large Pockets in Percy's memories, I took an involuntary step back.

143

Not only were my surroundings strange, but the furry creature was also so otherworldly, not to mention he looked like he could have ripped my arms from my body without a second thought.

He was dressed in clothing that would have befitted Nelson, all dark blue in hue. A long coat, britches to the knees, and white tights. The only thing missing was his tricorn hat.

"Hello, my name is Perfume Factory Large Pockets, or LP for short. Welcome to the Ministry."

"I like the library in the last room better." It was Gat who spoke. I realised he would have been more used to aliens himself.

I was more interested in how the misty smoke that emanated from behind the creatures ears got sucked into the little machine strapped to his chest. From which his voice could be heard.

"You have been though a lot, my friends. Come, I have prepared tea, and there are biscuits."

LP led us to a large sitting area, just off the strange control room, it was more to my liking, resembling a Soho gentlemen's club.

"The smoke I can see is your speech, isn't it?" This was Gat again, using up all the clever questions.

"Yes, it's my olfactory box. It translates my pheromones into spoken language. It's how we Zenobarts communicate. We have no vocal chords in our throats. Zenobartoosia has an oxygen rich atmosphere, the pheromones bond better to oxygen than nitrogen, so sometimes I can be translated wrong."

That was all he said on the subject, so we then exchanged a few more pleasantries, and we were down to business.

"I think you are right to be wary of Apollyon, beware that he doesn't double-cross you."

"Well, Apollyon seems very balanced..." I started.

"Yet he is a father who has lost his son. Once Apollyon has him back, do you really think he will leave this world? Where will he go, where does he exist? He is one of the Parthenon, yet the gods are only as strong as they are remembered. Who remembers Apollyon? Just his son, I would have thought, and those of you who have seen him now. How does he retain such power?" LP asked.

"Presumably his angelic birthright." Gat replied to the furry man.

LP nodded. "He resides on another plane. Hell is a socio-political construct to prevent the general population doing anything their feudal lord did not want them to do. It is more like there is a bubble world linked to this one, where he and his minions reside."

"I guessed that would be the case." Gat offered, pleased that LP agreed with his worldview.

"Yet Robert has a world he can step into, beyond the veil, as it were." Claire offered. "The Hopelessness."

"I have a feeling that Robert can tap into the natural order, and open wormholes to a similar bubble universe, one where ghosts and spirits get trapped. I presume, in this Hopelessness, you can travel awfully long distances with a mere thought. Try it now, Mr Waterfield. Take me with you."

LP travelled with me into purgatory. I noticed his musk as I looked around at the vast space, and its contents. He was amused. This place was a museum curator's dream. Full of treasures, and objet d'art. This *wasn't* the Hopelessness. LP had taken me to a similar bubble. One he controlled.

"Sorry Robert, a little subterfuge. Each one of the objects, books, and artefacts in this vast place link to another world or universe. This is the Room Between Worlds. It is attached to the Closed University, where my students, faculty staff, and close colleagues reside. It exists a few seconds outside of ordinary time, somewhere in Scotland, sometime in the 20th Century. Forgive me if I am not specific. One has to have some secrets."

I immediately thought of my Menagerie. It was on a smaller scale, but each rose jar and capture box were the link to an anchored soul. Like these artefacts were linked to worlds, and other dimensions. I understood LP's need to be cautious.

"We are alike, Robert. May I call you so?"

"Indeed."

"Are you going to ask why I have been watching you?"

"Presumably as a replacement for Percy, if I'm putting the jigsaw pieces together correctly."

LP laughed. Just after, the air was filled with the scent of apples and cinnamon. Like the apple pies my mother used to make.

"That is partly right. However, there is another reason. I have reason to believe you have come across Isabelle of Stafford?"

"The witch? Yes. How do you know of her?"

"It is a long story, with many aspects. Isabelle's magic will doom Earth eventually, in one possible future. She will soon, in your time, make a pact with a group of scientists called the Corvidae. A loose bunch of eternal youth seekers who will forge science with magic, and create creatures that will invade most of the universe. One of that group's antecedents is a man called Lord Ainsworth. The owner of Alexander's Castle. Yes, Percy sent me a message on her phone. I had it confirmed a moment ago. It's not a castle, but a walled Tudor mansion set back in grounds. Some size it is, too. It is not on any map of the capital. Ainsworth is definitely mixed up in this. There is some link to Isabelle, and I have never found out what that is.

"I need you to keep a look out for the signs. You are linked to the world's NET, however temporary, your senses are enhanced. By the way, the story of Earth's demise will begin in the house you currently reside in. I will go no further, for fear of you trying to alter the future. And, by the way, do not attempt to. I would rather not have to kill you."

More bloody prophecy. This creature is as bad as the thing Postlethwaite tapped into. Yet, LP was right. The day World War Two broke out, a man, George Wright (no relation to Claire) would ask me to sell one of the Legend Street houses to him.

That story is for another time though, reader. Back to *this* story.

"I'll try not to change the future, then." I said.

My week had been very strange, up to that point. Yes, I might be a slayer of demons, and a collector of dead things, but part of me didn't want to believe anything LP said; any more than I trusted Apollyon. His bubble was so like the substance of my Hopelessness, and I didn't want Isabelle spoiling my life in the future, or anywhere else for that matter. The thought of the Lantern Heads invading was even worse, though.

"We have encountered them before, in other times and places."

"Sorry?" I asked, making it clear I knew the blue *thing* had read my mind.

"The Lantern Heads, their master and I go back a very long time. I read your scent, not your mind, Robert. It's different. Well, mostly. I can tell that you love both of the women back in the library, as well as the man. Yet, you have been dishonoured. Your sweat smells of sadness, the sadness of betrayal."

"I'll take my chances. And you can tell all of that from how I smell?"

LP ignored me. "You need to put an end to Charlotte's machinations. Although I am certain she is possessed by another. Find out who is behind her treachery, and destroy them and their Lantern Heads. If the leader of the Lantern Heads is the same one as I have met before, then you could be in a lot of danger, Robert. Again, I will not chance the fabric of time by giving you any hints." LP nodded to reinforce my promise. I nodded back.

There was a glimmer in the corner of the room, as a portal opened, and a handsome, red-haired woman appeared. She was dressed in green leather, like one would expect Robin Hood to look if he were real, and knew a really good tailor.

"Longshanks, we have an infringement, can I call you away?"

"Elizabeth, welcome home."

She nodded impatiently, almost rude in her bearing, like she was royalty, and we were excrement on her shoes.

"Robert Waterfield. This is Elizabeth Tudor."

I shook the woman's hand before the name sunk in.

"Yes, the definitive article. Shut your mouth, Lord Robert. The flies will get in." She had a deep sonorous laugh.

"I will be with you shortly, my dear." LP said to Elizabeth Tudor, who opened another doorway in the air, and walked through it.

"Apologies. Elizabeth is not one for standing on ceremony, as you can imagine."

"Elizabeth Tudor leads your merry band?"

Again, the apple and cinnamon scents. "No Elizabeth works for me, under her own charter, as do quite a few of the ex-monarchs of Europe, and Asia. A couple of Prime Ministers and Presidents of various countries, from various times, and a few great scientists, like Stephen Hawking and fine role models like Mary Seacole. The former, you will not know about yet, but the latter should be familiar. Sorry, I am waffling, and filling your head with nonsense. Let's return to your present."

And we were back in the vast Library. No one batted an eye. It was as if we hadn't left.

"Percy, we need to assume that the power behind the Lantern Heads is the same as we have encountered before. I have warned Robert that we cannot divulge his future, so therefore we will keep the facts close to our chest until they happen. I am sorry for more dishonesty, Robert, but I dare not risk the future, as well as the present."

"You knew of the Lantern Heads Percy." It was a statement not a question. "But you couldn't tell me. In case it broke the future."

Percy nodded and quickly glanced at Claire. Claire's face gave nothing away.

"I am sorry, Robert. It seems I keep having to apologise."

I sighed. "There is no blame in obeying your elder's and betters, Percy."

I smiled at Percy more for Gat and Claire to see. They didn't need to be caught in more of my moroseness.

"I presume, LP, we also need to ascertain how the Lantern Heads are being created in this time, and destroy them." I looked at the big blue creature who nodded.

"Percy is an established part of this timeline, I am not, yet. She can act on my behalf. Until the time comes for me to intervene." He looked at his watch. "Forgive me, Robert, friends. I am required elsewhere."

LP quickly shook our hands, and then opened himself a doorway, which he stepped through. He was clearly able to do this without anyone knowing he had gone, yet, he was so polite he probably would have thought it rude to just disappear.

Percy asked for our patience whilst she went and gathered a few things from her apartment at the Ministry of Mirrors. We then travelled back the way we came, and back to our familiar London, via the War Office.

147

We took tea in the hotel, and planned our route for the next day, to try and track down Sammel. Percy had brought with her two sets of blueprints, LP suggested that we needed to look at - the plans of Ainsworth's castle and manufactory.

After tea, Percy led us through gaudy flock wallpapered corridors, to a conference room she and LP had hired for the day. There were Ministry of Mirrors staff laying out other maps and reference books for us to look at. How had they done all this so quickly? Then I remembered their time travelling abilities. The staff soon disappeared through doorways in the air, and left us to our own devices.

We had the maps of Lord Ainsworth's manufactory and castle laid out across two tables. We soon decided that Claire, with her military training and ability to translocate, would remain on point, at the hotel.

Candour had returned to us, after a brief commune with his master. In a very out of character way he revealed his two-handed broad soul blade, and outlined what he would do to Whisper's murderer.

He really was not himself following the death of his sister. In quiet tones, he commanded to join Percy, Gat, and I in the field.

The first part of the plan would be a double recce the following evening. Gat and Candour would try and find out where the Lantern Heads were based, most likely the Manufactory, and Percy and I would try and locate Sammel at Lord Ainsworth's stately property, just on the outskirts of London, near Windsor. Then we would meet back up for breakfast, and discuss our next plan.

It might be that Sammel and the Lantern Heads were in the same place. Although, the factory screamed creation of clockwork parts. Knowing Charlotte, she would be where the action was, and I would find her near Sammel, or those automatons. Would her possessor be the same?

"Do we need re-enforcements? Goodness knows how many of the creatures they may have, and with Charlotte having the ability to somehow kill or injure celestial beings, Candour and Claire will be helpful, but not above severe injury, or death."

"Remember, Robert, and I can tap into the planet's NET. We should be able to deal with most threats." Gat added.

Percy shook her head. "Charlotte has a power no-one understands. I have seen people wield your power on other worlds, ordinary soldiers or assassins killed them. A stray bullet here, or an arrow there. Do not forget the might of the Lantern Heads. They can spawn quickly, even when engaged in a fight."

Candour nodded. "Even my master knew nothing about Charlotte's ability to kill Whisper, or indeed injure the Order Soul."

"Then let's hope Charlotte can be defeated with an arrow or a stray bullet." Claire said, sadly.

"I'd rather see if she is being controlled by something else before we kill her. I allowed her twin to die. Charlotte can only be killed if we ascertain she is already dead, and then if there is no other way – or, one of us is in mortal danger from her."

Most of my friends nodded, but I noticed Candour sigh.

"Are you okay, Candour?" I asked knowing he couldn't lie.

"No. I have lost half of myself. It is Charlotte's fault."

"And Charlotte lost her twin. If she is in fact evil, and lost to us, I will not stand in your way, caveats in place as I said. Moreover, if she is now controlled by another being, or supernatural force, I would want to at least attempt to save her before we sacrifice her."

I held my gaze, and that was quite difficult when you are looking into the eyes of a being that was ultimately angelic. He nodded, and I relaxed a little.

"Should I ask the Strange Regiment to mobilise? We could have a battalion here in two days, maybe less." Claire sipped at a glass of wine, her beautiful face rosy cheeked.

"It's a thought, but let's have a good look around first. Then we can make some decisions about our reinforcements." Said Percy.

"Okay, it seems we are as organised as we can be. I'm going to get some sleep, after I have visited Raven and Postlethwaite. I am hoping there are no more prophetic surprises for us."

Chapter Twenty
Rattling Rose Jars

I found Raven exercising in the underground training area I'd spent very little time in recently. I was getting flabby, I would have visit the room more often in the near future.

"How is your injury?" I asked.

"It's healed." She said punching a long, large sausage shaped leather bag. Rags were tied about her knuckles. "Since *I* have become *me*, I can get injured, but I can also heal surprisingly quickly. I want to join you again in the field."

"I want you here. Safe. To look after things, I mean."

"I might have died when I was sixteen years of age, but I am ancient. My face belies my experiences."

"I would have said you looked about fourteen." I replied.

"I always looked young. It had its advantages. The Viking's slept with anything that moved and bled, if you see what I mean. I pretended for as long as possible that I was too young for sacrifice or sex. Can you imagine what a black-haired creature had to suffer in a predominantly fair society. They weren't all blond and ginger, lots of browns, but few blacks. My mother had been an Irish captive."

This version of Raven spoke so well. She wasn't the avatar of my bird Postlethwaite I had known her to be. I needed to recognise that.

"I want you as back up. If things get a little difficult, I want you there. For now, I need you here, healing."

Raven nodded reluctantly. She stopped punching the bag and unwrapped the rags from her hands. I helped her with a particularly difficult knot. She looked up at me, and smiled. It was heart-warming. She was so different now. The hard shell of Postlethwaite's supernatural personality was sloughing from her.

"Yes, I can now be injured, Robert. Normally, a sword would pass through me, even though before, I could transubstantiate myself, and hit someone. Then I began to change. But although my body has changed in the last few days, and not just from spirit to corporeal, I still know when it's at it's optimum." She blushed, which I had never seen her do before as an avatar. "Surely you have noticed I am more woman than girl."

I looked at Raven for the first time as a man, and felt the shock of my experience. Her girlish figure had given away to the curves of a young woman. It was my turn to blush.

"I'll need to shop for clothes. Everything is tight around my tits. My arse is too big for my leathers. My mother said I was a late developer, just before I was killed in battle, and now I know she was right. I thought I was just going to have a flat-chested, boyish figure, which would have been simpler."

I gulped. Where was Claire or Percy when I needed them?

"A man of your experience should know about a woman's cycle of development."

I cringed, we weren't that well informed back then, I am ashamed to say. "Do you know how to care for yourself? You can call on Percy or Claire they…"

"I fought with the maidens from the age of twelve until I died at sixteen. We were taught the right things about a body's development. Not like you tight English people. And so, I'm not stupid. Just unprepared."

"I would never suggest you are. We have all changed in recent weeks." I rolled my sleeve up and showed my wrist print, hinting at the power I could wield, but did not understand. The idea I was semi-immortal, too.

"We can face the future together."

"Thank you, Uncle Robert."

"Uncle?"

"Well, you aren't my father. He was a drunken bastard. So, I would like to call you uncle. We called respected men uncle in our settlement."

"I am not sure I ever broached the subject of your home, or your people. I am sorry for that."

She smiled, but looked on the verge of tears. "And now I fucking cry for no reason."

I must have looked shocked at her use of such language.

"Fuck was not a bad word in my time. It was just a functional one. It sounds rubbish in Anglo Saxon, anyway. Brutal language."

She sighed and I held my arms out and she embraced me. Raven sobbed for a time, and then she stepped away from me.

"I was raised in Vagan, Lofoten, North Norway. I hope you don't mind, but I have been looking at your maps. I needed to reconnect with that place, try to understand why my spirit was here, and not there. Then I remembered I died in England, in Lincoln, during a raid. I stupidly feinted to the wrong side, and the Saxon split my skull with an axe. I took three days to die, my brain exposed to the sky. I felt that death every minute when we were in Lincolnshire, and I had started to change. I think the prophecy has done this to me. I think, eventually, I will not be useful to it, and it will move onto some other untethered being."

151

"You should have told me."

"We fought non-stop for three days. Fighting the living dead, and the men with lights on their necks. You lost lovely Avery, and his bitch of a boy-girl sister killed Walter. You had no time for me. And I would not have expected it of you."

I sighed. "And now I know you, I am not going to put you in danger, ever."

That was when she pulled a knife from somewhere and flung it at me. It whispered past my ear, embedding itself in the wall behind me, or rather, putting out a candle in its sconce.

"I trained in the art of the warrior, from the age of eight. My mother was a queen. I fought my first battle on my twelfth birthday, and I died on my sixteenth. One mistake. I've killed men a head taller than you, Uncle, and drank others under the table. I am formidable, and never forget it. Treat me like a simpering violet, and you will never see me again." Raven winked.

I laughed. I couldn't help myself. How lucky was I to have such strong women in my life? Which led me to think momentarily of Percy, and then Claire, who I had only just met and had fallen in love with.

Love.

Not since Eliza.

"You are off with the fairies, Uncle Robert. Walter often said that to you. I will go and wash and change, and then we can talk some more."

Raven left me, but I followed her out of the training room soon after I had put out the candles. I was on the second level when I heard the tapping in my head. Tap. Tap. Tap. Like fingers on glass. Tap. Tap. Tap.

Was it coming from the room where I stored all the rose jars? I headed down the interconnecting corridor, to the weapons room, I then opened the door into the large storage area. There was a flight of steps down to cellar area three, on the northern wall. I touched the knob, and the door unlocked for me at Waite's bidding. I mentally thanked the bird, and descended. This area of the underground warren was always alight. Having electricity also helped us to detect abnormalities in the spirit world. The lights were flickering as I entered the Rose Jar Room.

All the jars were making tapping sounds. If it wasn't bad enough, Postlethwaite materialised.

The air tasted of phosphor, like a whole box of matches had been struck at the same time.

"I have warded the room. Nothing can get in. Nothing can get out." Waite said, matter-of-factly.

Then the world ripped. A hole was torn in the air like the split seam of a fat man's trousers.

Out fell Avery and Walter. Both flickering like the unstable ghosts they were. They could not manifest, they were too young. Avery's ghost was very feint, like a washed-out watercolour picture. I dragged both their souls into the Hopelessness, where I could control things better, snatching a jar from a shelf as I went.

Walter was substantial there, Avery was still flickering, and that was unusual.

"Bobby, we do not have much time. You need to get Avery into a rose jar."

"What about you? You both died. Passed over. No unfinished business. No curses. No anchors. You should be in Heaven."

"Avery was dragged back. I felt him screaming as I died, and so I remained as his protector. Charlotte has taken his soul. Well, most of it. He has managed to hold onto his nature, but his being is being sucked from him. Charlotte has taken his femaleness. She is trying to become female. She originally needed Avery's body, but clearly it was destroyed. Now she is trying to take his shape. His original girl shape. Without reciprocating. He will be a soul without a being. A ghoul. We need to get him into a rose jar, and ward him."

"Avery Curzon, you must sleep." My wrist imprint suddenly felt hot. I was drawing from Gaia for the first time.

The feint flickering being that had been Avery began to be drawn to a rose jar as I opened its lid. Avery's spiritual remains filled the small jar, and I screwed the lid back on. I said the warding words, and the glowing jar became benign again.

The tapping in the room increased.

"Is that you, Walter?" I said to my former batman.

"Yes. But please do not put me in one of those jars. I am not ready just yet.

I nodded, and Walter vanished. So, I stepped back into the real world.

The tapping had reached a frenzy, and then the noise changed in tone. It was resolving into a howl. A window opened in the air, similar to the one Walter and Avery emerged from. No one emerged this time, but someone was watching me from the other side.

It was Charlotte. Or the thing she had become.

"I hate you, Robert Waterfield. I will kill you. I will take your life, and I will have Avery's soul, and his being. I will be whole."

I hadn't noticed Raven appear until Postlethwaite cawed, and the young woman fired off an arrow at my niece.

"Be gone, bitch." Raven said. I winced as much at the coarse language as the fact she had shot at Charlotte. I knew my niece was inhabited by evil, but I did not think I was ready for her to die.

153

A Lantern Head stepped in front of Charlotte, and caught the arrow. It rattled at us with its ethereal burning mantle.

The second rip in the sky that evening closed.

Raven looked at me with sadness. "They have come back. Avery and Walter?"

I nodded, but I also sighed. "Wally is a true spirit, and he has gone his separate ways, for now, but Avery is torn. Charlotte is trying to take his female shape and if the gesture is not reciprocated-"

"...then Avery will be disembodied. A spirit without true shape. A ghoul." Raven cut in.

"I need you both to remain on guard, in this room. Any more attacks like that last one, call me through the Hopelessness." I said.

"There is no need, I can hold this place against Charlotte Curzon and the Lantern Heads." Raven said.

"I am more worried who is behind it all. This cellar has some of the vilest creatures from all of history locked up within its rooms. I cannot afford our enemies to have access to the worst of them. Re-weave the wards, Postlethwaite. I know it weakens you, but I need the extra security."

Waite cawed in irritation, but I knew she would obey.

We returned to the upper floors, where Raven made some tea, and we took a seat in the library. The maps of Norway were still out on the study table. A compass had been used on one to draw a small circle.

"So that is where you were born?" I pointed.

"Yes," she said. I noticed as we sipped our tea that, although she still dressed in a more masculine way, black leather trousers, high boots, now she also wore a dark green chemise. It was one of Avery's, no doubt.

"Would you like to return?"

"I have."

"Not as a spirit, but as a non-supernatural being?"

"Very much so."

"Then, when this business is over, I will take you to visit your ancestors."

"Unfortunately, with the onset of Christianity, Valhalla has been forgotten."

"I think you will probably find there are those who still worship the original Norse gods."

"I really hope so. I remember a boy in our village. It was the summer before I was killed. He was beautiful. Tall, strong, and red-headed. He had a mark on his chest like a lightning bolt. It was so clear on the day he was born. His parents named him Thor. He had a very big…"

"Perhaps don't share that with me."

"...hammer. He was a smith's apprentice. He could make the most beautiful swords and arrow heads. I would like to find out what happened to him."

"He might be difficult to trace. Even with my access to the Hopelessness. It is so exceedingly long ago."

"He would find me. With your help, I am sure of it. I hope he died honourably in battle, weapon in hand. Not in his bed, an old man."

"When we are done, I will take you there. We will try to find him."

Raven smiled her beautiful smile. The natural resting harshness was wiped from her face in those moments. She became more and more human, and less spirit as each day went by.

"I just want to know he is at rest. You can't bring back those who are not ready. I am not wanting to resurrect someone else. Just put my mind at rest. Dear gods and goddesses, I am so weak, now."

"It's called caring, it's what separates us humans from the monsters."

Raven nodded. "Are you sure you want me to remain?"

I sighed. It was getting a regular occurrence. I just felt I was leaning too heavily on my friends, new and old. "I need someone I can trust to hold the fort. I feel that I can trust you, Raven, probably more than I would trust myself, at the moment."

"That is a funny thing to say."

"You are a Shield Maiden. You will carry out your task, if I am unmistaken, even if it threatens your life."

"I am bound by honour. It *is* our way, Uncle."

I smiled. Hearing that filled me with so much pleasure. "I can't believe how you have changed, Raven. From an avatar to a corporeal being in such a short space of time."

"Odin fought his daughter, Hel, for my soul, it seems. It is his gift as well as yours."

"It certainly is another mystery. One that can wait. Enjoy your new life, Raven. It is a precious gift."

"Tea certainly tastes better now. But I do not like having to piss so much again."

"That is another word you may not wish to use in company. In fact, talking about ablutions is not held in high regard in polite society."

"Oh uncle, you English are so prudish. Not talking about something everyone clearly does. Its madness."

I finished my tea and took my leave of Raven. It was difficult to leave her. The current level of threat meant she could be in danger. We needed to find Sammel, or the world would be under threat from the minions of Apollyon. Then, we needed to deal with Charlotte, if things were not inextricably linked.

155

I went in to see Claire, immediately. She was sound asleep, so I moved back into my own room, and took a shower. I dried myself, and put on my pyjamas. I then went back to Claire and got into her bed.

"Pyjamas?" Claire said. "You can take those bloody things off."

Society might gasp, but who was I to argue? I might be dead soon.

Chapter Twenty-One
Reconnoitre

Percy and I stepped out of the Hopelessness, into a warm, clear, moonlit evening. It had been a warm week, as summer faded into autumn, only the leaves in their reds, yellows, and browns indicated that summer was almost done.

I let go of Percy's hand. It felt warm and too familiar now we had lost even our unrequited love.

We were standing within the high walls of Lord Ainsworth's property, on the borders of Windsor and Slough. Even the tall townhouses in the square opposite would struggle to see over those walls, as the ground within the complex had been purposefully lowered. Even though parts of Alexander's Castle were ancient, the sprawling property had been redeveloped fully in the nineteenth century, by the looks of it, apart from the odd border wall and flying buttress.

"This is grand." I whispered.

"It's bloody pretentious." Percy noted. There was a moonlit twinkle in her eye, and I had to silently chuckle. I had seen pictures of her parent's former pad, it was three times the size of Arthur's Castle.

"You had better keep hold of my hand. Any sign of dogs or guards and we will need to drop into the Hopelessness."

"What would the lovely Captain Wright think? Holding my hand twice already."

"It's a purely protectionist gesture." I said, and I must have had a bit of an edge to my voice.

"Bobby, stop. I was only joking. I am pleased you have someone, however quickly things are developing. It will stop you goggling my ankles so much."

"What, how dare-"

"Oh, come on, you silly bugger," she cut in. "You need to chill out a little."

"Chill out?"

"It's a phrase from the future. It was an ancient phrase, by then. It means relax. Bobby, I am so sorry I did not tell you all of my history. Even you can see that I couldn't. You lived some of it. You saw what was in my head. And most of my memories were left in storage on Nova Gaia." Percy squeezed my hand. "Look. I would never want to harm you, Bobby. Never.

You have to let go of me, or the faded romantic notion you had of me. We are good friends. Nothing more." Percy smiled at me, and I nodded in return. She squeezed my hand again. "As one of your very best friends, you need to let me take the piss every now and then."

"Charmed." I said, a little too loud.

A dog barked.

"Halt, who goes there?" A voice shouted.

I tried to drop us into the Hopelessness, but nothing happened. Percy looked at me and I shrugged.

"Run," I whispered.

There was something here that was dampening my ability to move through the veil, I was sure of it. I kept trying to move us there, but to no avail. It just wasn't working.

So, we kept to the shadows, out of the glare of the moon. We had messed up almost as soon as we had arrived. Or, I had, at least. We would have to try and get away, and then try this again in a night or two.

There was a smaller northerly gate set in the larger structure, probably used for deliveries and tradesmen. I took us in that direction.

I was loath to pull my soul blade - as the light would call all defenders to us. It was important that we did not do so until we were cornered, or could use the swords to cut through the gate. The swords had that ability, but they easily ran out of power if their energy was used against inanimate objects. The soul blades were powered by life, spiritual energy. They drank the power of their victims.

I tried to tap into my new power via the NET, but again that route was blocked. Lord Ainsworth's property was well guarded in reality, and supernaturally, it seemed.

The noise of the dogs, meanwhile, was loud as they were nearing, and, at a startling speed.

"They've let more dogs loose." Percy hissed.

"We won't have long."

We reached the large North gate, and surprisingly it was open, but, as you would expect, the drawbridge was up, but the portcullis was down. The only way we were getting out of here was for me to release the mechanism and for us to dive into a moat.

There were two heavy wooden doors set either side of the barbican. I pointed to the left-hand side for Percy to attempt to open it. I heard her turn the handle, but it was locked. I tried my side, and it was stiff, but opened. I pushed into a small well-lit room. It was the gatehouse control room. Percy followed me in, and we pushed through the entrance into a room with a small table, and four chairs. Three used teacups sat on the table, along with an ashtray, and a tobacco pouch.

158

I put my finger to my lips, and I concentrated. I could hear two men laughing in the next room. I held two fingers up to Percy, who nodded. She pulled her soul blade, but we certainly weren't going to kill innocents on my watch.

Then the dogs arrived, barking outside. I travelled over to the gas lamps and put them out one by one. I had motioned to Percy to grab the door handle, so it didn't just fly open. I did the same with the door to what I was expecting would be the mechanism room for the drawbridge.

"They are trying to get in Robert." Percy whispered.

"On my mark. One, two – three."

We opened our doors with the timing of people who had fought together in the field for quite some time. The dogs immediately made a beeline for the light, even thought they could probably smell us. The change in contrast had confused them.

They were not a breed of dog I had ever seen before. From behind the door, I saw two large red, lizard-spined things, with maws like something from a HP Lovecraft re-imagining of Hell. Steam came from their mouths. Made of the same mechanical magic as the Lantern Heads, no doubt.

I slammed my door. Percy slammed hers. Not before a Lantern Head had stepped in.

Its head lamp lit up the room with a gaslight gloom one would find in the streets of a big town on a foggy night. It rattled, its mantle-like voice flickering along with its illumination.

Death.

In the room beyond I could hear the screams of the men as those Hellhounds set upon them. They would not have stood a chance. There was a key in the lock. I turned it, realising the dogs were more of a threat than anything else we would face. I was hoping there was only two of them. Percy nodded as if in understanding, and drew her blade.

The creature was about to spawn another of its own kind, and it thought it had us trapped. It was mistaken.

Percy sliced through the creature as it tried to spawn, decapitating two heads from a twisted conjoined creature that was partially two torsos and one set of legs. It dissolved into energy as it fell.

The only light left was that of Percy's sword.

"Let's get out of here. We will have to try the north gate."

"Those dogs, what were they?"

"I have never seen anything like them before."

"They were not of this Earth."

"Ainsworth, it seems, has a way of warping people and animals."

We kept to the south wall which led us ultimately to where we needed to be. We were like mice keeping close to walls in order to navigate and avoid confrontation. There were more outbuildings scattered about, a summer house too, so we could find ways to hide or shelter if needs be. Although any sanctuary could soon become a cage.

Dogs barked again. I couldn't tell if they were earthly dogs or those lizard-like Hellhounds. I really didn't want to find out.

"They are going to be guarding the north exit now. We are going to have to draw as many of them out as possible. We can't avoid a fight."

Percy was right. She generally was, in the field. Brilliant, operationally.

Then a hound came at me out of the darkness. This one was black, rather than red, hence I had not seen it coming. It knocked me backwards, snapping at me as I fell. Its hissing steaming maw gnashing at my throat.

I saw the flash of Percy's soul blade and there was a noise like wet meat hitting a butcher's block, before the creature dissipated. Percy helped me up, and I faced the darkness with her, the looming, multi-eyed façade of the house at the heart of Alexander's Castle was grinning at me.

As I watched, first one, then two Lantern Heads materialised out of the gloom. The usual mantle-rattle accompanied them. I pulled my soul blade, and prepared to go into battle.

Percy ran at them. "Get them before they bud!" she cried.

I'd laughed at her dressed in boys clothes earlier in the evening, but she was as practical as ever. She looked like an up-market chimney sweep. She had said that she needed to have all of her movement, hence no long skirts. Her hair tied up within a black cap. Whatever her clothing, Percy was dangerous when cornered. I had seen it on many occasions.

Percy took the first one out with a diagonal stroke. It parted from left breast to right thigh before dissipating. Percy then stepped aside, and turned to skewer its partner, but it dodged and then spawned a fellow. That one ran at me, drawing duel soul blades.

Swordmaster Luigi Caruso, the spirit imbued within my sword, advised me of the moves I should make. Planting them in my mind well before I needed them.

I managed to stop double blades coming at my head with a horizontal parry. It was a defensive stroke that was stronger at the elbow and weakened further down the arm, so difficult to manoeuvre.

How a blank lantern head could leer, I did not know, but it did as those twin blades pushed down at me. Its glass-plated frontage, of which there were four, gave me a look of pure hatred. Maybe I was imagining it, maybe some sort of psychic assault was making me hallucinate? However, it did it, it was bally clever.

Luigi advised me to wait for the maximum pressure, and then step to my right, causing the creature to fall forward. It stumbled and lost one sword, it turned to face me, but I split it from head to mechanical groin.

Percy was struggling to fight off two others, and then I saw one of the dogs loping towards her.

I dashed over and stabbed one of the Lantern Heads in the back. It dissolved as I ran it through.

"Dog. Percy. To your left."

Percy, who had been fighting with only one sword, pulled another. She twisted in flight, with a ballerina's skilled pirouette. Her left arm took the head off the lantern creature whilst her right came up just as the dog jumped at her.

Her stroke missed, and so the dog fell upon her. Percy screamed, who wouldn't? Her two swords had been away from her for too long, and because they were entirely made of energy, other than the handles, they went out.

I kicked the dog. It was too near Percy to skewer. I did it just in time as it was about to bite her neck out.

It came for me, then, but I was ready for it. As it jumped at me, Luigi informed me of the best way to stop a jumping beast in mid-flight.

So, I despatched it. Expertly. Nothing of my own skill, just that of someone once dead, whose personality existed in a sword handle, or two.

Percy smiled at me, but her face looked worried.

Then two things happened. Candour linked with me just before I was knocked out. I had enough time to say *run* to Percy before I collapsed. I had been hit from behind.

Chapter Twenty-Two

Back to London

I was unconscious on one level, yet I was somehow able to see through Candour's eyes.

My Lord Apollyon has many wondrous gifts.

"Let me speak to Gat, please, it is urgent."

Ainsworth's manufactory was beside the Thames, and Gat and Candour had taken a carriage as planned to the east of the city. The sprawling site was set next to the water, with access to river barges. Whatever Ainsworth was doing it involved the transportation of goods in and out of the premises.

"How is it going, Robert?" Gat asked, his kind smile filling me with a little hope, despite my predicament.

"Not good." I said, through Candour. "We arrived but were immediately attacked by Lantern Heads, and some type of lizard-hound mechanical cross. Percy and I managed to face a couple of assaults, but I think I fell for the 'don't just concentrate on what is happening in front of you,' ruse. I have been knocked unconscious. I am hoping Percy got away. The odds aren't spectacular I am afraid. I think we need to ask Claire to call on her chums from the Strange Regiment, and get in touch with the ministry. Abort your reconnoitre, for now."

"An assault could prove disastrous." Gat wisely said. "We needed stealth. We needed to plan better."

"Give me twenty-four hours. If Percy and I both return, then hunky dory, if not, then if either one of us is still captive, you might have to go direct."

Gat nodded, and Candour seconded him. There was no way we could go in alone, or in pairs. The Manufactory was bound to be heavily guarded if it was in fact producing the Lantern Heads and the Hellhounds. I was desperate to find out where Sammel was, and I needed to bring Charlotte into custody before one of my friends killed her.

I began to feel myself fading. Hopefully, it was only unconsciousness, and not death.

"Remember, twenty-four hours." I said to my companions in the carriage.

Then darkness had me for a second time.

I awoke with what felt like the mother of all hangovers. I was in a bed, which was kind of them.

Then realised it was my own bed. I recognised my dresser. Claire's dressing gown was on the back of the door. How had that happened?

"I sent them all to go and rest." Raven said, she was sitting at the end of my bed, eating grapes. She smiled at me. I wasn't used to her smiling yet, so I actually laughed. It hurt my head badly.

"What happened?" I asked.

"You somehow tapped into the power NET, and forced a way into the Hopelessness. Candour tracked your dream, and brought you out. Odin knows how he did it."

"How long have I been unconscious?"

"Two and a half days."

We didn't have that time to waste.

"Percy?" I asked.

"Percy got out. She is back at the Ministry. Trying to look for ways to neutralize the barrier Ainsworth has in place about his home. The blue furry man came to see you. Nice, big though. And he smells."

"Yes, that is how he speaks to us. With the smells translated by a box he carries. All rather clever."

"I have some aspirin for you." Raven passed me two of the little tablets, and a glass of water. I struggled to sit up, but felt better for it. Lying down horizontal was not helping.

I swallowed the bitter pills with a long draft of the water, and sat back against the brass bedstead. I manoeuvred my, pillows to stop the cold brass from digging into my back.

"I want to come with you, next time." Raven said matter of fact and coming to lie next to me.

"I need you here."

"Claire said the soldiers have arrived in London. One or two of the more powerful ones will be happy to guard the house. Postlethwaite will alert me to any danger."

"No."

"I will be able to travel straight back through the Hopelessness."

I closed my eyes against the pain. "Fine. Let us consider the finer detail when I am up and about."

Raven nodded, and then moved the bowl of grapes onto the bedside table. "I will let you sleep."

"Thank you."

I slept sitting up for another two hours and then Claire came in with some broth for me. My head was no longer banging like an unlocked gate in a gale, and I was feeling much better.

"Feeling better, Bobby?" She asked. Claire was dressed in a simple blue dress. He red hair was pinned up, and she wore a pearl choker about her neck. She was beautiful.

"Yes, thank you."

Claire lay the tray on the bed in front of me and sat in the chair Raven had vacated.

"Raven has been very worried about you. I am sure she gets more and more human each day. Last night she even had tears in her eyes. I can sense she is much nearer to being human than she was this time last week."

"I welcome her emotional development, although I fear I have another ward on my hands who I might also let down. I was going to relax my parental responsibilities after Charlotte and Avery moved away, or got married and settled down." I sighed, feeling the weight of the world on my shoulders, as one probably does if one has to care for children, and keep a job and a roof over everyone's head.

"She needs emotional support, and some friends. Raven will be fine at that point. She *is* mature, being a thousand years old helps with that, I suppose."

The broth was wonderful, it was chicken and leek, and it warmed me and helped me to come round a little further.

I soon washed and dressed and met Gat in the library. He was looking through books, but my vision was not yet fully restored to read their titles.

Candour was standing to one side, by the fireplace, like a big ornament. I wouldn't have known he was there if he hadn't have spoken.

"Robert it is good to see you better." Candour said.

"Indeed, it is." Claire entered the library. "I have had cook whip something up, I hope you didn't mind, Robert?"

"No, of course not, I am famished." I replied.

"The regiment are now stationed in London at the Ministry. They are on standby, should we need them. Lord Holden is with them. He thinks, the sooner as we get Sammel back, he can have his HQ again. He is a simple soul."

"Thank you, Claire, that is helpful."

"I asked Abel whether there is any legal way we can enter both properties. He has said he will look into it." Gat said as he removed his glasses and closed the large book he was reading. "Do you think Lord Ainsworth would agree to a search of his properties?"

"Depends on if the judiciary are brave enough. You would only want to accuse a peer of the English realm if you had irrefutable proof." I said. Asking the Lord Chief Justice to sign a warrant against the Minister for War was probably pie in the sky, so a less legal approach would be needed. "We would be laughingstocks if I said we wanted to search the property for the son of Satan."

164

"Yes, but not for your kidnapped niece."

"That is an even trickier accusation. I am not sure how I feel about Charlotte, at present, so I wouldn't involve her in police issues for fear she would be exposed as a curiosity, or a homosexual."

"Does she not hold a full female form after what she did to Avery?" Gat asked.

I shrugged. "Without asking her, I cannot be sure. And then, I'm not going to make her prove it. So, I do think our task is about infiltration rather than legal challenge. We need to get in there, and get Sammel and Charlotte out."

"Percy rang earlier, Bobby." Claire said. "To see if you were up to a return to London. LP has apparently drummed up some support from within the Ministry of Mirrors."

"Yes, I think I'll be fine to return tomorrow. Claire, do you think a couple of members of the regiment *could* come and look after this house? Postlethwaite does a good job, but I need people who can actually defend it."

"Already agreed with Lord Holden and Percy. A further task force, additional to the few already here will be arriving in the morning. So, Raven can come back with us."

"She told you, then?"

"Pleaded with us, Bobby." Gat replied. "She really is a darling, now. Not so po-faced.

"Keep Raven safe. She is needed. In the future. When the Magpies and Ravens roam afar."

I turned. It was the voice of the prophecy, talking through Raven.

"A hundred and more years hence. When the Viking sounds the battle cry. You must write this adventure down for future audiences to read, Robert."

Then Raven was back in the room.

"Did the prophecy have me? Again?" She asked almost disgusted.

I nodded. I looked about for a fountain pen, but I already saw Gat had scribbled down what the prophecy had said. I smiled my appreciation at him, and he had nodded back.

We had supper and retired relatively early. I had the healing hands of Claire Wright who gave me the most luscious of massages before we went to sleep, well we did other things, but I will not embarrass you too much. Even though the prophecy said to keep you informed.

The Ministry of Mirrors, or rather Percy, had found us an abandoned office suite with accommodation for us to stay in. It wasn't far from Whitehall, and was a mothballed official town house belonging to the current

Governor of India who had no intention of returning anytime soon. Probably enjoying squeezing the life out of that poor country and its indigenous people.

I am such a republican.

Anyway.

The offices had been cleaned within an inch of their lives on the upper floors, and the offices on the ground floor were not that abandoned. We settled in quite quickly, and spent the rest of the day unpacking the maps and notes Gat had made whilst I was unconscious. We then pinned them up in the main room. The blueprints of Alexander's Castle, Ainsworth's residence, and Ainsworth's Manufactory.

Soon after tea, Gat and I were sitting discussing the planned approach to the factory in the main office when a hole opened up in the sky, and the blue furry man that was Large Pockets stepped through. He was closely followed by Percy.

"Bobby. How are you?" Percy said, coming over and hugging me. LP sat in one of the chairs that Gat offered our guests, and we settled down to parley.

The air filled with strange smells, like hay and apples, Bovril, and glue.

"I will support you from afar in your assault on the Manufactory. I cannot be seen to be working against a fellow of Whitehall." LP turned to me, and nodded. It seemed to me he was now incredibly serious, as opposed to before, when I had met him, and he seemed jolly, like a blue Santa Klaus.

"I cannot find out what Lord Ainsworth is warding his property with. I have tried to portal into his grounds, but to no avail. He is not tapping into the Gaia Net, I think his magic may be celestial. His power seems effortless. The wards around Alexander's Castle are impenetrable to my best applications or tools. We will need to find another way. I suggest we assault the manufactory first. This may well flush Ainsworth out, although officially the manufactory is registered with Companies House to a company called Midas Holdings. It seems that much of the funding comes from the Americas."

"So, we can hit the factory without rousing suspicions?" I asked.

Percy shook her head. "If only it were that easy. We need to plan the assault on the factory well, for we will have only hours between our application for a warrant to find your niece and Sammel before Lord Ainsworth is alerted. The most the Attorney General will give us is two."

"If we plan well, have the Strange Regiment at hand; then it should be straight forward." Gat was thinking aloud and was repeating almost word for word, the things I had in my head.

"If that place is full of Lantern Heads, as we suspect, then you will have a fight on your hands." The tall blue furry man said.

166

I looked at him more closely, and at that point I was sure my gaze was sliding away from him. Every time I looked, I struggled to memorize him. I knew he was tall, blue, and furry. I could not tell you what colour his eyes were, or what shape his nose was.

I smelt cinnamon again, like the last time I had met him, and when I looked back at him, he was bearing his fangs in a type of smile. Had he understood what I had been thinking? Indeed, I gave my thoughts away with my anxious smells.

"We need to discuss our tactics with Lord Holden, and then we will plan our final strategy." LP said. "I suggest you wait for the weather to turn in two days' time. Cloud cover. Fog. The moon will alert them to us otherwise."

"I have a small band of agents at hand, Bobby. They will go in and recce. the situation. They will plant timed explosives, if necessary. We do not need Lantern Heads running amok in London. We have to destroy them all." Percy added.

"The Prime Minister is not happy that we might be going up against Lord Ainsworth. Ainsworth is a major philanthropist, and benefactor to the PM and his party. Although, as it happens, word is out that Ainsworth is currently planning to oust the PM, who is quite obviously unhappy about this. Therefore, he and the Secretary of State for Home Affairs have informed the Attorney General to sign the warrant the Ministry of Mirrors has requested. It is subject to Official Secrecy, though, so will not be widely known. If Ainsworth has spies on the PM, Home Secretary, or the Attorney General's staff then we are in trouble."

"Do they know of the Apollyon threat?" I asked LP.

The blue creature nodded. "Indeed, the warrant application is all based on that. The PM knows we need to return Sammel to his father. Getting your niece out, Robert, is important, but not our actual focus. Percy has also informed her friend King Edward."

I must have started at that as LP held up one large hand to pause my ire.

"Officially Robert. We need to follow the rule book here. Of course, we will try and get Charlotte out of there. The official line is we need to get Sammel. Therefore, releasing a national threat. Of course, this will be all hush, hush. The general populace know nothing of our actions, or of some of the strange and celestial players involved."

I nodded, my business was a strange one, and far from in the public eye. As this adventure got stranger and stranger, it became even more important the general populace did not find out about the threat the world faced.

It was then that Candour materialised in the room. His chiselled features were a reflection of his calm nature. He was dressed in a smart suit, and his long curly hair had been cut to seem more officious. Thank goodness he was wearing clothes.

"Candour has offered to act as a liaison of sorts, Robert. He has re-confirmed Lord Apollyon's promise, that he will depart this realm once Sammel has been returned. Candour may well stay with the ministry and act as an Ambassador, if all parties agree."

"I look forward to the role with relish. His Lordship Apollyon has commissioned two more aides to act as his conscience. I am therefore somewhat redundant, I still have the full range of my celestial powers, I was born an angel and I can use the might of one once more. Heaven might disagree, but as we haven't seen anyone from the upper realm for millennia, I am claiming my right again until Gabriel or Peter revoke it."

Percy looked at me with her eyebrows raised. He had told us more in that eulogy than we had got in days from him. Although, not sure either of us really believed the angel stuff.

Then, I suddenly had a thought. Now that Candour was not just one side of Apollyon's conscience, could he now lie? He was such a gentle soul, I felt bad for thinking that. Unfortunately, many gentle souls had betrayed me in my forty-two years of life.

"Robert, in order to give our application for a warrant more credence, we have involved the police. In particular, they are interested in your niece's disappearance, as the Sammel side of things is a little more hush, hush. I have it on good authority that Chief Inspector Hugo Marble will oversee the missing person's investigation itself. Would you be inclined to meet Marble? He is a particularly interesting character."

I nodded. "Will that not muddy the waters, somewhat?"

"No. He is one of my own operatives."

Now Percy looked at LP with surprise. "Him?"

"Inspector Marble is an excellent agent. Forget you know, Lady Anna. It will be better in the long run."

"But he is as clumsy as fuck. You may as well have attached a clown to the investigation, not a copper. Couldn't Bertie have done it?"

"Bertie could not, and you know why."

"Pack all your ornaments away, Bobby, and your nice pens, Gat."

"Chief Inspector Marble has come down from Staffordshire Police to help out, in the absence of the incumbent, Lozenge, who, *accidentally,* ruptured a knee on the rugby field. My suggestion to the Home Secretary was welcomed with open arms."

Again, the smell of cinnamon that I was associating with LP making fun of people or laughing. Probably both.

"Right. I am wanted elsewhere. Lady Anna, keep me informed." LP stood as a coruscating hole opened up before him. He went through, and Percy followed him.

168

"I'll be back this evening." She smiled at me like the good old days, and it was heart-warming. Percy, it seemed, had sacrificed a lot helping others. Her life, her husband, fifty thousand years on another world. She stepped through with a wave.

Chapter Twenty-Three
Marble and Randolph

The Marble fellow had nearly fallen over twice getting to and from the bar. My pint of mild was a quarter empty before I took my first sip.

"Sorry." Marble said, wiping beer from the table with a bar towel.

Although he was clumsy, and I had been pre-warned, I hadn't been told about his intense grey-eyed stare and his intelligence.

Hugo Marble listened to my story without flinching.

"I work across the Artefact Worlds, Mr Waterfield. I am familiar with the Lantern Heads. Although from what you have said, they seem a little different here. I will go and drop in on Lord Ainsworth just before the advance on the manufactory. As soon as Ainsworth gets notice that the factory has been raided, then I will raid his home. I have a team of bobbies who used to be in the military, just waiting to enter the home of the Secretary of State for War. It just so happens that, with a little interference from LP, Lord Ainsworth had already invited me to a meeting regarding the policing of his estate and properties."

"That makes exceptionally good sense." I said to Marble.

"Yes, Mr Waterfield. I have dyspraxia, I am *not* stupid. I do, however, act up to it. It's an invisibility cloak. Stupid looking equals non-threat."

"I am sorry if I implied you were anything other than brilliant." I said, holding up my pint glass for him to chink. "If ever you want alternative employment, Marble, I could do with a little help from time to time keeping Britain safe..."

"You are a canny man, Mr Waterfield. I'd love to be linked to your Menagerie. I wouldn't want to put Lozenge's nose out of joint though. He said he loved clearing up after you, in the bar just before we began the inter police rugby match."

"You know each other?"

"Yes, he tends to look the other way, whereas I like to get involved."

"Is your approach always like this?"

"It is. But I wouldn't have it any other way. I needed Losenge out of the way for a bit. It was a high tackle, I didn't mean to injure him so, but I fell on top of him."

Marble raised his glass, took a sip, and looked at me directly.

"It takes a Lantern-Head three point four seconds to spawn another of their kind from the point they lock onto you and decide to attack. It is then that they are at their most vulnerable."

"But you have to take their lanterns in order to destroy them?"

Marble shook his head whilst he took another large gulp of beer. "No, if you get the timing right, and you get them at the point the glow appears, just here," he pointed to his chest, "where you and I would have a heart. Their creator, who I have met, but you can't know about yet, put pig hearts in them. Without a heart they cannot travel between the worlds. Only beings with hearts can. It's a bit of an issue for human agents of LP, as we can find ourselves in a bit of difficulty if we do not look after our cardiovascular systems. It's the same for the Lantern Heads. Their porcine hearts also trigger the budding or spawning process. They are very well protected, up to the point they start to glow. For about three point six seconds they are vulnerable there. Don't bother with their heads, go for their hearts."

"How many have you killed?"

"Millions. I have lived an awfully long life, Robert. Mainly sideways and diagonally. If I had lived a linear life, I would be close to three thousand years old. I know you know that Percy is much, much older. I admire the way she keeps her thoughts at bay. It helps to put them in the cloud from time to time."

I frowned. "Cloud?"

"Ah, sorry. I have felt so comfortable with you, Mr Waterfield, that I am talking to you as if you work for the University. The cloud is a storage method from where I come from. To be honest, when I first went to work for LP, you had to write them down in journals then have your mind wiped. This is far more humane."

I must have looked confused.

"Time will tell. I will reveal, one day, once LP clears you for forward travel. I cannot have you knowing things which might affect the forward flow of time and cause a paradox."

"That's Greek for contrary opinion?"

Marble laughed. "It's not far from the truth. It just means, if you know about your future, then there might be things you might want to prevent. If you did so, you might change events on your own timeline. If you interfere too much, or tried to put things right, you could end up looping a paradox back on yourself. Therefore, worst case scenario, you are trapped in an ever-repeating cycle. Many of the artefact worlds are the result of paradoxes that have become unstable and have broken off from the proper timelines."

"Surely, decision upon decision causes lots of timelines."

"Lots of versions of a timeline, usually. Time is not linear. Listen I have said enough. Ask me more about the Lantern Heads."

"Is there any other way of killing them? I get you could probably use a bow and arrow, and target their hearts, but is there a way of turning one off, having a look at what one is made of?"

"Bear with me a second." Marble said, and his eyes rolled up into his head.

"LP has just sanctioned a quick trip. Fancy a visit to another world?"

Fascinated, I nodded. "I'll need a pee first."

"Yes, its rubbish when you face your enemies, and wet yourself because you didn't have a safety wee before you set off."

Marble took me to the University, through a portal he summoned at the back of the public house yard. We were scant distance from the hotel, and I asked if Gat could accompany us, but Marble said only I could go along. I was in no position to argue. I needed their help to get Charlotte, and find Sammel, fast.

We stepped through the portal, and arrived in the chamber I had visited before with Percy and LP. The one which housed all of the artefacts. The area was vast, there were shelves upon shelves of objects, bottles, boxes, books, stones, scrolls, and paintings. Lots of doors. I'd never seen so many in one place.

Marble took me to a door. He reached for the handle, and it opened. I got the feeling it would not have opened for me.

"You have your soul blade charged?"

"Charged?"

"Is it in your back? What has Percy taught you?"

I nodded. The blade and handle slid into one's soul, it wasn't corporeal, so it didn't hurt at all.

"So, it is charging. It uses energy of the soul. It doesn't affect us, it just uses the power of our intentions, in either a good or bad way. A soul blade is neither good nor evil. The wielder gives it intent."

I had guessed as much, but politely thanked him. He seemed like a man who thrived on being useful.

"It's just in case I fall over. You will have to protect us both." Marble said, dead pan. I soon realised he wasn't being sarcastic, either.

We stepped into the gardens of Alexander's Castle.

"That was an *anywhere door*. It takes us via this version of Earth, then we can step through to ours. This new version of the Earth is a brutal place. Earth minus 125. The minus is because it is a side-parallel of a timeline, but here, humans are far more technologically advanced. Here, the Romans invaded Europe and the rest of the world, and stayed. Rather than

172

interbreeding, they subjugated and made slaves of 95 per cent of the world's population. It is a horrible world. It is policed by Lantern Heads. The Governor of Britannia funded their invention in order for them to be his spymasters and secret police. The ones on this world do not dissipate as easily when you kill them. Look, there is one. Follow me."

It was clearly just after sunrise, and it was hot - mid-summer. I followed Marble, and was sweating within moments.

"They have different grades of the things on this world. The more stupid ones patrol the streets."

He ran towards the Lantern Head, it was walking down the middle of the broad main street.

The creature was dressed in tight fitting robes, with a blue over toga on top. It moved towards us.

"One."

Marble sprinted towards it.

"Two." He shouted.

"Three."

He skewered the thing through the heart, just as it was about to do its spawning wobble.

A set of wormholes were activated, and other creatures stepped out.

"Quick, help me. Get its legs."

Marble had opened up his blue portal and was dragging the creature through.

"Wont they just follow us?" I took a look over my shoulder, and the creatures were spawning copies of themselves.

"No, the wormhole is encrypted."

"En what?" I asked, grabbing the creatures feet. It didn't have shoes, and its feet felt like a fresh cold corpse. Precisely how the boy Eliza had killed felt as I had wrapped him in a sheet, prior to burial.

"Right, I need to open a parallel portal."

"Well, you might have to hurry up." I said, the Lantern Heads were getting closer.

Marble pulled a device from his pocket, and clicked it between his thumb and fingers.

A portal opened up around us, and we were swallowed up, only to reappear in the exact same place, but in broad daylight. I was glad we had hidden our faces under masks. To be identified at this point would be disastrous.

"Right, we are back on your Earth, and this one is bait." Marble looked down at the creature. "It's still dying, its rattle will bring others, be prepared."

In seconds, one of the Lantern Head portals opened. Two stepped through.

"Draw. You get the left one, I'll get the right one. Go for the heart. Not the head."

Marble did his one, two, three battle cry again, and charged.

I had pulled my soul blade, but I was a little slow, my adversary was already spawning.

I rarely swear, but I did let out a crafty 'bugger' at that point.

I got the one on the right first time. I missed its heart, and ended up taking an arm off. It staggered as the other one came at me. I focused and the Swordmaster guided me to the spot I required.

With a parry, I knocked its weapon aside and slid my blade through its chest, although it didn't go all the way and so staggered backwards.

"I've got one, Robert, come on."

I saw Marble had opened up a portal and was in the process of stepping through. I turned to follow, but then the first Lantern Head I had engaged clattered into me.

I staggered, dropping my sword, it burned its way through the turf of the ornamental gardens. I turned and gave a hefty kick to the creature assaulting me. It staggered back. I picked up my sword handle and re-ignited it. Then I decapitated my assailant, messily carving half-way through its lamp. It dissipated noisily.

I then staggered off towards the hole in the sky. I heard barking, and the thought of those horrible Hell hounds made me run faster.

I arrived in the offices at Chelsea, Gat was looking over his books. Claire was seated next to him. Obviously assisting him, with something. Marble had only just arrived, despite passing through a few seconds before me.

Once I managed to step through behind Marble, the portal started to close.

Gat had already pulled his Soul blade. Claire dropped the cup she was holding, and it smashed upon the floor.

The portal winked shut just as a Lantern Head reached through, severing its arm. The arm felt like a wet mackerel onto a fisherman's deck.

"It's okay. This one is dead. I promise you. That one," he pointed at the arm, "is definitely dead. I'm Hugo Marble, by the way. How do you do."

Gat was already crouching down, looking at the Lantern Head. "So, they don't always dissipate."

"Not if you get them through the heart. It is organic, and cuts the creatures off from whatever enables them to dissipate."

Claire looked at me, a bit bamboozled. I just shrugged, explanations could come later.

"Let's get this bugger up on the table. I want to show you a thing or two."

Claire and Gat cleared the desk, and then we took an arm and a leg each and plonked the dead thing on the table. I heard the door to the office open and looked to see Raven enter.

"You have a live one?"

"No, it's okay, it is dead." Marble said.

"No, it is still alive. I can hear it screaming."

Marble looked at Raven as if she was an idiot.

"I killed it. Skewered its heart. It's the best way."

With a rattle, the creature's lantern lit up, albeit sputtering like the flame couldn't get a hold.

It grabbed Claire, who was nearest to it. Claire screamed.

"I can't dissipate."

Then something fascinating but repulsive happened. A mouth formed from the lantern plate facing us. It dragged Claire towards its ever-developing maw. It rattled horribly. It did sound like a faint scream. Did they scream outside of the frequency of human hearing? Were there nearby dogs going mad because of its high frequency sounds?

I was worried it would start to spawn too. I did what I thought necessary, and pulled my soul blade. I cut off the arm holding Claire. At the same time, Raven threw one of her hunting knives and pierced it through the heart. It fell back with a death rattle. The lantern smashed on one of the side facets.

Something emerged. Everyone else was ignoring it, but I could see it and, it looked spiritual. It started to hover above our heads, but it wasn't dissipating. No one else looked up.

"Can you not see it?" I asked those in the office.

Marble looked up, dusting his hands off as he released the creature. I think he thought it might revive again. Claire was over the other side of the room, clearly shaken. I should have held her, but I was watching the spirit.

"What can you see, brother?" Gat asked. He moved over to me, putting a hand on my shoulder as if to shake me out of what I was envisioning. For all they knew, it was a vision. Or possibly prophecy.

"A spirit left the creature through its broken head." I pointed to the ceiling where, to them, just a cheap glass chandelier hung. I could see the spirit circling it. "It should be moving on, yet it seems caught. Trapped."

As I watched, the thing took form. It soon revolved into the face of a young man.

"They have used the spirit of a teenage boy to animate this creature. Dear God, it is sickening." I said.

The insubstantial boy looked at me with tears in his eyes.

"That's horrible." Claire said.

"I have never seen a spirit emerging from one of those things before. Not in all the years I have been fighting them. It must have linked to something else in this dimension." Marble gasped.

The boy began to fade. He would be visiting the Hopelessness first. I needed to speak with him.

"Marble, let me now take you on a journey. Hold my hand."

Marble beamed. He walked towards me, and he took my hand. Then I stepped into the Hopelessness, pulling him with me. Raven had joined us, and Gat brought Claire.

The spirit who had been insubstantial and invisible to the others in the real world was firmly opaque. I'd never seen such a solid spirit in the Hopelessness.

The boy had jumped as we appeared. He burst out crying.

The boy wasn't very tall, and he was dressed in rags. Not rags of the Edwardian period, he was much older in age, yet not appearance. He looked like a Victorian guttersnipe, like the children who would play around the streets of Birmingham when I was a child.

"Mister, what is happening to me? I was in that bloody creature. They snatched me from heaven they did. I was on the way to see me ma. She died of the pox a while ago. Then I got stuck here, and then he came for me."

"Who came for you?"

"The Gold Lord. Midas himself, sir."

"What?" Marble screeched.

The boy jumped again, and started to cry.

"Shh. Let him speak." Raven hissed. "He is like I was. Alive, yet not alive."

"What do you mean, miss? I'm dead. I've been dead for forty years, or more. I couldn't move on. That's when Midas came. Trapping the strongest of us."

"What do you mean, the strongest of you?" I asked.

"He said he needed those who died at the hands of evil. We were stronger in our claim to be alive. Those who died naturally are faint. He said. We shone. The victims of evil. The Moribund. Those of us who had been murdered by evil men, and women. The oldest of us was thousands of years old."

I looked across at Raven. We would need to talk about the man who killed her on the battlefield before this was over.

Moribund. I would hear that word again, always with a capital letter much later in my life. And I know by the time you read this, you will know of it. Who would have thought an explanation would come from such a source?

"What is your name, boy?" I asked.

"Randolph, sir. Dolph."

"That is a grand name."

"My father was a Lord. An important man, apparently. Got me mum up the spout, then sacked her from his 'ousehold without giving a shilling or a shit."

I winced at such language from a young man, but managed to swallow my Victorian etiquette.

Raven had moved near to the boy again. She put her arm around his shoulder.

"You *are* like me miss. Ouch."

Dolph fell to the ground. I thought for a minute we were going to lose him, that he would just fade away.

"Look at his legs." Claire said. "It's like the reverse of one of my dissipations."

Dolph was screaming in agony as he was becoming more solid.

Raven got down with him and cradled his head in her lap. "It's okay. It's okay."

The boy wasn't only becoming more solid. He was aging. Only slightly, maybe one or two years. Yet he was definitely older now. The rags about his body tore under the strain as he grew taller. Buttons popped on his shirt. It was lucky his trousers had been loose, or the poor lad would have been further embarrassed.

We watched Dolph for a while as Raven stroked his hair.

"I'm the age I choose. The age I wanted to be. A man, now."

Dolph's voice was slightly deeper, or at least steady whereas before it was all peaks and troughs.

Clearly the boy's pain was gone. He smiled at Raven, who had tears in her eyes. Then he pulled himself up, a tall handsome lad of about nineteen, maybe twenty.

"We can step back though." Dolph said. "I can now be alive in the real world. Gaia has let me return. I have purpose. That is, to kill Lanterns. Lots of 'em."

Chapter Twenty-Four
Who is the Gold Lord?

"You are sure he said Gold Lord?" Percy asked me one more time. I could smell the smokiness of what I figured to be LP's inquisitiveness.

"Yes, he did." Claire said. She was irritated at the ongoing questioning, and was happy to have a chance to bite at Percy.

I looked from one beautiful red head to the other. Percy, whose love was out of reach, and Claire, whose love was real and tangible, but had come upon me so quickly.

"Bobby. I am sorry. The Gold Lord *is* involved, we are in trouble." Percy said.

I glanced at Claire whose face darkened at the use of the shortened version of my name.

"We have something far worse than Apollyon on the loose." LP's aromas became muted and angry.

"The Gold Lord is an enemy of LP's. Although he looks like you or me, he is an Oosian."

"That explains nothing." Claire bit. Claire was annoying me a little by then. I could speak for myself.

I sighed. "Percy or LP, please explain. Claire, please let them do so, without interruption."

I didn't look at Captain Wright, no, Claire, I corrected myself. I knew she would be angry, or upset. Percy looked at LP, who nodded for her to continue.

"LP comes from a world called Zenobartoosia. It had two dominant lifeforms. The Zenobarts were like LP, bipedal and all furry, and then there are the Oosians, who were insubstantial, like the spirits of this world.

"The Oosians were once the dominant race on Zenobartoosia, and tended to control Zenobarts like slaves, parasitically overwriting the Zenobart personalities with Oosian ones.

"Millenia ago, the Zenobarts found a way to rebel. They developed their pheromone translators and fought for independence for a thousand years. For a thousand more, war raged, with both sides almost wiping each other out.

"A localised skirmish narrowly missed destroying the only life-bearing planet of our Solar System, Earth, and during that battle, a lone Oosian pursued a lone Zenobart to this world.

"LP crash-landed on Earth in his shuttle sometime during the year 30BC, about the time of the early Roman settlement. The Oosian followed LP, and took on the body of a Roman soldier, who soon became the first Gold Lord, a despicable and greedy man who ended up seizing control of Roman interests in Britain for a time. LP has battled him ever since. Although we thought we had finally defeated him.

"Hiding away in an artefact world called Alberta, the last Gold Lord was called Humphrey Mortimer. Mortimer set a trap for LP, so me and a few other colleagues had to defeat the Gold Lord and pull LP clear of the binding machine that would have made him an Oosian slave once more. Arthur was with us then, too."

Percy had gone emotionally distant, and, for the first time, I saw the blue furry creature hold out a paw to sooth her. He patted Percy in a poor attempt at being human and comforting, Percy smiled sadly.

"The Gold Lord shouldn't be alive. He had an end point. We ended him." It was LP talking. His odours were like burning coal and railroad steam.

"We need to question the boy."

I sighed. We were sitting in the lounge of the rooms in Chelsea. We were all on comfortable seats, and we were all sipping brandy. Our offensive on the manufactory would happen the very next day. The arrival of Randolph had phased us all. I had spoken with the boy earlier that day, he was full of vim and vinegar, and he wanted to be useful.

We had got Dolph back to the rooms soon after he had solidified. He had asked if he could have a bath, then he would really feel human again.

Raven was all for going and joining Dolph in his ablutions, saying there was nothing embarrassing at all about it, and it was just the Viking way.

Dolph looked half horrified and half eager, until I reminded her that, in polite society, young men and women were not as free with their nakedness as the Vikings were.

So, Dolph had a bath. Gat went out for some clothes for the boy and, when he got back, we presented Dolph with his first set of clothes that weren't hand me downs or sewn up rags. The poor lad had tears in his eyes.

We brought him back out into the lounge, where Gat and I asked him, some questions provided by LP. Raven joined us, and I noticed that she was wearing something much more feminine.

Raven still had trousers on, but they weren't leather, she wore one of Charlottes blouses this time. It looked wonderful on her. She had pinned up her hair, too.

Dolph wouldn't make eye contact with her, whatsoever, and I knew instantly that they had a connection. I would have to watch them, with my suspicious Victorian morals.

179

I poured the lad a brandy. He took a sip and nearly coughed his lungs up. His second sip was more measured. Particularly as Raven had laughed and said she would drink him under the table at her first opportunity.

"What was it like being a Lantern?" I asked Dolph.

He started to fidget, and looked generally uncomfortable.

"I don't remember much, Mr Waterfield. Just flashes. I remember being taken by the Gold Lord. Well, it was one of the senior Lanterns. It had a strange gun. I got sucked into a jar at the end of it. I only know that because he did it to this girl spirit. I could see through the glass and see her spirit as it was sucked in. When I was got, the world around me was strange through that glass. I could then hear the pig."

I looked at Gat and then at the boy. "Pig?"

"Those things have pig hearts. I shared a mind with a pig. Pigs are strange. Fuck me. They'd be evil if they could comprehend it, sir."

"Please do not swear." I almost shouted. Stopping profanity came to me naturally.

"Bobby, let him say it in his own way." Gat snapped.

Gat always read people better than me. He always knew how to get to their secrets.

I nodded. "Sorry, my boy. Go on."

"I imagined a world in my mind. A world where the pig and I fought. But the pig always won. I used to get forced back into the corner of my brain. The pig mind/brain would try to make its pig noise, but it would come out as the rattle of the lantern mantle. I remember helping my uncle to change the things on a gas lamp. They rattled when you first lit them. It used to be familiar, now it bloody haunts me, sir."

"Do you have any particular memories?"

"No. But I remember always fighting the pig for control. It always wanted to kill. It killed a lot of people. Men, women, young and old, and kiddies. It liked to kill the young. It wanted to eat them and, every now and then, when the Gold Lord wasn't looking, the pig brain would make a mouth and take a bite. I could taste it. Oh god, I could taste..." Dolph started to sob.

"I think that might be enough, Robert, I do not want us to irreversibly damage his emotions." Gat was pleading with me.

I was about to nod in agreement when Dolph shook his head. "I need to get it out, sirs. Particularly as you have been so kind to help me. I must say, Mr Gat, I have never met a blacky. They said you were all savages, but you are a proper gent."

Gat nodded and smiled. I would pick Dolph up on his use of the word 'blacky' later.

"I remember going to the factory recently and there was a woman there. To be honest at first, she looked a bit like a bloke and if I had been

180

properly alive, I might have tested the theory in the lavatories, but then later when I saw her, she was much more ladylike. The bump in her throat had gone."

He was talking about Charlotte. Had she fully transformed into a woman? If I was interpreting things correctly, then it was true. In a way, I was glad, but couldn't forgive her for using her twin, or for murdering Walter.

"I am still going to kill her." Raven said harshly.

Gat put a finger to his lips. Raven shrugged. Even more human.

"Who else was at the factory? Do you remember seeing another boy, a young man?"

"The boy who felt old to the pig?"

He looked from Gat to me, to Raven. I think we all nodded for him to go on.

"There was a lad, looked about my age now, twenty or so. They kept him locked up. The Gold Lord tortured him. Wanted his power. The lad looked normal to me, although he was very handsome – that don't make me no nonce saying a boy is pretty, by the way. He was perfect. I took him food once, but the pig was far too much in control for me to work out where. The pig thought he felt much older than he looked. I think the pig was struggling. It was able to think better, I think it was growing off me, eventually it would have eaten my mind, or taken it for himself. The pig just imagined a sow and her babies, then their babies, on and on for like, hundreds of times. Giving birth, raising piglets, dying again. The pig was trying to represent age, old age, incredibly old age. Hundreds of years – I'm sorry, I can't count well; I don't know what comes after a hundred."

"Thousands."

"Yep, but many of those thousands."

He had met Sammel. I was sure of it.

"Does the name Sammel mean anything to you, Randolph?"

Dolph shook his head. "No, Mr Waterfield."

Percy looked at me horrified. "We thought they were just automatons. They have pig brains, and the stolen spirits of dead children inside them. How many have we dissipated, and not let those poor spirits free?"

Percy was on the verge of tears, LP held his hand up. "We didn't know Lady Anna. We have only just discovered this. It might be peculiar to this world. If this is the first time, they have appeared on this, the original version Earth, so maybe this is particular to Earth."

"Bound spirits need magic. Access to the NET might get you close, but this is old magic." Gat said. "My grandmother knew the old magic. She would recognise what this was."

"If we can find a way of dispatching the Lantern Heads and freeing their spirits-"

"You won't always have the time to do so, but I applaud the sentiment." Marble responded.

"Well, Chief Inspector Marble, we will try."

"Pulling rank Miss Percival?"

"If I must."

"Dead is dead. Randolph may be a one-off. We haven't the time to experiment. Let's find Miss Curzon and Sammel, and then we can think about experimenting with the release of spirits from Lantern Heads."

"I agree with Marble." LP said. Percy gave him a look that could have turned the furry creature to stone. LP continued. "We are here to support Mr Waterfield in freeing his niece and the son of Apollyon. Rome wasn't built in a day."

Percy nodded reluctantly. "We will need to take the boy with us when we raid the Manufactory, he wants to fight them, and might recognise Sammel."

"Mr Marble, can you return to the Ministry, and hold the fort there for me until I send for you?"

Marble nodded. I would have liked the fellow with me for the assault, but now he had other duties, it seemed. I would speak with him about working with us again.

"I will prepare Dolph for battle, Uncle Robert. You will be busy enough. He needs me with him. We are the same."

It was my turn to reluctantly nod, I had come to the same conclusion, myself. Raven and now this boy were a bit special.

There was a knock at the door, and one of the Ministry of Mirrors staff popped her head around the door. She was a mousy girl of indeterminable age. I must admit, like her colleagues, your eyes seemed to fall off them as if they were the opposite of sticky.

"Excuse me, sirs, milady. Brigadier Lord Holden is here, as requested."

It was time for a war council.

Brigadier Lord Holden was as bright and breezy as ever. He could see an end to the occupation of his HQ in Lincolnshire, and was up for a military manoeuvre.

"So, Ainsworth doesn't have a clue?"

"No, sir." Claire answered on behalf of us all.

"And we have the correct warrants and agreements from the Attorney General, the Chief Lord Justice, and the House of Lords, Magnus?" This request was put to LP who had assumed a human appearance again, and he nodded."

"How many troops have you bought with you, Brigadier?" LP asked in return.

"I have brought a company of about a hundred. I hope that will be sufficient. I can bring others down if necessary?"

"Let's see how we go. Can I ask that you do not alert your fellows in the House of Lords that you are here. We will station you within the mirror overnight again."

Lord Holden nodded. "It is extremely comfortable inside the Ministry of Mirrors, I wouldn't mind a term as its Secretary. If you ever were unable to carry out your duties, or felt bored, Lord Magnus."

LP ignored him, so he continued eyebrows raised.

"So, when we raid the manufactory, half the company will go with you, ideally those handier with a sword. The other half will join the raid on the house, some two hours after, or when Ainsworth flees to attend the manufactory site."

"Thanks, Brigadier." Percy replied. She pointed to the layout of the factory site on a large blueprint. "The East and North sides are both bordered by the Thames, and so, can only be accessed easily by boat. If your soldiers embark and move up to the north side, then we will have made a hole in its wall for you to come through.

"Me, Gat, Raven, Dolph, and Robert will enter under cover of darkness, to look out for any dangers or defences we were not aware of. Although I will say your troops will be facing Lantern Heads."

"Yes, I have briefed them. Damned ugly beasts, we need to wipe them out." Brigadier Lord Holden snapped.

"I agree. So, then we identify whether the targets are on site, if not, Robert will transfer to Alexander's Castle with Raven and Dolph and meet up with you my Lord, and LP. Gat and I will secure the site, and possibly burn it down."

"I'd say." Brigadier Lord Holden nodded profusely. Then he said. "Right, I think I am well enough briefed." He reached into his left waistcoat pocket and brought out a lovely shiny gold pocket watch. He flicked open the lid and shut it carefully once he had read the time. "Time we got some rest. Deployment in minus eight hours."

The hours had flown by during the briefing. I was feeling tired. It was gone eleven thirty by the time I was ready for bed.

There was a knock at my door. It was Claire. She was dressed ready for bed, no doubt something quite revealing under her dressing gown.

I had mixed emotions. My body reacted to her presence in a carnal way, despite my Victorian soul.

Then Claire's face turned to Eliza's.

I shook my head to rid myself of the image of that murderess.

"Are you okay, Bobby?"

183

"Could you call me Robert, at least in company? It is a little over familiar." I asked.

Claire frowned. She dissipated and ended up manifesting on my bed. Naked. Claire had always been forward, but never this blatant. I felt uncomfortable.

"You don't really love me, do you, Robert? You haven't let go of Percy. I can see it when you look at her. Who is more beautiful, Robert?" She was pronouncing my name very succinctly.

Beware.

That was the voice of Apollyon. He hadn't linked for a while.

I looked at Claire, but she was now Eliza.

"Hello, Bobby. I've been talking with your niece. Pretty girl."

"How can you be here?"

"Charlotte re-took my rose jar. She let me go. Well almost, she has anchored me to one of these things."

Eliza dispersed and materialised as a Lantern Head. The rattle was despicable. Then she phased back again.

"Charlotte should not have let you go."

"Possibly not. I just need to find myself a new body to possess, and I'll be out of your hair. You used me, Isabelle used me. I will be my own woman again. You might want to go and look in on your Captain, Bobby. She is literally in pieces."

Eliza laughed, and then she vanished.

Horrified, I ran across the apartment living room, towards Claire's bedroom. Gat came out to see what the commotion was.

"Eliza is free." I shouted, bursting through Claire's door.

Captain Wright was in her bed, but it was blood-soaked. She had been decapitated. The Lantern Head assailant had just dissipated a moment before.

I screamed.

No.

Raven appeared, and beside her was Gat.

"Bobby. Come away."

"Wait." Raven said.

Claire's remains dissipated, but she did not re-materialise. Her spirit departed downwards.

Don't follow me, Bobby. My soul goes to the Earth. I love you.

I was too numb to cry.

And Eliza was free.

184

Chapter Twenty-Five
Assault on the Manufactory

My head was foggy for more than one reason the next morning. I was still reeling at the death of Claire, at the hands of Eliza. Percy had also fed me enough brandy to fell a horse.

I had no time to grieve, as we had to begin our offensive. That might seem stupid to one of the modern era, but we did tend to bottle things up, have a stiff upper lip, then get admitted to the asylum shortly after, in those days.

Percy, Gat, Candour, Raven, Dolph, and I were soon in the Hopelessness, emerging right by the factory. I couldn't feel any wards, this time. Not like Alexander's castle. It was either serendipity, or a trap.

Was the appearance of Eliza real? Was it Eliza, or had Charlotte released a spirit infused Lantern Head? Had the whole dastardly event been choreographed by this Gold Lord that Percy, LP, and the strange Chief Inspector Marble knew so much about?

We needed to get Charlotte and Sammel first, then it seemed, face the Gold Lord. More and more villains were being added to the piece. Ainsworth wouldn't let us take his factory down without reprisal. Nothing was going to be easy. And just what was Ainsworth's role in this?

Gone were the days where I would trap a spirit in a rose jar, or send it back to Hell. It was never going to be so simple again.

I couldn't get rid of the image of poor Claire. I could hear Eliza's words about Claire being in pieces, over, and over.

Percy squeezed my hand. I looked at her and nodded, trying to hold back the tears.

"Right, are we ready?" I said, pushing my emotions to one side.

"Let's kill Lantern Heads." Raven cried.

"Indeed." Gat and I said at the same time.

It was a dull dawn, overcast and muggy. Light was reduced because of the cloud cover; there was no hustle and bustle in the immediate vicinity, I then realised it was the Sabbath. Oh, how I had lost track of the days.

Gat, Dolph, Candour, and Raven left us. Dolph was carrying the bag of explosives, the eager-to-please young man had been shown how to rig them the previous evening, by Percy.

185

They would blow the North wall when asked, and then the half a company of the Strange Regiment would pour in.

Then LP and Lord Holden would be serving Lord Ainsworth the court warrant with Marble and his bobbies.

We had no time to lose. Percy and I moved over to the warehouse building on the south side. It looked well-constructed, unlike the timber frame buildings that riddled the City of London docks. This was steel frame and brick.

As we approached the factory, we could see a flight of steps that lead up to the offices over the main shop floor. It was common, during industrial times, to have elevated offices with the work going on below. The offices were normally high enough not to be disturbed by smoky, or cotton-filled atmospheres, particularly within textiles mills.

Percy signalled with her hands, opening and closing her fingers. I knew immediately what she meant. There was light emanating from the building, but it looked like it was on the ground floor.

At the top of the stairs Percy made a short work of the door, although the mechanism made a click that carried across the courtyard that felt like it could have woken the dead.

I heard Percy take a deep breath.

Then there was the howl of a dog in the distance. It was a large site, so the north wall was quite some way from where we were. Nevertheless, I felt the howl came from there. I hoped our friends were okay. Candour would protect them.

Then in the distance, more barking and the light of soul blades appearing.

"Come on, Bobby. We have to hope they are okay."

I nodded, but I didn't want to lose anyone else. I wanted to get Charlotte away from there, and try to cure her of her evil. I laugh now at how stupid that sounded. The same mistake I had made with Eliza.

We entered the building, and it was as quiet as the grave. Light from the factory played across the walls of the large office like the reflection of water on the walls of a lido on a sunny day.

The main office was surrounded on three sides by other smaller rooms. Opposite us was a door which opened up onto a viewing gallery.

We made our way out and immediately we were hit by a wall of sound. The factory was clearly sound-proofed. It was as if you had imprisoned a thousand banshees or sirens. The screaming and wailing was horrific.

"Dear goddess." I heard Percy say, even against the din.

The factory floor was full of biers. On each was an unanimated lantern head, except for the far row, which was empty, waiting for more creatures to be laid out. The empty biers were by a large crystalline machine. It had

186

many facets, and looked as it were made out of the largest ruby in all the world.

From the machine came what looked like strands of spider-web, iridescent and flickering. Yet I realised it was because we were so high and far away. They were clearly thin cables attached to helmets, which someone was putting onto the creatures heads.

That person was Charlotte. She was moving like an automaton, herself. Moving from one creature to the next. She would put a helmet on one of the bodies, it would wake up, then sit up and get off the bier. It would then walk to the back of the ruby machine, and disappear, clearly into one of the two massive storage hangars that sat behind the factory itself.

As Charlotte carried out her work, the machinery coughed and spluttered steam.

"Are those rose jars, Bobby?" Percy asked, pointing to a skip, of sorts, filled with the heart-shaped, glass storage vessels.

As we watched, a young boy was taking the jars from the skip and throwing them into the ruby machine. The screams and wails came from the machine. It was extracting the souls of the dead, and putting them into the lantern-head bodies.

I then realised the screams and wails were purely those of children.

"We need to get down there, Percy." I whispered.

Percy nodded solemnly.

"There's no sign of Sammel."

"I'm not joining up with Holden and LP unless I've at least tried to rescue Charlotte."

"You know it's probably too late, Bobby?"

"Boo." Said a deadpan voice behind us. I jumped, and Percy swore.

It was Raven.

"Why are you here?"

"Gat and Dolph are fine. Candour is tearing Lantern Heads apart, and taking children into the Hopelessness. I had to come, I smelt Charlotte's evil. There's the bitch." She said, pointing at my former niece.

"Do not kill her." I almost spat. Raven actually grinned at me.

"You are in control here, Uncle Robert. I will do as you say. Unless she threatens your life."

I nodded. For the first time I didn't trust that Raven would keep her word. I had a problem with trust, it seemed.

The viewing gallery peeled round to the right and, as we walked on, hidden by the shadows, we noticed a stairwell leading back down onto the shop floor.

We descended in silence. My heart went in my mouth when one of the wooden steps creaked and groaned under my weight. But the noise on the shop floor, of all those screaming, tortured souls, intensified as we walked on.

It seemed gloomier as we reached the bottom, the stairwell ended behind a stack of storage containers, all piled up higgeldy-piggeldy. I guessed they had the raw materials for the Lantern Heads inside. I wondered where they put the pig hearts in the things, and animated them with spiritual magic, surely the organs would atrophy before transplant if they were not stored in a cool, dry place.

Not that I thought of it as a transplant, the thought of putting the organs of another person or animal into a recipient was still very Mary Shelley, in my time.

Percy motioned to me that she would go left if I went right around the storage containers. Raven followed me. If I'm honest, I was pleased to have a Shield Maiden backing me up.

The containers were seven or eight across, and piled as high, I wonder the exact count of things that were inside them. These were the ingredients for an army, not a handful of weird assailants.

After the sixth row of containers, they were a little less packed together. Raven tapped me on the shoulder, and pointed upwards. She started to climb. I was about to call her back down when the noise in the factory stopped.

It was so quiet you could hear a pin drop.

Then I heard the rattling mantles of Lantern Heads behind me.

The cacophony started back up, and I jumped as I turned, just as the first one came at me. It's soul blade passed my left ear, and embedded itself in one of the containers. I kicked it away, and it took the sword with it. I could smell burning wood and something else. Flesh.

Then the other one came at me. It had two swords, and it looked a little different. It had more stripes on its peeler-like uniform. It was a bloody sergeant Lantern Head. Someone had a sick sense of humour, or there was a strange hierarchy.

The Swordmaster Caruso who had taken up temporary lodgings in the corner of my mind calculated the exact parry to stop the scissor cut that came at me. Then as I kicked that one away, I sidestepped and backhanded the other cutting into its torso. I wasn't sure I had time to skewer it through the heart, but I would try.

The Swordmaster in me was trying to calculate a route to the heart of the one with two swords. From the carnal way it attacked, I devised I would get it in three moves. Block, parry thrust. I got it.

It squealed and fell backwards, its lantern free of magical protection smashed and the spirit of a child emerged. I briefly stepped into the Hopelessness.

It was a young girl. She looked ancient, yet so young.

"Do you understand me?"

She nodded as her form became more solid.

"I will send others here. Look after them, and tell them to wait."

Candour, can you get here to protect the young ones?

Ancient ones, you mean. I will send him for they need angelic company. Some of these children have been dead hundreds of years. Find my son though, human.

I will.

I stepped out of the Hopelessness, on to one of the boxes. I guessed I could assail the other from up there. I jumped down, and the second Lantern Head turned. It started to spawn. The other one, the sergeant, hadn't done so.

I had surprise on my side, and I skewered it. Or rather, the Swordmaster in my mind did.

It fell, but its lantern didn't smash, so I stamped down on it, oblivious to the fact I might cut myself. Adrenaline was pumping.

The child spirit circled above my head like a beautiful white corona before moving to the Hopelessness.

Then there was a massive explosion that lit up the windows. Dolph and Gat had clearly blown down the North Wall.

The factory silenced once more. I could hear the sound of soul blade on soul blade. Raven and Percy had clearly engaged the enemy.

I made my way past the boxes to be met with an incredible sight. A frightening sight.

Raven and Percy were engaged with six Lantern Heads off to my right. To my left, and from behind the ruby crystal machine, poured more and more Lantern Heads. One after the other. We really needed those soldiers here.

I stabbed one of the creatures from behind. It fell, and its lantern smashed. A child spirit was released.

Percy and Raven were dispatching the things as quick as they could, but would soon be overrun.

"Get Charlotte." A voice came from behind me.

Gat and Dolph had now joined us, and pulled their swords as I charged, I made my way through row upon row of biers that had the Lantern Heads upon them.

I looked up at Charlotte.

She looked female, and I don't mean that disrespectfully. The male line of her jaw was gone. Where she once had a flat chest, a bosom filled her bodice. She had transformed. She had clearly used Avery's soul to effect the change.

She was in a trance. The power of the machine was actually flowing through her, then into the helmet she had been putting on the Lantern Heads to reanimate them.

She was also flickering. Like a spirit. As the power was going through her.

Why?

I surveyed the scene. There was a large cable coming into the ruby machine. It carried electricity. Where the cable met the wooden base, it crackled. Above that was a large lever that looked like it needed two hands to operate, it was like a railway signal switch .

I needed to turn it off.

So, I set off at pace. I ran through the biers towards that infernal machine. The hairs on my head, neck, and hands were rising because of the power in the air. It was making me dizzy.

The machine was on a tiered wooden dais, it was like a small South American ziggurat, but with another large crystalline feature atop it. That ruby pulsed quicker as I neared it.

I then saw the boy who had been throwing rose jars into the machine looking at me fearfully. He was no more than nine or so. He was dressed in dirty clothes, filthy, in his own muck, and chained to the machine.

I pulled my sword, and he screamed, covering his face with his arms, but all I did was sever his chains as near to his body as possible.

"Run as fast as you can. Get away from here, your life depends upon it."

He ran as best he could, he probably hadn't walked further than a chains length in an age. At least he was alive.

I took a look at the large wooden container that held the rose jars. There were still hundreds of the subtly glowing heart or tear-shaped bottles inside. All made by the same few glass blowers. No doubt they'd had a recent dividend with all the demand for their goods.

I would have to recover these spirits at some point later.

I ran up the steps of the dais at the back of the machine, to where there was a control panel next to the big switch. There were all sorts of dials and gauges, like something out of a Jules Verne novel.

I just grasped the handle of the big switch. Depressed the trigger and pulled the lever.

The machine was just about to start up again, but as I pulled the switch, the dynamo inside, that was wailing upwards, decreased in pitch.

I could hear again. I could also hear the charge of the soldiers who I could see coming down the stairs. The doors on the other side of the factory blew in. The percussion rocked me.

Not as much as the back-handed slap from Charlotte.

I was thrown back into the ruby machine's control panel. It damn well knocked the wind out of me. But I recovered.

"Charlotte. It's me, Uncle Robert."

She was in a total daze, and not totally corporeal. I reached for her, but she knocked my hand back. Her strength was amazing. She was obviously not fully alive.

"You should have stayed away, Uncle." Charlotte said, in a pleading voice. Then it changed, and she said. "Stupid man, I am going to enjoy killing you."

To be honest, I am rather good, usually, at judging situations, even very strange ones. Charlotte presenting like this was making me wonder. Had I guessed the situation correctly?

This was Charlotte's spirit, but not her corporeal form.

"You aren't Charlotte. Where is her body?" I pulled my soul blade.

The thing that looked like Charlotte laughed. "You silly man, Uncle Robert. You think you know what is going on. Yet, you do not. You are a narrow-minded fool."

I was even more surprised when Candour appeared next to me.

"Celestial. Have you come to play?"

"Robert. I need to kill this."

"What is it? I asked."

The Charlotte-thing laughed. "I *am* your niece, but not all of her, and not all of me. A nice hybrid. I improved her. She's dead now, but I made her a girl. Finally. It was all she wanted. I gave it to her because she begged, then I took hold of her."

"What are you?" I screamed at it.

"It is a splinter of another being." Candour said.

The Charlotte-thing laughed, it was unhinged, a little past insane.

"Cut the riddles, Candour." I said.

"I do not know…" Candour replied.

"It is the Gold Lord." Apollyon said. Yet it wasn't from inside my head.

I looked left, and Candour was changing into a cloven beast, the head and torso of a man, from his waist downwards he was a hooved creature. He flickered once between this form and a being of the purest white light. This was Apollyon in his truest guise.

"Just a fallen angel, Robert. I am no more evil than you. Someone has to keep the demons in order. I just broke the rules."

Apollyon pushed out a hand, and Charlotte flew backwards.

"This isn't all of me, Robert. Just a part. Candour has sacrificed himself to become me for a short time. I will honour him. I need to separate the Gold Lord splinter from your niece, and then you need to take her to the Hopelessness. Candour has made sure your child spirits are safe, and he has protected them all with a ward. It is his final act. He has given his angelic energy to protect all of the children."

"What do you mean, he has sacrificed himself?"

"You will see. It is the only way."

191

Charlotte pulled a soul blade, and came at us. Candour/Apollyon pushed me out of the way.

The soul blade came crashing down towards Candour/Apollyon's head. He just caught the blade with two flat palms. Smoke, and the smell of cooking flesh filled the air. Candour/Apollyon screamed.

Apollyon snapped that weapon of purest energy. Then he punched Charlotte. Hard.

"Remember, this is not your niece, just part of her spirit in one of those pig-controlled bodies."

I realised then Charlotte hadn't got the woman's figure she had always wanted. I felt sad, then realised she hadn't got her life anymore either. Like Avery. Yet she was so utterly feminine, not like a Lantern Head.

Candour/Apollyon punched it again to knock it back.

"Don't grieve now, Robert. There will be plenty of time during your long life." Candour/Apollyon said, as Charlotte came at him again.

He just batted her aside.

The Charlotte-thing, laughed, and a golden glow surrounded her. She seemed to be effused with more power.

The Charlotte-thing came at Candour/Apollyon more slowly. Her head cocked to one side, like an inquisitive puppy. Her hands grew longer. Talon-like nails grew from those withering appendages. Her face morphed and became, at first, oblong, then square-ish, and then lantern-shaped.

Finally, a mouth appeared in the front-facing glass.

"Interesting match, Apollyon. The King of Hell versus the King of Gold, King of the Hopelessness."

The Gold Lord. King of the Hopelessness?

"Did you think you were lord of my domain? The Hopelessness was mine. I was its lord, for a time. Until today, when I become myself once more."

"Robert is the Veil Lord. He is the current Keeper of Purgatory?" Candour/Apollyon screamed.

"I will squash him, Apollyon. After I make you scream. I can kill angels you know. I'm going to kill you for certain." The Charlotte-thing screamed.

Apollyon screamed in anger back at her.

The Lantern-headed Charlotte-thing clapped its hands together, and a thread of pure golden energy shot into Candour/ Apollyon. This time his scream was one of pain.

"Pull it into the Hopelessness. If you have all of the Veil Lord's powers, you will be able to. Step through. Pull on the threads. You should see both of us from there."

I stepped through the veil. I could then see the threads of an angel. Apollyon's were bright white, and that surprised me. There was no evil at all about him. He had yellow threads of purpose, and the green thread of his life spurred off into the distance, to connect with the earth. The Gold Lord had a twisted cable, black as coal. In the distance, I could make out that it was connected to a much thicker tree trunk of a cable which was probably the Gold Lord himself. This was a fragment after all.

Use the Net. Connect to Gaia. We are her children. All of us. Except him. He comes from elsewhere. From the future of an evil world, back to haunt her.

I hadn't given the arm patch a second thought. However, as I linked to it, I became aware of another.

Yes. Good idea. Bring Gat. He will help.

Gat. I thought. Come to me.

And my friend appeared.

"Thank goddess for that, I was sick of killing Lantern-thingies."

"Pull on the net. Aim it at the black thread." I said.

We both drew Gaia's power, and concentrated. Gat was surrounded in a green glow, much like the power that surrounded Claire when she dissipated. Then I felt Gaia's anger at the remembrance of the death of one of her tree spirits.

"Aim." I said. "Now."

We poured power into that black thread, and it radiated outwards towards the thick, black trunk. Wherever the Gold Lord was, he would be hurting.

You can step away Robert. Come for Charlotte. Gat, you can continue.

Gat nodded at me, understanding what Apollyon meant, and I walked into the real word.

The thing that was part Gold Lord, part pig, and part Charlotte, was screaming. A gold lantern atop its shoulders, now.

I couldn't get near the fighting pair. Blow after blow came from Apollyon. The Gold Lantern just took them. It moved backwards, down the steps of the dais. I could see over its shoulder, that Raven and Percy were there. They had disengaged, to come and see what was happening. Over my left soldier, the noise of the Strange Regiment was loud as they engaged with more of the creatures.

Blow after blow, Candour/Apollyon rained down. He was beating the thing into submission. He knocked it to the ground. He then watched it as it sprawled in the dust.

Percy, by now, had reached me, and she put a hand on my arm. I looked at her quickly, and gave a worried smile, but couldn't pull my gaze away from the fight.

"You are done for, fragment. Leave. I am coming after my son. If you get in my way, Gold Lord, or whatever you are called, I will kill you."

The creature held up two normal-ish hands in supplication. It stood upon wobbly legs. Apollyon followed its movement intently. No doubt to knock it down again if it attacked.

193

It began to vanish. The Gold Lantern cracked, and the spirit of Charlotte moved towards me.

I didn't kill anyone, Uncle. It wasn't me, it was...

I cut her off. *Go, I will be with you soon.*

The Gold Lantern was fading.

Candour/Apollyon walked towards it.

I noticed that one hand had not faded. A hand that was quickly growing into a claw.

"Apollyon!" I shouted.

With a fading laugh, the Gold Lord skewered the Apollyon avatar that had been Candour.

It disappeared as Apollyon fell to his knees.

Now you know what I mean about Candour's sacrifice, Robert. I will not help you further, until I have my boy. I hoped to save him with you, but this was Candour's last battle. And his first.

Then the body that had been Candour/Apollyon started to flake away, like the ash of a well-burned fire on the wind.

I immediately stepped into the hopelessness and towards Charlotte. She was solidifying. Becoming opaque.

She was still in a feminine form. She would live again like Dolph if I had anything to do with it.

"I am becoming whole again, Uncle. How is that?"

I shook my head. I didn't understand it, myself. Then I realised I had willed it, with the power of Gaia.

"Avery." She screamed. "Walter."

Two tears in the Hopelessness opened to yet another place. Two threads of energy came through. They started to solidify.

"Uncle," Charlotte said, screaming with pain. "The Gold Lord. He took me when I was young. All that time, I fought with him in my mind. I am sorry for killing Walter. He made me do it. Yet now I make my amends."

The streams of light burned like magnesium in water. Avery, from his rose jar, and Walter, back from visiting his Lizzie, appeared slowly, outlines at first, and then more solid. Just as Charlotte was coming back.

I pulled on the NET. I added Gaia's power.

LET THEM LIVE!

I spoke with Gaia's voice. Then suddenly I was myself again.

"Wall lead the twins back home. Ask Waite to let you through the veil."

Charlotte nodded and came towards me. She kissed my cheek. She had insubstantial tears on her cheeks. She went over and grabbed the hands of the materialising pair, one her brother, one my friend.

"What is happening?" Gat asked joining me.

194

"I used some of Gaia's power to bring Avery and Walter back. I've now got to go and get Sammel."

Gat walked towards me, and clasped my hand. "Whatever I can do."

I nodded.

"Apollyon's avatar Candour is dead. It is up to us to free Sammel. He must be at Alexander's Castle."

I stepped us out of the Hopelessness, towards a rendezvous with our brave-heart friends.

Chapter Twenty- Six
Finding Sammel

The warehouse smelt of death.

Fortunately, many child spirits had been released, and many of the Lantern Heads had dissipated. We had saved many souls, and that was pleasing.

Percy was tired, I could see it upon her face as Gat and I materialised. Holden's soldiers were being organised by a Captain Wallis, a man of mixed Indian and British heritage, a handsome lad of proud bearing. Wallis was making sure all the Lantern Head corpses that remained were being burned. He also had orders to torch the warehouse as soon as we were all clear, the Lantern Head making machinery, too, there was a fear it might fall into the wrong hands.

I would have like to have studied it, and Gat said so, too, but there was too much to be done.

Dolph was standing wide-eyed at the newly blown-through ground floor entrance to the factory. Raven was with him, he looked like he'd had a fright. Well, we all had. He'd been dead since the day before and had, on the day of his re-birth, learned to blow massive holes in things with dynamite.

My mind was struggling to keep up with the eventualities. Claire was dead, Candour was dead. Although Charlotte, Avery, and Walter may well have returned to the land of the living, at that time, I wasn't sure I believed it to be true, in that haze.

Gat hugged me as soon as we appeared from the beyond. I hugged him back, gratefully, yet slightly uncomfortable in the presence of so many others.

"I don't think it is over, my friend." I said, pulling away.

We were led outside the factory, and I ended up accepting a cup of tea from a young-looking soldier with a beaky nose who looked a little green around his ears, like Claire had.

"At least we know that Ainsworth will have the boy at Alexander's Castle, where else would the Gold Lord have kept him?"

I nodded. It seemed that way.

"The Gold Lord must have taken control of Ainsworth, too. There could be no other explanation." Percy said, joining us. Her normally immaculate, if tomboyish, look was suffering somewhat with her hair coming out of place, breeches cut in many places, not to mention a nasty gash on her arms that had been hastily bandaged by one of the soldiers.

"How are you, Bobby?"

"I've had better days."

"But at least you have Charlotte and Avery's spirits back. Charlotte's memories were lies, Bobby, take solace in that. The Gold Lord must have rearranged them."

"Not all of your memories, though." I said before thinking.

Percy looked at the ground, and quietly said, "No."

"Percy, I'm sorry. I'm just so…"

"Tired, grieving? I am not surprised. And we haven't finished."

"Ainsworth didn't come here. He surely has stayed at the Castle." Gat said.

"He was tipped off." I said. "I had my suspicions, but I wanted things to play out rather than voice them."

Percy nodded.

You need to get me my Sammel, Waterfield.

Apollyon. He seemed vexed. It must have been the loss of his avatar.

"Raven are you ready? Dolph?" I asked.

The young/old Shield Maiden nodded and so did the boy. He was scared out of his wits but still very brave.

I looked at Percy and Gat. "Ready, my friends?"

They nodded. I got them all to hold hands, while I caught on the end of the chain. Then I stepped up into the Hopelessness. Then I took us to Alexander's Castle and stepped us out of that realm, into the land of the living, at the precise location LP had told us to rendezvous - in the gated recreation field. It was a stone's throw away from the castle.

The sky was grey over this part of London. The air was thick and heady. It felt like there was going to be a thunderstorm. That was a portent of doom, if ever I saw one.

LP stepped out of one of his blue coruscating portals. He was in his Lord Magnus form. Brigadier Lord Holden was with him.

"My boys did the trick then, what?" The old soldier said, proudly.

"Brave men. I would fight with them again, Brigadier." This was Raven. She wasn't the dark shadow anymore, her experiences over the last ten days, or so, had changed her.

"Excellent. The other half are scattered, ready to engage as and when *we* are ready.

There is something amiss. I am blocked from seeing.

Apollyon seemed nervous. Was that why he was snappy earlier? All the other times he had communicated with me had been matter of fact. Maybe he was concerned for his son?

Let's see how we get on when we get into the Castle grounds.

197

"We tried to deliver the warrant, but it seems Lord Ainsworth has been tipped off. He would not let us in. Sensibly, he didn't make for the manufactory. He must have known it was a coordinated attack." LP said, in his smelly way.

Robert. This is Large Pockets. There is someone among us who is feeding Lord Ainsworth information, it would seem.

Is Ainsworth the Gold Lord?

It certainly seems that way. I have blocked Apollyon. It is taking all the energy I can muster, but we cannot have him interfering, at the moment, not until we have breached the walls. Something feels wrong. I need to capture the Gold Lord. Death doesn't hold him. He will just jump to another body.

Okay. We get in. Find out where Sammel is, get him away, and to Apollyon. Then we engage the Gold Lord. It may not be as simple as that.

It will not. Humphrey always has a trick up his sleeve. Although it seems he is no longer Humphrey Mortimer, but Lord Ainsworth. I will remain here with Lord Holden, and the back-up troops. I will keep this link open.

I want Gat to stay with you, LP, as protection. He can call on the NET.

I am able to protect myself, Robert.

I know, but strength in numbers. Trust me, LP.

The exchange was over in milliseconds, and LP, in his human disguise form, nodded at me.

"Are we ready, Minister? We have orders from the Attorney General to carry out."

"Gat, you are to stay with the Minister. Percy, Raven, and Dolph with me."

Gat nodded, but I sensed reluctance. I smiled at him. I tried to convey that I needed someone on the outside, should it all go toes up and we needed rescuing.

"Captain Davies." Brigadier Lord Holden called.

A soldier appeared out of the trees, to our left. "Sir."

"Blow the gates. We have work to do."

LP moved over to Percy, Gat, and I. He pulled us to one side as Holden barked orders. "I will open a portal. I have got around the ward-block. Robert, the block to *your* ability to use the Hopelessness in this *vicinity* is not coming from the castle-wards. I can feel a powerful being stopping you from going in."

"Sammel?"

"Possibly, but probably the Gold Lord."

"Yet, we got in the warehouse, and the factory buildings." Percy said.

"Does Sammel not want us to rescue him?"

I looked at Gat. I thought, at the time, he had hit the nail on the head.

"Has the Gold Lord helped Sammel to get away?" Percy followed up.

I could feel the presence of Apollyon back, so I put my thoughts away. As you know, I can compartmentalise some of my thoughts rather well. That was when it began. A gift from LP, it seemed.

LP opened up a portal. Percy, Raven, even Dolph had pulled a soul blade. Raven must have given the boy one of hers. The boy's confidence had lifted. I hoped we could cope until the backup arrived. We stepped through. The portal fizzed shut.

Thunder cracked the sky and I could feel the pressure of the atmospherics in my sinuses. Spots of rain began to fall. Rain would make the assault more difficult. Although it would also confuse the Hell hounds, and hopefully the Lantern Heads.

We headed for the main house. There was no reason to skirt in the shadows. We engaged no one at all. We made it to the extended Tudor mansion, and we skirted around to its rear.

"I can feel him." Dolph said. "I remember what he felt like."

The boy is right, Robert, he is in this building. Apollyon sent.

I nodded to Dolph, and we entered the back of the house via the small door set in a larger gate that probably would normally be for tradesmen. The house, not really a castle, at all, was formed about a courtyard. It was and still is huge, mind you.

We shut the gate behind us.

Then there was another much louder bang. It wasn't thunder, this time, it was the gate house being breached.

That was when the dogs started to bark.

The gravelled courtyard must have been over a hundred yards across, probably larger than a football pitch, or the Oval cricket ground.

In the distance through the darkness and the burgeoning rain we could see the glowing red eyes of the Hell hounds.

"Raven, we will hold off the dogs. I was suddenly linked once more to Apollyon. *Where is Sammel*?

He is in the Northwest Tower.

I looked a Dolph, who pointed to the very spot. It was diagonally across from where we were standing, in the middle of the southern wall.

The dogs were coming. Their baying was so deep, it was horrible. I could hear them loping through the rain.

"Raven, are you ready?"

"Yes, Robert."

"Percy. Dolph. Run."

I made myself big to attract the dogs, and try to distract them from Percy and Dolph. Hopefully, the rain would cover their scents.

Raven had engaged the first dog. As I have said more than once, she was incredible to watch in battle. She had thrown a knife, then followed up with a sweeping downward cut of her soul blade.

199

Its fellow changed course towards her, instead of me, and leapt.

I couldn't get purchase on the cobbles, I could only watch in slow motion as it tore at Raven, I could only hit it with just a glancing blow. It whelped and skirted away. I heard further barking. And that was not all. Lantern Heads were appearing, too.

Raven went down on one knee.

The dog then came at me. It jumped awkwardly, as it was injured. It was a Hell Hound, and they rarely went down it seemed, unless killed outright. It hit me in the chest, and knocked me down. It came at my throat, but I just managed to hold it at bay with my sword. I could feel its breath as it snarled. It would have torn out my throat if Raven hadn't skewered it, at that point.

Raven was limping, but she helped me get upright.

We turned, and faced the Lantern Heads. There were twenty, or more, although they were spawning all the time.

Use Gaia's power. Apollyon said. *My ward protects the little ones.*

I was wary of using the power. I'd had no training like Gat. Then I felt it come to me. I decided that I would probably be better off facing the creatures on my own terms, on my own ground.

Good idea.

I pulled on Gaia's power. I sent the power out from myself. I linked with every Lantern Head in the place. There were very few others, I couldn't sense any in the buildings.

Then I heard the screams, felt the fear of the child spirits bound up in those things. The merciless pig brains wanting to constantly feed.

"I'll save you." I said. It was the most certain thing I had ever said.

I then pulled all those creatures and Raven into the Hopelessness.

I could now see the cords of oily blackness that linked them all. Gaia's power didn't work so well there, so I just mastered my own domain.

If the Gold Lord had been the temporary guardian of this realm, in the past, he was in control no longer. I had been master here since I was a seven year old boy.

The question was why? But I didn't have the time to cogitate.

I seized all the black cords that linked those creatures together. Then I pulled.

I struggled to make purchase, at first, as the things were as slippery in this domain as the real world.

Raven had other ideas. She was bleeding from the bite to her right upper leg, but she was able to cut through those black cords. She separated the nearest Lantern Head from its link. Just as the others came at her.

Her victim stopped. Its lantern shattered, spraying glass in our direction. Raven went down.

I had purchase, so I pulled.

I pulled all those cords with the help of Gaia. I pulled as hard as I could with my mind, like when I thrust away evil spirits there. I was soon straining as if I was trying to physically pull them.

My wrist, where what Gat called the NET imprint, became burning hot. I screamed.

But I also pulled harder on the power.

The cords split like snapped elastic bands. One after the other.

Lanterns popped and shattered, one after the other, in a staccato cacophony. The pigs screamed, the child spirits felt elated.

Each of those evil, pig-controlled forms started to fall away as they dissipated. Turning to ash. From each shattered lantern the child spirits coalesced above my head.

And there were others. I must have freed all the trapped spirits in all the Lantern Heads all over London.

Calm settled over the Hopelessness as children appeared all around us. There must have been hundreds, maybe a thousand.

There was one distant scream left. It was coming from the end of the large pustulating black cord the Lantern Heads had been joined to.

There is something wrong. Follow the cord, Robert. Raven will be well.

I traced that thick, pus-filled cord out of the Hopelessness. Back into the real world. Back to the Recreation Field.

I stepped out.

Lord Holden had a sword raised.

Gat looked at me with one last sad parting glance as the Brigadier, or rather the Gold Lord, took Gat's head from his shoulders.

Another of my friends was dead.

Chapter Twenty-Seven
Sammel

Brigadier Lord Holden was laughing.

Large Pockets was down, also dead, by the looks of it.

The rest of the Strange Regiment company, too. Holden, it seemed, had killed them all before they had been able to enter the grounds of Alexander's Castle.

Holden's skin shimmered.

"You are a tricky fucker, Waterfield." Holden said, breathing heavily.

I really hoped Gat had given him a good fight.

Holden was now surrounded by a diffused glow. "Clever trick, with the Lantern Heads. I'll have to wring that out of your devious little head. There's more of them on other versions of Earth; I'll get me some more. There are billions of dead children out there, too. An almost endless supply."

"I will end you." I spat.

"Ha. I am made of energy. Many more suited to killing have tried."

He was certainly sure of himself.

I pulled my soul blade and approached him. He did likewise, and caught my downward thrust.

"I don't have a little voice inside my head controlling my moves, you fucking cheat."

Despite my predicament I winced at his repeated use of foul language.

"What are you?" I said.

"Ha. Come now Bobby dazzler. Perfume Factory Large Pockets has told you. More interestingly, do you know how he got that name?"

"I want to know about you."

"His olfactory translation unit fused on his first diplomatic mission to earth. That was how his name translated into Anglo Saxon, hundreds of years later. King Alfred shit his breeches when he first saw the blue furry bastard."

Such a vile creature, in many ways.

"I'm an Oosian. I am a superior being. I ascended from the physical plane millions of years in your past. I am the scourge of the Zenobarts." He flicked an effete hand at the body of LP.

"I can wear bodies like clothes from a wardrobe. I have worn Holden's on and off for a few hours, and the lovely Charlotte's before that. What a confused creature she was. They usually die when I discard them, but Charlotte's spirit was too strong. So, I put her soul in one of those pig homunculi. Tragic. Oink-oink."

"You are an evil creature." I said, launching another attack. He blocked me, and I all but wheeled away before he did me an injury.

"I lived in your house hiding in Charlotte's mind for years. I watched. I know your secrets. I let Eliza out. She will be coming for you soon. I just know it. I have found out about Isabelle. I will be having a conversation with that witch soon. What fun we will have. Side by side. Isabelle and I."

"I will save Eliza, and Isabelle will betray you. She will want you to be one of her Magpie's." I was apoplectic.

"Isabelle's magic carves the future. Be warned. That witch will cause the Earth's downfall. I have seen it. Her spawn will ravage the Parallel. I will one day be her disciple – yes, sounds great. For now, I will lead. The deaths I can lay at her feet will make her a goddess."

That last sentence was said with supplication, as he muttered his nonsense. This creature was as mad as a box of frogs, as you would say, these days.

"You would have to live in order to do such things."

"I am pure energy. I am the stuff of the universe. Energy cannot be destroyed. Just transferred. Imagine my power when I take over the body of the Nephilim."

Sammel.

Kill him.

"Ooh. Is that the King of Hell on the line? Morning Father of Lucifer, Shaitan, Apollyon. Whatever fucking name you have at the moment. Do you know, I've eaten scarier Kings of Hell for breakfast and shat out their horns. I'm going to take your little son, invade him, and carve out his mind. I *will* have his powers."

The Gold Lord came at me with his sword, like a thing possessed. I stepped to one side, it was amazing I had got away unscathed. I cut across his back, and he shrieked.

Suddenly, I felt very peculiar. It was like I was feeding from the well of Gaia again, but judging by the different type of pain, that source of power was gone for now. This power was different.

It's all I can give.

Thank you, Apollyon.

I charged at the Gold Lord, but he managed to jump over me. Now, that was a trick I'd like to learn.

"Like the gymnastics? I've just broken Holden's ankles and he's screaming like an injured bitch inside. Oh, didn't I say? They die when I leave them. Not when I go in. Ha-ha."

203

I held up a hand, and fire shot from it. I felt no heat, no searing pain, just strength. If Apollyon had this power, why did he not rule over the world?

Because I am a man of honour. But if my boy is hurt, I will destroy you all. Ending with you, Robert.

Why is Sammel so important?

He carries the Goddess Seed.

What?

He will beget the new Goddess. Heaven will sing.

What happened to the old God?

He is out there, somewhere. A little bored. She will be his successor.

"When I take over Sammel's body I will sleep with a nice specimen, and then, when my daughter is of age to use her powers, I will invade her, too. You know I can hear you, Apollyon."

Kill the abomination.

The fire of Hell shot from my hands, and it hit the Oosian Gold Lord, formerly Brigadier Lord Holden, in the chest. His body started to burn, or at least Holden's clothes did.

The Oosian screamed. But it was laughing too.

"You think a little fire from Hell can take me down? You foolish things. Apollyon, I am disappointed. When I am Goddess, you will be the first redundancy."

My hand shot out of its own accord. The fire spat from it. Then I holstered my soul blade, and my other arm extended. Fire shot from it also.

The heat consumed the Gold Lord. He was still laughing like the last inmate of the last asylum at the end of time.

Then his noise stopped, and I could hear burning bones cracking.

So sorry, Lord Holden.

He was dead already, Apollyon replied.

The noise was sickening, the smell of burning flesh worse. The pillar of fire roared like a cremation furnace. It didn't last long. The body of Brigadier Lord Holden was nothing more than a pile of fatty ash in seconds, such was the heat of that balefire.

Then it was over. The ash that flew on the post-thunder breeze was all that was left of the Gold Lord. I looked around me. Death and destruction.

The noise of a portal opened up, and Marble appeared.

"Robert, are you okay? Something was blocking me coming… Oh my god, LP."

Marble rushed to the furry giant's side. It seemed in death the creature had reverted to his natural form. I hadn't noticed in the melee.

"Thank god. He's alive. I'll need to get him back to the Ministry."

"I can give you some help."

"I'd rather you helped Percy. My son would never forgive me if his wife died."

"You are Percy's father-in-law? Arthur's father?

He nodded.

Find my son.

"I'll see you soon, Marble. We need to talk."

The man was busy, though, trying to care for his employer. I strode towards the hole in the wall.

The streets were bizarrely deserted. I looked up. The sky was clearing, but it was a strange kind of blue. I could see a flickering film of magic or some protective barrier. Had LP kept the outside world out?

It's the work of the Gold Lord.

Yet surely if he is dead, then....

The Oosian isn't dead. He is going after Sammel.

LP appeared beside me. I jumped. I'd seen it happen with Percy, so it shouldn't have been a surprise.

"Better?" I asked, sort of nonchalantly.

"It took a few weeks but yes. Sorry about Gat. I couldn't stop The Gold Lord in time. I tried."

"I have many to mourn. Yet I do not have the time."

LP put his hand on my shoulder. I suddenly felt calmer. Focused.

"Have you been keeping my grief at bay?" I thought of the times he had touched me on my arm. I had always felt calm in his presence after those moments.

LP nodded. "You were needed. We needed you focused. I am sorry."

I nodded in acceptance. God only knows I would pay for the postponement of my sorrow.

Make haste. If he gets my son. I will destroy this world.

I started to run, and LP kept pace beside me. His recuperation must have been lengthy, or his race were fast healers.

We made our way thought the grounds to the tower.

LP waved a hand, and a portal opened up. We stepped through into a grand hallway, at the bottom of a flight of stairs.

We raced up the stairs, to where the wide tower intersected the first floor.

"No!" Came a scream. That was Dolph's voice.

We dashed through the corridor which led to a large circular room.

There, I saw Sammel for the first time.

Save my son.

Sammel looked about twenty. A tall muscular boy. He was naked, and tied to a pillar. He had been tortured, judging by the state of him, and for a very long time.

We took in the scene, LP and me.

Percy was trying to hold the Gold Lord at bay. He was Lord Ainsworth, now.

Dolph was on the ground. His soul blade was fizzing off to one side. Raven was circling the creature in his new form.

"I will engage it. You free the boy." LP said, and he pulled the biggest soul blade I had seen. It was like a broad sword. It looked mighty in his hands.

"Oh shit. You didn't die, blue bollocks." The Gold Lord said. He knocked Percy's sword out of her hand, and backhanded her. Percy was thrown, but she managed to land well, balancing herself.

I ran towards Sammel. He was barely conscious.

Touch his head. My interaction is now limited. I grow weak. I will give him the last of my strength.

I did so, and the boys eyes fluttered.

"Help. Me." Sammel murmured.

"That is what I am here for."

Then I felt an almighty force pick me up and throw me against the nearest wall.

I couldn't move. The pain, but moreover, a force was holding me there. I was sure it wasn't the Gold Lord.

As I watched, the Gold Lord was fighting with LP and holding the blue fellow at bay with one hand. The other was pointing towards Sammel. Energy shot from that hand connecting with the boy.

"That energy would have killed you." Sammel said. "However, it has revived me."

His smile was angelic. Which is ironic, as that was exactly what he was. Well, fifty percent of him.

Then he stepped out of his body.

He wasn't a thing of energy, like the Gold Lord. He was a thing of blue heavenly fire, yet recognisable as Sammel.

The Gold Lord disengaged with LP, then punched the Zenobart. LP went down. Raven engaged again, and he disarmed her, then she was also slapped aside.

"You are going to have to do better than that. Oh, and guess what I did? I found a box of Lantern Heads I'd left in a safe place."

A portal opened up in the air and a dozen or more of the horrible creatures appeared, each pulling their soul blades.

Then everyone stopped.

They didn't merely stand still, time itself had paused.

"There's one of you with your strange powers, Oosian. But there's two of us with a celestial gift.

Then Sammel dragged me and the Gold Lord into the Hopelessness.

Strangely I relaxed. This was my domain.

Sammel turned to me. "We need to finish it."

The Gold Lord was giggling, amused by something.

There he stood in the Hopelessness, a thing of energy and flesh. He was no different from any of us. Well, except for the large, evil-looking cord that stretched from him, and off into the distance.

"I knew your mother, Sammel. I took this realm from Evelyn . I invaded her, and took the Hopelessness. The bitch fought back though, before I killed her, she handed this place to Waterfield's people." Again, he giggled like the last resident of Bedlam.

I noticed Sammel take a step back. His confidence had waned.

"What do you mean, alien?" Sammel said, confidently.

The Gold Lord laughed hysterically. "This is where the story really twists, Robert. Sammel, you've got a twin brother."

The Gold Lord held out a hand. A portal opened and a boy identical to Sammel fell through.

No. Apollyon hissed.

The Gold Lord burned away the shell of Lord Ainsworth. He became a figure of burnished metal, like Midas of the myths. He then stepped into Sammel's twin.

"No, this is all deception, Robert. The prophecy." Sammel whispered.

"When an angel and Eve's sister pair, the child begat will pour forth a goddess. And she will destroy eternity."

"It's not you though, Sammy. Their first born twin was called Mantus. I've just devoured him. Sammy, I am now your older brother. Well, I've just ate your oldest brother. Ha! He has been hidden from you and your father for thousands of years. I once invaded a woman called Lilith, she told me of all the living Nephilim."

No.

His power will be formidable. We may not survive.

"You still have me and Robert, father," Sammel said.

207

Chapter Twenty-Eight
The Prince of Lies

The Gold Lord was laughing.

"Lie upon lie upon lie. Neatly woven to bait you, Apollyon. I'm the heir to Hell. Not Sammel"

He gave a little dance.

Sammel. I am sorry.

"Which son was it you wanted to rescue? Your true heir, or the goody two shoes, over there? He doesn't even have any horns. Well, apart from the one between his legs. I wish he'd put it away. You see, the power of a Nephilim is huge, they can kill angels. And, when you add the power of a Nephilim and an Oosian together..."

You do not have to do this.

"Listen to Mantus, Apollyon."

Another keening voice arrived in our heads.

Did you check daddy? Did you look for me, like you looked for Sammel? No. And he wasn't gone as long. Mother took me as her reward for giving you a son. She lied about me being born. Then when she was killed Lillith tortured me for my power, experimented on me. She tried to wring the god seed out of me, tried to make me impregnate her. She wanted to control the Goddess. You abandoned me to her."

Enough.

There was a strange noise, almost as if reality were ripping.

Apollyon appeared.

Reader, he had come in person. I could feel his godly power, it was ancient. Beautiful, but terrifying. He had abandoned Hell.

The Gold Lord must have felt the same, but he just laughed.

"Oh Apollyon, what have you done, you can't return. Hell will open now, you silly billy. Ha, but now I've got you and Sammy. Right where I want you."

The Gold Lord screamed insanely, and I took a step back. Even Sammel jumped.

"I will rule this world, all the layers of Hell, as well as the Purgatory you call the Hopelessness. I will strip Gaia of her power." The Gold Lord gasped like an actor delivering the last soliloquy of a play. Spittle on his lips.

"Well." I said, feeling really brave, when my bowels just wanted to void themselves. "I am glad you brought us to the Hopelessness. Because here I can end you."

"No." Sammel whispered. "Don't antagonise him."

Don't be a fool, Robert. I will end this foul creature.

"Do you know how I took control of your realm?" I said.

"Pray tell."

I didn't have a clue how I came to take over the Hopelessness as a seven year old boy. I didn't even realise I had taken it over. I just thought I could traverse its ghostly paths un-assailed.

The Gold Lord laughed as I paused.

"You are playing for time." The golden creature said. "Now, I am just going to demonstrate my power, boys. Let me show you how the Nephilim and Oosian power work, in tandem. My power is now - almost limitless."

The Gold Lord reached both of his hands towards the fathomless sky in the Hopelessness.

"Father-dear, now you are released from your Hell-Bond, I can have some fun with that realm."

You killed my son. You are an abomination.

I was struck by the cold at that point. I had not noticed how cold the Hopelessness was before. Shadows approached me. The evil wraiths and soulless spirits appeared to taunt me. I could always keep them at bay. Now they were clamouring for my soul. The Gold Lord was stripping away my influence.

That was when Apollyon went for the Gold Lord.

Yet the once-Angel couldn't move, his aspect changed from demon-like, to the sharp-suited incarnation I had first met, to an old, bearded man in chains.

"Look at the poor bastard. The angel that God threw down. The horror of as many religious books as I'd care to mention. Odin's child Hel. Pah. He. Is. A. Pussy."

Apollyon looked up at me and winked. Sammel touched my shoulder again.

"You *are* an abomination." I said, suddenly filled with the power of the Apollyon and Sammel. I looked for Gaia's power once more.

Shine, my son. Gaia said.

Apollyon was somehow shielding the Gold Lord from our intentions, from the knowledge of accessing the combined power of Heaven, Earth, and Hell. I reached out. I focused on the cords.

The black evil cord of the Gold Lord, and the jade umbilical of Mantus.

Reality stuttered as I suddenly pulled.

I regained full control of the Hopelessness again.

The Gold Lord laughed but nervously this time.

"Do you think I don't know what you are doing? Father? Half-brother? You are aiding this puny creature."

A sword of blue light appeared in the Gold Lord's hand. As ethereal as a thought blade – yet more powerful. The blade of a Nephilim.

I looked to Apollyon.

With my last breath. I give you my powers of protection over Sammel.

"Stop muttering, *father*." The Gold Lord tittered.

The smiting power of a demi-angel came to pass with that fiery blue sword. The Gold Lord took Apollyon's head.

I knew it would happen. Apollyon knew it would happen. Sammel, too.

There was a bloom of white light. The life force of an angel escaping to whichever heaven it came from. The Hopelessness glowed for a second. The wraiths hissed and the soulless screamed, some evaporated like water on a hot stone. I tapped that power. I could do anything in the Hopelessness, it seemed.

Thank you, Robert.

"I take control of the Hopelessness. I take control of Hell. I will take control of Heaven, and Earth. I leave you with nothing, Sammy." The Gold Lord sang.

I was surprised at how controlled Sammel was. He had watched his twin, then his father killed, impassively. I was surprised that Sammel had not gone for the Gold Lord.

Well, I found out later, Apollyon had said two words to Sammel.

Goodbye, and *Timing.*

"As for you, Robert. I gave you friends who deceived you. I gave you a path that deceived you. I gave you your adversaries. I gave you your successes. I gave you your Menagerie, Robert. It was all me. I messed with the twin's memories. You should have never come to the Hopelessness as a boy. You should not have taken the Hopelessness from me when I was at a low ebb. This was my Kingdom."

"It was Mantus's kingdom, and you killed him. You never had control. He always did. He still has."

I then had an image in my mind of Sammel's brother in his prime, a beautiful demi-angel, a fearsome being shackled. Tears of blood formed in Mantus's eyes. He nodded at the seven year old boy who had stumbled into his realm.

Take control my young one, then one day, please release me.

I had remembered.

The Gold Lord screamed his last. He was glowing with his power, but he was struggling to hold the power of Mantus, the Nephilim.

"I walked into the Hopelessness, Gold Lord. I didn't take control of the Hopelessness. Mantus wanted me here. I was invited. I was its saviour. Obviously, you were not the rightful heir. You had killed its mistress, prevented her heir from his Kingdom. You are wrong, and you shouldn't exist. I *am* the Veil Lord."

210

I summoned the power of Apollyon, Gaia, and the Hopelessness. Sammel touched me again, a friends hand on my shoulder. I tapped the power that had been Mantus.

Then.

I pulled.

I tore at the Gold Lord's cord.

I was intent on destroying the creature.

As I started to dissolve those evil threads.

I thought.

Like a God.

I acted.

Like a God.

The next thing I did was bring back the rest of my dead friends.

Gat and Claire.

I knew I could.

The second thing I did was make Avery, Charlotte, and Walter fully alive.

The third thing I did was give my nephew and niece their rightful bodies.

The fourth thing I did was bring back the dead children, tapped in the remaining rose jars.

The fifth thing I did was find Eliza's soul in an abandoned rose jar. I sealed her away in the very depths of Hell.

The sixth thing I did was locate Arthur Poke and I brought him back to Percy.

The seventh thing I did was bring LP to me. I felt in my bones I would need him.

Then I sealed Hell.

Then I started on the Gold Lord.

I had the background energy of the Hopelessness, I had the protection power of Apollyon, the warmth of Sammel and Mantu's Nephilim energy. The anger of the spirits around me. The NET's power filled me. Gaia was there, too.

My, it was starting to hurt.

The Gold Lord sheathed his soul blade. He walked towards me. I sensed him raising the balefire, the god killer, and he smote me.

Ordinarily, I would have been burnt to a crisp. But I wasn't really there. I was one foot in the Hopelessness, and one foot in the real world. I could always step between them at will – well ever since I was seven. Now I existed in both, and didn't exist in either. Schrodinger would have loved me then.

I hit the Gold Lord with everything I had.

I poured power into him. The power of purpose.

211

I channelled the love of my friends. I forgot their betrayal. The Gold Lord had manipulated me for too long.

Separate him.

Separate his cords.

The Gold Lord screamed as Mantus was torn from him. Again, the bright flare and I tapped into the Sammel's twin's remaining power.

The beautiful figure of Mantus, so like Sammel, looked at me, and nodded.

Thankyou. I go to be with my father. Sammel. Live well.

For the first time, the Gold Lord's face revealed his doubt. He knew what I was doing.

I *had* done it to Susan Smart's brother as a lad. I had done it to the *Lantern Heads*. I cut cords.

I pulled at the threads. I separated a gold cord from the black one.

"I've got a container for the Oosian spirit." LP shouted. "Percy!"

Percy stepped through a portal, a young man with her. He couldn't have been more than twenty. Arthur. Her husband.

"Bobby. LP, Arthur and I can take the Oosian spirit. Unravel it."

I felt elated. I pulled the tiniest thread that made up that gold cord. Even the smallest pull could unravel a garment.

The Gold Lord, The Oosian, screamed. It had been integral to him. A part of his being. I had taken any residual physical form of that creature and I pulled it apart. It was thousands of strands of physical being. What we would call DNA. All the people Sukthet the Oosian had ever inhabited.

I pulled the energy form of Sukthet towards me as it screamed in defeat, and the device Percy held. It was like a rose jar held in a wooden frame.

I will end you, Waterfield.

Percy slammed home the trap. The sense of that evil power was gone.

The Gold Lord was trapped.

It was over.

For now.

Chapter Twenty-Nine
An End of Sorts

So, that was that.

I stepped out of the Hopelessness fully.

I greeted all my friends, and relations. All so alive. There were many tears.

It was my forty-third birthday. I had forgotten. We didn't have cake. Instead, we slept.

We had cake two days later when my beloved Claire baked a chocolate sponge. As she sang "happy birthday" She smiled at me, her red hair was tied atop her head, her lime green evening gown fitting in all the right places.

"Happy birthday, Bobby."

We kissed.

Apollyon, Gaia, and Sammel had helped me to bring back my love.

Yet, none of the powers I had been able to summon to shred the Gold Lord remained with me. I couldn't sense any residue from what Sammel had given me to aid my destruction, nor his father.

The imprint on my arm was dull, so it seemed I was unlikely to commune with Gaia's NET again.

I wasn't so bothered. I just liked being human. That is not to say I didn't wield other powers during my successive adventures. But you will have to wait and see about those.

Two months later I sat in the library at Legend Street. I had a brandy to my left and this journal to my right. My hand was aching from writing within it. Gat was reading in one corner of the large book strewn room.

Charlotte brought me tea, and Avery bought me biscuits.

Raven, my young Shield Maiden was, on that day, sitting on a couch, sharpening her knives, her eyes flitting between Dolph, who was dozing, and Sammel, who sat by the fire with a copy of 20,000 Leagues Under the Sea. That love triangle promised some fireworks, it seemed. Raven was dressed as a girl too. Charlotte had taken her shopping at my expense.

I had profusely apologised to Sammel for sealing Hell. He said it would be fine without him for a Millennia, or so.

Walter was on rota, chasing down a particularly nasty demon in Nuneaton. He eventually caught it with a fishing net and some glue.

A few weeks before, Charlotte and Avery had said that they would like to explore the world, and would be leaving the Menagerie to travel for a time. Their life and death experiences had driven them apart, and they needed to come back together as twins, in their own destined bodies.

Walter eventually accepted a senior role looking after the Strange Regiment, which was now aligned to the Ministry of Mirrors. He took over from the honoured Brigadier Lord Holden, who had given his life to the cause. Colonel Trevithick and I would work together again, many more times.

The night before this memory was written, I was visited by LP, Percy, Arthur, and Marble. I still have to stifle a sob to this very day when I think about it.

It was the last time that I saw Percy for nearly seventy years. She was off to make a life with her husband. When she did return, our adventures were crazy, and poor Arthur was dead. He'd aged and, for some reason, Percy hadn't.

I occasionally saw LP when he commissioned the Menagerie to carry out a piece of strange business, and we shared a brandy, or two. He remained distant. He was too busy with something called the Whampyri. He never elaborated. I found out what they were when Percy came back.

Raven, Dolph, Claire, Gat, and I became the new mainstays of the Menagerie in late 1906.

So, another reason why I began to write these journals, reader and why I sent them to you.

One day, I did something foolish. And it wasn't very long ago.

I returned to a place called Magpie Farm. But not until you had defeated Isabelle. Not until she had become corporeal, and had died again.

I needed to understand if that evil was still there. If it remained after her death.

It filled me with horror.

When we next meet Maisie, we will need each other. You will need Raven more.

The End

To be continued in The Legacy of the Magpie Book Two : The Raven's Message

Afterword

I had planned to put The Lure of Magpie Farm in as the prologue to The Ghostly Menagerie, but then felt Robert needed to reflect backwards, and so the story – the second from Impossible Fruit – would have detracted from the narrative. For those of you who have not read Impossible Fruit, Lure is presented here as a coda and a treat.

The Lure of Magpie Farm

Elizabeth looked at me across the room and smiled as she pulled out the knife from the boy's chest. The blood fountained under aortic pressure like a geyser.

I stared back, locking that horrible tableau in my sight. I loved her, yet now hated her at the same time. I had opened the bedroom door; she was atop a young man and smiled, stabbing him repeatedly whilst she rode him. That poor young man. A coital knife through his hairless chest.

Would I ever kill a woman? Kill Elizabeth? I wondered this as I ran towards them, seizing the knife, pulling Elizabeth off him. I was more embarrassed that I couldn't stop the pumping blood, rather than at the young man's post-aroused nakedness.

After he had passed, I turned to her. Elizabeth's eyes were shallow pools in a bloody landscape. I could tell from the way she was looking at me that behind the display of haunted composure, she might one day kill me too; and this might be that day.

She sat there in the farmhouse for a further hour – mute- whilst I had washed the blood from her and rolled *his* body in our bed sheets. I then made us both a cup of tea. I immersed myself in the day's broadsheet, trying to take my mind off things momentarily before I faced up to burying a fellow human. The Hopelessness would not have me.

I heard a click and looked across to see she had my handgun cocked and pointing at my head. I knew the gun contained two bullets.

Elizabeth was backlit by the early morning sun, like an icon - a Madonna. Motes of dust and fibre reflected the light, like planets orbiting a flaming star. She was smiling - a lustful smile, the smile of an angel or a devil, depending upon your perspective.

The ghost of the boy she had just killed stood behind her, but by the nature of ghosts, or most of them anyway, he had no corporeal sway over the proceedings. What played out on Magpie Farm on the 14th of August 1904 was between Elizabeth and me. The lure had brought her here.

216

"Put the gun down Elizabeth. There's no need for you to point it at me all the time." I *was* nervous, but I thought her love for me was stronger.

"I don't need your forgiveness." She was distant again. Charmed by faeries, as I used to think, but now I knew better. Elizabeth was governed by demons. Or witchcraft.

"I will forgive you, but you need to tell me what I have to forgive."

A tear escaped her left eye, like a sole escapee from Bedlam. Her left gun-hand trembled, but remained fixed in position. The tear tracked down her freckled face, ploughing a deeper, bloody wound, like a blossoming scar.

"I am not ready." Her voice rose in pitch and volume, the determined toss of her head disturbing the motes, causing them to eddy to and fro. It was as if those bright angels now knew her purpose and could not bear to be near her.

We were due to be wed the next morning. A rushed courtship, my parents had said. *To a farming wench?* Well, that had become my mother's favourite phrase.

Elizabeth was much more than that, and far wealthier than my nouveau riche parents believed. They had worked hard, saved hard and forgot their working-class roots hard. She had lived in the farmhouse in recent times to write her book, but before that Elizabeth had resided at Bell Manor.

Her white wedding dress still hung on the parlour door. The guests left uninvited, with cries of "told you so" as subtle in their whispered tones as the thankful prayers of the ghosts around me.

"I'm going to kill you, Robert. If you forgive me."

"I do not think you will." I hoped.

Then I felt a feeling of utmost dread. Those feelings radiated from the dead around me. They were legion. I felt the breath of the bullet coming towards me - I jumped at the percussive sound tearing through the barrier between silence and noise, just before the bullet was about to hit. In a flash of finality, I saw my pathway to Magpie Farm and reflected upon it.

It was rare to have a man in his late thirties unmarried in 1901. Queen Victoria had educated the population of England to live a

217

life in godly marriage, then Edward the VII had led by example by taking every opportunity to rut in secret. I hadn't done either.

I remember my father taking me aside in my late twenties. He had been very awkward and nervous, and he had never ever been like that with me before; he was habitually a monster of self-assurance. All he asked me, late one night in a St Paul's gentleman's club, was whether I liked the taste of a different sort of apple.

It wasn't until years later when I met my good friend Arthur - who did like the taste of other apples, particularly the tall handsome African type - that I laughed myself silly, mainly at the thought of my stiff old bastard of a dad squirming to ask me if I was homosexual.

The ghosts had permanently kept me away from long relationships, but I was no virgin. It's difficult to keep a relationship going, if you can see their dead ancestors clambering over each other for gossip. It's true, I had occasionally committed the sin of sex outside of wedlock. I am assured that the gods do not see it as sin - according to the ghosts - neither is lying with your own sex. They see sin in other forms: murder, slavery, rape, and abuse.

As my life flashed before my eyes, I admit under God – or gods plural, as the ghosts are quite clear to remind me- that I put too much stall in those dead relatives. I let many a lovely potential Mrs Waterfield go by the wayside due to what they told me, rather than trusting in my own choice and perceptions. And look where that's got me: moments from my brain decorating the Welsh dresser in the farmhouse.

I had also found in my discussions with the ghosts that *they* were not the problem; it was the other thing, which they feared too. The Hopelessness. The almost entity that lived in the place between life and death. What my mother would have called purgatory, but what I know now to be much more horrific than that Biblical waystation.

I'd had my first brush with the Hopelessness shortly after my seventh birthday.

Grandfather lay dead in the main parlour and had been there for two days. A swarm of well-wishers and what Father called carrion crows filed past his open coffin. Edmund Waterfield had been born in a workhouse, but that had been forgotten by the time he was to

218

be buried in his lead and silk-lined oak casket, with gold leaf handles and ornate fittings.

Grandfather had been a violent, miserable man who everyone had hated, and he had been vile to all of them – except his wife and his little Bobby.

"Come sit on my knee, Bobby." He would tap his lap and I would trundle over. Daily, he would secret a florin into my hand when no-one was looking and tell me to hide it in a strong box away from prying eyes, before my father gave it all to prospectors in America.

Father said, one day in anger, that grandfather was as tight as a starving man's arsehole and was amazed he had given me anything. I went on to buy my first piano with that money; my secretive, squirreling nature buying some grudging respect from my father - and a puritanical lecture on avarice from my mother.

As Grandfather succumbed to senility, he would slip back into his workhouse ways. His accent would deepen, closer to Black Country than affluent Birmingham. He began to hallucinate enemies all around and once, following an entertaining argument with a myriad of hallucinations, he called those visions "a bunch of cunts". It was a while before I knew what that word meant, and I had almost a lifetime of blushes once I found out. I only ever used it once; my nanny fainted when I had called my rocking horse that particular "c" word one day when it rocked over my toe.

Anyway, I'm digressing- and the bullet is coming.

One night, I crept down to the parlour. I wanted to see Grandfather one last time before they nailed the lid shut. What I found surprised me. A little woman, beautiful but petite, standing by his coffin. She looked pregnant; at the point she had died, she was. It was his wife, my grandmother, staring at me. I stared back and smiled. She looked back flabbergasted. How could I see her? It was a rude awakening for her and me. I wonder why the woman, who until now, had only appeared in the photo frame on the living room mantelpiece, was standing in her translucent glory next to my dearly departed beloved grandfather. I suddenly realised why he might have been so angry; he had loved her so and she had gone.

"Beatrice, this is Bobby. Our grandson."

I jumped as Grandfather appeared next to her. I looked from his body to his ghost, puzzled but not scared - as if it were the most natural event in the grieving process.

Then they were gone, and I was in another place. The same place but different. I suddenly felt scared. Ghostly Grandfather and Grandmother were gone. The corporeal coffin and corpse of Grandfather were also not present in this place.

It felt like a dream, but one I would remember forever. The Hopelessness was there, a gaping void of eternity, more evil than the places where curses lay in wait for their call. I was a young boy and yet I understood. That was what terrified me most. It still does.

I ran from the room into the hallway to escape the Hopelessness. Infinity stretched that journey. I thought, at that time; if I set foot on either path, forwards or backwards, I would be lost forever. I did not want to become part of that rank Hopelessness - where the monstrosity laughed and cried equally at a heinous act.

I looked across into the waiting room, where Father kept his working guests before he met with them. I ran to that door as part of my escape from that void of a hallway and turned the handle. The room before me opened like a fusty grave on a frosted night. My breath crystallised and my lungs filled with fog.

I felt it there - the Hopelessness, a personification of uncaring thoughts, a voided optimism. It wasn't strong enough to trap me. So, the Hopelessness welcomed me without words. It took my hand without touch and sat me down. My heart thumped, as if it were trying to spend its allocation of beats and be away from this place. This thing was beyond evil. It had evil for breakfast and expelled horror from its faecal end.

"Robert." It didn't speak, I represent it as speech for my own sanity. "Robert. You should not be here. Why are you here?"

The answer was obvious like asking a pious priest why he did not appear regularly on stage in vaudeville alongside a group of tarts.

"I do not know, Sir." Goodness knows why I called it "Sir". Manners, perhaps.

The Hopelessness un-laughed; it was of course without gender, so the absence of laughter was strange neutrality. Within that one were-laugh, it showed me the evil within. No, I am mistaken. Thinking of the Hopelessness as evil meant there was polarity. This thing was an absence of anything: faithful or faithless.

I saw in it the hatred between the pain of tortured innocents. I saw the feelings sexual depravity gave its victims, without knowing what it was. I saw the way in which men and women used children for their sin and how those children were broken. I saw the bad luck of the unlucky and the horror of the first witness at a murder scene. I saw trees of corpses all rotting, yet laughing at their own plight- and I saw the hope of the un-rescued leach away.

That was the Hopelessness. The gap between good and evil, where the indifference lived. The Hopelessness did not care if you lived or died, killed your victim, or let them live. It wanted the bits between. The victim's knowledge of impending death and the murderer's fleeting regret.

It revelled in the lack of effect it had on me. It was clearly testing me with the images. At that point, I think it feared me too.

Then I was back in my body, waking in the armchair next to grandfather's coffin. The spectres of him and my grandmother were still there, smiling at me.

I would often spend time with them as a child, long after the funeral.

When I was sixteen, I encountered the Hopelessness again.

I had gone on holiday to my uncle's house in Cornwall with my mother, whilst father took care of business in the good old US of A. It was six blessed weeks without Father's constant quips about my aptitude at schooling and my ability to be a man.

By my sixteenth birthday, I was what they called "strapping". I was six feet tall and looked at least three or four years older, because of the dark shadow of whiskers that had come thick and fast after puberty.

Exploring the village on my own, I came across a young woman who had fallen off her bike. She was probably in her early twenties and was holding her leg. She had her petticoats rolled up, which both surprised and aroused me; she was dabbing at one knee with a handkerchief. I noticed quickly that there was a very faint apparition standing over her, a young man. It was her late brother, I just knew it. He glared at me, but was too translucent for me to be bothered with.

"Are you hurt Miss?" I asked politely.

She looked up, her pale drawn face and streaked with tears. She had a crown of jet-black hair and green eyes that blinked a lot, probably because she did not want to be seen to be crying.

"Just my pride." When she smiled, it was like the sun coming up for the second time that day. His Lordship the ghost suddenly became more opaque and rushed at me with his fists up.

Then I was in that place again. The Hopelessness.

The experience was different this time. There was all the nauseating horror of my first visit, but being in the open, the Hopelessness felt even more expansive, even more infinite.

"He is the ghost of her guilt," it un-said. "Holding her back. Not a curse, but worse, a promise. A promise to look after him that was never kept."

Either I must have looked confused, or it was irritated that I wasn't scared, so it continued.

"She promised she would sit by his side as he got over the flu, instead, she went out to play and he died. Drowned in his own sputum."

"And she is haunted so? Did you do this to her?" I knew she had been but a girl when her brother had died, responsible for nothing.

"I cannot interact. I only wait. I wait for others not to care. Her brother appears as a ghost in her dreams. She is tormented. She fell from the contraption because she drinks fermented liquids to try to chase away the pain. We then feed upon her drunken apathy. Pain that feeds us, the pain of indifference. "

"She does it to herself, then?"

It didn't answer, but I felt an absence of sound that was an affirmation.

Then the tableau changed. The woman who had come off her bike was now translucent and the man or older boy that had stood behind her was coming for me. He was as solid as I was. He charged me with an expert rugby tackle. Arms about me like a fleeting lover- head tucked into my lower stomach.

I had the bally wind knocked out of me, I'll tell you. We both rolled away and stood. I nodded an acknowledgement, as I would on the field. He had done well, being much smaller than I.

"Lucky, I have a lower centre of gravity," he announced.

"Unlucky that you are dead. Stop haunting her. Or the Hopelessness will have you both," I told him, although I didn't know how I knew. He was as handsome as his sister was pretty, with the same dark-haired Irish look.

"I cannot." He crouched, like he was going to come at me again. That was when I saw the shining black rope, a length of polished, malleable coal, out of the corner of my eye. It was an umbilical cord linking him to his sister, but it only appeared once I thought of it. I might have missed it if we hadn't had been in the throes of what was likely a wrestling match, a show of strength. Once I knew it was there, it became more visible. I tried to grab him by that thick vine, but my hand slipped away.

"I need her not to care. Or I will have to go."

"She needs her life. She needs hope." I retorted.

The pustulating black cord stretched from the boy to his sister, pulsing like a swollen varicose vein, undulating like the most venomous of black snakes. It was the link of a broken promise. Normally the cords of promise looked bright, like a cable of sunshine, unless they were unfulfilled: then they were as black as ink. Once more, the Hopelessness had fed me its un-knowledge.

I checked my back pocket. My penknife was there, substantial. I approached the boy.

It was like hitting a low brick wall or a baby rhino. He was strong, this lad. Strong in his attempt to keep his sister in her drunken apathy. He knocked me back and then rabbit-punched me. I staggered. It bloody hurt. I fished the knife from my pocket and flicked it open. Knowing then what I was about to do, he turned and ran.

I took chase, and he ran faster. I could feel the Hopelessness starting to fill him; it wanted our suffering, but it wanted his sister, with her drunken indifference, more. What was I doing? In a moment of inspiration, I stopped and ran back to the woman, who had lived for years with the guilt of her little brother dying whilst she'd played.

I reached her and found where the link buried itself between her breasts. Her brother was a raging, snarling mess behind me by now. He was slashing with his hands and fingers, like the shattered branches of trees, razor-sharp pitchfork prongs.

I asked forgiveness for ripping open her blouse, then I took hold of the link and gasped at its coldness. The man launched at me, taking me down. I felt a claw rake my chest, rippling my shirt;

the knife skittered away on the road, knocked loose from my now-frozen grasp.

He came at me again, but I hit him with hope. Hope for this young woman - his sister. All the hope I could muster. I pictured her happy, content, a long life ahead of her. I visualised her chance encounter with a sixteen-year-old boy on a road in Cornwall when she was twenty-two; how she stemmed the blood flow from a terrible injury and probably saved his life. And then I imagined how that grateful boy went back to visit her a year or two later and lay with her, giving them both a start on the hopeful pathway of love.

He screamed as I cut the cord, but I slipped and slashed my hand, then Susan Smart forgot her woes and tore those petticoats to make a bandage and helped me home.

Before he vanished, I saw him whisper, "Thank you." He was as much of a victim as his sister had been, but now he was free.

The Hopelessness un-howled.

The bullet missed me. I had subconsciously retained some of the hope I had for Susan and projected it. I remembered being in her arms once again.

Elizabeth looked at the smoking weapon as it backed up, as if it was the gun's fault. Grimacing, she fired again. I threw myself backwards this time and hoped that bullet would sail over my head.

The pathway to Magpie Farm was writ large again.

Elizabeth Bell had always been an independent woman.

I met her for the first time in London, on Fleet Street. It was the summer of 1901. Elizabeth had caused uproar, turning up at the offices of *The Times*, where she verbally attacked the Editor-in-Chief for not offering her an interview for the position of reporter. I had been in the interview earlier and it was I who had secured the post. She was fundamentally independent, and Women's Rights were her bag. She was horrified they wouldn't offer her at least a chance to meet with them. I had sympathy with her for that.

Elizabeth was the daughter of the Bells, a wealthy Lichfield family. Bell Manor stood just outside the small Cathedral city, near the old Roman ruins at Wall. Bell Manor was a product of the age

when the nouveau riche had made money out of the Enlightenment and Industrial Revolution.

I hailed from Birmingham, a growing centre of industry itself.
I was the urban gentleman; she was the rural duchess-in-waiting.

After the Editor's heavies had manhandled Elizabeth out of
The Times' offices, I followed and placated her. I turned down the
job later that day because of their mistreatment of her. I would
never have taken gainful employment with such beasts. Instead, I
took on editing work for a local publisher. I had plenty of money,
I just wanted to be a writer. Father didn't see it that way, but from
beyond the veil, Grandfather approved and showed me the places
he had secreted monies for a rainy day - or a Bolshevik invasion.

Both the Waterfields and the Bells had townhouses in London,
so after we struck up a friendship, we could meet easily. As our
love grew and we started to explore each other further, we had the
Waterfield town house in which to carry out our illicit affair. Our
property was always empty, as Father was constantly overseas.

Elizabeth showed nothing of the strangeness then. It wasn't
apparent until we announced our engagement, and I visited Bell
Manor. Lord Bell wasn't a nice man. He looked haunted most of
the time. He was obsessed with birds, especially magpies, crows,
and ravens. Edmund Bell refused to accept our engagement and
his simpering wife Agatha just did as she was constantly bidden.
No wonder Elizabeth was so fiercely independent.

When Elizabeth and I announced our engagement, I was sum-
marily banished back to the farmhouse, never to set foot in Bell
Manor again. I had the money to set us up after marriage, so there
would not be any concerns about our financial independence. Lord
Bell knew that. In those days, however, if you were female and
unmarried, you were your father's chattel, no matter what your
thoughts. Elizabeth hated that.

The farmhouse itself was interesting. Elizabeth refused to
come to it at first, declaring it "evil." I'd tried to enter the Hopelessness the first night I was there on my own, following my ban-
ishment from the mansion. I needed to find out whether I was safe
here.

I could always access the Hopelessness, but I found there were
parts of the estate I could not explore via that world as if there were
a block. Part of me felt an urge to try and break through. One night,

225

one of the first I was there, I tried, and upon transference, I was suddenly filled with an insane lust.

From the shadows, a woman appeared: tall and beautiful. I blush to recall the effect she had upon my body.

"Hello. I am Isabelle and you are a strange one, Robert Waterfield."

"Strange? Interesting opinion from a ghost."

Her laugh was laced with cruelty.

"Too weak to be my Magpie, too strong for the Hopelessness."

What did she mean?

"When your concubine eventually comes to see me, she will be a better Magpie than her father. He has not yet killed for me. So, I remain like this." Isabelle waved her arms about her person, as if to illustrate her insubstantial aspect.

"I will not let you have her."

"Oh, I will. Or what you call the Hopelessness will."

Then Isabelle vanished.

When I came back from the Hopelessness, Elizabeth was there. After that night, she would never leave the estate; not once in the nearly three years that I travelled back and forth from London to Lichfield did she leave the Manor. What she needed from outside, the servants sourced for her; she became nothing more than a recluse.

I loved her for her strength and independence. She had been turned into a wreck by her own choices.

One cold February, mere weeks after she moved into the farmhouse, Elizabeth's father died in mysterious circumstances. Apparently overcome with grief, shortly afterwards, her mother fell down the stairs and broke her neck.

Elizabeth was their sole beneficiary, but not once at that point had I suspected her of foul play. Her father was, as his father before him, an only child. No male heirs lurked, ready to take the Bell estate away from Elizabeth.

The day before Elizabeth shot at me, I knew there was something wrong as soon as I entered my home. Someone else's accoutrements lay scattered about the place: male clothing, shoes. I climbed the stairs and found her in bed with a local man. Charlie Spent, the nineteen-year-old son of the Bell estate gardener.

Spent, I remembered, was a handsome young man; because Elizabeth had been so lonely, I almost understood as I confronted her. But almost before I could process the image of her and Spent together, she had driven the knife through his chest.

After the bullet sailed over me and the next empty barrel clicked, Elizabeth declared that she had previously killed six young men, as well as both her parents. Spent had been her ninth victim. She had lured all the men to the farm from far and wide.

In a rage, I took us to the Hopelessness.

As soon as we arrived, Elizabeth broke down. I stepped away from her; knowing that I would never hold her ever again.

"Bobby, those terrible things. She made me do them."

"Isabelle?"

Elizabeth looked at me horrified.

"You know of her? Then you can't forgive me."

I thought about it for a while. "Now why would I not?"

"You are my fiancé. You are meant to be my protector. I will be damned if you forgive me".

"You are evil. Yet you are not beyond god's mercy" I had loved her so, but the hope of a future with her, of a loving marriage, was fast draining away. The Hopelessness un-laughed.

"Forgive her. Forgive her, then Hell shall have her for eternity. She is of no more use. Her killing days are over." Isabelle appeared halfway through that speech. My lovely Elizabeth froze, as if captured in a photograph. Still beautiful. How had I not noticed her flickering around the edges before?

"You already have her, don't you?"

Isabelle giggled. "Such a clever Bobby."

"When did you kill her?"

"I didn't - not fully. I have this trick of suspending my people between life and death. That's how *we* were able to rut. I can transfer myself into Elizabeth's body at whim. When she first came to you in this farmhouse, we were linked. When she first put you in her mouth, I had taught her that act."

That had been a surprise and it rocked me to my very foundations, mainly out of embarrassment. One did not discuss sexual acts with others.

227

I looked closely at Isabelle and imagined the lines of power that had joined Susan and her brother. There were thousands joined to the witch. And then thousands stretching to the Hopelessness in turn. She was equally a servant of the Hopelessness, caught in its thrall. It had realised Magpie Farm was a good source of food.

A single cord joined Isabelle and Elizabeth. I held my thoughts, wrapped them in secrecy. Walking to the far end of the room in a pretence to look at my Elizabeth. I picked up the gun Elizabeth had been pointing at me.

I knew what all the ropes meant in the Hopelessness. I could feel the Hopelessness did not like Isabelle. She kept a lot of false hope for herself.

I whipped around, firing at the link between Isabelle and Elizabeth. Knowing there was one chamber stuck in the gun, I had pocketed a bullet or two earlier that day and had quickly reloaded. The bullet that did emerge under percussion ripped through the link and Isabelle screamed.

"You could have been a beautiful Magpie, Robert. Had you killed for me I should have lived again. Death magic and your love would have healed me."

Then the ghost-witch dissipated. I would see Isabelle once more, but it wouldn't be for another hundred years.

I moved across to Elizabeth; she looked like all her troubles had been washed away. Hell-bound, I supposed. Was I right to let her go, or should I save her? No, Elizabeth had taken so many lives. Something else could have her.

I opened myself up to the Hopelessness; I had reeled it in, purposefully lowering my optimism, so it would think it had me. Elizabeth couldn't see the insubstantial cord that linked her to the Hopelessness itself -now it was growing thicker.

"You can't have her. I forgive her." I announced to the Hopelessness. With that, the blackened thread fully materialised between her and the void.

"I didn't know what I was doing, Bobby." She was crying, yet fading.

"Go to Isabelle, Elizabeth, you are too evil for the Hopelessness."

She screamed as she slowly faded. I never saw Elizabeth again.

It's the year twenty-twenty two. I am over one hundred and sixty years old. I have never aged, nor have I grown ill. I am standing on the fringes of Magpie Farm. There is nothing to hold people any longer; the evil has gone. There are police about and the manor house is burning. A man and a woman walk across the yard to their car. A BMW.

He holds her tight.

That man was you, Harry Morton and she of course is you, Maisie Price. I know one day I will make your acquaintance properly. Isabelle's curse walks the world on different paths now. You will be the solution. Then I will finally find out the reason why I can't die.

I had been lured to the farm so I could finally see you both, not to send Elizabeth into the Hopelessness. That had been my own action.

I turned to my companion, the woman in yellow, who I think you know. She smiled. Then we stepped into the Hopelessness.

"You think you can control me?" The Hopelessness un-said.

"I have done so before. I will do so again."

"You foolish man. I allowed you to do what you did. Did you think by purely channelling hope you defeated me? I am nothing, you cannot defeat me. I am the conduit for the one to come. Forget the Magpies, Robert. Beware the Crows instead. They are legion."

I laughed as we disappeared, and later, I wrote this letter to you both, because I heard that, like me, you both like strange cases.

Acknowledgements

Firstly, I have to thank the author Gavin Jefferson for helping me to read this beast within an inch of its life. His eye for detail surpasses anything I have in my locker. His friendly commentary also helped to polish this manuscript into a better book. I bet you wished you'd never offered Gav.

I'll pay it forwards. I'll also buy the beer if we ever meet in the real world.

I would also like to thank my other beta readers, authors Alan K Dell and Jennifer Maglio, for insights and advice, particularly Jennifer's observations from the LGBTQ+ community, and Alan's correction of Raven's Viking surname.

As ever, love to Jacey, my ever suffering wife, and our three sons N, C and E.

Finally, to Jason P Saunders, the best of mates, recently gone to Valhalla. Save me a table Jase; order the pints, ill pay when I get there.

September 2023

Printed in Great Britain
by Amazon